D1583567

GYFFORD OF WEARE

GYFFORD OF WEARE

BY

JEFFERY FARNOL

LONDON
SAMPSON LOW, MARSTON & CO., LTD.

TO

ERNEST V. CHANDLER

MY TRUSTY FRIEND

I DEDICATE THIS BOOK.

JEFFERY FARNOL,
   June.   Sunnyside: 1928.

CONTENTS

CHAP.   PAGE

I. TELLETH HOW ONE ENTERED AND TWO DEPARTED BY A WINDOW . . . 1

II. TOUCHING SIR RICHARD, HIS SINS . 8

III. WHICH INTRODUCES ONE, ANGELA, THE PRIMARY CAUSE 14

IV. DESCRIBETH THE BREAKING OF A HORSE-WHIP 20

V. OF THREE FINE GENTLEMEN AT BREAKFAST 27

VI. INTRODUCETH DIVERS GREAT FOLK, PARTICULARLY A DUCHESS . . . 37

VII. WHICH IS A CHAPTER VERY FULL OF SUGGESTION 48

VIII. TELLETH AMONG OTHER MATTERS OF MORNING SUNSHINE AND—A BACONY FRAGRANCE 56

IX. DESCRIBETH A BREAKFAST 'AL FRESCO' AND A SIGNET RING 64

X. BEING A CHAPTER BEAUTIFULLY SHORT . 72

XI. WHICH IS EVEN SHORTER AND THEREFORE—— 76

XII. A SOMEWHAT LENGTHY CHAPTER BUT ON THE WHOLE, READABLE. . . 79

XIII. TELLETH HOW JULIAN GYFFORD WENT A-WALKING 93

XIV. TELLETH HOW SIR RICHARD FLED AND WHITHER 102

XV. TELLETH HOW SIR RICHARD FOUND SANCTUARY IN THE WILDERNESS. . 109

XVI. IN WHICH THE DUCHESS MAKES A PROPHECY 123

XVII. TELLETH HOW THE MARQUIS WENT FORTH ON A PILGRIMAGE OF FRIENDSHIP. . 129

XVIII. TELLETH MORE CONCERNING A CERTAIN OLD MILITARY CLOAK . . . 140

XIX. MAKETH YET FURTHER MENTION OF SIR RICHARD'S OLD CLOAK . . . 144

XX. WHICH IS A CHAPTER OF RECRIMINATIONS 149

vii

CHAP. PAGE

XXI. IN WHICH SHALL BE FOUND MENTION OF ANOTHER RING . . . 157

XXII. WHICH HATH A SHADOW AT THE END . 163

XXIII. TELLETH OF A NIGHT AND A RADIANT DAWN 168

XXIV. BEING A CHAPTER OF NO PARTICULAR INTEREST 177

XXV. WHICH IS CHAPTER SUGGESTIVE OF MANY THINGS 182

XXVI. IN WHICH TITUS OLDCRAFT COMES UPON A CLUE 191

XXVII. GIVETH SOME DESCRIPTION OF THE ODD MAN 196

XXVIII. GIVETH A SOMEWHAT WORDY DESCRIPTION OF FINE COMPANY, A GARDEN FÊTE AND WHAT BEFELL THERE. . . . 207

XXIX. DESCRIBETH A NIGHT OF INCIDENT . 218

XXX. TELLETH OF THE MORNING AFTER . . 227

XXXI. TELLETH, AMONG OTHER MATTERS, OF ROSE BUSHES AND ONE IN PARTICULAR 233

XXXII. OF RUMOURS AND A SECRET KEPT . . 241

XXXIII. TELLETH HOW THEY HEARD A CRY AT MIDNIGHT 248

XXXIV. TELLETH OF ONE DEAD THAT WALKED . 261

XXXV. GIVETH PARTICULARS OF ONE DAY— MORNING 274

XXXVI. WHICH HINTS OF DANGERS IMPENDING . 286

XXXVII. TELLETH WHAT HAPPENED AT THE "HAUNTED MILL" 291

XXXVIII. RELATETH A CAPTURE 296

XXXIX. WHICH RELATETH YET ANOTHER CAPTURE 301

XL. CONCERNETH ITSELF WITH TWO CAPTIVES 309

XLI. IN WHICH MASTER TITUS OLDCRAFT RIDES OUT OF THIS NARRATIVE . . 316

XLII. TELLETH HOW TWO RODE HOMEWARD TOGETHER 321

XLIII. GIVETH FURTHER PARTICULARS OF AN APPARITION 328

XLIV. TELLS HOW OLD BENJAMIN MADE A BET 333

XLV. WHICH, BEING THE LAST, NATURALLY ENDS THIS BOOK 336

GYFFORD OF WEARE

CHAPTER I

TELLETH HOW ONE ENTERED AND TWO DEPARTED BY A WINDOW

THE flash of a face glimpsed beyond opening door, a puff of breath, and the candle, suddenly extinguished, choked him with its reek. Rigid he stood, peering into the engulfing darkness, every faculty keenly alert, every nerve and muscle strung for swift action; thus for a long moment he waited, grimly patient, until there stole to him a vague rustle of stealthy movement, then, dropping the candle-stick, he leapt—to grasp draperies that tore in his fierce clutch—to hear a faint cry, a stumbling fall.

Uttering a smothered exclamation he started backwards to the door, locked it, groped feverishly for another candle-stick, took out tinder-box and struck a light, all in as many moments.

She crouched within a yard of him, her face and form hidden in the folds of a long cloak.

"Well, who—what are ye?" he demanded.

"Your prisoner 'twould seem," she answered; and he frowned to hear her voice so smooth and untroubled.

"Ay, I have ye fast enough," he nodded grimly. "But who are ye? Here's to see!" With movement incredibly quick he stooped and plucked back the hood of her cloak. . . . Grey eyes, black-lashed, that stared up at him from the pale oval of a face framed in dark tresses of lustrous hair; vivid lips firm-set and resolute like her smooth-rounded chin. But it was her eyes drew and held his regard, eyes wide-set beneath low-arched brows, eyes that met his unquailing and never a sign of fear. She viewed him serenely, from his disordered wig to muddy riding-boots; his sombre eyes deep-set beneath thick, black brows, his dominant nose, the sardonic bitterness of curling lips, the grim line of jaw; a middling tall man, all lean strength and supple poise despite the careless slouch of broad shoulders, who met her calmly appraising scrutiny with a half-sullen, half-mocking air, and whistled softly between white teeth.

"You must be Julian Gyfford!" said she, at last.

"Ha, must I so?" he answered, scowling suddenly. "Why then—so be it. And what then?"

"You will help me, sir, to avert shame and misery from one I love."

"A man?"

"A woman, sir, and very young—very guileless."

"Guileless?" he repeated. "Breathes there such woman indeed?" And seating himself upon a corner of the table he lounged there, swinging muddy riding-boot to and fro. "And pray, ma'm," he went on, seeing she would deign him no answer, "why should I help you?"

"For your mother's sake.'

"She's dead."

"She lived once."

"But died ere I could know her. So this plea fails you."

The grey eyes flashed him sudden anger, the red mouth was eloquent of disdain, but when she spoke her voice was soft and smooth as ever.

"Then I ask your aid because you are a man."

"But a man that scorns womenkind!" he retorted.

In one lithe movement she was upon her feet facing him with chin upflung, viewing him beneath drooping lids, a very figure of scorn.

"I doubt but some dairy-maid hath flouted you of late, poor youth!" she murmured. "'Tis possible years shall heal the smart and bring you a little manhood!"

The muddy riding-boot stilled suddenly, the black brows frowned, then he laughed harshly and bowed:

"*Touché*, madam!" quoth he, slapping his knee, "I protest 'tis most palpable hit. A little manhood, says you—hum!"

"Mr. Gyfford, are you a man of honour?"

"Faith ma'm, I fear not——"

"For shame, sir! Have you indeed no sentiments of kindliness and generosity, of that quality of sympathy that lifteth man above the mere brute?"

"None, ma'm, not one! Question those respectable gentle-folk my neighbours and they shall assure you of the fact, with divers deplorable particulars. Howbeit, you will perceive I have at least the virtue of candour."

"Nor do your looks belie you, sir."

"My looks, ma'm? Ha, you'd say my poor visage matches my reputation! Egad, am I so satyr-like? Pray was it to brow-beat a disreputable dog or plead his aid to some unknown purpose that you broke into his house?"

"Neither, sir, 'twas merely to steal."

"Gad, so here's more candour, i'faith!"

"To recover a letter addressed to your cousin Sir Richard Gyfford."

"Addressed, says you, to my cousin? To—Sir Richard Gyfford. So—ho, damn my cousin!"

"Heartily, sir!" she murmured, nodding at him fiercely. But he was staring at the candle, whistling softly between his teeth again, quite lost in gloomy thought; whereupon she surveyed him anew with quick feminine eyes. His age? Anything between twenty and forty. And was it, indeed, the face of an evil man? In puckered brow, grim mouth and indomitable chin was there not an air of latent power—and more, a hint of something nobler? And, despite sullen look, his features were good enough, also he was younger than she had supposed. Now was he truly an evil man or bitter disillusioned boy? His age should be about thirty—and then all men were children——

"And yet," said he suddenly, "I have neither seen nor heard of such letter!"

"How should you, sir? 'Twas addressed to your cousin Sir Richard, and he is away in London. But 'twas delivered here this afternoon to a man in livery with a scar on his face."

"Ha, this will be Tom Pitt! And he received the letter, you are assured o' this?"

"Beyond all doubt."

"And you came hither to steal it, ma'm?"

"Or buy it back at any price before Sir Richard should receive it."

Reaching out to a bell-rope beside the chimney he jerked it violently and a distant bell tinkled.

"What would you?" she exclaimed.

"We will question a rascal, ma'm—nay, if you fear to be seen, get ye behind the curtains," and he nodded towards the deep window recess. For a moment she hesitated in frowning perplexity, but, at the sound of approaching footsteps, vanished behind the draperies, as, crossing to the door, he unlocked and threw it wide, and there entered a man who bowed and peered with narrow, close-set eyes.

"Tom Pitt, I want the letter was brought you to-day, a letter inscribed to Sir Richard Gyfford."

"Letter, sir? There was none, sir, none indeed."

"However, I want it, Tom, a letter that was put into your claws this afternoon. Do I get it?"

"O impossible, sir, quite impossible indeed, there was no——" Tom Pitt's sleek head rapped sharply against the panelling, and he gasped and choked in the sudden gripe of sinewy fingers.

"Do I get it, Tom, lad?"

With feverish haste Pitt thrust hand into bosom, and, drawing thence a heavily sealed letter, gave it up without a word.

"Exactly!" nodded the other, glancing at the superscription, "Now begone, Tom, and close the door after you."

He was turning the missive over and over when she parted the curtains, her serene assurance whelmed in a tremulous eagerness.

"You—you will give it to me, sir?" she questioned.

"I wonder?" he answered, his saturnine features twisted in sardonic smile. "'Tis Sir Richard's property true enough, here is his name very fairly inscribed."

"Julian Gyfford," said she, sinking her voice to passionate whisper, "'Twas writ to a villain by a foolish

girl who bitterly repents her folly. Should it come to
his, to Sir Richard's hands, only God knoweth what of
evil and how much agony it may work. Sir, you as
Sir Richard's cousin, must be sensible of his ill repute,
but, for his soulless cruelty, his wickedness and black
deceit none but a woman may know——"

"You are well acquaint with this right villainous
Sir Richard, 'twould seem, ma'm?"

"Enough to hate his name and run this hazard to-
night that I may snatch one poor victim from despair."

"Faith, ma'm, you paint him monstrous villain—a
blacker rogue, begad, than—even I had thought him.
You shall tell me more of his sinning."

"Nay, 'tis vile subject! And I am expected—I pray
you give me the letter."

"Aha, the letter!" he sighed and, in that moment,
broke the seal, unfolded it and began to read. "Pah!"
he exclaimed, and turned to glance at the signature.
"Are you 'Saccharissa'?"

"No!" she cried, fiercely scornful. "And what
manner of thing are you so to dishonour yourself—to
pry—O shame!"

"Considering you are a thief, ma'm, a housebreaker
caught in the act. I prove in you a singular absence
of fear, a deplorable lack of confusion! A very arrogant criminal, a most imperious gallows-bird!"

"Will you give me the letter, sir?" sighed she wearily.

"Do you know the purport of this missive you hazard
that white neck for, eh, ma'm?"

"I know 'twas writ by a poor distracted girl."

"Have ye read it?"

"Nor do I wish to!"

"Then be seated, ma'm, and I'll read it to you."

"I'll not hear it."

"Then cover your ears, ma'm." And holding the
letter to the candle he read aloud:

"Dear Sir Richard, I will meet you to-night at the
hour you appoint by the old Mill House trusting to
your honour to return my letters. But oh, Richard,
you have promised so often, pray God you will keep

your word to-night and return the letters. I think
it would be my ruin, my despair and lasting misery.
Indeed, Richard, they was wrote you before I knew
what love was—but I do love at last with all my
heart—do not break this poor heart I pray thee and
return these letters and I will rest your grateful,
loving friend Saccharissa."

"Well, sir, the letter speaks for itself. Are you
satisfied?"

"And here is your letter, ma'm," said he, handing
it to her with mocking bow. "Our Sir Richard is
proved a very complete knave, ma'm. What manner
of letters are these she pleads for, think ye?"

"Romantic folly writ by an innocent school-miss to
a designing villain, trifles of none account, 'tis this
letter might work the harm!"

"Trifles? Yet she would seem vastly anxious for
their recovery. The old Mill House—hum! Now for
yourself, ma'm, you break into this house which was
desperate folly, hoping to steal this letter, which was
madness, such letters as this do not lie waiting to be
stole! How then did you hope to recover this letter?"

"Sir, I had two alternatives, the one was bribery."

"And the other?" But at this moment, from some
chamber above, rose a waxing and hideous uproar of
drunken voices wailing the chorus of a song to the
accompaniment of thudding heels and ringing glasses.
"Hark ye to the poor wretches, ma'm! These unhappy
souls have, each and every, suffered by reason o'
woman's faithlessness, and gather round me, betimes,
to drown their sorrows in the flowing bowl—sworn
dispraisers o' the Sex one and all. And yet were I
to show you to 'em now, your eyes so bright, ruddy-
lipped, egad, so tight and buxom. . . . I wonder?
Come, let's try 'em."

But as he moved, forth from the folds of her cloak
flashed a white hand that grasped a small pistol in slim
yet resolute fingers.

"At your peril, sir!" said she, high and disdainful,
"Touch me an you dare!"

"Madam," he retorted with his slow, dark smile, "I earnestly desire not to touch you at any cost! Woman hath resistless appeal to most men, but for myself—I much prefer dogs, ay, and horses, to be sure."

From somewhere adjacent came the sound of unsteady feet, and therewith a bibulous voice calling plaintively:

"Oho, S'Richard, come back t'us! Dicky—Dicky, O Dick Gyfford, come back t' y'r fr'en's!"

"Sir Richard?" she repeated, glancing around in sudden alarm. "Sir Richard is here, then?"

"He is, ma'm."

"But I heard—they told me he had ridden for London this morning."

"He had, ma'm, but then he changed his mind and rode back again."

"I must begone—he must not see me!"

"Indeed, but he must, ma'm, since, having eyes he may not help, alas!"

Now meeting his grim, unsmiling look, she recoiled, the pistol slipped her lax fingers and lay unheeded.

"You mean," she faltered, "You mean——"

"That I am Sir Richard Gyfford, ma'm, yours—up to a point—to command."

"You?" she faltered, "you? Then suffer me—to go, sir."

"None shall let or stay you, lady, least of any I. You came by the window, I think?"

"Yes!" she murmured, not looking at him.

"Then by the window will we go."

"You? You will come?" she questioned, staring, as he took hat, cloak, and sword whence they lay.

"Indeed!" said he, bowing. "My poor wretches up aloft are already happily drunk, but wine, like so many other things, hath lost its savour for me. . . . You are forgetting this second alternative—your pistol, ma'm, most unwise!" And picking it up he set it in her unready hand. "Come now, I shall see you to your carriage, or horse, or friends, or whither you will and, while we walk, you shall tell me more concerning Sir Richard Gyfford, his monstrous sinning."

CHAPTER II

It was a warm, still night, lit by the soft radiance of a rising moon and full of the languorous fragrance of honeysuckle, while from the shadowy coppice stole the soft, bubbling notes of a nightingale.

Sir Richard, glancing at his companion, espied a glistering tendril of hair, a slim, proud-arched foot and, between these, voluminous cloak; yet in every fold of this enveloping garment, and in her every motion, he sensed an ineffable disdain, wherefore his grim lips smiled a little wryly.

"Aye me, ma'm," he exclaimed, sighing heavily.

"List ye to lonely Philomel, yon amorous fowl! Gaze on Dian, her fair loveliness, pale lamp for languishing lovers—how think ye, ma'm?"

She merely hurried her step a little.

"Faith, ma'm, I protest; 'tis night most apt to sighful dalliance, how say you?"

"That I would be alone, sir."

"Nay, but consider yon bright orb."

"Indeed 'tis very bright," she answered in her smooth, soft tones. "Too bright for some folks—highwaymen, for instance!"

"Gad—so!" he exclaimed. "Doth that fly buzz? 'Highwaymen!' says you. Now I wonder why?"

They had reached the high-road by now, stretching white before them, a silver track fretted, here and there, with the far-flung shadow of tree and hedge.

"Here, sir," said she, turning and glancing at him at last, "I will give you good-night!"

"Which I return, ma'm, with all my heart," he answered with careless bow. "'Tis night to be enjoyed, let us go on."

8

"Sir, I would go alone."

"Then, madam, alone with me you shall go, and we together will look on chaste Dian yonder and converse o' highwaymen and—housebreakers, in especial one!" At this she turned her back upon him.

"So you will afflict me with your presence, sir?"

"Gladly, ma'm—until I weary, or you reach your friends or carriage, or inn, or——"

"And you will so plague me because I am defence-less?"

"Because thou art indeed mine own particular house-breaker, ma'm."

"Is this a threat, sir?" she inquired, glancing at him over her shoulder.

"Nay, a bond rather. . . . Will you walk, ma'm?"

"Alone, sir."

"Lady, you harp on the word to none avail for thy way shall be my way until——"

"Sir, you grow but the more detestable."

"Perfectly, ma'm! And our nearest inn is the Gyfford Arms, two miles hence. Walking at a mean speed of three miles to the hour thus gives you but half an hour to endure the infliction of my company, and in half an hour yourself, being a woman, may tell me more of myself, my sins and frailties, than I am at present sensible of. So with the monstrous Sir Richard for your theme—recount, ma'm, discourse, recapitulate—mine ears attend you."

"So be it, sir, and now shall they tingle if there be any shame yet in you." And speaking, she tossed back her hood with sudden angry gesture showing him all the proud scornful beauty of her face.

"'S bud!" he exclaimed. "'Tis a fine-spirited, proud, handsome piece!"

"Indeed, Sir Richard," said she with bitter con-tempt, "thus should rustic lout flatter village hoyden!"

"Precisely, ma'm. Here in the country I am heartily rural, were we in town now, I might put it more elegantly thus: Here walks proud Prudery artfully provoking—man's sweet madness and abiding misery. For here you are, ma'm—'spite your proud arrogance and high imperiousness—a mere feminine lure to the unwary, and therefore of sex abhorred."

"And you, sir," she cried in sudden fury, "you——"

"Ay, ma'm, and now o' me! Yourself, that hath known me scarce an hour, tell me of my monstrous self and spare me not. Begin, ma'm! . . . Firstly?"

"I know you, Sir Richard Gyfford, for one of infamous life, a menace to all purity and innocence."

"Egad!" he exclaimed, shaking his head, "and I know myself a very Cato, fleeing Woman like a plague! . . . Continue, I beg!" His calm gravity seemed but to infuriate her the more:

"I know you for drunken satyr—a cold-hearted libertine——"

"Now 'pon my soul, ma'm, you shock me."

"And O, most vile—a blackmailer of women who——"

"God's death!" Even as she gasped at this fearful oath she was stayed and swung by powerful hand to behold a face so transfigured that her courageous spirit quailed at last, and, bowing proud head, she covered her face against these awful, glaring eyes. Then he loosed her, and she heard him laugh harshly.

"Did I fright ye, ma'm? A little rough, I fear? Well, put it down to my rural manners. I may appear somewhat over-sensitive but we rustics are a little more squeamish than town folk. . . . A blackmailer—precisely! And what more, ma'm?" But instead of answering she was staring up at him with troubled eyes.

"You are indeed Sir Richard Gyfford?" she inquired in voice strangely hushed.

"Never doubt it, I am he, ma'm, upon my honour—tush, this were vain to swear by! I will swear upon my life."

And now as he went beside her, his sombre eyes staring down at white road, or up at brilliant moon, she looked at him often and with ever-increasing unease.

"But—if you live in the country, sir——"

"I am frequently in London. . . . Pray continue, ma'm. And do not walk so fast lest we part ere all

my sins be known to me." Here she stole another
searching look at him. A saturnine face yes, with its
glooming brow, sullen eyes and mouth and aggressive
jut of chin. . . . And yet . . .?'

"Come, proceed, lady, I beg!" And now his eyes
were twinkling, his lips twisted in their sardonic smile;
she would have remained dumb and meaning not to
speak, met his eyes and—spoke, yet in her tone was
subtle change.

"'Tis said, Sir Richard, that you was a rebel of the
15, a Jacobite taken in arms and—condemned to
death?"

"All true, ma'm. Being younger then, and greater
fool, I, for sake o' one frail as fair, 'listed for the Pre-
tender, was taken at Sherriffmuir, clapped in prison,
'scaped the axe by a miracle—and was finally par-
doned.'

"You did this—for a woman?"

"Well, 'twas ten years since, ma'm, and most boys
are fools!"

"And—the lady?"

"O, married, ma'm, married. But what more o'
myself? Keep you to me, I beg."

"Nay," she answered, averting her eyes, "'Tis
become a weariness."

"Yet soon to end, for yonder is the village, so
haste to complete my sinful catalogue. . . . Nay, I
insist."

"Well," said she unwillingly, and keeping her gaze
upon the distant lights of the village, "'tis rumoured
you do consort with thieves—highwaymen——"

"Nay, nay, gentlemen o' the High Toby, rather!
'Twas one such saved my head for me, contrived the
miracle of my escape, a clever dog and hath my abiding
gratitude. And yonder is your inn." And he nodded
where, across the village green and close beside square
church-tower, rose the chimneys of the Gyfford Arms,
a great, rambling place of jutting gables whence came
a sound of voices and laughter, with a rosy glow from
latticed windows which, like the wide, hospitable door,
stood open to the balmy night.

" Ay, there's your inn, ma'm, and gay wi' company, strangers hereabouts, I fancy, quality from London and cheery souls, list to 'em!"

They were close upon the inn when, from the wide-flung casement of an upper chamber, rose a sudden tuneful roar and the words, these:

> "Of Helen we the praises sing,
>   Our love and worship tellin',
> To Helen let our glasses ring
>   To Hel, to Hel, to Helen——"

" Ay, hark to 'em!" repeated Sir Richard, for his companion had stopped suddenly, and was staring up at that open window. " Poor fools, sorry, misguided wretches, tossing down bumpers to some regardless she who is probably smiling on another at this moment. Egad, what a contemptible thing is a man in love, what a——"

Here, finding the lady had gone on and was walking swiftly away, he ceased rhapsodizing and hurried after her.

" But the inn, ma'm—will you not enter?"

" No, sir."

" Eh, because o' yon poor wretches' dismal howls?

" Because I am going home, sir."

" Home?" he repeated, " Hereabouts?"

" O, is it so marvellous?"

" Astounding, ma'm! You are out o' place amid things rustical!"

" And I am living in the lane beyond the toll-gate, And, with submission, sir, I love the country."

To this he made no answer, but walked in frowning thought; and when he had gloomed beside her thus some distance, she laughed suddenly.

" You are, I think, by nature a morose creature?" she inquired.

" Why, I'm better company when drunk, they tell me," he answered. " And I suppose the worst name any woman may answer to is—Helen!"

" O sir! And why?"

" Well, she was a wanton, which is no great matter for wonder, but——"

" Sir!"

" But, ma'm, she brought ruin and destruction on a brave people. A somewhat wholesale lady, for your ordinary woman is——"

"Too good for your ordinary man, sir."

" Hum! Now, touching yourself, ma'm. You ha' never met that complete man o' fashion my—ha—dear cousin, Julian Gyfford?"

" No . . .! And here is my house, sir," said she, pausing at a lych-gate set amidst a very high, thick hedge. " I bid you Good-night." Sir Richard took off his hat and bowed:

" Y'r servant, ma'm," said he, turning to be gone, but she stayed him with a gesture. " Sir Richard, I think perhaps you may send back those letters—some day?"

" I think, perhaps, I may, ma'm."

After this they remained silent awhile, he staring up at the moon, she studying his face.

" You have never asked my name, sir."

" 'S-life, ma'm, it never occurred to me."

" I am Helen D'Arcy."

" Helen!" he repeated. " Ay, I feared so! And a reigning toast it seems . . . ' to Hel, to Hel, to Helen!' Madam, I salute you."

Then he bowed, hat a-flourish, and strode away.

CHAPTER III

WHICH INTRODUCES ONE, ANGELA, THE PRIMARY CAUSE

It was in very black and evil humour that Sir Richard went his way, fists deep thrust in capacious side-pockets, and scowling gaze upon the dusty road. Once he cursed aloud fiercely, and once he halted suddenly and glanced over his shoulder as though half minded to go back, then, laughing harshly, went on again.

He had turned aside from the high-road, meaning to take a short cut homewards, when he was arrested by the whinney of a horse at no great distance, and, glancing up, beheld, above tall hedge and tangled thicket, the mouldering ruin of the ancient mill; moved by sudden impulse he went in among these thickets and presently came on what he sought—the fresh imprint of a horse's hoofs in the soft earth, and followed these tracks until he heard a murmur of voices and beheld the speakers. They were standing in the full radiance of the moon, between the grim shadow of the ancient mill and the deep, still waters of a shady pool; he was a slim, handsome, extremely elegant young gentleman entirely *à la mode*, from flowing periwig to silver-spurred riding-boots, and she seemed very young, and of a soft and gentle loveliness as she stood looking up at her companion, while her small hands clasped and wrung each other.

Sir Richard halted and, leaning against a tree, watched them sullen-eyed, whistling softly to himself between his teeth. . . .

The gentleman drew a packet from the breast of his embroidered coat, at sight of which the girl reached out eager hands; the gentleman seemed to consider, smiled, shook his handsome head, and, finally, thrust the packet into his breast again, whereupon the girl uttered a pleading cry and cast herself upon her knees before him, arms up-flung in passionate supplication; smiling still, the gentleman took these pleading hands, kissed them gallantly and, swinging lightly to saddle, bowed with graceful flourish of hat and cantered away, leaving the girl upon her knees, her slender loveliness shaken by great sobs. At last, uttering a desolate, wailing cry, she rose and began to stumble towards the pool, and was within a yard or so of these deep and stilly waters when, hearing a footfall behind her, she started round and shrank, staring with eyes of terror.

"Tush, child," said Sir Richard, a little peevishly, "I am no ghost!"

"Who—what are you?" she whispered.

"Faith, 'tis a somewhat vexed question, 'twould seem," he answered, viewing her trembling loveliness keen-eyed. "But what o' yourself now—hum! Are you child o' innocence indeed or woman o' wiles? However, here is no place for you, also you would find the water unpleasantly cold and wet, and our Helen expects you and will be in fine taking an she find you not. Egad, I can vision how her black brows will frown on thee, the flash of her eyes, the cock of her imperious head! Moreover she hath recovered your foolish letter."

"My letter? . . . The letter I writ Sir Richard to-day? . . . Oh, sir, is it true? Is it true, indeed?"

"Come and see for yourself—child!" he answered, and smiled down into her troubled face; beholding which smile, all her fears of him seemed banished, her small hand crept within his arm and the eyes, upraised to his, were bright with joyful tears.

"Thank God!" she whispered.

"And Helen!" he added.

"Yes—yes, indeed! My brave, beautiful Helen! And you—you, too, sir, for had you not come——" Here, she glanced at the stilly pool, shivered violently and clung to him the tighter. Now looking down at these small hands that clasped his arm so confidingly, he began to whistle softly between his teeth.

"Come," said she, "let us go; prithee take me to Helen."

"To Helen!" he repeated. "To Hel—to Hel—to—hum! Come your ways, child, lest she slap thee, pull thy hair and savage thee—come thy ways, Saccharissa."

"Ah, no, prithee never—never call me so. 'Twas thus—he named me."

"Who, lass?"

"Sir Richard Gyfford. Is he friend to you, sir?"

"Not so, child."

"I am glad, for he is—O wicked! I hate, fear him."

"Then talk we of Helen the heroical, our dame undaunted——"

"Tell me, sir, are you one of her suitors?"

"Hath she so many, the poor soul?"

"O sir, a veritable host! And small wonder for she is so proud and beautiful and rich."

"Beauty and riches—a plague o' suitors! So wags the world, child. Doth she favour any?"

"Nay, alas, she contemns and flouts 'em all—even Lord Brocklehurst and Viscount Carberry, that hath writ a song to her, she vows she'll not be wed."

"Ay, faith, a stout soul is Helen, wi' the heart of a lion, the pride o' Lucifer, the courage of a paladin! Egad, she's so flintily unfeminine she might become almost endurable——"

"Endurable, sir?"

"Except her name! Helen likes me not; she should be called Penthesilea."

"O, pray why?"

"Because she is creature truly Amazonian, bold for battle, stern for strife, a Roland for any Oliver, in fine, and despite her petticoats, a very 'roaring boy!'"

"Nay, indeed, sir, ah—no, no! Helen is vastly brave and if a little fierce in her tempers—yet can she be very tender. O, very infinite, gentle. I have seen her weep for——"

"Never tell me she can weep, child. I'll not believe it."

"Truly, sir, she can weep right piteous for another's sorrows! She wept for me only this morning when I told her all my griefs."

"Thou'rt over young to be so grievous, child."

"Nay, sir, I am nigh upon eighteen. As for my beloved Helen, I would she were married, but she swears——"

"Ay, I'll be sworn she swears, child, I'll warrant me she can swear as blythe, and rap out oath like any tarry mariner!"

"Indeed, and she can't, sir! Helen never swears—save when she is mightily put out—and then vastly prettily, and—why, there's our old Ben looking for me with a lantern and the moon so bright!"

"Ay and begad, there's your Helen! Beware her potent fists, her rending claws, my poor child. As for me, having legs I'll use 'em." And, running across the road, Sir Richard vaulted a stile and was gone, leaving his companion to stare after him amazed; then, crying Helen's name, she kilted up her voluminous petticoats and sped light-footed towards that twinkling light—to cling and be clasped in Helen's protecting arms, to be kissed and scolded, slapped and fondled, all in a moment.

"O Angela, dear child—thou devilish imp to run such risk! I'm all distraught for thee——"

"But you have the letter, my Helen! You have the letter—he told me so!"

"Did he forsooth! Well, for once the villain spake truth, I have the letter."

"O thank God! Stoop—stoop and let me kiss thee."

"So you met Sir Richard Gyfford—at the old Mill House, Angela?"

"Forgive me, dearest, but I had to go. . . . He showed me those other letters, but would not give them back, and left me despairing and then—O Helen, hold me tight—it seemed death was the only way for me, and I would ha' jumped into that dreadful pool and then—he came."

"You mean Sir Richard, back again?"

"No, no, a strange, great man that scowled, yet with gentlest smile too. He seemed a friend o' thine— I wonder which?"

But Helen was silent, her abstracted gaze bent where old Ben hobbled on before; and, staring at the unnecessary lantern he bore, she visioned instead the grim and sullen visage of Sir Richard Gyfford, but a face marvellously transfigured by her own imagination to what it might have been.

"Yet is he rogue!" she exclaimed with sudden strange vehemence and angry toss of proud head. "Yes, a mere scheming, sordid villain!"

"Nay, truly, Helen, he doth not seem such——"

"And is therefore the more dangerous, my Angela— an odious wretch!"

"He talked much o' thee, Helen."

"Did he so—the viper! . . . Well, what said he?"

"Asked if you favoured any one o' your suitors."

"An impertinent monster! And what said you?"

"That you flouted them all, and he vowed you were a 'stout soul'—though methinks he meant it kindly."

"Kindly, miss? The man's a hellish reptile! What more said he?"

"Nay, dear Helen, I ha' forgot."

"Tell me this instant, miss!"

"Then be not angry, dearest love!"

"Angry—I, my sweet? Never with thee, 'tis but the natural indignation I prove against this—this devilish wretch—nay, I am calm, my love, so tell me all the fellow said o' me, bate not a word or syllable—come!"

"Why then, dear Helen, he said he'd warrant you could swear——"

"Swear!"

"Like a tarry mariner."

"The inhuman monster! O just Heaven——"

"Nay, but he said it kindly, Helen, and lauded thy bravery, called thee lion-hearted, an Amazon and a roaring boy in petticoats, yet always his voice seemed——"

"O, the cockatrice!" exclaimed my lady, clenching white fists, "The venomous serpent—the basilisk! O, 'tis damned fellow this, a runagate villain, a very hell-hound."

"Nay, dear Helen, an you miscall him so bitterly I shall begin to think—ay, I shall!"

"What, miss, what?"

"That you shall come to——"

"Well, ma'm?"

But Angela laughed, and, reaching the lych-gate, sped away into the house.

CHAPTER IV

DESCRIBETH THE BREAKING OF A HORSE-WHIP

MEANWHILE Sir Richard, reaching the inn, turned into the yard, and, taking care to avoid the stables where horses stamped and snorted and ostlers hissed and whistled, made his way to a door behind the inn, a small, discreet door, in shadowy and unexpected angle, that seemed, as it were, to hide coyly from all chance observation. Taking a key from his pocket he opened this door and stepped into a narrow passage, dim-lit, and panelled from floor to raftered ceiling; having closed this door which fastened itself with a spring lock, he stood a moment listening, for all about him was astir, a blend of vague sounds—footsteps that came and went, a distant, high-pitched, giggling laugh, murmurous voices, sudden creakings, soft rustlings— a stirring that seemed above, below and all around him. Half-way along this passage he paused and reaching out assured hand, slid aside a certain panel discovering a dim flight of stairs up which he mounted, the panel closing behind him, and so came into a small, odd-shaped chamber with many unexpected corners and deeply recessed angles; also, although this strange room possessed four several doors, it had not so much as a single window. Upon oaken table lay a horseman's cloak, very dusty, a pair of long-barrelled pistols, and a heavy riding whip; beholding these articles Sir Richard laid his hand upon the latch of one of the four doors when, from somewhere nearby, rose a querulous, high-pitched voice speaking in quick, staccato sentences:

"No—no, damme! I refuse—I refuse, I say!"

Ensued now the smooth, soft murmur of another voice whereat Sir Richard frowned, turned from the

door and, crossing to a particular corner, lifted a sec-
tion of the moulding, thus discovering a "judas"—
two peepholes whereby one might look into the neigh-
bouring room.

At a table heavily laden with glasses and bottles
mostly empty, sat a gorgeous young gentleman, elbows on
wine-dabbled cloth; his great peruke was all awry, and
his face, framed between slim, tight-clasping hands,
was just now contorted by rageful despair. Seated
behind him, frowning and a little aloof, was an older
man, keen-eyed, high-nosed, intent; and, fronting these
two, stood a tall, elegantly-slim, smiling creature who,
for all his languid air, seemed to dominate the situation;
his face, modishly pale, was almost hidden in the blond
curls of his lofty peruke, a richly-braided coat of delicate
green velvet offset his slender, shapely form, and now,
though his lips smiled, his sleepy eyes were a menace:

"My dear Brocklehurst," he murmured, "I shall
be happy to afford you another week o' time and
then——"

"But ye know—ye must know—'twould mean my
ruination, Gyfford!" and in the speaker's haggard eyes
which glanced this way and that, was sudden, glaring
hate.

"My lord, you exaggerate the fact!"

"It's true—'tis too dev'lish true—you know it is!"
cried his lordship, and now his furtive eyes stole a look
towards the small-sword in adjacent corner. "Don't
—no, don't push me too far, Gyfford."

Sir Richard closed the judas and, taking up the
riding-whip, viewed it with thoughtful frown. Then
a door opened suddenly and there entered a fine, handsome girl who wept but, espying Sir Richard, she
checked her sobs, dried her eyes and dropped him a
curtsey.

"O, sir, thank God you'm here!" said she.

"Why, Penelope, lass, what's amiss?"

"'Tis Nick, sir, 'e do be that rampagious I be come
to hide his pistols."

"Nick? Ay, he's come to earth, I see," and Sir
Richard nodded towards the dusty cloak. "But what's

the trouble? Are the officers on his heels again, or is he only drunk?"

"O worse, Sir Richard, he be—jealous! An't please you, sir, it be all along o' they London gentlemen— they—they—O me they were for kissing me, sir. I told father, and father told Nick, and Nick do be a-goin' to—O Sir Richard, 'e do swear to be shootin' some o' they gentlemen—but you'll stay him, sir, won't 'ee?"

"Where is Nick?"

"In the kitchen, sir, along o' feyther—no, he be a-coming up here for his pistols sure! I can hear him— O Sir Richard, you won't——" As she spoke was a quick, light tread and in came a tall, well-featured man, a comely fellow, from neat wig to dusty, spurred boots, who might have been anything rather than the notorious character and dreaded night-rider he was; to be sure bright eyes and jutting chin seemed truculent, yet his clean-shaven mouth had a good-natured and humorous twist notwithstanding.

"Oho—is't you, sir?" he exclaimed, and stood hesitant.

"Myself!" nodded Sir Richard. "And leave your pistols alone, Black Nick."

"But, sir, d'ye see 'tis a matter o'——"

"Don't be a fool, man!"

"Lord, sir, fool I must be being in love wi' lass as loveth not poor Nick! But dog bite me, sir, if any man shall treat my Pen anyways disrespectful whiles Nick can twitch trigger, 'tis matter o' conscience wi' me."

"And who," demanded Penelope, frowning at him over rounded shoulder, "who give 'ee leave to name me 'your' Pen? Beant as if I were promised to 'ee."

"And it beant for lack of askin' of 'ee, Pen—ecod, I've axed 'ee often enough, as Sir Richard do know."

"An' you can go on axin' of me, Nick, but——"

"Ay, I will so, lass!"

"'Twill be no and no so long as you be—what you be. They'll take an' hang 'ee one day, Nick, and then, O then——"

"Why then, dear lass, I'll ax 'ee no more."

"And why are ye here to-night, Nick?" inquired Sir Richard drawing the whip-lash through his fingers thoughtfully.

"Ill luck, sir. My mare, good lass, cast a shoe, or I should ha' made pretty work on't wi' so much grand company on the road, fambles and tattles not to mention cole—O pretty work, sir."

"Wicked work!" cried Penelope.

"So, sir, thinks I, having missed 'em on the toby-consarn, and them trying to kiss Pen, dammem, what's to stop me——"

"Myself, Nick. I forbid it!"

"But, sir, my conscience!"

"Damn your conscience, Nicholas, and mind your neck! You'll leave these frolicsome gentry to me."

"Eh—what's to do, sir?"

"Watch!" answered Sir Richard, and strode from the room.

Thus, Mr. Julian Gyfford, smiling so amiably at his two companions (the one who muttered and plucked nervously at stained tablecloth, the other who sat so tensely still and silent, yet both so alike in their impotence), Mr. Julian was in the act of inhaling a pinch of snuff when the door swung open and Sir Richard entered.

"Wha—what—who the devil?" queried Lord Brocklehurst, and got to his legs with an effort; the dark, silent man scarcely glanced round while Julian Gyfford hailed cheerily:

"Greetings, Dick! 'Tis my joy to present these two dear friends o' my bosom, Lord Brocklehurst—Captain Despard. Gentlemen, my esteemed cousin Sir Richard Gyfford."

The Viscount bowed, a little unsteadily, the Captain merely nodded, Sir Richard did neither, nor did his sombre gaze leave his cousin's handsome face; conscious of which scrutiny, Julian's smile faded:

"What the devil ails thee, Dick, art drunk?"

"Never more sober."

"Well—what d'ye want here?"

"You."

"Ay, you bring me my letter, I think?"

"Not I."

"Well, but what's this Tom Pitt tells me of a letter?"

"The lying rogue tells truth for once, maybe."

"Where is my letter, Dick?"

"'Twas addressed to me."

"What o' that?"

"So—you'll mask your damnable practices under my name, will ye?"

"'Sdeath!" exclaimed Julian, opening his sleepy eyes wider than usual, "Are you mad?"

"No, merely sober."

"Then let me die, but I prefer you drunk!"

"So you'll cloak your villainy beneath my name, eh, Julian?"

"Villainy, d'ye say—you? Why, damn you, your name is so devilish smirched and blown upon that one peccadillo more or less can pass unnoted. The world knows you for no saint, Dick, and expects you'll act accordingly. . . . But enough o' this!"

"I'm but beginning, cousin Julian."

"Ha—damme, then if you must quarrel let us at the least ha' the decency to do it in private."

"No! These so dear friends o' yours shall learn the loathly villain you are and see ye flogged."

With the word, he leapt to action incredibly swift. . . . Vicious blows—a cry, and Julian Gyfford was squirming beneath his cousin's dusty riding-boot. . . .

"Gentlemen—O stap my vitals—!" gasped the Viscount, floundering to unsteady legs; but Captain Despard pulled him down again, whispering sibilantly:

"A way out for us—a way of escape, Will, I see a light! Wait, man, wait—let be!" And then was the vicious hiss of flailing whip-lash, a passionate cry repeated again, again and yet again. . . . Stifled groans, wild imprecations . . . a raving voice that grew shrill, grew hoarse while the Viscount, crouched in his chair babbling futile oaths, flinched to every hissing stroke, and Captain Despard, lips curled in gloating smile, watched with eyes that glittered between narrowed lids.

The whip broke at last, and Sir Richard, panting a little, let it fall, and nodded down at the awful shape writhing beneath his foot, a wild creature, dishevelled, torn, a smear of blood across his pallid cheek, and all hell glaring in his eyes.

"Cousin Julian, to-night I was named a 'blackmailer' of women! From to-night I refuse to father any more sins o' yours. And now I'll have—these!" So saying he thrust hand into Julian's breast and, snatching thence the packet of letters, dropped them into his own coat-pocket.

"You—you shall rot—in Newgate—for this!" gasped Julian. "I'll watch you—hang."

"However," nodded Sir Richard grimly, "in the meantime you will leave my name alone." Then he turned towards the door, but in that moment Julian was up, a small pistol in his hand, but even as he levelled it, Captain Despard caught his wrist; a passionate oath, a shattering explosion and, reeling to the table Julian leaned there, left arm a-dangle, glaring at Sir Richard through a swirl of smoke, while, like an echo to that ringing shot, came a sudden uproar of excited voices, a hurry of feet.

"What, cousin, is it murder, then?" said Sir Richard, smiling into that haggard, passion-distorted face. "Why, very well, seek me when you are more able, and we'll slaughter each other for the betterment o' the world in general." Turning to be gone, he saw the place a-throng with people, fine gentlemen who stared, plain folk who gaped, but one and all made way for him, and with never a word.

Then Julian laughed oddly, and, still supported by the table, raised his left arm and showed a hand red and dripping. From this he glanced at the Captain and laughed again.

"My arm, George," said he, "'tis only my arm alas! A few more inches and 'twould ha' been my heart. As 'tis I'm merely winged. Still wert mighty quick, George. And now I'll thank somebody for a sup o' brandy."

Meanwhile, Sir Richard returning to the secret chamber there found Black Nick at the judas.

"By Goles, sir," exclaimed the highwayman, shaking comely hand, "'Snoggers, Sir Richard, Mr. Julian meant to kill you I rackon!"

"We shall probably kill each other, one o' these days," sighed Sir Richard, sinking into deep elbow-chair. "But, Nick—when we were little lads I—used to—kiss Julian 'Good-night'! However—I ha' spoiled thy whip, Nick. . . . And now, pray ha' them send up ale, plenty on't, for to-night I intend to be very comfortably foxed."

CHAPTER V

OF THREE FINE GENTLEMEN AT BREAKFAST

THROWING wide his casement, Sir Richard leaned out into the fragrant morning; the day was young, the dewy world all a-sparkle in the early sunshine, birds made joyous clamour, but Sir Richard, clasping heavy head, groaned by reason of last night's deep potations, and gazed about him haggard-eyed. Immediately below lay the pleasance, a riot of weeds, its yew-hedges untrimmed, its winding paths over-grown, a desolation, like the rose-garden beyond, now little more than a tangle of briars; yet this had once been the joy and care of that young, long-dead mother he had never known, she whose gentle spirit was said to haunt it in the full of the moon. He looked above him and around upon this goodly house but, finding everywhere the same signs of neglect and decay, groaned louder than ever, whereupon the soft-moving personage in the bed-chamber behind, ventured to speak:

"I would suggest a glass of Mrs. Abigail's cordial, sir, a draught of her Surfeit Mixture, 'tis marvellous good against the spleen, megrims or vapours and can tackle a man's liver better than any pill or bolus of Doctor Samson or——"

"O, man Gregory, come ye here. Here, beside me!"

The person obeyed, a tallish, lean man whose sedate visage was offset and dignified by the trim curls of a small, neat wig.

"Tell me, Gregory, what d'ye see?"

"An uncommon fine morning, sir.'

"Tush! Look about you—this home o' the proud Gyffords—a wilderness, Greg, and all my doing! A fair heritage run to seed like its owner, damme! You'll

27

"The poor soul would prove me an infliction, I fear. . . . And yet—not for very long, mayhap—a month or, say, three weeks. Who is she?"

"The Viscomptess de Champfleuri, sir."

"Ah, a Frenchwoman!"

"Nay, extremely English, sir. I knew her father, the title was bestowed on the family years ago by the Grand Louis. In English she is the lady Helen D'Arcy."

"Well—sink me!" exclaimed Sir Richard.

"Your father and hers were great cronies in their youth."

"Rabbit me!" murmured Sir Richard.

"My lady Helen's parents died young, leaving her to the care of Madame la Duchesse d'Estouteville."

"Helen!" quoth Sir Richard, "Gad's life, Greg, you'll tell me you know her, next."

"I did, sir, years ago."

"Thou'rt constant surprise to me, Gregory. Ha, the still tongue in the wise head! Howbeit this particular heiress shall never do; she is altogether too heroical, too handsome, too proud—too superlative in every way. And then her name—Helen! No, she'll never do, Greg."

Sir Richard's ablutions duly accomplished, Gregory brought his newest periwig freshly ironed, adjusted it with dexterous fingers and, stepping back, bowed:

"Now, sir, I beg to inform you my lord the Marquis of Merivale waits below."

"Merivale? At such preposterous hour! 'Tis not seven o'clock."

"No, sir. His lordship is asleep."

"And small wonder."

"On the kitchen settle, sir."

"In heaven's name what brings him there?"

"The Surfeit Mixture, sir."

Forthwith Sir Richard descended to the kitchen, a cosy place from raddled stone floor to low, beamed ceiling, and bright with the sheen and glitter of copper and pewter, yet with nothing in it brighter than the eyes of pretty, buxom Mrs. Abigail who, curtseying to Sir Richard, finger on rosy lip, nodded towards the great high-backed settle where, outstretched in peaceful slumber, lay a slim and very resplendent young gentleman snoring gently; at Sir Richard's touch he moaned plaintively, sighed deeply and opened a pair of languorous, blue eyes.

" S'there y'are at last, Dick!" he murmured, extending languid hand. " Here's me like th' early worm, I mean bird."

"A thousand welcomes, Ned! But how comes it thou'rt so far from St. James', thou pink o' fashion? And Gad's my life, lad—why so marvellous early abroad?"

The Marquis who, being young and extremely modish, was a perpetually weary soul who found the exertion of movement and articulation an effort almost beyond his powers, nevertheless contrived to sit up, by degrees, and to speak again:

" T'offer m' services, Dicky. T'act for you in y'curst affair wi' Julian. Has he sent his cartel yet?"

" No, but——"

" He will, Dicky, lemme perish but he will!"

" Of course, Ned. . . . So you've heard o' the business so soon!"

" Heard o't, man? All London'll ring wi't in week, Brocklehurst babbles!"

" Viscount Brocklehurst is a great friend o' Julian's—eh, Ned?"

" S'much so, Dick, that if—I say ' if '—you should chance, b'some miracle, t'pink Julian, friend Brocklehurst would sing f'joy, ay, an' so would that f'low Despard."

" And yet Captain Despard is another of Julian's friends! Hum! 'Twould seem Julian hath queer friends, Ned."

" Julian's a queer soul, Dick! Split me, but y'made sore bones of 'm! Brocklehurst says y'nigh killed 'm, and begad Brocklehurst giggled f'pure rapture while he told me. Friend or no the Viscount don't love Julian, and if—I say ' if,' Dick—you should happen to give cousin Julian his quietus, Brocklehurst's joy—stupendous!"

"You did and I was grateful, old lad, but fools
should pay for their folly. . . . However, you were
telling me o' this Captain Despard."

"Well, Dick, seein' he killed Tony over the cards—
he's amazin' lucky at cards—seein' he persoos the peerless Helen like a beast o' prey 'n' she fears him——"

"Fears him, Ned—not she! Your Helen is an
heroical Amazonian creature far above such weakness."

"Yet, Dick, I'll lay m' life she fears him. Some
folk can't abide cats, 'n' are terrified b'toads, slugs,
snakes 'n' so forth, and this f'low's worse, split me if
he a'nt! So I'm waitin' opportunity o' tryin' on him
my pet thrust in quarte, 'tis sufficiently baffling, not
t'say deadly, 'n' hath served me prettily once or twice—
ha, b'heaven, I'll show it to thee, Dick! See, here's
the manner of 't!" And, forgetting modish languor,
up sprang the Marquis with surprising agility, out
flashed his delicate small-sword and he fell to a posture
of offence.

"See, Dick, I bear my point—so! You meet me in
quarte, I feint in the low line, you parry—I drop my
wrist, up comes my point, I straighten my arm and you
—egad, you are in your second's arms and they are
howling for the surgeon. Go get your sword, Dick
and let's to't, for man I—O dem!" A rap at the door,
and Gregory appeared to announce:

"Mr. Anthony Trumpington!" Forthwith in stalked
a tall, somewhat cadaverous yet highly ornate young
gentleman, whose eyes were wistfully soulful and who
spoke sighingly:

"Greetings, gentle souls! Woe's me, though so early
I'm late, it seems, for here is Ned afore me, and both
o' you rehearsing scenes of blood and sudden death."

"'Sbones, Tony!" wailed the Marquis. "Who's
talking o' death?"

"Myself, Ned—even so, for death's in the circum-
ambient air, alas—why baulk it? Julian is a madman,
raving for Dick's life, yet a cold, purposeful, devilish-
deadly madman! And thus I mourn for thee, Dick."

"Mourn?" repeated the Marquis indignantly. "Y're
demd early about it, 'n' altogether demd dismal, Tony!"

"O naturally—naturally!" sighed Mr. Trumpington, his soulful eyes reproachful also. "Would ye have me rejoice in the prospective loss of a friend? For, why deceive ourselves, our Dick is surely in the Valley o' the Shadow!"

"Enough—ha' done!" cried the Marquis. "Here's no season for y'r dismal Jeremiads! If y' must wail go out 'n' do 't t' th' cows 'n' cabbages, 'n' so forth."

"Nay, sit down, Tony, and eat," said Sir Richard, carving at the ham; but at this juncture Gregory knocked for third time and opened the door; said he:

"Sir Richard, Captain Despard begs a word with you."

"Desire him to walk in," and, setting down the carving-knife, Sir Richard got up and turned to greet his visitor:

"Your servant, sir," said he, bowing as the Captain entered.

"Sir, yours humbly to command!" answered the Captain, saluting all three gentlemen in turn with grave ceremoniousness.

"You are from my cousin Julian, I think, Captain?"

"Indeed, sir. I have the honour to represent Mr. Julian Gyfford, and to hand you this letter on his behalf."

Sir Richard took the letter and laid it upon the table.

"Its purport is easy to guess, sir," said he.

"Precisely, Sir Richard. . . . It will be small-swords, I presume?" Sir Richard nodded. "And the place, the time?"

"These particulars you may discuss later with my friend the Marquis of Merivale, who will act for me."

"My lord!" said the Captain, his grim mouth faintly supercilious as he bowed to the Marquis, "Your very devoted, obedient!"

"O sir," lisped the Marquis, bowing languidly to the Captain, handkerchief a-flutter, "Yours to command!"

"Have ye breakfasted, Captain?" enquired Sir Richard.

"Thank you, yes, sir. And now, by your leave, I will return to my principal." So they all bowed again

My lady hurled a pillow with such unerring aim and vigorous arm that Betty staggered and clung to the bed-post.

"Now take a deep breath, child, straighten your cap and—speak! Their names, wench! Nay, first the pillow to my back—now, tell me!"

"Well, my lady, 'twas that wildsome, wicked gentleman, Sir Richard Gyfford——"

"Ah—!" nodded my lady. "Well?"

"Nay—ill, ma'm! A beats his poor, young gentleman cousin most shameful cruel—Mr. Julian, such pretty man as eye ever see!"

"His cousin—so? And wherefore, my Betty?"

"O ma'm, 'twas in's cups—disgustful drunk were Sir Richard by accounts."

"Ay, the man's a sot, I know."

"Nay—worse, ma'm! For though a gentleman he don't get drunk properly among gentlemen on wine, ma'm, as gentleman should, but a drinks—ale, ma'm! And among they common village folk!"

"And how didst learn o' this, Betty?"

"Well, ma'm, this morning I chanced to pass the time o' day wi' Mr. Meagles, my lord Viscount Brocklehurst's gentleman, what see the outrageous act commit with his two very own eyes, ma'm! And besides everyone's a-discussing on't, my lady, as I stand on this identical spot! There's Mrs. Weatherby below stairs, as lives at The Gables, ma'm, and Sir John Parret and his lady, and my lord Viscount Brocklehurst and Captain Despard all a-waiting to tell ye about it, and setting in the garden with Madame. Will I send word you'll join 'em anon, ma'm?"

"Do and I'll scratch thee, woman! And yet, I'll hear their chatter, ay, I'll to 'em." And forth of bed leapt Helen, supple and graceful as the young Diana. "Lay out the taffety and new French head," she commanded.

Thus, in due season out into the radiant sunshine stepped my lady, very gracious, very dignified, very handsome and completely aware of it.

The visitors were grouped about Madame la Duchesse

d'Estouteville, who sat throned beneath the great
cherry-tree, a hook-nosed, sharp-chinned, formidable-
seeming lady she, of very uncertain age, with hair
preternaturally curling and abundant, complexion too
vividly red and white, but with glorious eyes, undimmed by years, of a wonderful blue, deep and dark
and variable, beautiful eyes, indeed, that, in their quick
changes of expression, matched the too-wide but
generous mouth below.

As Helen approached the company rose, the ladies
rushed delicately to greet, to pat, to kiss her, the gentlemen bowed, fluttered hat or handkerchief, shot ruffle
or tapped snuff-box; as for Madame la Duchesse she
inhaled a copious pinch of snuff and snorted; quoth
she:

"And is this yesilf, Helen, an' your company waitin'
this half-hour! Art here at last, me dear soul? 'Tis
hoping I am ye didn't distress yesilf wi' any passion
o' haste or hurry."

"Dearest Beloved," smiled Helen, patting Madam's
nearest hand, "I'm all breathless and twittering with
my speed."

"Howbeit, dear Madam," quoth Sir John Parret, a
very solid, red-faced, full-necked gentleman. "I protest
you—ha—you come like the Spirit o' Summer, the very
soul o' beauty!"

"Vastly poetically true on my life!" simpered
Viscount Brocklehurst, Captain Despard merely bowed
and gazed.

"And now, me Soul o' Beauty," said the Duchess,
opening her large fan with a snap, "you find us sitting
in solemn judgment upon a wretch, a monster, an ogre,
and a villain and consequently—'tis dying I am to
meet him!"

"Him?" repeated Helen, sinking gracefully upon
rustic seat.

"Himself, my dear; shure he is but one though he
sounds like a regiment, and his name is Richard Gyfford.
If ye'd learn more of him, and himself our landlord, it
seems, here's the Viscount shall discourse; the dear
man tattles moighty engaging."

"Julian's bound to challenge the fellow, has challenged the fellow, the duel's good as arranged."

"A duel!" repeated Helen. "Then pray why should Captain Despard speak of murder?"

The Captain smiled and shook his handsome head gently:

"I said 'battle, murder and sudden death,' madam. Sir Richard seems desperate determined fellow, whilst his cousin vows to make fatal work of this unhappy affair and, one way or t'other, I believe he will."

"Och, me dear souls," exclaimed the Duchess, smiling round upon her visitors with show of remarkably sharp, white teeth, "shure we've arl been deloightfully malicious, 'tis quite uplifted I am, for 'tis moighty comforting to us poor sinners to know of someone more sinful than ourselves. Sir Richard now—the dear, sinful monster—is so infinitely iniquitous that, compared with him, we are all angels o' light and saints o' holiness. So 'tis, we should all be deeply grateful to the wicked crayture, I am—and yonder he comes, I think, through the herb-garden."

Looking whither the Duchess's levelled fan directed, the company rose incontinent; Mrs. Wetherby shrieked faintly, Lady Parret shivered and shrank, the gentlemen stared, fumbling with hat or snuff-box, and Sir Richard, halting beneath the arch cut in carefully trimmed yew-hedge, stood a little at a loss and very much surprised, staring at them, one and all, with his most sullen expression. Then the Duchess smiled and beckoned, whereupon he bowed in perfunctory manner and stepped forward, hat in hand; but as he advanced the company retreated, so that when he stepped beneath the wide-flung boughs of the ancient cherry-tree, the Duchess and he were alone.

"So you are the ogre!" said she, looking up at him with her strangely beautiful eyes.

"Faith, ma'm, 'twould seem so," he answered, his gloomy gaze upon the distant, chattering company.

"A pariah and outcast—eh, Sir Richard?"

"Which nothing grieves me!" he answered, turning his back upon the company as the Viscount's high-pitched giggle rose again. " I am here, madam, in answer to your strangely urgent letter, pray how may I serve you?"

" First by sitting down, sir, lest I get a crick in the neck o' me—sit ye here! Och, shure ye greatly resimble your father, sir."

" Eh, ma'm?" exclaimed Sir Richard in quick surprise. " Faith, I scarce remember him. You knew him?"

" Shure he kissed me frequently, the dear man, but 'twas long ago, and I was Eileen O'Malley then! Ah, but 'tis with the eyes o' your mother you look at me —me dear, loved Barbara."

" My mother. 'Tis strange word on my lips. . . . She died so very young—knew you her well, ma'm?"

" Passing well, sir. She was me dearest friend—me much loved Barbara. I knew her years ere she met your father."

" I pray you tell me of her?"

" Not now, sir. You shall tell me of yoursilf.'

" Myself?" he repeated and scowled. " Nay, ma'm, twere merest waste o' breath. You'll have learned all about me from the good folk, yonder. Sir John Parret and his lady, for instance."

" Ay, indade, and they were eloquent, however now I'm for hearing yesilf, sir."

But he sat mute, scowling down at the toe of his riding-boot.

" 'Tis listening I am, me dear Richard."

He started and glanced up, so wonderfully, kindly soft was her voice: " Richard Gyfford, suffer your dead mother's dearest friend to peep into her son's heart— speak Richard!" Then looking into these strangely beautiful eyes, Sir Richard leaned forward impulsively and began to talk, as he had never done even to the faithful Gregory, speaking from his very heart.

Thus, after some while, the company having departed, when Helen approached the shady cherry-tree it was to find the Duchess and Sir Richard seated side by side (to her no small surprise) with their heads very close together, absorbed in murmurous conversation, nor were they conscious of her presence until her shadow fell between them:

"Ah, Helen, me jewel!" smiled the Duchess, "behold the Monster! Make your riverince to Sir Richard Gyfford."

"Nay, madam," sighed my lady, curtseying to him with extreme formality, "we ha' met before."

"O miss and indeed ma'm, and will ye discover the hour and where of it?"

"Why yes, Dearest-Loved," answered Helen, seating herself on the other side of Madam, "I broke into Sir Richard's house to steal a letter."

"Saints and angels o' grace!" exclaimed the Duchess.

"A letter which may perchance explain how Sir Richard broke his whip——"

"And is it a riddle ye'll be tellin' me now?"

"Though, indeed, I think the matter should have been conducted in more usual and less brutal fashion. How say you, sir?"

Sir Richard merely bowed.

"Tare an' ages!" cried the Duchess, rapping each in turn with her fan, "And phwat's all this I'm hearing o' letters and thievery? Speak one o' you—both, any of ye, or is it die of curiosity I must?"

"Nay, Dearest-Beloved, but 'tis Angela should speak for 'tis her secret."

"But 'tis yoursilf knows Angela is away to Lewes, and here's mesilf and you and Richard——"

"'Richard,' madam?" repeated my lady, eyebrows arched in surprised reproof. "Such sudden familiarity."

"O miss, and why not? 'Tis son of his own father and blessed mother I find him, so ' Richard ' is he when not ' Dick.' And now then, miss?"

"As you will, ma'm!" answers my lady, disapproval in every line of her.

"And now this letter, speak, miss—explain, child— this moment, ma'm, or I vow, me dear Helen, I shall burst something."

"There, there!" said Helen, taking Madam's somewhat large but very capable hand and patting it, "Shalt not burst, Dear Heart. no—not even a stay-lace.

Here's poor Angela's silly story: A year ago she met a villain."

"Aha, that demure, pretty piece o' pink and white modesty! Well?"

"A villain—and, Dear One, do not interrupt me! A cold-hearted, calculating villain and the poor, sweet innocent scarce out o' the nursery! Well, being in love with love she writes him foolish letters, and presently forgets both them and him. But, scarce two months ago, she meets my lord Althorp and scarce is their betrothal announced than the villain reappears threatening exposure of the letters. Then, Dear Beloved, we come home, back to England, thou and I, and in London poor distracted Angela flies to me in her terror. I learn the villain is in Sussex, so to Sussex we come."

"Aha, so here's the reason ye fled the Town in such haste, me dear?"

"Indeed, my love. But scarce are we here, and before I can do aught i' the matter, Angela writes the villain another letter, behind my back, a wild letter full of frantic supplications and then tells me."

"And boxed her silly ears ye did, I'm hoping?"

"Soundly, my dearest soul! Then I borrowed Betty's cloak, and, with golden bribe in one hand but loaded pistol in the other, I crept to the villain's house, slipped through the villain's window and met the villain—in the dark."

"Mordieu—And Gad love us all—why i' the dark, Helen?"

"Because I blew out the villain's candle."

"Eh? *Nom d'un nom!* Phwat then?"

"The villain knocked me down."

"*Alors ma mie, quelle horreur! Ventreblue!* And then?"

"I recovered the letter."

"And who was the vile wretch? Phwat is the black villain's name?"

"Sir Richard Gyfford."

The Duchess fell back in her chair the better to stare up at Sir Richard, who had risen, and now stood looking down at her sombre-eyed, his shapely mouth curled in sardonic smile. . . . And so for a long moment they remained, eyes of blue, keenly questioning, staring up into eyes of hazel steadfast yet very wistful. Then the Duchess swore a great French oath and shook her head.

"I don't believe it—no, never of thee, Richard Gyfford!"

The bitter smile vanished from his lip, his eyes seemed suddenly very bright and he made her a stately bow:

"Madame la Duchesse, I—I am grateful!" said he, his speech and tone so altered that my lady Helen glanced at him in faint surprise.

"Sir," said the Duchess, smiling up at him, "ah Richard, 'tis not stone-blind I am, ye'll ha' noticed the good God gave me eyes?"

"Ay, I've remarked 'em, ma'm!" he answered, whereat these same beautiful eyes that saw so much, grew so singularly kind that Sir Richard took her hand, fan and all, and kissed her bony knuckles with such sincerity and reverence that my lady Helen's grey eyes opened somewhat wider than usual; yet when she spoke she contrived to sound very coldly aloof.

"Howbeit, madam, all these letters were superscribed to Sir Richard Gyfford——"

"Och, me child, then 'tis plain the villain used Dick's name. Now amn't I right, sir?"

"Then perhaps Sir Richard will tell us—who?"

"To what end, ma'm?" he retorted, "Since Madam is assured that my father's son hath not stooped to such infamy—what matter? As for yourself I beg you'll think no worse o' me than you will. Also I regret the knocking o' your ladyship down, and vow to do so never more."

"Your jesting is out o' place, sir."

"Like myself, ma'm, so I'll be gone. . . . And here are Mistress Angela's letters." So saying, he thrust the somewhat bulky packet in Helen's white fingers, and rose to take his departure.

"Richard," said the Duchess, looking up at him thoughtfully, "'tis the dog with a bad name, y'are."

"Faith, ma'm, you've said it!" he answered, smiling a little grimly. "And such beasts are best left to themselves.'

"And so, mon Richard, you will ever be an honoured guest. 'Tis come again ye will—and soon!"

He stood silent at this, and when at last he spoke his voice sounded harsher than usual:

"No!" said he. "No, madam! I thank you from my heart but—'tis impossible."

"Indeed, Rick, and pray why?'

"Because," he answered slowly, "I—am a man— with a shadow. . . . Listen, madam, and judge: Some six years ago I had a friend, but—one night— we quarrelled bitterly, and would ha' fought there and then but were prevented. . . . That same night he was found—murdered within a few yards of my lodging. . . . I was suspected and shunned by all save two o' my friends. . . . Well, this was six years agone, but the shadow of suspicion dogs me yet. . . . Here, madam, is reason sufficient, I think, why I am indeed pariah and outcast, and must so remain until——"

He ceased suddenly, and with a hurried gesture of farewell turned and strode away.

even to pleasure so kind and loving a friend as—
thyself . . . Nay, spare me thy protestations, let us to
business—how speeds heiress-hunting?"

"Nay, Julian," cried my lord, flushing, "I swear
now thou'rt scarce——'

"Well, how goes your wooing?"

"Excellent well, Julian, though I could wish her
something less—majestic. Yet give me but time to
contrive the matter with due deliberation and no
unseemly haste and she's mine, Julian, mine!"

"I wonder?" retorted the invalid, fixing the speaker
with his brilliant eyes. "Whence this sudden assurance, my lord? By all accounts she is no puling,
bread-and-butter miss to blush at your lordly beck,
or come simpering to your so masterful embrace, nor
languishing madam to weep or wail, sink or swoon and
wed you in vapourish fit of outraged coyness."

"True enough, Julian—but," and here my lord's
eyes narrowed and his loose-lipped mouth took on
an expression of unexpected, ruthless determination,
"consider, Julian—a solitary house, an ardent wooer
—a day and night and—final discovery! Such methods
may bend the most stubborn of feminine wills—eh,
Julian? For where is the woman that won't sacrifice
fortune, freedom, her very self to save her reputation?
You, of all men, should be well aware o' this, my dear
fellow. As for 'the D'Arcy' she was all graciousness
this morning, the dear creature! Sink me, but I begin
to think Despard's scheme may prove unwanted."

"How? Despard's scheme, d'ye say?"

"Why, I'll admit 'twas he suggested the—the
method."

"What you mean this kidnapping, this lonely house?
Tis a somewhat age-worn method, a little hoary, eh,
Will, lacking somewhat in originality, ha?"

"Can you suggest a better, a surer method, then?"

"Not I, faith, not I! Love, force or strategy, win
and wed her as you will, make her securely your spouse,
her fortune your property—the sooner the better for
your sake and—mine, eh, Will? But Lord, man—what
ails ye? Cease your tramping and sit down!"

The Viscount dropped into the chair, and uttered a sound between sigh and groan.

"Well, what—what o' to-morrow, Julian?" he questioned.

"To morrow?"

"Ay—your promise—what o' your promise?"

Julian laughed gently and shook his head, while the Viscount, writhing in his chair, watched him beneath close-knit brows.

"So you won't, eh—eh?" he questioned suddenly. "It's to be 'no' again, is it?"

"Positively no, Will."

The Viscount's narrowed eyes drooped, he licked his lips, his small, shapely hands fluttered:

"Oh, damme, but 'tis ever the same!" he cried in high-pitched, querulous complaint. "Every year you promise and every year——"

"Thy fellowship becometh dearer, Will. These latter years ha' knit us close—in a bond o very brotherhood——"

"A bond!" cried the Viscount, and his fluttering hands clasped and wrung each other. "A bond?" he repeated in harsh whisper. "By heaven, ye name it well, Gyfford."

"A bond, my dear Brocklehurst, that nothing shall ever break."

The Viscount's head drooped until his face was quite hidden in the flowing curls of his long peruke, but his writing hands became sharp-knuckled fists while his narrow gaze crept along the bed-valance up and up to the small table standing at the invalid's elbow; then, leaping to his feet, he crossed to the wide hearth where a dim fire burned, and stood a while staring down at the smouldering embers.

"I was a fool!" cried he suddenly. "I was a mad, a damnable fool to sign the cursed thing!"

"Tut, my dear Will, tut-tut!" murmured Julian, taking up the silver-mounted pistol from where it lay on the little table, and glancing from it to the Viscount's unconscious back. "Never miscall thyself to me, Will. Besides, you acted for the best, egad,

"You have, George. And I heartily commend you therefore!"

"Ah, and pray why, Julian?"

"Because, whereas Brocklehurst is foredoomed to failure being only Brocklehurst, thou'rt almost as certain to succeed, and I desire to possess a friend so superlatively wealthy as 'the D'Arcy's' spouse will be."

"To—possess him, Julian?" murmured the Captain.

"Precisely, George!" sighed the invalid, and for a tense moment each watched the other as they might have done above the glitter of deadly steel; then Julian smiled, nodded, and continued: "To own a friend, my dear George, of such enormous wealth would be an asset of corresponding worth to such as I."

The Captain closed his snuff-box gently and, staring down at it thoughtfully, began to tap it softly with one white finger.

"Friendship," said he in his pleasant, slumberous voice, "friendship, more especially such as yours, Julian, is a jewel—of price, it seems?"

"'Tis beyond rubies, George!" The Captain tapped awhile.

"And yet," said he, finger arrested, "the thought occurs to me that, given certain circumstances, friendship—even such as yours, might perchance come to a determination, languish and—alas—die?" Here the Captain, lifting heavy lids, looked with sudden fixity at Julian who, lying back among his pillows, looked as fixedly at the Captain:

"My dear George," he sighed reproachfully, "how can you contemplate such impossibility? Friendship such as mine, overleaping all sins of omission and commission, shall never end but with my life."

Here the Captain glanced at his snuff-box again, and again he tapped it gently.

"Your life! Julian?" he murmured.

"My life!" repeated the invalid, and, watching the Captain's tapping finger, he saw it rise, poise a moment suspended to fall slowly, slowly, light as thistledown. Julian laughed softly and stared up at the bed-tester again. "But, George," said he, "life being so uncertain, I have made particular provision, should Death leap on me sudden and unannounced—a statement documentary, George, that shall to the world declare in clarion tones the wherefore and precise reason for such friendship as this of mine for thee. And so, George, as thy friend abiding, Heaven speed thy wooing, say I?"

The Captain pocketed his snuff-box and, crossing to the open casement, leaned there.

"Referring to your duel," said he suddenly, "art so sure, so confident o' the outcome?"

"'Tis beyond all doubt, George. I shall pink cousin Richard precisely how, when and where I will. Dick and I have fenced together since boyhood, and I could hit the fool howso I would. . . . Ah, George—George, 'twill be joy to feel him writhe upon my steel, to watch his dying spasm, hear his parting sigh! . . . And yet —the public ignominy of the hangman's noose! The gaping crowd! To watch him die kicking for the delectation of the mob—why, this were sweeter!"

Captain Despard turned from the window and, coming to the bed's foot, surveyed the speaker with an expression of wondering interest:

"Heaven refuse me!" he murmured, "but I discover in you at times, Julian, a sublimity that awes the mere human."

"My dear George, such appreciation from such human as yourself is infinitely flattering. And speaking of yourself brings me to poor Tom Allinson, who was found dead outside Richard's lodgings—his sudden demise. Could we not resurrect him for the nonce, raise him from the grave, as 'twere, contrive new evidence, and damn our Richard to the gallows? Advise me, friend George."

"Not I, Julian, not I, you are sufficient unto yourself. I'll out into the air and get me an appetite for supper.'

CHAPTER VIII

TELLETH AMONG OTHER MATTERS OF MORNING
SUNSHINE AND—A BACONY FRAGRANCE

THE *Black Horse* was a low-browed, tumble-down little ale-house which, standing alone, seemed to crouch, as it were, sulkily aloof from the village, scowling across the wide green towards the lofty gables and clustered chimneys of its grander neighbour the Gyfford Arms.

And here, that is to say on weather-worn bench before this tavern, Sir Richard sprawled with a mug of ale at his elbow though the day was so young that dew sparkled in the grass and gemmed every leaf and twig, indeed a glad, brave morning, yet Sir Richard's sullen gaze was fixed on vacancy and, being lost thus in gloomy reverie, he whistled softly and dolefully between white teeth; and his peruke was askew, he wore his oldest coat, a shabby garment whose wide skirts and tarnished silver lace proclaimed its age, into the huge bulging pockets of which his fists were deeply plunged. Divers villagers, sons of the soil abroad thus early, espying this so solitary and familiar figure turned thither, eager to touch their hats in salutation, but, beholding his dark, abstracted gaze and lowering brow, hastened silently upon their way. Jonas Watt, the landlord, peering furtive through open lattice at this same disconsolate figure, shook gloomy head at his buxom wife who, sighing, shook hers back at him.

Thus Sir Richard, sitting in this glory of sun, felt it not, and, staring upon this goodly world, saw it not, for his mind was wholly obsessed by the consciousness of his own futility, the slow but sure degeneration of these latter years; wherefore he scorned himself very heartily and, scowling thus upon creation, yearned amain to vent his spleen on all and sundry.

At last he stirred, jerked hand from pocket, and had grasped the half-emptied tankard on the table before him when my lady Helen, touching her spirited mare with riding whip, came galloping joyously across the green, to rein up within a yard of him. Now beholding her thus suddenly, and herself radiant as the morning, he started, and getting to his feet made her a profound obeisance with wide-armed flourish of slopping ale-mug.

"Ma'm," quoth he, "all hail!"

"Sir," she retorted, pointing disdainfully at his tankard with her riding-switch, "why the aspirate? 'Tis ale you mean, surely."

"Faith, ma'm," he laughed, "then in ale I hail ye—to Hel—to Hel—to Helen!" and he raised tankard to lip.

"O poor wretch!" she exclaimed, shaking handsome head at him in scornful reproof. "And on such fair morning, and the world so glorious!"

"Is it, ma'm? Then God give ye joy on't."

"And what o' yourself, sir? Ay, what indeed?"

"Never better, ma'm. Never so merry. Say but the word and egad, I'll sing!"

"How, sir, are you so shamefully fuddled—thus early in the day?"

"Hardly so, yet, ma'm. Howbeit, give me but time and——"

"Odious!" she exclaimed, "You look sufficiently sottish and dissolute, sir. I bid you Good-bye!" and, wheeling her horse, she cantered away, leaving him to sit and frown at nothing in particular, blacker than ever.

Suddenly he heard a shrill scream and, glancing up, had the vision of a small, flying shape, felt his booted leg clasped by a panting, sobbing creature who looked up at him through tumbled, raven hair with great, black eyes a-swim in tears. So, for a moment, the child gasped and sobbed distressfully, staring up at him in passionate appeal.

"Why, how now," said he, stroking back her long, disordered curls, "who are you?"

C

"Curst—if I do!" gasped Mr. Battleby, sitting up and feeling his chin with anxious solicitude, while the little gipsy watched him with a fearful joy. "Ah, but you shall pay for this!" he cried, ordering his rumpled attire. "I shall instantly impart the matter to Sir John Parret himself!" At which dread name the little gipsy, quite forgetting her jubilation, began to whimper. "Ay, you may snivel," quoth Mr. Battleby fiercely threatening, "but you shall be whipped yet, Sir John Parret shall see to it." The child cried shrilly, and with a supple bound, clasped Sir Richard by the leg again and, crouched upon her knees, drew the skirts of his shabby coat about herself.

"O brother," she wailed in muffled tones, 'you won't suffer 'em to beat poor Shuri—not again? O pretty Gorgio gentleman, O kind brother, not again!"

"There, there, child!" said Sir Richard, and, feeling how she trembled, set his arm about her, "none shall harm ye."

"And I say, ' cried Mr. Battleby, clapping on his hat defiantly, " I say that Sir John Parret shall——"

"Peace, chatterbox, and hearkee, thou man o' straw! Should you, or Sir John Parret, or any other lay a finger on this child in the way of unkindness, I will lay ten fingers on him, and make that man the sorriest dog that ever howled. Pray tell Sir John this, with my compliments and now—begone lest I kick ye hence."

Mr. Battleby hesitated, made as if to speak, thought better of it, gulped and went; whereupon the little gipsy, peeping forth of enveloping coat-skirt, hooted in shrill derision until Sir Richard closed her rosy mouth with finger and thumb.

"Not so, madam!" said he, smiling down into the great eyes upturned to his. "Suffer the fellow to go, 'tis something unlady-like to hoot."

"But, brother, I allus hoots at them kind o' folk, if there's no chance as they ketches me. And him's worser than a plastremengo, a bad, bad customer for Shuri, big brother."

"And were you poaching Sir John's rabbits, Shuri?"

"O no, brother! O never—no, no!" Shuri shook her little head so violently and opened her great, black eyes in such wide innocence that he pursued his enquiry:

"And why must you poach rabbits on Sir John Parret's land, Shuri?"

"Lor, brother, Shuri wasn't! Shuri never don't poach, not never."

"Won't you trust me, child?" he enquired, gently.

The big, wistful eyes questioned him eagerly, every feature of his square-cut, comely face, then the long lashes drooped and she shook her head:

"Shuri's a Romany, one o' the poor folk, brother, as has nothing o' their own, and you'm a Gorgio, one o' the rich folk as has everything, and rich folk and poor folk can't never trust one another my grand says. . . . And they wasn't rabbits, brother."

"Then what were they, child?"

"They was only—partridges."

Sir Richard whistled in dismay and shook his head at her.

"And they wasn't on Sir John's land—leastways, brother, 'twas only just over the boundary from Gyffords."

"But, Shuri, if you must poach, why not keep to Gyffords?"

"'Cause there be's so precious little to poach there, brother!"

"Ay, true enough, child," he answered with rueful laugh, "true enough!"

"And there be's a fine, great lady staring at we!"

Sir Richard glanced up swiftly and saw Helen approaching across the green; she was leading her horse, the long skirt of her habit in her arm; and, beholding her noble form, her gracious walk, his mind instantly recurred to the Marquis's description of her, and he thought of Juno and Minerva. . . . But, marvel of marvels, she was smiling, while in her grey eyes was such a look as woke in him a growing wonderment. Hither came she and, having tethered her mare, stood looking down on him with the same unexpected kindness.

CHAPTER IX

DESCRIBETH A BREAKFAST "AL FRESCO" AND A SIGNET-RING

LIKE Janus, the double-faced, this tavern of the *Black Horse* opposed two very different aspects upon the world; thus, while it scowled so forbiddingly upon the dusty road, seen from this sunny garden it seemed to smile in kindliest welcome, its bright lattices twinkled in such downright friendly fashion beneath deep-thatched eaves, more especially one, a small, lop-sided casement that winked and blinked down from impending gable like some very jovial and vastly knowing eye.

In a shady corner of this garden, deep-bowered in honey-suckle was an arbour, beholding which Shuri laughed and capered in elfin joy, and, grasping a fold of my lady's habit in one brown hand and Sir Richard's shabby coat-skirts in the other, thither she drew them; and here presently came Jonas, the landlord, bearing a well-laden tray, his cheery visage more jovial than ever:

"Lord love, 'ee, S'Richard," quoth he, setting down the tray, "this be a occasion, sir, sure-ly, what wi' you and your lady so honouring me and my Mary, and you a-wolloping Sir John's new bailiff so 'earty as ever was—wot I says is, Lord love you, sir—and your lady to be sure! Yon Battleby be an 'ard kind o' chap by all reports—ay, 'ard as Sir John Parret hisself. 'Tis luck for me and my Mary as you'm our landlord, sir."

"Egad, Jo, d'ye think so, and the house yonder going to rack and ruin!" sighed Sir Richard, shaking his head at it ruefully. "Sir John's tenants are better housed.'

"Ah—and pays for it!" nodded Jonas. "And sir, the old *Black 'Oss* might be a sight worse! And here," said the cheery landlord, wrestling fiercely with something in his pocket, "here be the bell, your honour, if you lacks for ought, you rings and I comes. May you and your lady and missy yonder eat 'earty, sir." And the beaming Jonas, having touched eye-brow to each in turn, left them to their breakfast; but:—

Sir Richard, forgetful of the savoury viands on the dish before him, sat viewing my lady with thoughtful eyes and she (of course) supremely conscious of his scrutiny, gazed across the sunny garden at a row of stately hollyhocks, quite heedless of the steaming coffee-pot for all its delectable aroma, while little Shuri, glancing at Sir Richard, the bacon and eggs, my lady and the coffee-pot, sighed, wriggled and finally spoke:

"O brother, be's us never going to eat?"

Sir Richard started and took up knife and fork, my lady laughed and commenced to pour the coffee while Shuri, looking pensively from him to her, questioned Sir Richard again:

"Be's this lady your lady, brother?'

At this my lady glanced at Sir Richard merry-eyed.

"Not so, Shuri," he answered gravely, "The lady is, I believe, completely her own as yet, though she is for ever threatening."

"Threatening, sir?" repeated Helen. "Who, sir— and what, pray?"

"Matrimony, ma'm, to some adventurous male."

"And I likes the taste o' this stuff!" said Shuri, sipping her coffee.

"And indeed," said my lady, "'tis marvellous to be drinking such rarity so far from town, sir."

"Ay, but we are in Sussex, ma'm, a county that lacks for little that comes over-seas."

"Ah, you mean—smuggling?"

"Madam, 'tis word never uttered hereabouts."

So they breakfasted together right merrily by reason of little Shuri's trilling laughter, impish looks and odd questions; a truly memorable meal, more especially for Sir Richard, who beheld the transformation of stately goddess into very human woman, and woman into unaffected girl, her modish airs all laid by a-while; indeed my lady was a revelation, wherefore he watched her and forgot all else.

C I

him still oblivious of her, finally contrived to slip it off altogether and sat staring at the shining thing in gleeful ectsasy, polishing it on small, rumpled apron, trying it on each little finger and thumb in turn until it slipped, fell to the floor and rolled out of the arbour.

Thus Sir Richard was presently aware of a startled cry:

"Prala, prala—O brother!"

"Eh!" he exclaimed, startled and glancing about, "Why, where's the child?"

"O brother, here I be's—come quick! A big man goes for to prig your vangustri—your ring! Here be's wafoden-pen, prala, so come quick!"

Up rose Sir Richard wondering, stepped out of the arbour and came face to face with Captain Despard, a resplendent figure from top to toe, who stood with the ring on his palm surveying it with curious interest. For a moment they fronted each other thus, then the Captain tendered the ring with a profound obeisance:

"Ah, Sir Richard,' said he in his pleasant, sleepy voice, "your property, I understand. 'Tis a quaint piece." Sir Richard took the ring, slipped it upon his finger and bowed in turn, though a trifle stiffly:

"I thank you, sir," he answered. "Though of small value, 'tis trifle I should regret to lose." So saying, he turned to re-enter the arbour, but the Captain's smooth voice stayed him:

"I protest, sir, 'tis charmingly sequestered nook this, for a meal al fresco with flowers a-bloom for you, birds to carol and beauty to adore! . . . My lady Helen— madam, the very humblest of your servants ventures to salute you!" and he bowed gaily to my lady where she sat half-hidden in the arbour. Sir Richard scowled, the Captain smiled, my lady laughed, and little Shuri, staring up at this strange and so magnificent gentleman, hid herself beneath Sir Richard's shabby coat-skirts again and, from this safe retreat, hooted in sudden, shrill defiance:

"Ya—boo!" cried she, "Shuri don't like ye! Go 'way! O prala, O big brother, send the man away.'

"Hush, child!" said Sir Richard.

The Captain merely raised slim eyebrows and smiled; then my lady stepped from the arbour, her serenest and most stately self.

"One wonders how you discovered us here, sir?" she enquired.

"By your animal, madam, your beautiful mare," answered the Captain with another bow, "she, like her mistress, is unmatched in this South Country—or any other where. So hither come I, completely and most humbly at your service, to escort you home or where you will, when you will." So saying, he reached out his hand with a gesture half-pleading, half-commanding, but, ere my lady might reply, forth from Sir Richard's coat shot another hand, small and sun-burned, that clutched a fold of my lady's habit in little, quick fingers:

"No!" cried Shuri, with vehement tug, "don't ye be a-going with the man, my pen—you stay along o' we, pen."

"Why do you call me 'pen,' little Shuri?"

"Bekos you be's my pen—my sister, and I likes you, same as I——"

"Shuri!" cried a voice, and they beheld an old woman watching them—tall and gaunt she was, and bore herself with a strange pride—at sight of whom the child uttered a shrill scream of joyous greeting and next moment was folded in the gaunt old woman's long arms; for a moment they talked together in strange tongue, then, clasping Shuri's hand, the old woman approached with the same stately carriage and paused before Sir Richard; now looking into her strange, bright eyes, he saw that, despite her upright figure, she was much older than he had thought.

"For my dearie Dubbleskey," said she, raising one hand above her head with solemn gesture, "Truffeni Camlo calls a blessing on ye, Gyfford o' Weare. A tatchey Romany well-wishes ye—you as takes pity on my Shuri. Old Truffeni as be the 'wise one' calls a joyful dukkerin on ye, kind gentleman! . . . But old Truffeni as has 'the sight,' warns ye. Look ye now, and mark! . . . One!" and she stabbed bony finger at Captain Despard. "Two!" and she pointed at my

CHAPTER X

"DAYS ago," said my lady, frowning up through the branches of the cherry-tree, "I gave the man your message. And the man comes not. Well, confound the man!"

"Ha!" exclaimed the Duchess, opening her snuff-box.

"Fie, Helen!" murmured Angela, glancing up, meekly reproving, from her tambour-frame. "Remember, my sweet soul, how wickedly we have misjudged the unfortunate gentleman, how cruelly we have wounded his sensibilities."

"Say rather, his detestable pride!" cried my lady.

"And shure," quoth the Duchess, "pride is always so very detistable—in other folk!"

"And alas," sighed Angela, shaking her pretty head, "O me, the poor gentleman so soon to die!"

"Die, child—to die? Is it Sir Richard Gyfford you mean?"

"Indeed, Helen! They say he is certainly doomed."

"Who says so, miss—who?"

"All the world, and especially Mr. Trumpington! Mr. Trumpington mourns him already——"

"O, Mr. Trumpington is always mournful! 'Tis dismal creature, a moping owlish person. But—Lud, Angela, two gentlemen may surely fight without killing each other."

"Ay, ay!" nodded the Duchess. "Thrue enough, me dear, some gentlemen may but these won't; shure, here will be murderous business, as Captain Despard said, and nothing but dith itself shall prevent 'em killing each other."

"Nay," sighed Angela. "If either kill t'other 'tis poor Sir Richard must die."

"Heavens above!" exclaimed my lady, "You croak, miss, you croak! And why must you be so sure, little fool?"

"Nay—why, Helen, O my dear, why so angry with poor me?" cried Angela, opening big eyes to stare amazed at Helen's sudden gust of passion.

"Because, miss, if anyone be killed 'twill be all your doing!"

"Mine? O Helen! O my dearest!" wailed Angela, sobbing, her innocent eyes suffused with great tears. "Heaven aid me! How—how am I to blame?'

"For writing your three times accursed letters, for mixing up your villains, Mrs. Addlepate. O heaven and earth, when I think of it all, I could almost lose patience with you!" cried Helen between snapping white teeth. Whereat Angela bowed meek, pretty head and wept softly.

So Helen, leaning back in her chair, frowned up through the shady branches of the cherry-tree again, Angela wept and the Duchess, finger and thumb suddenly arrested in her snuff-box, watched Helen's abstracted face with a singular interest; thus was silence awhile save for Angela's gentle, and very lady-like weeping:

"Ah, kind heaven aid me!' she moaned at last.

"And him!" exclaimed Helen. "And him!"

"Who?" demanded the Duchess, sharply, "Which?"

"Whoever lies in most danger," answered Helen.

"Ha!" exclaimed the Duchess, and took her pinch of snuff with great gusto. "Angela, me dear choild, don't snivel: 'twill make your pretty little nose like a strawberry."

"O I know—I know!" wailed Angela. "And my poor eyes will blear, and Mr. Trumpington expected! But how may I help my tears and Helen so cruel? And how was I to know Sir Richard was not Mr. Julian—I mean that Sir Julian was—O, my poor heart is breaking, I vow!"

My lady Helen uttered a sound that in any other might have been termed a sniff; whereupon Angela

CHAPTER XI

WHICH IS EVEN SHORTER AND THEREFORE—

MEANWHILE Helen, standing before the largest mirror in her bed-chamber, stared at the reflection of her loveliness with troubled eyes, vexed, surprised, wondering; and viewing herself dispassionately, feature by feature, questioned herself, thus:

" Could it indeed be true?—Preposterous!"

" Had she ever thought of him as . . .?—Absurd!"

" Could she ever endure to think of him as . . .?—Impossible!"

" Then Angela had been the merest cat?—Assuredly!"

" Yet—why was her colour so high?—Natural indignation!"

" Still, why had the thought of him recurred so persistently of late? . . .!"

" And why must she remember the loose button on his cuff; the sudden way he had of lifting his chin and looking at her as if about to ask some question that never came; the quick vitality of his brown eyes; the small scar that made a dimple beside his mouth; his odd trick of whistling softly between his teeth—why? Why under heaven must she needs remember all this? . . .!"

My lady's wonder and unease nothing abated, she turned her back on the mirror in swift petulance and, leaning forth of the open lattice, gazed dreamily round about upon the pleasant, sunny country-side, shady road and by-lane, rolling meadow, leafy copse and darkling wood with the blue swell of the Downs beyond. And when she had viewed this tempting prospect a while and sighed over it, she rang for her maid.

And after some while my lady descended the stair, the folds of her riding-habit over her arm, and so to the stables, there to wait impatiently what time old Ben and one of the grooms saddled the Witch, her powerful, glossy-coated mare.

" A bit skittish she be, m'leddy," quoth Ben, as the mare pranced and sidled. " A bit playful-like but bootiful—O, bootiful! Jest look at 'er! Lordy, there beant nowt on four legs nowheres can ekal th' Witch for looks or pace."

" 'Tis why I love her, Ben," said my lady, patting the animal's sleek coat. Then, slim, booted foot in old Ben's hand, up she sprang to the saddle, gathered the reins, settled herself lightly, gave the word; the groom let go, the Witch tossed her shapely head whinnying softly, reared gracefully, and was out and away through the grassy paddock.

But scarcely were they upon the open road beyond the village than was a clatter of pursuing hoofs, and my lady found Captain Despard beside her, smiling into her eyes, hat in hand. Helen frowned, the Captain bowed until the long side curls of his periwig touched his horse's mane.

"Madam," said he, "I vow you bloom fairer than the day!"

"O sir," she exclaimed in sighful mockery, "I protest you flatter me!"

"Faith, madam," he languished, "I swear upon my soul I speak the veriest truth!"

"La, sir," she simpered, "then I vow y'are vastly polite indeed . . . and I bid you a very good afternoon."

"Helen . . ." said he, gently. My lady glanced at him, chin aloft, and gathered her reins. "Helen, I love thee!"

"And so 'tis I wish you Good-bye, sir!'

Captain Despard smiled:

"Good-bye?" he repeated, watching her with his intent, unswerving regard. "And yet, Helen, I dare venture to think you will be my wife sooner or later. I wonder when?"

My lady merely glanced at him and wheeled her mare, but out shot the Captain's long arm and he

curved to sudden smile; then, as horse and rider drew
level, he sprang and caught the bridle.

A sudden wrench . . . a stamp of hoofs and
up reared the mare and was away—riderless, for
my lady lay swooning in Sir Richard's arms—that
is to say her eyes were fast shut, and her supple
body lay very soft in his embrace and unusually
limp.

Thus stood he gazing down into the face pillowed on
his shoulder, studying it feature by feature—the wide,
low sweep of brow, the sensitive nostrils, the vivid
mouth; to be sure her deep bosom rose and fell somewhat quickly, but her face—how utterly serene, never
the quiver of an eyelash!

So Sir Richard bowed his head and kissed her, and he
did it with a singular deliberation; he kissed her hair,
one eye, and her mouth and, finding her yet a-swoon, he
kissed her mouth, one eye, and her hair and, indeed,
was in the act of doing this for the third time when she
looked at him and frowned.

SHE: Where am I?

HE: Upon my heart.

SHE: Sir, I believe you kissed me.

HE: S'life, ma'm, I'm sure of it!

SHE: Sir, 'twas wholly detestable act!

HE: Ma'm, 'twas the blissful aberration of a happy
    moment.

SHE: And I a-swoon! O shame, sir!

HE: But, ma'm, a-swoon so gracefully apt!

SHE: Have you no better excuse to urge?

HE: Only the best of all—yourself, ma'm.

SHE: How, sir, how? D'ye take me for one to be
    lightly kissed—a thing so shameless, a creature so
    light?

HE: Ma'm, on the contrary you are convincingly
    heavy!

SHE: Then put me down, sir! Set me down this very
    moment!

HE: But, pray, are you sufficiently recovered to stand
    alone?

Here my lady had the grace to change colour.

"I will do my utmost, sir!" she answered haughtily as her posture would allow.

So, with the extremest of precautions, he set her feet to earth, bowed and stood back while she ordered her attire with deft, feminine touches.

"You find yourself nothing faint, I hope?" he enquired solicitously. "No possibility of a recurrence?"

"None, sir, I never swoon without due reason!"

"Dare I hazard a guess at your present reason?"

"No, sir. . . . And 'tis vastly odd you look without your wig, extreme uncouth, I vow!"

"Why, faith, ma'm," he answered clapping hand to close-cropped poll a little ruefully, "'tis truly deplorable, I know, but I rarely entertain company these days and you . . . dropped upon me something unexpectedly, as 'twere!"

"So you think I tricked you?" she demanded, dimpled chin out-thrust.

"Also that you have beautiful hair," he answered gravely. "I am heartily grateful for sight of it."

"But why," demanded my lady, drawing off her gauntlets and dropping them, "why, pray, should I stoop to trick you? Tell me that, sir."

"Ah, why indeed?" he sighed, and picking up the gauntlets drew them gently through his fingers. "Here is mystery beyond my poor wits, ma'm."

My lady frowned, and began to put up her shimmering tresses, the while he watched her with profound interest, whistling softly through his teeth.

"What is yonder, sir?" she enquired suddenly, nodding towards the hedge he had been trimming.

"Come and see—if you will?" he answered, a little diffidently. "Your mare seems quiet enough, remarkably so."

"Nay, tis deceitful creature, pray secure her, sir, whiles I seek my hat.'

And so, the mare safe-hitched, and her hat found after no great search, since my lady knew exactly where to look for it, Sir Richard brought her into what had once been a fair garden enclosed by yew hedges, but the seat, she drew this cloak about herself, beckoning him to sit beside her.

"Come," said she, softly, "prithee tell me of your mother—if you will.

Thus, inspired by her unwonted gentleness, by her quick sympathy and ready understanding, he forgot his taciturnity and told her of the mother who was to him only a revered dream, and, led on by her subtle questioning, described his early years: himself a lonely child in the ungoverned household of his careless, widowed uncle, Julian's father. He told of his impish childhood and wayward youth, the follies of his early, reckless manhood; of all this he spoke until, catching himself in the act, as it were, he broke off with sudden, rueful laugh:

"On my life, ma'm. I amaze myself!"

"On my soul, sir, and why, pray?"

"Faith, I babble, I chatter, I prate o' myself. I am the merest rattle!"

"Nay, Richard, thou art a friend talking to thy friend here in thy mother's garden. So prithee talk!"

"Garden? 'Tis a desolation!" he sighed. "And yet, for her sake, I would have it bloom again, and by my own labour if it might be."

"And why should it not be?"

"'Twill take time . . . there is much to do!" he answered evasively.

"Well, and why should you not do it?" she persisted. Now at this he glanced up a little apprehensively to find her regarding him beneath puckered brows; so up he got and reached her his hand:

"Come," said he, smiling, "and I will show you how very much is to do, ma'm."

"Richard," she answered, shaking lovely head at him in reproof, "do not be-ma'm me! Being my sworn friend thou shalt call me Helen. Also, when I ask a question I am usually answered. Now, what shall hinder, what shall stay your labours in this garden? Is it . . . ah, can it be that Mr. Trumpington will prove true prophet?"

"Ha, Trumpington—he is a dolorous ass!" said Sir Richard, and picking up the shears he stood frowning at them until my lady took them from him and laid them out of his reach.

"Richard Gyfford!" quoth she.

"Well, ma'm?"

"Say 'Yes, Helen'! Speak my abhorred name at once, sir!"

"Yes, Helen?" he repeated obediently.

"Richard Gyfford, pray look at me!"

"'Tis a joy!" he answered lightly.

"I know you are to fight a duel, Richard. But Mr. Trumpington declares this meeting can end but one way . . . fatally to yourself. Now, Richard . . . nay, look me in the eyes, sir! How think you?"

"That Trumpington's Christian name should be Jeremiah!" smiled Sir Richard. "'Tis a sad, dismal soul, Trumpington."

"Surely, Richard, duels seldom end fatally?"

"Heaven bless you," he answered, seeing the trouble in her eyes, "such accidents are extreme rare, so pray let your apprehensions sleep!" And then, almost ere she knew, he had caught her hand to his lips. "O faith," said he, smiling somewhat self consciously as he met her eyes, "a woman's anxiety for my welfare is thing so novel that I find myself preposterously grateful. Come, my lady Helen, suffer me to show you the home of the proud Gyffords—heaven save the mark!"

So he led her by weed-grown paths and across lawns shaggy for lack of scythe until all at once she stopped, for before them was the great house that rose so stately from its noble terrace; but the westering sun's level beams showed up and made so pitifully manifest its many signs of neglect that Sir Richard flushed and scowled and gestured towards it, smiling in grim mockery; quoth he:

"Behold the house of Weare! And i'faith, it seems more forlorn and desolate than usual to-day . . . thus was it not in my good father's days! So, there it stands—a reproach to his unworthy son!"

"But then I gave him some cause for resentment against me."

"Ay, with your horse-whip! O, I wonder you did not beat his wicked life out!"

"And, Helen, I wonder if you are blood-thirsty as you sound?"

"I repeat such a man were better dead!" she retorted; and then, clenching passionate hands, uttered words which, though he little heeded at the time, he was to think upon very often in the future:

"And, Richard, I vow to you, should he ever give me cause, I would shoot him—and joy to do it!"

"No, no!" said he, shaking reproving head at her fierce loveliness.

"Yes, yes!" cried she. "D'you doubt me?"

"Nay," he answered gently. "I only doubt your capacity for murder."

"'Tis odious word!" said she frowning.

"Murder? Ay, true!" he nodded. "More especially on a woman's lips."

"Nay, Richard, but Abigail tells me——"

"O, Abigail!" sighed he.

"Tells me, sir, that Mr. Trumpington's dismal forebodings are shared by many—yes, and even by you yourself, Richard! She says that you ha' put all your worldly affairs in order—she tells me that you are prepared and quite resigned to meet your death . . . to being killed at the end of the month!"

"Tush and a fiddle-stick!" said he smiling. "Sure, Helen, you know 'tis only usual to make some such preparations before a meeting. And then, besides——"

"Nay, Richard, here is the reason you doubt if you will live long enough to see your mother's garden bloom again. You expect to die—is it not so? Come, answer thy friend. . . . How think you in your heart?"

"That what is to be—will be!"

"And thus," said she in sudden anger, "thus I am to be robbed of my friend by an unworthy creature, a revengeful wretch, a dastardly villain!"

"Nay—faith, I hope not. . . . But enough o' this, choose we a better theme."

"Then, Richard, sit down and let us talk of Friendship, and how I, thy friend, may avert this danger from thee."

"Not so!" he answered gravely. "Here's matter beyond the reach o' friendship—even thine, so let be, Helen, let be! No more o' this——"

"And so," she continued serenely, "because I am thy friend indeed, determined am I to speak with Mr. Julian Gyfford this very night."

"How—you will see Julian? And to what purpose? S'life, madam, would you stoop to plead with him on my behalf?"

"No such folly, sir! I would appeal to the cupidity o' the wretch. . . . I shall bribe him."

Sir Richard laughed, so suddenly and with such unfeigned enjoyment that my lady stared in angry amazement:

"Y'are pleased to be merry, sir?"

"O faith, Helen, thou'rt creature of infinite jest, I perceive."

"Then, sir, you must needs be stone-blind and the merest addle-pate, for I was never more serious! I shall see your cousin as soon as I may."

"What, ma'm, you mean actually to offer Julian money? You will pay him to . . .? Zounds! . . . to spare miserable me?"

"I shall offer him money to quit the country immediately!"

Sir Richard was serious enough now, eyeing my lady in ever-growing wonderment.

"Gad's my life!" he exclaimed. "Your gold for my blood—is that the fact of it?"

"Howbeit," said she, head high and imperious, "I mean to prove my friendship."

"So so, ma'm! And, pray, at how much do you price this carcass o' mine?"

"Lud, sir—I protest you sound like a butcher: so coarse!"

"And I feel like a marketed lamb! How much are you prepared to offer for me?"

"Sir, I shall pay your detestable cousin as little as possible, you may rest assured."

D

Sir Richard rubbed his chin, and surveyed her very much at a loss:

"Now, confound me!" he murmured. "But I almost fear you intend this folly."

"Folly, sir! D'you dare name my friendship folly?"

"Ay, I do!" he nodded. "Such friendship is out of all reason. Can you think I would suffer anyone—any man, much less woman, to interfere in this matter?"

"Then neither will I suffer your foolish pride to rob me of my friend, wherefore I shall see Mr. Julian anent the matter so soon as I may."

So saying my lady rose and, coming to her mare, mounted with Sir Richard's assistance.

"So then you will persist in this, even though I tell you 'twill be labour in vain?" he questioned.

"Howbeit, I shall have tried my best!"

"Even though he laugh at you—even though he make your name a by-word?"

My lady sighed, drooped meek eye-lids and endeavoured to look a martyr:

"This," quoth she, "this will I endure for friendship's sake!"

"Even though I beg you to forgo this whim?"

"Ah, call it not a 'whim,' Richard."

"Why then, Helen, I positively forbid you to hold any such dealings with my cousin."

"Forbid?" cried my lady, forgetting her meekness all in a moment. "La, sir, you may forbid until you are breathless and black i' the face but—" here she sighed and became meeker than ever. "Ah, Richard," she murmured, "thou shalt prove friendship such as mine no light thing!"

"Light?" he exclaimed. "A light thing? 'Fore heaven, 'tis ponderous as a mountain, overwhelming as an avalanche! 'Tis a very cataclysm . . . it crushes me, stifles me! 'Tis an incubus wholly insupportable . . . in a word, ma'm, I find it something embarrassing!"

Gone was the meek martyr, lost in the raging goddess. . . . Flashing eyes, gleaming white teeth, clenched hands:

"I am ponderous as a mountain? . . . I thank you, sir! A cataclysm? . . . Sir, my gratitude! I overwhelm, crush, stifle you? Alack, poor wretch! So then will I relieve you of these hateful embarrassments —thus!" So saying, she leaned from the saddle and, with swift, passionate gesture, wrenched the little cross from his neck.

Sir Richard bowed:

"So ends our new-born friendship, ma'm, like a whirlwind, leaving me, I vow to heaven, dazed, breathless and——"

"Take back your ring, sir—take it!"

Sir Richard obediently held out his hand, my lady drew the ring from her purse, held it above his expectant palm and dropped it into her purse again.

"Sir," said she, looking down at him with the utmost disdain, "as I took back my cross, do you take your ring—if you can!" And then, with trampling of sudden, eager hoofs the Witch tossed proud crest and was off and away.

Sir Richard, smiling a little grimly, watched until mare and rider were out of sight, then, as moved by sudden impulse, turned and hurried towards the house but, beholding Gregory in the kitchen garden, strode thither.

"Greg," said he, "prithee go saddle me the bay."

Now my lady, reaching the highway, reined her mare to a canter, to an amble, to a walk and often glanced back as if expecting pursuit; thus evening had come and shadows were deepening as she reached a place where the road narrowed between high banks topped by trees. . . .

"Halt, ma'm!" cried a voice, harsh, fierce, yet vaguely familiar, and a masked man swung his horse across her path and she caught the dull gleam of a pistol barrel; also, despite the gloom, she saw this grim figure was shrouded in an old, military cloak turned-up and faced with scarlet. Thus, she laughed a little scornfully as she drew rein.

"How then, sir," said she in lofty disdain. "You would fright me with your mask and pistol? You will

With sudden effort he raised himself and seemed to listen with straining ears. "Hearkee, Samson!" said he at last in sibilant whisper, "stoop—stoop your head, man—nay, first see the door is shut and—bolt it, bolt it!"

Wondering, the doctor obeyed and came back to the bed-side, his look more anxious than ever.

"Now—listen, Samson! Bend your head—lower, damme, lower . . . every night o' late I've been—haunted!"

"You mean, sir, that you dream?"

"Dreams? Dreams, d'ye call 'em? I tell ye I see visions . . . hear creeping steps go up and down . . . feel hands touch me i' the dark! And every day I am worse—mark that! . . . Well, my good Samson, worthy doctor, put 'em together, add two and two—and what d'ye get? How—don't ye see it? Must I tell you? Then, hearkee again, in your ear—murder, Samson, murder!"

Doctor Samson recoiled, staring in horrified dismay:

"Mr. Julian!" he gasped, "my dear sir——"

"Eh, eh, Samson, do I shock ye, m'dear, good soul? . . . How long have I lain here?'

"Eight days, sir."

"Aha, and wherefore, Samson? Why? For what reason? . . . Have I any bones broke? Not one! Am I cursed with any deep-rooted disease? You, that have known me all my days, can swear I am hale and sound! Have I contracted any virulent ailment? No! Then what the devil ails me, Samson—what, what?"

"Sir, I make it no more than a general debility induced by the immoderate heat and passion o' your temperament."

"Oho, most learned Aesculapius!" mocked Julian, wagging a finger. "Then I am in no danger?"

"None that I apprehend—at present."

"Then bring me my clothes and I'll go a-walking."

"Impossible, sir! Quite out o' the question."

"You'll find 'em in the press yonder . . . my clothes, d'ye hear?'

" Mr. Julian, twould be madness! Your strange weakness . . . this constant fever——"

" Ha—they puzzle ye, do they, Samson?"

" Sir, I confess it—although——"

" Then I'll resolve ye this mystery, and in one word —poison! . . . Ay, poison, my good fool! They're killing me by inches, I tell ye! They're dragging me nearer my grave every night! . . . killing me, Samson, killing me by degrees, slow but sure, damn them! But I'll up and cheat 'em yet, ay, I will! Bring me my clothes . . . my clothes!" The quick, whispered speech ended in a gasp, and the sick man sank back trembling while Doctor Samson, silent and aghast, stared down at him, his fever-bright eyes and passion-distorted features.

" Mr. Julian . . . sir . . . sir,' he stammered, at last, " 'Tis dreadful accusation, this! Who should . . . who . . . whom d'you suspect?"

" Villains, Samson, villains! An arch-rogue, a cold, sneering devil. . . . Beelzebub in velvets and a Ramillies wig! Where is mine own particular scoundrel?"

" You mean, sir?"

" My snake, Tom—Tom Pitt. Crawls he hereabouts?"

" No. I saw him in talk with one o' the maids from the Moat House——"

" Ha, 'twill be the D'Arcy's woman! So, the plot marches. . . . My clothes, Samson."

" Mr. Julian," said the doctor, viewing his patient in ever-growing apprehension, " let me beg you to compose yourself. These horrid suspicions, these evil dreams are but the outcome o' your malady, a fevered mind."

" Tush and the devil!' cried Julian in swift passion. " I'll up, I say! I'll quit this cursed inn——"

" Sir, to go abroad may prove fatal."

" And to be here, Samson, to be here surely means my grave. So I'll out into the sun and die i' the open air if I needs must. . . . Here's for it!" And, slipping out of bed, Julian took two steps, reeled, clutched the bed-post and clung there, shivering.

this pistol than meets the eye!" Then, slipping the weapon into wide coat-pocket, he took the doctor's arm, and, having slowly descended the wide stair, came forth into the sunshine and paused to gaze about him eager-eyed, breathing deeply of the balmy air.

"Life's an excellent thing, eh, Samson?" he enquired a little wistfully. "And yet, to the truly adventurous, the sick or soul-weary, death is none so ill if it come quick—a bullet, say, or steel truly driven! But the sun is strangely pleasant—let us walk. Go with me a little way."

"Assuredly!" answered the doctor solicitously. "But pray whither are you going?"

"Egad, Samson, that is the question—where? Whither go I indeed? Who shall say? Perchance—up! Most likely—down! A walk i' the sunshine or journey i' the dark! Who knows? Not I, in faith, not I. Meantime I'll seek out cousin Dick!"

"But, sir!" cried the doctor, "great heaven, Mr. Julian, you don't mean . . . you won't . . . you'll never attempt to cross blades with him in your present——"

Julian sat down on the bench before the inn and laughed.

"No, no!" he answered. "I meant to kill him— once on a time, but to-day my thirst for his blood is strangely abated. I dreamed we were boys again, playing together, perchance this explains it. Howbeit, my present desire is but for a word with him. Yet Weare is a good step hence. I cannot sit a horse and doubt if my legs shall carry me so far, damn 'em! Yet I'll walk to the stile by Fallowdene Wood."

"But, sir, 'tis a mile beyond the village and——"

"True! You must lend me your arm, Samson."

So they set off together, the doctor suiting his stride to Julian's faltering step; and often Julian paused as if to catch his breath, at which times the doctor noticed how he would glance behind him and round about with eyes alert—expectant, so much so that when they reached the stile at last, Dr. Samson ventured to question him:

"Mr. Julian, what is it, sir, what, whom do ye look for?"

"Lord, man," gasped Julian fretfully, as he sank down upon the low stile, "Lord, man, don't I tell you I'm haunted! Haunted? Ay, by that which may not be eluded, by one I cannot escape, fly where I will! Nay, my good soul, I am not mad—at least I'm as sane as another, in proof whereof—take this!" and drawing the pistol from his pocket he thrust it into the doctor's reluctant grasp; quoth he:

"Lookee now, Samson, you shall at your convenience seek out my cousin Richard and give him this weapon —into his own hands, mind, and say I bade you tell him there is more in this than meets the eye! . . . And now, my good doctor, you may leave me."

"Nay but, sir, you are not——"

"I shall sit here awhile to twiddle my thumbs and watch the sunset . . . and so . . . farewell! Off with ye, man . . . begone, I say!"

Unwillingly and with many ominous shakes of the head Doctor Samson bowed, turned and trudged heavily away; long after he had gone Julian sat there, alert of eye, yet very still, as if listening eagerly, and on his face that same dark look of expectancy. At last he arose and, climbing the stile with some labour, went on into the wood, walking slowly and often pausing to rest, yet pushing on again ever deeper into the tangled mazes of the wood. Once, as he leaned breathless against a tree, he started and turned to stare towards the denser undergrowth whence had come a vague stir, a faint leafy rustling, and he smiled faintly, because here was no breath of wind to cause such stir.

Smiling still he walked thitherward until he reached a path that wound amid leafy thickets. Here he halted once again to fetch his breath, and presently went on along this path, but more slowly; and now he began to whistle softly a merry jigging air, keeping his gaze upon a certain lofty and wide-straggling bramble bush. Thus whistling he approached this bush, drew level with it, stepped past it—to be deafened, blinded, smitten through by a sudden keen agony that

CHAPTER XIV

TELLETH HOW SIR RICHARD FLED AND WHITHER

THE obtrusive branch of a tree sweeping off hat and wig, roused Sir Richard from his most bitter meditation to find himself deep amid tangled woodlands and with night coming down.

Reining in his horse, he sat awhile to look about him ; trees whose leafy canopy shut out the sky, tall, fronded bracken and dense underbrush, that hemmed him in save for the narrow alley or ride that opened before him, depth on depth of whispering green. All this he surveyed vague-eyed, for his mind was still obsessed by this one tormenting thought—he had been so wantonly sacrificed. . . . His ring, that sacred bond of Friendship (Heaven save the mark!) had been made the proof of his blood-guiltiness, the evidence which should drag him to the horror of noose and gibbet! His ring! . . . And she had sought him out in his solitude, had named him her friend . . . and he (sorry fool!) had begun to dream of a future . . . happiness. He that was no more than the "dog with a bad name" to be suspect of all and bear the stripes for another's sinning, a miserable scapegoat! . . . And she had avowed herself his friend! At thought of this he laughed suddenly, and, teeth still bared in mirthless smile, he dismounted, took up hat and wig, clapped them on and turned back to his horse; but paused with toe in stirrup, for whither should he ride? The hue and cry would be up with the moon, for the murder could not long remain unknown. By dawn to-morrow the country would be roused, every town and village astir to hunt him down, his dishonoured name on every lip, and all hands eager to drag him to his doom.

"Ha, Cæsar," said he, smoothing his horse's arched and glossy neck, "'tis thou and I 'gainst all England, lad." The horse turned shapely head to look at him large-eyed, and touch his cheek with velvety muzzle. "Well, shall it be the coast, boy? Cuckmere Haven or Burling Gap? I might creep aboard some smuggling craft, as coward murderer should, and steal away to France and exist henceforth an alien and outcast, leaving behind a memory most vile . . . my very name a reproach. . . . Again, I might yield myself up and go to shameful death a very heroical martyr, enduring in silence for that which she named Friendship. But such friendship is but hateful mockery, and I am neither hero nor martyr. Third, I might live here i' the wild an outlaw and fugitive, a furtive haunter o' the night, yet fugitive that scorns to be driven forth of his own land. . . . Eh, Cæsar, how think ye o' this? Shall we bide here and juggle wi' Death and Destiny, how say you lad, ay or no?" And speaking, Sir Richard pulled Cæsar's ear, whereupon that petted animal whinnied softly and nodded sleek head as he ever did when so caressed.

"Then so be it, boy!" said Sir Richard smiling grimly. "Here in the wilderness we bide, come what may. So now let us reckon up our resources. Here then, we have a gold chronometer, a gold and tortoise-shell snuff-box, nigh empty alas! A pipe and tobacco to our comfort, a purse with . . . three broad pieces, a florin and a groat—which is damnable insufficiency, considering! A brace o' pistols and silver-hilted small-sword to our defence, divers garments somewhat the worse for wear, and saddle and bridle. So, all's told, boy. . . . And now, my Cæsar, come let us seek some likely corner where we may pitch our camp for the night."

Seeing the boskage too dense for riding, Sir Richard slipped the reins over his arm and strode along the narrow alley, his head aloft and Cæsar's velvety muzzle across his shoulder.

Thus went they, these fugitives, the man and the horse, while dusk glimmered dark and darker, pushing ever deeper into this leafy wilderness until, all at once, they halted together and stood, both staring in the one direction like the hunted creatures they were, for in the hush and brooding stillness was a distant rustling, a faint sound of muffled hoofs at rhythmic gallop.

"Can they be upon us so soon, boy?" quoth the man; the horse snorted, and both stood listening until these faint sounds died away and were lost in the soft, mysterious noises of this far-flung woodland. Then the fugitives went on again yet moving each with an added caution—on and on until glimmering dusk deepened to night, a thick darkness around them and above, save for the fitful twinkling of some star apeep through the dense foliage overhead. But after some while Sir Richard halted a second time; before them was a glow, the dancing, ruddy light of a fire. Having surveyed this for a long moment, he advanced thitherwards, nor paused until he reached the edge of a small clearing where blazed the fire, crackling merrily, whose cheery beams showed him divers dingy tents pitched in the shadow of a large, weather-beaten caravan and near this, a small pony whose shaggy sides laboured as with recent hard going.

And then one spoke in voice strangely rich and sweet: "Who creepeth yonder? Who seeketh the Romany? Up Tornapo and see!" Into the light of the fire sprang a tall, swarthy fellow who advanced fierce-eyed and peering; then Sir Richard stepped forth of the shadows and thus beheld old Truffeni, the gipsy woman, seated upon the steps of her caravan and staring at him across the fire.

"Mrs. Camlo," said he, saluting her with smiling bow, "I bid ye a very good evening!"

"Ah," cried she, "'tis the kind Gorgio, the noble Gorgio gentleman as is friend to the Poor Folk and as the Poor Folk bids welcome!" And rising with stately gesture, she beckoned him near.

"And pray, dame, where is my small friend, where is little Shuri?"

"She is away, sir, with Wentzelow. . . . But for yourself, my Gorgio rye that is friend to the Romanys shall find the Romanys friends in your need. . . . Tornapo, tend ye to my lord's gry, and let no one come a-nigh us here until I bid 'em!"

The swarthy man nodded, patted Cæsar with knowing touch, and led him away with the shaggy pony.

" Be seated, sir," said old Truffeni, pointing to stool beside the fire " —so! And now—why doth the proud Gyfford flee hither to the Romany, to Truffeni, the old, wise one?"

" I am here by the merest chance, Mrs. Camlo."

" Chance say ye, sir, chance? Then what o' the dukkerin, the bloody dukkeripen as I foretold, noble sir? A dead man! Blood i' the grass! Ha?" Sir Richard rose from the stool, staring down at the ancient gipsy in sudden, frowning perplexity.

" What do you know?" he questioned, wondering and disquieted.

" I knows, my Gorgio rye, as there's one lays dead and one as comes riding into the wesh, the wildwood wi' death behind him!"

" 'S bud!" he exclaimed. " What more do you know?"

" Reach me thy hands, lord, both of 'em that I may dukker drey thy vast. Be seated, sir!" Sir Richard obeyed, and, sitting thus, began to whistle softly through his teeth while old Truffeni peered into each palm by light of the fire.

" Well," he enquired at last, " what d'ye see, ma'm?"

" That thy vangustri is gone—thy fine ring."

" Ay," he nodded. " I left it beside a dead man."

At this she glanced at him with her quick, bright eyes, and so for a long moment they gazed on each other unwinking, then slowly she nodded at him thrice:

" And yet 'twas fool's act, my chavo!" said she in tone strangely soft and caressing. " 'Twas a wrong to thyself and will cause wrong to—others . . . and yet "—she was silent again and for so long that at last he questioned her:

" Speak, good dame! Are my hands foul or clean? See ye any blood there?"

" No so!" she answered. "Here is dangers and trouble, ah—tungnipen, my chavo, much affliction, but likewise I sees here a great joy!"

At this he shook his head, smiling a little wistfully:

" Joy?" he repeated. " Nay, 'tis stranger hath but nodded and passed me by."

" Patience, thou man!" she nodded. " For yet shall joy nestle in the heart o' thee. Happiness shall be thy bed-fellow by reason of a rawni."

" Rawni, ma'm?"

" Thy dear lady."

" Tush, dame! I ha' no lady, I! There is no woman in my life nor ever shall be such plague; by heaven, no!"

" However I sees her near thee, my chavo, her white arms clasping thee . . . her bright hair all about thee."

Sir Richard laughed harshly, and freeing his hands gently from old Truffeni's clasp, clenched them fiercely and buried them in the deep pockets of his riding coat, while the gipsy, drawing up her stately figure, surveyed him with wise, pitying smile:

" How then," she demanded. " D'ye doubt old Truffeni's dukkerin, my noble Gorgio rye—you—that is no better than a blind child i' the dark? I tell ye by this lady shall ye 'scape shameful death, and for her shall ye vainly seek until——" she stopped and turned as a tall, grizzled man stepped suddenly into the firelight and, pointing towards Sir Richard, said something in the strange Romany tongue, whereat Truffeni questioned him sharply; so they talked awhile in their outlandish dialect and with hushed voices. At last Truffeni nodded and, obedient to her imperious gesture, the man stepped aside into the underbrush and vanished sudden as he had come.

" So, my chavo," said she, shaking her head, " ye was spied riding into the greenwood."

" 'Tis like enough!" he nodded.

" Aha! And where shall the avengers o' blood come a-seeking first but among the Romanys, the Poor Folk as be blamed for every ill."

" Why then," he answered, rising, " the sooner I'm away the better, ma'm."

" Ay, but whereaway shall ye ride? "

" 'S death, and that's the question! " said he glancing about somewhat vaguely. " And yet what must be, will be—so what matter? I'll follow my nose."

" And it shall presently lead thy innocent head through Jack Ketch's hempen collar, my chavo! "

" What must be, will be! " he repeated. " Where is my horse, pray? "

" I knows o' them as might hide ye, my chavo, safe and sound, where none should dare seek ye."

" Most excellent dame, tell me who—tell me where? "

" 'Tis goodish ways from here, sir, and hard to find."

" Faith, ma'm, I'll do my best. Pray direct me."

" 'Twould none avail except old Truffeni go with ye."

" Nay but, good dame, 'tis vastly kind in you I vow, but if the way be long——"

" 'Tis no matter! " she sighed.

" Also to help such as I may perchance bring trouble on your head."

" Ah, sir, trouble is no stranger to old Truffeni. Moreover, Richard Gyfford y'are one o' the few as deals kindly by my people, and ye were friend to me i' the matter o' Squire Parret and my little Shuri. Also have I not named thee ' my chavo '? "

" And pray what is that? "

" Sir, in the Roman tongue it means ' my son.' For here i' the wilderness the proudest Gorgio gentleman is no more than a man! "

" Why, faith, that's true enough! " he smiled, and taking off his hat he bowed to her. " God bless thee, mother! " said he.

Now, because she read sincerity in his voice and look, Old Truffeni smiled on him suddenly, in fashion that transfigured her wonderfully, and, rising, she acknowledged his salutation with slow and stately curtsey; then, beholding his look of wonder, laughed softly and sighed thereafter:

hallowed grave, for he was a proper youth and a kindly
to the Poor Folk."

"Ha, you knew him?"

"Ay, ay," she nodded. "James Ahearn, he was."

"What, the highwayman?"

"Even so, my chavo, of the boro-tobbar-killipen, of
the High Toby game were he indeed, and overly young
to die . . . a kindly soul."

"And now, poor wretch, a thing to shudder at!
Come let us go!"

"Nenny!" said she, shaking muffled head. "For
'tis here ye must hide, my fine gentleman, lest they
choke out your innocent life and hang ye aloft for a
warning like poor James Ahearn yonder. For the
Shadow o' Death is all about ye, Gyfford o' Weare, by
reason o' that the which should be on thy finger and is
not! So come thy ways now."

Forthwith she led the way down through a little
dingle where tall bracken grew with, here and there,
a gnarled and stunted tree, until before them loomed
a ruined arch flanked by crumbling masonry thick-
shrouded in ivy that stirred in the wind with stealthy
rustlings. And now they rode across smooth turf
shut in from the blusterous wind until old Truffeni
stopped suddenly in a deep recess beneath a narrow
opening in the masonry, that had once been a noble
window, and where the ivy grew very thick; leaning
from her pony she groped amid these leaves and presently drew thence a cord, the which she tugged at,
once, twice, thrice, and thereafter sat very silent and
motionless. And after some while the ivy leaves, in
this particular corner, stirred, parted and from the
very ground the pale oval of a face glimmered up at
them, where-to the old gipsy addressed herself:

"All's bowmon, pal," said she. "'Tis Truffeni
Camlo with a friend!"

"Aha!" answered the face in jovial tones. "Greetings, Gammer! What's to do? Who is't ye bring,
old ma'm?"

Sir Richard leaned forward, peering, for this was
voice he knew well.

"One as I'll swear by!" said Old Truffeni, "and one as be-eth in peril o' the noose!"

"Oho, the nubbing-cheat, gammer?" quoth the voice. "What then, is't a roaring boy o' the High Toby!"

"No so," answered Sir Richard, "'tis merely myself, Black Nick."

"Lord!" gasped the voice in breathless amazement; then was sound of scrambling, the ivy-stems were plucked apart and Black Nick himself stepped lightly into the moonbeams.

"Why . . . Sir Richard!" he exclaimed in changed tone. "Lord love us all! What's amiss, sir?"

"Murder, Nick! My cousin Julian lies dead and I am running for my life."

"Murder, sir!" repeated Nick, shaking his comely head. "But sure 'tis killed in duel, ye mean?"

"It is murder!"

"Why then, Sir Richard, how can the matter touch yourself?"

"Very nearly! Ye see, Nick, my ring was beside Julian's body, and this shall be sufficient evidence to damn me!"

"Mebbe, sir, to them as don't know ye, but to them as do—'twon't signify, in especial to one as do know ye pretty well, your honour, and that's myself, sir."

"God bless thee, lad!" said Sir Richard, clapping him on shoulder. "Such faith should hearten any man. Howbeit, a fugitive am I and must so be it seems until the hue and cry abate somewhat. So hither come I seeking sanctuary."

"And Lord love ye, sir, you're heartily welcome! Moreover there ain't another such likely place as this in all the South country—or anywheres else, as ma'm Truffeni knows——"

"And faith," said Sir Richard, thrusting eager hand into pocket, "Mrs. Camlo, I am infinite obliged, vastly grateful . . . pray honour me by accepting this!" And he proffered her his purse.

"Nenny!" said she, shaking her head. "Though the Romanys be the Poor Folk yet they are also the proud folk—sometimes" battered lanthorn whose flickering beam showed a wide paved floor whence sprang row upon row of squat stone columns supporting groined arches.

"A Norman crypt!" said Sir Richard, glancing around with eyes of eager interest.

"Our stables, your honour! My mare's yonder. This way, sir. Look now, your Cæsar will do well here, plenty o' bedding and fodder!" Having thus stabled Cæsar and littered him down, Nick blew out the light and, grasping Sir Richard's arm, led him across this echoing crypt, through a narrow passage, up rough steps, along another passage that, trending ever upwards with many sharp turns right and left, showed a narrow opening whence shone a mellow light.

"Two steps down, your honour, and—here y'are!" A roomy chamber or cavern panelled with massive and aged timbering against which hung many and divers articles as,—whips, rusty spurs, a saddle, a weather-worn cloak, two or three swords, a brace of long-barrelled pistols, an old hat, and the like, while in opposite corners were two pallet-beds which, together with a roughly-contrived table, an ancient and richly carved elbow-chair and sundry barrels and boxes, completed its furniture; all this Sir Richard saw by light of an oil lamp affixed to the wall.

"'Tis rough, sir, for the likes o' your honour," said Black Nick, shaking his head, "but then 'tis safe, d'ye see, and when the fire's a-going 'tis pretty cosy. And now, sir, what d'ye say to a dish o' tea, a bite o' supper?"

"Tea?" repeated Sir Richard.

"Or coffee, sir. Then we've French brandy, prime Jamaickey rum, hollands, wine and a butt o' strong ale. Also snuff, your honour, and tobaccy, sir."

"'S life, Nick—here's riot o' luxury!"

"Why, sir, we don't lack for much, thanks to the lads o' the 'free-trade'—in partic'lar friend Potter. What'll you take, sir?"

"Ale, I thank ye!"

"Then please to be seated, sir, in the cheer. And likewise if you're minded to eat I can offer you cold ham, also a cut o' prime beef or——"

"Both, Nick. 'Fore heaven, now you mention it I find myself ravenous."

And so, waited upon by this quick-footed, neat-handed highwayman, Sir Richard supped and made hearty business of it.

"And pray," he enquired, after some while, "where is your partner, this man Rob?"

"Why, sir, having the . . . misfortun' to shoot a harmen beck, London way, and the queer cuffins being arter him very determined in consequence, he's come South. To-night he's a-working the toby 'twixt here and Lewes. But, sir, we ain't partners. Y'see I don't hold wi' his methods, me never having shot a man yet."

" I rejoice to hear it, Nick, and hope you never will."

" So do I, your honour. Though, mind ye, I won't say as I ain't used my popps now and then, butt-end, sir—but I ain't never shot nobody, though Lord love ye, 'twould be all one if they took me—Tyburn Tree, sir, the nubbing cheat. There be only one man as I'd like to be the death of and that's Wild, damn him—Jonathan Wild!"

" What, the thief-taker?"

" Thief-taker and thief-maker, sir! Jonathan raises all manner o' criminals, bless you, boys and girls, and sells 'em—thirty odd pounds for every thief 'e takes, lives by the gallers does Jonathan. 'Twere one o' Wild's constables, and a black rogue, too, as Rob shot last . . ."

" And what," enquired Sir Richard, laying down knife and fork, sighfully content, "what o' thyself, man, how goeth thievery these days?"

" Why, so so, sir, like most other perfessions it hath its ups and downs."

" Yet can have but one end for thee, fool-Nick, I fear. Gad's life, man, but you trouble me!"

" What—I do, sir?"

" Ay, lad, and well ye know it. You're too good a man to end in a noose."

" Lord, sir," said Nick, with reassuring smile, " we don't all get ' topped,' f'rinstance take Captain Archer, clenched upon Nick's arm, the other dangling and dropping blood.

"Sir . . . and a curse on't . . . they call me . . . 'The Parson,' and you being Nick's . . . friend, I give ye hearty greeting."

"At your service!" answered Sir Richard, and rising he aided the wounded man to the arm-chair.

"God bless . . . ye!" murmured the Parson, with upward roll of swooning eyes.

"A bullet through the arm, sir," Nick explained, reaching sponge and basin from a shelf.

"Have ye any scissors?" enquired Sir Richard, tucking up his ruffles. "I'll slit up his sleeve and——"

"No . . . damme . . . no!" gasped the Parson, "'tis woundy good coat this . . . took it from . . . a bishop . . . only last week . . . sober black and . . . suits me. S'let be, sir . . . with a curse!"

"But how may we come at your hurt?" demanded Sir Richard, shaking his head at the sodden velvet.

"I'll doff it," groaned the Parson. "But first a sup o' brandy, Nick." Heartened by the liquor he arose and, gasping maledictions, contrived to struggle out of the garment, scornful of assistance; then, sinking feebly into the arm-chair, sat shaking neat-wigged head over the blood-stained sleeve.

"Spoiled, alack!" he sighed. "Ruinated, damn their eyes! And fitted me like my skin! Wash it for me, Nick—soak it well, lad, mayhap 'twill be well enough until I can achieve another—if I ever may."

"Ay, but," quoth Nick, "what o' your arm, Rob?"

"Arm be damned, look at my coat—with a curse!"

"Nay, Rob, coat be cursed, show us your arm!" So saying Nick perforce examined the ugly wound and fell to work with sponge and water. "Here's no bones broke," he announced presently, "the which is mighty fort'nate considering."

"Ay, Nicky lad. Verily the hand o' Providence was over poor Rob this night as ever, wherefore have I lifted up my voice in praise and thanksgiving— albeit one o' my barkers missed fire, plague on't! Yet is my faith such that I can fold my hands, bow meek head and say—even so, 'twas for the best! And moreover—ha burn thee, Nick!"

"What, do I hurt ye, Rob?'

"Ay—but 'tis no matter, lad! Heed me not for, though my vile flesh curse ye, my soul poureth on thee benedictions. . . . Lord love thee, Nick! Heaven bless thee, good lad! . . . Oho, curses on this rascal, quivering flesh, say I——"

Thus Black Nick washed, anointed and bound up the ugly hurt what time the Galloping Parson alternate cursed and prayed; while Sir Richard viewed this man whose desperate affrays and ever-ready pistol-hand had made his name a terror far and wide.

A slim, small, strange man was he, black-browed and of saturnine visage yet whose long, melancholy nose, deep-set, gloomy eyes and peaked chin contrasted oddly with his wide humorous mouth, which expanded in sudden smile as, meeting Sir Richard's glance, he nodded towards Nick's solemn visage.

"How now, Nick?" quoth he. "You'll be thinking by to-night's work I've more blood on my soul as well as my coat—eh, lad?"

"I'm thinking you're too spry wi' your barkers, Rob."

"Maybe so, lad," he sighed, "'tis ever a word and a shot wi' me more's the pity, but such my nature is. No man shall let or stay me so long as I can pull trigger. And the Galloping Parson shall never kick in noose at Tyburn. . . . There's David and Jonathan in my holsters for all and sundry, 'twas Davie missed fire to-night—but for me—here's little Joseph!" and forth of his bosom he whipped a small, silver-mounted pistol. "Here's little Joseph shall waft me hence when needs must, translating me above reach o' human law—a flash, a pang and I shall be standing at the Tribunal o' the Almighty, and 'tis a Judge o' Justice He, so all's well."

"Ay but, Rob, how came ye by this hole i' your arm?"

"I met a young springald t'other side o' Lewes pike. 'Stand!' says I. 'The devil!' says he and claps hand to holster, so I let fly with Jonathan and down goes his horse. 'Now the favour o' your purse,' says I, 'and a grateful soul's blessing!' 'Take a bullet!' says he and, firing from the dust, wings me. Then David misses, folk come running and I'm beset, so it's whip and spur. . . . Never a guinea and my good coat spoiled! 'Tis curst trade ours, Nick. So lad, let me that is old enough to father you be warning to you. Quit—quit the game, Nick, lest 'stead o' taking it in the flipper as I—thanks to a merciful Providence, you get your innards blown out-ards, or are taken and duly hanged which is surely a death very odious and unseemly. . . . There's poor James now—hark to him! He sounds devilish uneasy to-night! Ay, I must out to him, give me the Book.''

"Nay now, Rob, why not do it here?'

"Because 'tis cosy here, and my cursed flesh would fain sprawl here in comfort, therefore I'll out to him. James was my friend, the only one poor Rob was ever blessed with! Reach me the Book—in my coat-pocket yonder!" So Nick gave him the Book, a small, thick, much tattered volume, whereupon the Galloping Parson sighed, struggled to unwilling legs and stumbled, moaning, upon his way.

"Nick, what's he after?" enquired Sir Richard.

"Your honour, he be gone up for to read a verse or so o' the Book and say a prayer over poor Jimmy."

"Eh—to pray, Nick? Zounds, and he a rogue so desperate!"

"Why, he were bred a parson, d'ye see, sir. And now if this corner will suit your honour, I'll make ye a shake-down for the night."

"Doth he know me, think ye, Nick? Didst mention my name?"

"Nay, sir, I told him you were friend o' mine, and my friend is his'n."

"The wind," said the Galloping Parson, reappearing after some while, blinking down at them from the narrow opening which served as doorway, "the wind is gentling and so poor James will be easier and I sleep the better. . . . And now, brothers, let us pray!" So saying, he closed his eyes and lifting clasped hands, spoke reverently thus:

"Spirit Almighty and Everlasting, reader of all hearts, show mercy on us three sinners—first on me, the greatest, an Ishmael, Lord, a lonely soul outcast from his fellows, being, in my deeds a man of blood, but in my soul a very innocent, a child for Thy care, yearning for better things—angel and devil, Lord, yet framed in Thine own image. Second, on Thy son Nick that is better than he thinketh and cleanest rogue that ever stopped coach. Let Thy light shine on him that he may forswear the error of his ways and, repenting ere it be too late, find that happiness I may never know. Third, this gentleman o' quality that is, as I guess, suspect o' the horrid sin of murder and whether innocent or guilty only Thou and he do know, yet I, being unworthy child o' Thine, give him Doubt's benefit and beseech Thy blessing on him. So bless us all this night and give us sleep in the shadow of Thy wings—Amen!' And now, Nick lad, gimme a hand wi' my toddling-cheats and I'll to roost!"

So Nick pulled off the wounded man's long riding-boots who thereupon sank down upon his pallet-bed with sigh of satisfaction, while Sir Richard eyed him in an ever-growing wonder.

"You stare at me, Sir Richard," quoth Rob, with sudden, whimsical smile.

"And you know my name, it seems!" answered Sir Richard, smiling also.

"Nay, sir, I but guess at it."

"You guess rightly, but how, pray?"

"By seeing two things found together in a little wood, sir, your signet-ring and the body of a murdered man."

"Ha—you saw them found?"

"With these two eyes, sir. I chanced to be hiding in that wood . . . and they were found by a lady and gentleman a-horseback."

"Zounds!" exclaimed Sir Richard, in frowning perplexity. "Now who should they be?"

"Sir, I heard her name the gentleman Captain Despard." Sir Richard started.

E

"Despard?" he repeated. "Then she could only have been——"

"He called her Helen, sir.'

Sir Richard was dumb awhile, staring blindly at the panelling opposite, and when at last he spoke his voice was hoarse, his speech halting:

"Who . . . who first . . . touched it . . . my ring?"

"'Twas the gentleman took it up and instantly knew it for yours, sir."

"Yes, and . . . and then?'

"He gave it to the lady."

"Why?"

"Because she pleaded, ay, begged for it, she did."

"She . . . begged for it?"

"Ay, she did, sir, mighty persistent. 'For' says she, 'it must not be found!' And on my life," cried the Galloping Parson in voice suddenly loud and bitter, "I've known many a poor wretch hanged on less evidence—ay, have I!"

After this, Sir Richard sat with head between his hands so silent and for such long time that Nick ventured to touch him at last.

"Ecod, sir," said he, nodding, "here's heartsome news, for if your ring an't brought in evidence agin you who's to suspicion ye?"

"S'death, man!" exclaimed Sir Richard. "What matter for that? But who may ever understand a woman?"

"Nary a soul, sir, and you can lay to that!" answered the Parson. "And for why? Hearken!

' The mind of a woman can never be known
  You never can guess it aright.
Shall I tell ye the reason? She knows not her
      own.
  It changes so often ere night.'

And now, douse the glim, Nick, I must sleep, and if you must think, Sir Richard, why thinking is easier i' the dark. So douse the glim, Nick lad, and the Lord have us in His holy keeping. Brothers, good-night!"

CHAPTER XVI

IN WHICH THE DUCHESS MAKES A PROPHECY

HELEN sat staring with eyes of horror at the signet-ring upon the table.

" And now, me dear," said the Duchess, staring also at the ring, " now that y'are more composed tell me arl over again."

Helen shivered, bowed her head between clasping hands, yet with wide gaze still upon the ring, and spoke in voice hushed and toneless:

" Last evening as I rode I met Captain Despard, and I would have left him, for I hate the man, but he persisted. We reached the little wood they call the Fallowdene Dingle, and he suggested we ride through it——"

" Ah—'twas himself suggested the wood, me dear?"

" Yes, Aunt. I did so because 'tis the shortest way back to the village. . . . And there . . . beside the bridle-path lay Julian Gyfford—dead! His pale face . . . all bedabbled and yet . . . smiling still —smiling up at me as if in mockery! And beside his dead hand—this!" And she pointed trembling finger at Sir Richard's signet-ring.

" And," enquired the Duchess, " shure the Captain saw it too?"

" 'Twas he picked it up, Aunt."

" *Fort bien, ma cherie!* And then?"

" He asked me if I recognised it."

" And what said you?"

" Nothing—I could but stare in horror."

" And small wonder!" nodded the Duchess. " So then phwat says our gallant Captain? Tell me his very words!"

"He said: 'Surely I have seen this ring before . . . these letters R and G? Ay, by heaven, this is Sir Richard Gyfford's signet!'"

"Ay, he knew it, I'll warrant me! Well, and then phwat says you?"

"Not a word, Aunt. I could only watch the Captain, turning the ring on his open palm. 'Sir Richard's ring!' he said again, and then, 'Here is evidence shall verily hang him—if found! He quarrelled with this unfortunate gentleman so bitterly! He assaulted him so viciously! And now we find his ring beside the murdered body of this poor gentleman! If found here, this shall assuredly hang Sir Richard!'"

"An' that was twoice he'd be hanging Sir Richard! Now tell me phwat you said, and he said, and both said to each other, every word, 'bate not a syllable, me dear."

"Then, Aunt, I told him it must not be found, and tried to snatch the ring from him. 'Not found?' says he, and shuts his hand on it. 'No!' said I, 'Give it to me.' And he not complying I—I——"

"Well?" demanded the Duchess, bouncing in her chair. "Well?"

"Then . . . Oh, my Dearest, I found myself . . . stooping to plead with him." Here my lady frowned and clenched her hands fiercely.

"And phwat says he to your humble pleading?"

"Shook his head, Aunt, and grew most virtuously shocked! 'But Helen,' says he—ay, he called me 'Helen,' damn him!—'if we suppress such evidence we condone this bloody crime, we make ourselves accessories after the fact, which is grave and most heinous offence!' 'No matter!' says I. 'Give me that ring!'"

"And then he gave it thee, av course, for here 'tis. But he'd be after making ye some foine spache, I'm thinking?"

"Yes, Aunt! He said . . . he could refuse me nothing, and would even screen a murderer from Justice and jeopardize his own fame and liberty to . . . to pleasure me."

" And so, gives ye the ring, eh? "

" He did," answered Helen, with a little shiver,
" he gave it and—smiled at me! ' Take it, Helen,'
says he, ' henceforth we are fellows in crime, bound
together by our secret guilt!' And he—smiled!"

" And no wonder!" nodded the Duchess, frowning,
' for fellows in crime y'are, indeed, miss!"

" But, Aunt!"

" And then he comes riding to the gate with ye and
kisses your hand. Egad, and mighty impressive about
it too!"

Helen nodded miserably.

" And will call and kiss your hand again to-morrow,
shure! And in a week, will be kissing your lips, me
poor soul!"

Helen shivered and stared at the Duchess wide-eyed.

" Ah! . . . what do you mean? " she whispered.

" That y'are to be the proice o' this gentleman's
silence—ye poor innocent!"

" Nay. . . . O Beloved, what . . . what must I
do? The man daunts me! He is so persistent, so quiet
and hatefully assured? What can I do? "

" First—give me this ring."

" Take it! Ah, hide the hateful thing!"

" And now, my dear Helen," said the Duchess, her
homely brogue giving place to the coldest of precise
English, " I take leave to say that you have comported
yourself like a witless wench, an addle-pate, the merest
fool, and a very simpleton!"

" O!" gasped my lady, all sudden, pleading humility,
her haughty fine airs quite abashed, " O Aunt, what
other could I ha' done——? "

" Well, you might ha' left this lying ring—lieing."

" Lieing ring? Then, O then you think it would ha'
borne false testimony? You don't think he—you
think perchance it—O Darlingest—loved—dear what
do you think? "

" Whirroo, Nell! Phwat I do think and phwat I don't
think is neither here nor there—'tis phwat I know!"

" And what . . . O dear Heart, what do you
know? "

"Vanished? . . . what . . . do . . . you . . . mean?'

"Only what everyone's a-saying, ma'm, how as S'Richard on the very night o' the horrorful deed, my lady, mounts his fastest horse, ma'm, and gallops away! And no eye nor yet ear, they say, has seed him since, my lady."

Here, at imperious sign from her mistress, Betty curtseyed again and closed herself out of the room.

"To—run away!" whispered Helen, "why should he? O, why? Dearest, if this be really so, what doth it mean? What can we do?"

"Nothing!" answered the Duchess, frowning up at the carved ceiling. "Nothing at all . . . now! But we'll have him paying us surprise visit one o' these foine nights if—y' do as I bid ye.'

"What? O tell me!"

"Whist, me dear—let me whisper!'

CHAPTER XVII

TELLETH HOW THE MARQUIS WENT FORTH ON A PILGRIMAGE OF FRIENDSHIP

THE Marquis of Merivale sighed, moaned, murmured a plaintive anathema and, opening unwilling eyes, blinked at the beam of sunshine that fell athwart his bed, and showed him the face of his sedate servant, Francoise, whose baptismal name was Tom.

"'S matter, Francoise?" he enquired drowsily. "'S time o' day?"

"My lord, it vergeth on the hour of ten."

"Ten o'clock!" wailed the Marquis reproachfully, "'S plaguey early! Why an't I asleep? Who . . . what waked me?"

"I did, my lord. Sir Richard Gyfford's gentleman, Mr. Gregory waits below, 'Twas at his earnest solicitation I ventured to arouse your lordship."

"Gregory—eh?" quoth the Marquis, pulling off his night-cap and blinking at it. "'S early too! I wonder what——? Send him up, man, send him up and let nobody disturb us!"

"Why then, will your lordship partake of breakfast?"

"No—yes, y'may bring me a morsel t'peck at when I ring."

The Marquis had achieved complete wakefulness when Gregory entered, bowed, closed the door and showed a visage unwontedly troubled, beholding which the Marquis seemed troubled also.

"Well, Greg, what news?"

"None, my lord."

"Eh? Y'mean?"

"Sir Richard has not come home."

"Odd, Gregory, curst odd—eh?"

"Sir, I . . . I cannot understand it!"

"friendship is a very holy and a—ha—vastly serious obligation—eh?"

"It is, my lord. But pray where are we going?"

"On a Pilgrimage o' Friendship, Greg, to track base rumour to its loathly lair and muzzle, pink, or choke it into silence."

"But, sir. Rumour hath a thousand tongues!"

"Maybe, Greg—but——" the Marquis smiled happily and laid one slim finger on the chiselled pommel of his colichemarde, "if we silence one or two—t'others will wag less glibly, I'll warrant me."

"My lord, d'ye mean . . . fight?"

"If," sighed his lordship, "if only Fortune prove so kind. Nay, look not so austerely, man, what I do is all in Friendship's sacred cause. . . . This way!"

"What, to the Moat House, sir?"

"Indeed, Greg. 'Tis there we are most like to find that fellow Despard, he haunts, y'know the 'Handsome D'Arcy'—or her money, or both. A hawk, Greg, Beauty and Fortune the lure. So come other birds o' prey, fine gentlemen all, from town or country, hovering over the spoil—egad, and I with 'em. She holds her court daily at twelve o'clock, we shall be early."

"My lord," quoth Gregory, his tone apprehensive as his look, "Captain Despard is, I judge, a dangerous man with sword or——"

"Faith, 'tis my hope, Greg. I burn t' try him wi' that thrust o' mine, the one I showed ye, last week."

"'Tis deadly if—well-timed, my lord, but——"

"'Tis sure as death, Greg! In m' last affair I pinked m'man in the first rally. Lookee again!" said the Marquis, stopping suddenly to illustrate with his cane. "Your own play is masterly as we know, Greg, though a little out o' date. See now we are in tierce—so. . . ."

They had reached that deep and tall hedge beyond which rose the gables of the Moat House and now, as the Marquis poised himself in graceful fencing attitude, forth of this leafy hedge shot a small, slim brown hand that clutched his embroidered coat-skirts. . . .

"Gad love me!" exclaimed the Marquis, and whirled about to see a small, elfin, child-face peering up, wistful and a little frightened, from amid the leaves.

"O pretty gentleman," said she in soft, pleading tones, "if y'please I'm Shuri."

"Stap my vitals!" said the Marquis, staring.

"Kind Gorgio rye, I'm Shuri Camlo o' the Poor Folk as wants to see the pretty lady, please."

"Sink me!" murmured the Marquis.

"I brings her a message from Truffeni Camlo, but I dassent go in."

"O? B'gad! Why?"

"'Cause he's in there. I sees him go in. Sir John Parret."

"What, d'ye know him, my child?"

"All the Poor Folk knows him, sir, and—hates him. He had me whipped once, he did!"

The Marquis, having pondered this, nodded down at the small speaker and reached her his hand:

"I'll take y'in," said he, and on they went together.

The lawns at the Moat House were a feature, being shaded by great trees and shut in by tall hedges of clipped yew. Now it was from just beyond one of these hedges that Sir John Parret chanced to be speaking, his far-reaching, throaty voice very plain and distinct:

" . . . and as everyone knows, Gyfford, alas, hath long been a—hum—a disgrace to his and our own order, I say a constant—ha—discredit, nay, a positive menace to us o' the County! To-day, gentlemen, to-day he stands suspect, I say—ha—very gravely suspect as a—hum—a malefactor befouled by a kinsman's blood. . . ."

The Marquis, beholding little Shuri's terror by reason of this imperious voice and its nearness, smiled reassuringly and, leading her to a rustic seat in secluded corner, bade her wait there; then, nodding to Gregory he stepped out upon the sunny lawn and beheld Sir John Parret, solid legs wide planted and fist on palm, holding forth to a silent and approving auditory, gentlemen who glanced at each other, nodded, and chorused frequent assent to Sir John's rolling periods:

Gyfford, if he be guilty then hang him, my dear Sir
John, but to know him guilty ye must have proof.
Well now, phwat proof have ye?"

"Why, madam, his so sudden flight, his continued
absence, the present mystery of his—hum—his whereabouts."

"Ah, the silly man!" nodded the Duchess. "Shure,
he should tell us all where he goes—every time he
goes there!"

"But, ma'm, bearing in mind his—ha—his recent
bitter hostility against the murdered man, remembering
they were actually to fight a duel, surely 'tis but
reasonable to suppose——"

The Marquis coughed behind slim finger, and meeting
Sir John's responsive glance, bowed:

"To s'pose—what, sir?" he enquired, gently. Sir
John drew a deep breath and turning, addressed himself to the Duchess again.

"As to proof, madam, I have it. Such proof indeed
as might warrant any and every suspicion. As a
magistrate I had meant to—hum—to keep it back
until the official—ha—enquiry, but under the present
circumstances, feel that I am justified in—ha—hum!
Know then, madam and gentlemen, that I have the
sworn testimony of a witness who deposes he saw Sir
Richard Gyfford gallop furiously out of the Dingle—
just about the fatal hour."

For a moment was a hushed stillness, even the
Duchess was silent, then Captain Despard, shooting a
ruffle gracefully, enquired:

"Ay, but, Sir John, who knows the fatal hour?
Who can be sure of the precise moment o' the crime?"

My lady Helen, who chose this moment to appear,
returned the Captain's salutation with curtsey far
more gracious than usual, and smiled upon the bowing
company, bright-eyed, while the Duchess nodded
approbation; as for Sir John Parret, being at a loss,
he pursed his lips, puffed out his cheeks and rolled
his eyes from Mr. Magnus to Mr. Threep and never
a word to say. . . . And in this moment came a demure
young footman who, halting beneath the Duchess'

window, very stiff in the back, proclaimed, in voice unnecessarily loud:

"If you please, madam, Sir John Parret's ead-keeper, ma'm, to see Sir John—very important!"

Even as the young footman spoke a burly fellow stepped out from the yew hedge but, beholding the fine company, paused and stood abashed, knuckling his forehead to all and sundry.

"By your leave, ladies," said Sir John, "I'll hear the fellow's business."

"Let us all hear it!" cried the Duchess, whereat Sir John bowed, and with wide imperious gesture beckoned the man to approach:

"What is it, Grimes?" he demanded.

"Why, Sir John, me and Jarge ha' been a-searchin' of the Dingle as you so ordered, sir, and we found this here, y'r honour!' So saying, from beneath his arm the keeper produced a dingy bundle and, unrolling it, held it up: An old weather-worn military cloak turned up with scarlet; but, as they gazed on it, there went up a shocked murmur, a sound of inarticulate horror since all eyes might see this old garment was stained by more than weather—awful smears, dark and ominous splotches there was no mistaking,—beholding which, my lady Helen clenched her hands, closed her eyes and opening them, after a moment, found Captain Despard watching her ere she turned and sped away into the house.

"Blood!" cried Sir John, his voice loud with triumph. "Ha, and 'fore heaven, I know this cloak! 'Tis Richard Gyfford's; I'd swear to it anywhere! Ha, you—Gregory, step forward! You recognise this as your master's cloak, come now—confess!" Gregory merely nodded.

"Excellent!" cried Sir John. "And, Grimes, you found it near the fatal spot?"

"Within a dozen yards, y'r honour.'

"And stained with his victim's blood!" quoth Sir John. "Here is proof on proof——"

"No, no!" said the Captain. "Sir Richard may not have been inside it."

"Not inside it, sir—not in't? Ha, what d'ye mean sir, pray?"

"I mean, my dear Sir John, that it may have been upon another man's back."

"Ay, sir," snorted Sir John, indignantly, "it may have been on my back—or yours! Tush, sir, these are idle speculations! We know this cloak for Gyfford's, or many of us do. . . ."

"I for one!" boomed Mr. Magnus, peering at it.

"Refuse me!" piped Mr. Threep. "Heaven refuse me if I didn't see him in't to-day se'en night or there-abouts!"

"Demme," quoth Viscount Brocklehurst, viewing the garment through his glass, "demme if I hadn't seen him in one very like it!"

"Gentlemen," cried Sir John, smiting fist to palm, "here's evidence shall bring a murderer to his doom, we ha' but to find him. Ay, and find him we will if we have to turn out the military and beat the woods from hence to Battle and the coast! Grimes, fold up that damning evidence and follow me! Madam, y'r servant, gentlemen—yours!"

So saying, Sir John bowed and turning on his heel strutted away and his company with him.

"Gad—so!" murmured the Captain. "Sir John would seem plaguy full o' zeal!"

The Marquis took out his snuff-box and stared at it absently.

"Captain Despard," he enquired, "are you still o the same mind regarding my friend Richard Gyfford?"

"Precisely, sir," answered the Captain.

The Marquis sighed heavily and opening his snuff-box tendered it to the Captain with a bow.

"Sir," he murmured, "favour me!"

So they snuffed together and bowed to each other very ceremoniously. Then, the Duchess having van-ished from the lattice and my lady remaining invisible, Viscount Brocklehurst sauntered towards them from the house and slipped his hand within the Captain's arm, and together they departed. So presently all were gone except the Marquis who stared up at the blue sky, and Gregory who frowned down at the green turf.

"So, Greg," said the Marquis, nodding gloomily after the Captain's retreating form, "it seems I'm not to try my thrust on him, after all. . . . Come, let us begone!"

"Stay!" cried a voice, and Helen came hasting, light-footed to give them each a hand and look from one to other with eyes of dreadful speculation. "You are his two friends," said she in strange, hushed tones, "and never did Richard Gyfford need them more than now, for . . . Oh . . . that cloak! Its awful stains . . .!"

"My lady," said Gregory with hushed vehemence, "I can swear he was not wearing that cloak when he rode away."

"Ah, Gregory—Gregory," she whispered, "but I . . . I can swear he was! I . . . saw it on him when he stopped me in the lane . . . that same cloak, Gregory but . . . there were no . . . stains on it then!"

So stood they, all three, gazing mutely on one another and the dread in her eyes was reflected now in theirs.

CHAPTER XVIII

TELLETH MORE CONCERNING A CERTAIN OLD MILITARY CLOAK

Now as they stood thus, looking upon each other in a dismay far beyond words, the Duchess approached unheard upon the soft turf and, crossing mittened hands upon crutch-stick, she stood and snorted at them:

"B'the Powers!" she exclaimed as she met their startled looks, "Three images o' tragedy! Such gloom! Like three mourning mutes—and arl b' rayson o' wan dirty ould cloak!"

"But, alas Aunt, he wore that same cloak in the lane!"

"Pah, me dear soul and tush! Who's to say twas himself left it in the wood? So mighty convaynient to be found! Come into the arbour out o' the sun for 'tis minded I am to talk, discuss and sit in council."

So to the arbour went they and there seated, waited for the Duchess to begin.

"Edward," said she, turning to the Marquis, "I'll thank ye for the loan o' your snuff-box.'

The Marquis tendered it with a graceful flourish.

"Now!" said the Duchess, here she inhaled a copious pinch, "Now—you, Edward, and you, Mr. Gregory, ha' known Richard Gyfford arl his days—now, is there wan of us belaves he could stoop to murder?"

GREGORY: My lady, such idea is——
DUCHESS: Quite so, Mr. Gregory, not wan of us.
MARQUIS: Madam. I'd lay my life on——
DUCHESS: Shure ye would. So would I. Very well, then——
HELEN: Nay but, dear Aunt, how if 'twas a duel and——

40

DUCHESS: Pray, miss, suffer me a word! We may know 'twas not a duel or Richard would never ha' run away.

GREGORY: Very true, my lady. Beyond all doubt 'twas cold-blooded mur——

DUCHESS: As you say, Mr. Gregory, 'twas murder shure. And O Lud, what truly amazing murderer! So careless! He scatters his possessions arl about the fatal spot! So reckless!

MARQUIS: (*sighing and shaking head gloomily*) Ay, faith, you mean his cloak!

HELEN: (*sighing also*) His ring.

DUCHESS: (*nodding*) To-morrow they may find his hat and his boots. O, 'tis an astonishing murderer! So supernaturally sly! So very infinite careful!

GREGORY: Careful, madam? Sly? May I ask——

DUCHESS: Too, too careful, methinks! Richard's cloak, like his ring, was there to *be* found!

MARQUIS: (*brightening*) Ha, madam, strike me dumb but I believe you've hit it! You mean, O sink me! You think 'twas placed there by other hands than Dick's—ha?

HELEN: (*shaking head*) But how may this be, when Richard was wearing the cloak and the ring?

MARQUIS: (*sinking back into depths of gloom*) Ha, rat me but there goes that hope! For 'tis imposs——

DUCHESS: (*closing snuff-box with loud snap*) S-a-a-cré! Am I never to speak?

GREGORY: Ah, my lady, pray do—indeed you inspire me with hope of——

HELEN: But, Dearly-beloved, I gave Richard back the ring! I saw the cloak upon him! How then can they——

DUCHESS: O Miss? And who's to say he was not waylaid—hurt, wounded, stripped and robbed——

HELEN: God forbid!

MARQUIS: (*brightening*) Ha, faith, this would explain the riddle! And—by heaven, I vow 'tis most likely. The highwaymen! They ha' been busy enough o' late. I myself was sto——

HELEN: Richard hurt! Wounded, perchance dead!

CHAPTER XIX

"NICK's late!" said Sir Richard, frowning at the blue wreaths of his tobacco pipe.

The Galloping Parson reverently closed The Book, and, turning to the shelf at his bed's-head, placed it beside David and Jonathan, those two formidable, long-barrelled horse-pistols:

"Friend," quoth he, shaking his head, "the High Toby concern is profession as no man may play fast and loose with."

"Faith, Rob, thou'rt at least a conscientious robber!" smiled Sir Richard.

"Friend, I am so—for Highway Robbery should be taken seriously as I've warned Nick many's the time, but he's too light-minded, is Nick!"

"And should ha' been here an hour ago!" said Sir Richard, glancing at his watch for the third time in as many minutes.

"Ay, friend, but then—Nick's . . . in love!" Here the speaker shook grim head in scornful disparagement. "And Love hath been the ruin o' many a promising High-Tobyman as should have neither friend, sweetheart, nor bowels—any o' the which shall bring him to the cart and Tyburn tree. A true Tobyman should work alone, ride solitary and keep his own counsel; he should warn once and pull trigger, and have faith abiding in Providence."

"Nay, Rob, surely Providence and robbery be but ill assorted?"

"Ah, verily, friend! But I, though sinner by trade, am religious by instinct and reverent by nature. Bred to the Church was I, and should ha' made a notable good parson, but a cruel destiny decreed otherwise.

So 'stead o' taking holy orders I took to taking purses,
and ha' gone on taking 'em ever since, and so must
do—more's the pity!"

"Why not give it up?"

"Because on a day, friend, I shot—and killed—a
perjured rogue had sworn away an innocent, honoured
life, and vowed to live and die by the road. And an
oath is an oath. 'Twas long ago, since when, six
sinners vile have I made to cease from evil by means
o' steel and bullet, translating 'em to a nobler living,
I pray. . . . See yonder!" and he jerked bewigged
head towards a small battered, leather-covered box
or casket upon the shelf. "I call it my *memento mori*
—ha' the goodness to set it in my reach." Sir Richard
did as requested, and opening the box the Galloping
Parson gazed into it smiling a little grimly.

"Lookee!" quoth he and held up a rusty spur. "This
was Sylvanus Todd, one o' Jonathan Wild's perjurers,
as black a rogue as ever sold man or woman to the
gallows. I killed him on Kennington Heath about
dusk of a November day . . . it was snowing, I
mind. This," said he, showing a large plate coat-
button, "this was Timothy Dwyer, another o' Wild's
crew, I stabbed him wi' my sword under the arch o'
Clifford's Inn one night, whereby two poor souls won
free o' the noose awhile. Here now," he continued,
drawing from the box a bunch of seals, "here's William
Shand, another of 'em. I shot him on Blackheath.
This," and he showed a gold ring, "this was Thomas
Collison—Tom was a mistake . . . however. This,"
and he held up a yellow lace ruffle, "this was a murderer o' quality, Sir Ralph Markly, that dodged the
gallows thanks to Wild, who set another dangling in
his stead—I ended Sir Ralph on the Hownslow road.
And that, friend, is all . . . for the present. But
some day, Providence aiding me, I'll rid the world of
Wild—ay, of Jonathan and Titus Oldcraft . . .
some day belike." So saying the Galloping Parson
replaced his mementoes, sighed and closed the box
while Sir Richard, his pipe forgotten and out long
since, watched him in an ever-growing wonder.

"Are these so great, brother? Birth and death are our common lot, and cloaks and rings well nigh as common."

"Nay, Rob, vastly uncommon, rather—for this cloak that I left miles away is yet found on the scene o' the crime, and this ring that I found and left beside the dead, vanishes as——" he caught his breath as memory rushed upon him.

"Aha!" exclaimed the Galloping Parson with stab of bony finger. "'It must not be found!'" quo' she —and, lo, it vanisheth! Ergo, she is thy friend, this haughty dame, like him that rode with her and picked up the ring, this gentleman ornate that, if Providence prove kind, I will yet ha' the picking of, he is thy friend also, this Captain Despard."

"The which," said Sir Richard, rising to pace up and down, "mightily astonishes me. . . . Pray, what manner o' night is it, Nick?"

"Fair, your honour, and with a moon." Sir Richard put on his wig and reached for hat and riding-coat.

"Eh?" cried the Galloping Parson. "Friend, ye're never venturing abroad?"

"Rob, I am so. I've tryst with one shall tell me more news."

"Sir . . . your honour," protested Nick, "the country hereabouts is plaguy unhealthy for the likes o' we, and especially you, just now."

"No matter," answered Sir Richard taking up his pistols and glancing at their primings. "Nay, faith Nick, I shall go warily."

"Ay, brother," demanded Rob, "but how if you be pursued?"

"I must take my chance. Howbeit, I should lead the chase away from here."

"Nay but, sir," cried Nick, "there be constables coming from London. Titus Oldcraft himself is with 'em and——"

"Ha, d'ye say so, Nick lad, d'ye say so?" cried the Galloping Parson in glad voice. "Why here's famous news, joyful news—all praise and glory be! For hearkee, brothers, 'tis in my mind that if ever Titus goeth back to London-town he'll go—feet foremost . . . in a box."

CHAPTER XX

IT was a mighty tree, gnarled and rugged with un-numbered years, vast of girth and with great spread of writhen branches whose myriad leafage cast much shade; a tree that in its slim and tender youth had mayhap shaken to the quick, armed tread of hard-marching Roman legionaries.

With his keen gaze upon this stately giant, Sir Richard checked his horse and whistled a soft trill of rippling notes; and instantly from the shadow of this great tree rode a man, at sight of whom Sir Richard spoke in joyous greeting:

"Ha, Gregory, old lad!" and, leaping from saddle he hurried forward, hand outstretched, then halted suddenly and swung round, peering.

"Richard!" said a soft voice, and into the moonlight rode my lady Helen; reining up her mare beside him, she leaned down, her handsome face seeming wonderfully gentle in the silvery radiance:

"Richard!" she murmured again, and in such tone as no man had ever heard from her lips ere now. For a long moment he stood dumb and motionless, then he bowed, hat a-flourish, and, turning from her, seized Gregory's ready hand.

"Well, Greg, and how wags the world?" he enquired lightly. "And Abby, the good, dear soul, how is he?"

"Mrs. Abby is well, Sir Richard, though like all our friends, sadly concerned for you and this . . . his ugly——"

"Ay, ay, the murder—and faith, 'tis small wonder or murder is grave offence, take it how you will, nd——"

looked back at him, then, that he might see her loveliness the better, doffed the coquettish riding-hat she wore:

"Why wilt decry Friendship, Richard?" she murmured, leaning towards him, wherefore he, very aware of the appealing beauty of her, scowled hard at his horse's ears.

"Friendship?" he repeated. "'Tis a canker—a pest, a very plague!"

"Why didst run away, Richard, why dost hide thyself?"

He stared at her, dumb with anger and amazement.

"Why didst leave thy ring in the Dingle, Richard?"

"'Sdeath, ma'm!" he exclaimed. "You mock me!"

Once again Cæsar reared to the unwonted prick of spur and bounded forward, and once again his rider heard the quick, rhythmic pounding of the mare's fleet hoofs in determined pursuit; therefore, espying a narrow, leafy alley to his left, Sir Richard wheeled his horse in full career and, stooping low against whipping twigs, drove on through leafy tangles, yet still, hard behind him was the sound of The Witch's galloping hoofs. . . . And thus he rode until Cæsar checked suddenly and stood quivering, his further course barred by a dense thicket. Sir Richard swore peevishly, my lady, close behind, tittered.

"Pray whither now, sir?" she questioned.

Sir Richard scowled at the impenetrable boskage that barred the way, but spoke not.

"We had better ha' kept to the open rides," she suggested.

Sir Richard scowled up at the bright moon and round about him a little wildly, and ground his teeth.

"Ah, Richard," she murmured in voice tender as cooing dove, "why didst ravish from me thy ring in manner so ungentle?"

"Oh, ma'm," he answered harshly, "if talk you must and will, speak plain and to the point, I beg, for I protest you weary me sadly."

She recoiled as from a blow, then up went haughty chin, slim hand clenched tight upon her riding whip.

"Indeed," quoth she at last, "'tis evident the wilderness makes you more boorish than nature hath already."

"Forsooth, ma'm, a very oaf-like murderer, I. But what o' my ring?"

"You took it, sir—stole it from me in the lane that fatal evening."

"Now, faith, and did I so?" said he, and laughed oddly, while his eyes narrowed upon her.

"Can you—will you deny it?"

"Not I, 's life—not I! Yet tell me more and be explicit, I beseech. What said I? Smiled I or frowned I? How looked I?"

"You went masked and——"

"I' faith, ma'm, 'twas cunningly contrived—masked! And yet you knew me?"

"Ah, yes, yes!" she cried passionately. "'Twas for very reason of your mask I recognised you."

"Why so, ma'm, why so?"

"Because upon a time I named you highwayman, wherefore masked and armed like highwayman you stopped me that evening. And you rode in your old military cloak—the cloak I had folded about me in the rose-garden that same hour. . . . And you whistled soft twixt your teeth—as you are doing this very moment!"

He ceased whistling to view her twixt narrowed lids, then he laughed gently, and eyes and laugh stung her to flare of anger.

"Well, sir, well? Are you dumb?"

"With wonder, ma'm, with awe!" he answered gravely. "So here then was the way of it! And I vow and protest it hearkens rarely, ay—'twill do, ma'm, 'twill do!"

"Dare you . . . will you deny it?" she demanded, quick-breathing.

"No, lady, no! Heaven forbid I should question tale so apt, so purely convincing."

"Convincing, sir?"

"Why 'tis tripping narrative, madam, reasonable to admiration and shall serve you infinitely well, for——"

"How, sir, how?" cried she in choking voice. "You think—O, do you dare suggest—what do you think —what?"

F

"Lady, my poor thoughts are mine own, what matter for 'em? And now, shall we seek the so patient Gregory?"

"Answer me!" she cried, with passionate gesture. "You must—you shall! Was't you stayed me that evening? Speak!"

"Lord!" sighed he, shaking reproving head at her. "Thou'rt wild creature—a very fury!"

"And thou," she retorted hotly, "thou art fool, stubborn as a fool—as an ass!"

"An ass?" he repeated. "Ay, faith the simile is just, for the ass is beast of burden—even as I. Ah well, ma'm, I have shouldered my burden, and, repining not, fathered this crime, playing murderer to the best o' my poor capacity, and thus, with ass-like patience, do plod my way whithersoever it shall bring me. . . . And now shall we seek——'

"Dear God!" she exclaimed, and, swaying towards him even as she spoke, was staring at him with eyes of horror, begauntleted hand twitching upon his arm:

"So—you think," sighed she in dreadful gasping whisper, "you think—'twas I—murdered your cousin?"

Sir Richard was silent, and for a long moment they stared mutely on each other, eye to eye.

"Oh—hateful!' she cried. "You would put off this crime—on me . . . foul me with your kinsman's blood. Is it thus you would retort on me? Oh—most shameful! Ignoble man, odious wretch, how dare . . . how can you?" Sir Richard merely looked at her until she, impatient for his answer, driven by his grave immobility, shook wildly at the arm she clutched

"Speak—speak!" she panted. "Your vile suspicion . . . how dare you so misjudge me? Speak, I say!"

"Ma'm," said he gently, "did you not threaten poor Julian's life more than once? But—mum for this, 'tis no more to me than the babble of a brook."

"I . . . I threaten him?" she stammered, and uttering strange, broken cry, she shrank away "Ah, sweet mercy of Heaven . . . I mind me now I did—Oh, I did!" Then, cowering in the saddle she hid her face in clasping hands.

Now beholding her swift abasement, he stared up at the moon again, stole a glance at her distressful figure and fidgeted with reins and stirrups:

"Madam," said he, at last. "I should not have spoke o' this, indeed I had not meant to, for what is past is done with—and shall be so for me, henceforth."

A long, shuddering sigh.

"My lady, I do not reproach circumstance, indeed 'twas but natural suspicion should fall on me. 'Tis so my fate it seems for I have lived suspect before and 'tis burden I'm well broke to."

A painful, gasping sob.

"Helen . . . forget, as I do—for I am thy friend now as ever. . . . And, moreover, killing is sometimes justifiable and therefore no murder."

"Cruel! Oh—cruel!" she sobbed wildly, "to deem me such blood-guilty creature . . . a wretch vile enough to use your ring to such base purpose! To think me such detestable craven, shielding myself at another's peril! I deny your loathed suspicions, I——"
Here my lady, being beyond tears, took deep breath and, while he stared bewildered, reproached, denounced and reviled him, scorned, rated and derided him until even words failed her at last and, uttering bitter, inarticulate cry, she struck him with her riding-whip so heavily that his hat spun to earth. So they fronted each other a while, she panting and desperate, he motionless and grim.

"'S bud!" he murmured at last, teeth a-gleam between sardonic lips. "Bellona and Penthesilea rolled into one!"

"You doubted . . . you doubted my word!" she stammered. "You . . . ah! you suspect me yet . . . I see it in your look. You dare to think——"

"Ma'm," said he harshly. "I dare to think yon was a right shrewd, murderous stroke, very worthy of ye!" and he pointed down at his fallen hat. "I dare to think that had you grasped sword 'stead o' whip you had surely ended us Gyffords once and for all."

"Oh!" cried she, in weeping tones. "May God forgive you!"

"Yet surely, madam, surely his motive was generous and well intentioned."

"And yet I abhor him—O, vastly!"

"Then, madam, alas——" Gregory paused for she was looking at him through a glitter of tears.

"Ay, Gregory," said she between laugh and sob as she met his look of bewilderment, "and should this abhorred wretch be taken or come to any harm, I think 'twould break my heart. . . . So I pray God be his sure defence now and always."

"Amen!" quoth Gregory fervently.

"Years agone," said she gently, "thou wert my friend and playfellow, Gregory, and time hath but mellowed thee . . . and so dear friend, Good-night."

Off came Gregory's hat and, speaking no word, he stooped to the hand she reached out to him, kissed it reverently and thereafter sat bare-headed to watch her safely indoors. Even then he remained staring at the house as if lost in profound meditation until— the hedge rustled behind him, a spur jingled and starting round, he reached instinctively for his pistol-holster as a masked man stepped into the moonlight.

"All's well!" said a familiar voice, and, slipping off the hideous half-mask, Sir Richard smiled up at him.

"God save us!" exclaimed Gregory. "This is madness!"

"Nay," laughed Sir Richard, "here rather is sanity, reason, common-sense. And yonder went rare creature, Greg, and—prayed for me—wept! Ha, 'tis sweet, good world!"

"But, sir . . . your honour, there be men from London to hunt ye down."

"Ay, I know, Greg man, I know. But—she prayed for me, and sure such prayers cannot but be answered. Howbeit, I'm come home again, old lad."

"Home . . . home again?" stammered Gregory.

"And I left Cæsar farther up the lane, yonder!"

Now as they went, Sir Richard looked up at Gregory riding so gravely beside him.

"Ha, Greg," he said, clapping him on the knee, "'tis like thyself not to trouble me with questions nor even ask why I fled like guilty rogue."

"Sir," answers Gregory, very conscious of that hand upon his knee, "we have lived together so long that no need is there for questions twixt us, for as I knew the boy so do I know the man, thus I judge your flight was to some good purpose.'

"'Slife!" exclaimed Sir Richard, smiling up into the wistful eyes above him. "There spake Friendship's very self, Lord love ye, Greg! And yet my running away was all to no purpose, it appears. For in jumping to conclusions I cracked my addlepate 'gainst Circumstance soundly, ay, faith I set my numbskull in reach o' the hangman and all, as I say, without just cause or need, for the which, God be thanked."

"Amen!" quoth Gregory fervently.

"'Twould seem I woundily misjudged her, the fierce, sweet, fiery, gentle soul—wherefore she vows me hateful, scorns and contemns me, and very naturally, Greg. Wherefore, unless they hang me, I am determined to follow your advice and make her my wife, heaven help her! Ay, faith I'll wed her, soon or late, maugre her money bags, the poor wretch!"

The usually solemn Gregory actually chuckled:

"And pray doth my lady guess aught o' this your determination?"

"Not she . . . as yet!"

Gregory laughed suddenly, and was instantly grave again, at the which unwonted exhibition of feeling Sir Richard viewed him a little askance.

"And yet, sir, I dare to suggest she favours you.'

"Zounds yes, she hath already whipped me."

"Whi—whipped you?" repeated Gregory in shocked voice.

"Heartily, Greg. The which doth argue her not altogether insensible, nay I protest it promiseth well. Faith 'twill be a right merry wooing."

"Sir, are you truly serious, indeed?'

"As death!" nodded Sir Richard with grim smile. Here, reaching his horse, he mounted and they rode on together at a hand pace.

"Sir," said Gregory at last, "there be divers other gentlemen do protest the same desire of wedding her."

"Why, she is become the fashion, it seems, Greg, and these be all the merest sparks o' fashion."

"Yet there is one at least who shows mighty determined, sir, I mean Captain Despard."

"Ha!" said Sir Richard thoughtfully, and took himself by the chin. "Why then, Greg, 'tis high time I set about my wooing seriously and the sooner the better."

"Sir," said Gregory the cautious, peering about them, "pray let us take to the grass, our horses' hoofs might be heard."

So they presently reached the village where none stirred and no light beamed; cottage, inn and tavern, all lay hushed and dark with sleep long since, and never a sound to disturb its peaceful silence save the whisper of their horses' feet on the soft green and the creak of their saddle-girths.

"A pretty place, Greg, and homely!' sighed Sir Richard drawing rein to look about him. "Ay, a good homely place and looks innocent and harmless enough even to hunted fugitive such as I. And yet here, at this moment, sheltered 'neath one o' these familiar roofs, lie they, few or many, that plot my ruin, though who or why, is beyond my guessing. Yet here lurketh some secret foe, thus here will I hide."

"Here, sir?" demanded Gregory, starting.

"Or hereabouts. To-morrow is the inquest on poor Julian, it seems, and to-morrow I shall assuredly be pronounced the murderer, so here needs must I be."

"Nay, sir, 'twere wanton risk! There are these catch-polls from London . . . they have searched Weare from cellars to attics."

"Ha—dammem!" murmured Sir Richard.

"The whole place is watched for you. There is even talk of calling out the soldiers to beat the woods . . . the hunt for you grows but the keener."

"Well, so much the better, old lad. Faith I shall e'en be safer here under their very noses, as 'twere, and to succeed in my purpose, here must I bide."

"Nay, what desperate thing do you propose?"

"To dog my hunters, Greg. To haunt the neighbourhood o' nights—flit like spectre, glide like ghost, skulking mid the shadows. A ghost—ay, but I vow to heaven, a mighty purposeful one. The which minds me— what o' Tom Pitt, hast seen the rascal o' late?"

"Once or twice, sir. He hath taken service with Viscount Brocklehurst, I hear."

"Brocklehurst? He was one o' poor Julian's friends."

"Sir . . . your honour . . ." said Gregory in pleading tones. "Oh, Master Richard, never venture yourself hereabouts I do entreat."

Now Sir Richard, perceiving his passionate anxiety, clasped and squeezed him in long arm.

"Greg," quoth he, "good my friend grieve not thyself for me, for did not She pray for me? Art thou not mine assured and faithful friend?"

"God knows it," muttered Gregory.

"So then all's well wi' me, man. Howbeit here- abouts goeth the murderer of Julian . . . poor Julian that died even as I found him and, dying, gasped out strange warning . . . ay, by heaven, with his last breath spake mighty strange thing, Greg, a thing hath sore puzzled me."

"What, sir—what said he?"

"'Ware, Dick,' he gasped, 'ware, Dick—a cat's- eye——'"

Sir Richard checked himself with hissing intake of breath, and turning swiftly to stare at Gregory found Gregory staring at him, and each in that same moment reined his horse to a standstill, and gazing thus on each other, wide-eyed, were silent a while; when at last Sir Richard spoke it was in hoarse and broken whisper:

"'Sdeath, man . . . he . . . he was not raving then! He had been shot from the bushes . . . at close quarters! He had seen! A hand 'mid the leaves . . . the cat's-eye ring! . . . You saw it also—where, Gregory—where?"

"Sir," whispered Gregory, "I saw it . . . in the Rose garden . . . on—her finger. But, sir, she may have lost it later."

"Or had it stolen from her, Greg, like mine—like mine! Ha, the devil! So here's another ring, then! Two of 'em! . . . And Julian died trying to tell me

—what?" Sir Richard stared up at the moon with haggard eyes that saw it not. "And yet . . . " he muttered after some while, "killing may . . . be no murder . . . sometimes. It may be justifiable, Greg."

Then, all at once, he was off his horse and had thrust the reins into Gregory's lax fingers.

"Howbeit, Greg," quoth he. "I wed her . . . cat's-eye or no! Take now my Cæsar, away with him to Fallowdene or hide him where ye will, and be ready o' nights to open to my ghostly rapping. Nay, argue not, Gregory man, for I'm determined on my course. Should you not see me awhile, Landlord John shall give you word o' me, and so—farewell—wait! Take these jingling betrayers," and stooping, he did off his spurs.

"Ah, sir," sighed Gregory, dropping them into his pocket, "'tis desperate risk you'll be running."

"Why then, also I'll take my pistols. And now away with ye, Greg, shalt see me over at Weare one o' these fine nights, and so fare thee well!"

Shaking troubled head, Gregory sighed again, gripped the hand extended to him and rode off leading Cæsar with him; once or twice he turned to wave his hand to that desolate, solitary figure upon the green, but Sir Richard never heeded, since his head was bowed in distressful thought. At length, starting from this dark reverie, he crossed the wide green and, halting before the Gyfford Arms, stood a moment to survey its many latticed casements each and every vague and dark, then, swift and light of foot, he turned into the yard and crossed to a certain shadowy corner where, deep in the angle, was that small and unobtrusive door which seemed to hide from chance espial.

Drawing key from inner pocket, he was in the act of fitting it to the lock when he stood suddenly motionless and rigid, for his sharp ears had caught a stealthy sound hard by, his quick eyes beheld a shadow that moved amid the shadows on the opposite side of the wide yard, a dark and furtive shape that yet stole at purposeful speed. . . . Sir Richard turned and, moving on soundless feet, followed grimly in pursuit, his face once more hidden beneath black half-mask.

CHAPTER XXII

WHICH HATH A SHADOW AT THE END

THE Duchess sat up in bed very wide awake despite the late hour, though with night-cap somewhat over one eye:

"And is it see him ye did, me sweet soul?" she demanded.

"Ah, Dearly Beloved," sighed Helen, tossing aside hat and gauntlets and frowning at the candle-flame. "I saw the odious wretch!"

"Eh?" cried the Duchess with a sort of pounce. "And didn't your 'odious wretch' kiss ye then?"

Helen merely looked and turned away with gesture so superbly disdainful that the Duchess chuckled.

"Arrah now, me dear, didn't ye go in the fond hope and expectation o' kisses?"

"For shame, Aunt!"

"Well, but didn't ye, now?"

"Fie, madam! I vow I'd sooner ha' died! I protest to heaven I——"

The Duchess snorted.

"Tush, girl! Have done wi' your high tragedy airs, miss! Here's none to see 'em but yourself and myself, so—be yourself. Ye've seen him and he's disappointed you—tell me how, tell my why, and tell me quick!"

My lady's magnificent disdain wilted and, uttering a sound that was neither laugh nor sob yet something of both, she sank upon the great bed and hid her face.

"Oh, Aunt," she whispered, "he thinks me a . . . murderess!"

"Ah, shure!" nodded the Duchess. "Och the dear man how he must worship ye!"

"Aunt?" cried Helen, lifting head from pillow the better to look her amazement, "I tell you . . . he thinks 'twas I killed his cousin Julian."

"Av course he does, ye sweet simpleton! The riddle grows plain. Ha, don't ye see? Is 't stone blind ye are? Here's the true reason for his flight, our Dog with the Bad Name fathers the crime, runs the hazard o' shameful death, braves gallows and gibbet—for thee, Helen, all for thee!"

"Oh, Aunt!"

"B'the Powers, girl, this poor dog, this Richard, this Gyfford o' Weare is noble gentleman, ah—and what's more, a very man!"

"Ah, Belovedest, if this indeed be so——"

"Pest!" cried the Duchess, nodding her night-cap more askew, "if me no ifs, 'tis beyond all doubting, it is the only explanation. And proud ye should be o' such brave devotion, humble and thankful for the love of such a man."

"Humble? Alas, Aunt! Oh, my dear, I—struck him!"

"Eh—struck him, did ye?"

"With my whip!"

"Ah!" sighed the Duchess, sinking back among her pillows, "then I'll thank ye for me snuff-box."

"But, Aunt!"

"Me snuff-box. . . . So—a man perils his life for ye, sullies his proud name for ye and ye show your gratitude with a whip! Well, the method was original and 'tis well to be exempt."

"But I . . . I struck him with good reason, Aunt."

"And a whip, me dear soul."

"He . . . he accused me of using his own ring to cast suspicion on him—yes, he dared suggest I was shielding myself at peril of his life. Such base imputation! Oh 'twas cruel, wicked, odious and shameful . . . and I'm glad, very infinite glad I struck the wretch."

"Ay, but this wretch is a Gyfford, me poor soul, and if I know aught o' the proud Gyffords—and, mark me, I do—this Gyfford will surely cry for 'quits' for that blow."

"Oh?" enquired Helen, cocking defiant chin, "how, pray?"

But the Duchess merely inhaled a pinch of snuff with great apparent gusto; thereafter she abruptly changed the subject.

"Your maid Betty 's a sly minx and will bear watching."

"Oh, Gemini, Aunt, why? Betty's a rattle-brain, a simple creature yet faithful and devoted——"

"So I watched her!" said the Duchess somewhat grimly. "And, what's more, your devoted, faithful creature can read and write!"

"Why, yes, Aunt, but——"

"And consequently she writes and she reads. Faith, me dear, she reads your letters and she reads my letters, and writes to somebody she names 'dear T——'"

"Aunt!" gasped Helen.

"There's a letter writ to 'dear T,' hidden in the arbour at this moment."

"'Tis but a love-letter, belike."

"Hum!" quoth the Duchess. "It is and it isn't!"

"Aunt, you never bothered to read the thing?"

"Every word, me dear."

"And what said this letter?"

"I'm wondering who 'dear T' may chance to be.

"La, Aunt, some rustic swain, be sure."

"Oh b'the Powers, I'll be sure, me dear. . . . Angela's come back—on a flood o' tears."

"Angela? Why, Aunt, you know she——"

"Having parted with her lordling for ever, and quarrelled with her mother for the present, she's come t'us to weep and grieve in comfort."

"But she was to ha' been wed next month! Whatever can have——"

"Och, me dear, she'll tell ye all to-morrow, and take all to-morrow to do't. . . . Then Viscount Brocklehurst called this morning——"

"He!" exclaimed my lady, supremely disdainful.

"Himself! And mighty curious and insistent to know whither you had ridden and with whom."

"Brocklehurst?" exclaimed my lady again in contemptuous surprise. "'Tis a doting wind-bag, full of empty nothingness, a mincing clothes-horse!"

"'Is she with Despard?'" says he, and shure the man was all of a shiver. 'Maybe,' says I, and the man frowns and bites his lips—I saw him in the mirror —and such dark, murderous look as was marvellous to see in a 'mincing clothes-horse,' and put me to some wonder. Afterwards, in shady corner—they didn't see me—your faithful devoted Betty told him something concerning yourself, though what I couldn't hear, not being close enough, but I caught whisper also of Richard Gyfford's name."

Once again my lady gasped, but this time in a very real and growing terror:

"Aunt. . . . Oh Aunt—the perfidious wretch!"

"Whereupon, me sweet, confiding soul, your mincing clothes-horse swore a fierce, great oath and vowed 'twas time to act."

"To act how, Aunt, how? What doth it all mean?"

"That mischief's afoot. But b'the saints we'll outwit 'em, thou and I."

"But Betty—the wicked, false wretch! How came she to know?"

"Why, me innocent child, it seems she has the same powers o' stealthy observation as I possess—almost."

"And what—what must we do?"

"We must wait and we must watch."

"Ah, so we will!" nodded Helen. "Yet, oh, Dearest —beloved—this Betty! This slimy serpent, this stinging asp that I've nurtured in my bosom, this hateful scratch-cat! She shall pack, the faithless, treacherous reptile shall pack and go to-morrow morn!"

"Ah me, dear Helen," sighed the Duchess, closing snuff-box with a snap. "You've the face and form of a goddess, the wit of a sparrow, and the guile of a woolly lamb."

"Oh, indeed, ma'm!" quoth my lady and instantly became majestic.

"Lookee, Helen, we must meet guile with guile, we must use our eyes and ears, we must act a part, but —above all we must cling to our Betty—she is the toasted cheese to our trap, the lime to our twig, the worm to our hook. And now enough—kiss me good-night, mavourneen, forget not thy prayers, and pleasant dreams attend thee."

"Nay, first," said Helen suddenly tender, "will I smooth thy pillow and straighten thy night-cap—so! And now Good night, thou dear, wise, guileful Aunt!"

So they clasped and kissed each other and Helen, taking lighted candle, went to her room, but paused often in her disrobing to stare dreamily at the sinking moon, and so to bed. Yet scarcely had her head touched pillow than all hope of sleep was banished by the hurry of her teeming thoughts, also the moon's bright beams were all about her; therefore she rose at last to draw the curtains, but being at the open lattice, leaned forth to breathe the languorous fragrance of the midsummer night and to gaze down into the garden, a place of mystery, of silvery radiance and far-flung inky shadows cast by motionless tree and hedge. Now as she stood thus, awed by the deep and brooding stillness, her heart made a sudden leap and, instinctively drawing the curtains about her loveliness, she stood breathless and wide of eye, for amid those black shadows something had moved.

CHAPTER XXIII

TELLETH OF A NIGHT AND A RADIANT DAWN

A TALL figure it was, Sir Richard noticed, that flitted silently in the dusk of hedgerows, but sped crouching through every patch of moonlight; and as silently, as cautiously, Sir Richard followed whither it led. So came they to a lane, to a gate set in high hedge, to the Moat House garden and there, by grass-bordered walks, to a rustic arbour wherein the figure vanished, soon to reappear and, crouching in the moonlight, unfolded a slip of paper to scan it with eager eyes; then Sir Richard recognized the reader and, with his gaze on this sheet of paper, stepped behind a tree as the man thrust paper into pocket and hasted away, swift and silent as he had come.

For some while Sir Richard leaned there against the tree, arms folded and head bowed like one who puzzled over some abstruse problem, then, moved by sudden thought, he stepped into the arbour and peered about him. At some time or other the interior had been painted white and by reason of this, and the moon's radiance, the place was fairly luminous; by which vague light he began a laborious search, passing his hands to and fro across the timbering, thrusting fingers into every crack and crevice until at last his care and patience were rewarded, something rustled faintly, and from behind one of the uprights, he drew a folded paper, and spreading this to the moon, read these words very plainly written and in a familiar hand:

"Dear B. but do as I bid thee and our fortune is made. My L. is pleased with thee and I have lace for thee French point mighty fine. Should you hear aught of his whereabouts, haste to tell me, for naught

is well till he be took. So be watchful to see and
hear all you may and act when I give word. My L.
is for the haunted mill and tis likely spot being so
desolate. Do your ladies drink a posset of nights?
Encourage them to it. To-morrow is the inquest
so no more until we meet, same hour and place.
I've much to tell.

"Thy ever-dear T."

Sir Richard was still conning this screed when a
vague sound startled him, and glancing round he espied
a cloaked and hooded figure speeding to him across
the wide lawn.

"Helen!" said he, in glad surprise.

Breathless she was with haste and now stood before
him, panting a little, her face a pale sweet oval beneath
drawn hood.

"Helen?" said he again and reached forth his hand.
Whereupon she fell back a pace, one shapely arm out-
flung against him in swift repulsion.

"Ha!" quoth he, viewing her from hooded head to
slim, be-slippered foot apeep beneath voluminous cloak.
"Why such offended majesty? Thus might have stood
the proud Diana before bold-eyed Actæon! Yet I
am no prying hunter-lad and you, i' faith, no goddess
but merest human woman for—how runs the ditty?

> On land or sea
> Our toast shall be—
> To Hel, to Hel, to Helen!"

"Odious!" she exclaimed, drawing her cloak with
petulant gesture.

"Why, so I think!" he nodded.

"What do you here, sir?"

"Trespass, ma'm, beyond a doubt."

"And run deadly peril to come at your—your billet-
doux!" And she pointed disdainfully at the open
letter in his hand whereupon he looked at it also. "You
found it hidden in the arbour yonder?"

"Ay, I did, ma'm."

"Sir," said she, chin aloft, contempt and disdain in every line of her, " twas writ by my maid!"

"Alack, madam!" he sighed, then chuckled, and yet bowed with such grave punctilio, such leisured elaboration of gesture that her next question faltered:

"Can it be that you—you are her . . . 'Dear T'?"

"Let us suppose it, ma'm, and what then?"

"There is no more to be said, sir."

"Nay, faith, ma'm, there is so much that we are like to talk until dawn."

"So will I bid you good-night, sir!" But, even as she turned to be gone, he had her by the cloak.

"A good night indeed," said he. "'Tis a balmy air and kindly warm; moreover this cloak is stout the which is well seeing y'are so scanty clad below. Now as to your feet—nay, seek not to hide 'em—those white, slim feet, should they grow cold, for the grass is dewy, I'll chafe 'em in comfortable hands or wrap 'em in my coat-skirts. Howbeit, this night we come to an understanding."

"Loose me, sir!"

"I have much to say, and you to hear.'

"Loose me or I scream!"

"Attempt it, ma'm, and I kiss you breathless.'

At this she stood mute and with head averted, and supremely conscious of his grasp upon her cloak.

"So you will deign me an explanation at last, sir?" she demanded.

"Freely and most fully, Helen, for whereas the world deems me no more than cowardly murderer, you suspect me of an intrigue with your maid! Now which, I wonder, should you prove the greater offence, my Helen?"

"What brought you here to-night?" she demanded, speaking with head still averted.

"Pure villainy," he answered lightly, "it crept before me all the way, it brought this letter in its pocket, a missive mysterious addressed 'Dear B' and subscribed 'dear T.'"

"Oh!" said my lady, coming a little nearer. "'Twill be for Betty, my wicked maid."

"And T," nodded Sir Richard, "is for Thomas, Tom for short, though himself is something long and very rogue, poor Julian's erstwhile servant. You'll mind Tom Pitt, my Helen, you saw him the night these eyes first looked on thee, the night you——'

"Yes," she answered, coming nearer yet. "Yes, I mind how you rapped his head against the wall. Now, pray, show me this letter."

"Why so I will and divers of my thoughts o' thee, but not here."

"Where then?"

"Yonder, 'neath the old cherry-tree—come!" and, stooping suddenly, he swept her up in his arms before she might prevent.

"Why . . . what . . . ?" she gasped, kicking feebly.

"The dew,' he explained. "It lies heavy on the grass and I fear for thy pretty feet. . . . Strive not, my Helen, 'tis vastly unbecoming in creature so dignified and, i'faith, I might drop thee."

"Oh, 'tis hateful in thee to so abuse my helplessness, tis cruel, 'tis monstrous! Ah, where do you take me? The cherry-tree is yonder!"

"Ay, but I keep to the shadows to 'scape censorious eyes and talking tongues."

"You know there's none to see us, sir—all the world's asleep."

"Save thou and I," said he, pausing to look around him. "'Tis sweet thought, my Helen."

"I am not thy Helen!"

"'Twere hard to credit since here stand I and——"

"Then stand not but go—go——" and here she kicked again, vainly yet with passion.

"And in my arms, upon my heart, thy proud and peerless self!"

"Set me down, sir, set me down for I do feel myself supremest fool."

"Faith, my Helen, this new and sweet humility becomes thee mightily."

"And you go so slowly!" she wailed.

"For good reason," he answered, coming to another pause. "Thou art no slim and airy sylphid, and I, what he was and deeming thee proud and fierce as Bellona's very self I . . . I feared . . . I thought——" He faltered and stopped, wherefore her hand, being yet in his, nestled itself a little closer.

"Say it, Richard, say it!" she sighed.

"No!" he answered gravely. "I was merest fool!"

"You thought I had murdered him," she whispered. "So you left your ring where you found it, the ring I had lost to one I thought you . . . you left it to ward suspicion from me at peril of your life . . . wherefore?"

"You were my friend."

"And would be so, still," she answered, "thy ever grateful friend."

"Then Helen, in Friendship's name, I bid you tell me where now is your cat's-eye ring?"

"I lost it," she answered, turning to him in swift surprise. "But why do you——?"

"I pray you, Helen, tell me how you lost it and when?"

"Nay, I'm not sure, yet I think 'twas when the masked man stayed me in the lane. But what matter for such——"

"Did you give it up with my signet?"

"No, indeed. Mistaking this man for you I grew angry you should play me such sorry trick, and dashed my purse 'neath his horse's feet, and so fiercely that my gauntlet flew off and with it, as I do think, my ring, though I missed it not until next day. But why so grave? Why trouble for the foolish trinket, 'twas of small value?"

"Because with his last breath Julian spoke me this warning: 'Ware, Dick, the cat's-eye!'"

For a moment they sat utterly still, looking upon each other and never a word.

"Oh, Richard," sighed she at last in awful whisper. "Then you think he saw it . . . on his slayer's hand . . . my cat's-eye ring?"

"Such rings are scarce hereabouts," answered Sir Richard in the same hushed voice.

"My cat's-eye ring!" she repeated, and shivered.

" Would it fit a man's finger, Helen? "

" No—yes. . . . I'm not sure, but 'twas loose on mine."

" These white fingers!" said he and took her hand into his warm, vital clasp again.

" But—my ring!" sighed she. " I wonder where now it is? "

" I'd give much to know!" said he thoughtfully. " Mayhap 'twill be found, soon or late. . . . But enough o' this, no more o' the past. I'll tell thee of the future."

" What canst thou know of the future, Richard?"

" That I shall woo thee," he answered. " Ay—and I further prophesy that this thy Richard, *me mihi*, shall suddenly vanish awhile and yet, so vanished, be nearer than thou, or any, dream. I prophesy that because thou art absolute woman and thy heart very tender and compassionate, thou shalt yet come to think on thy Richard with an ever-growing kindness, until one day perchance, shalt be glad to know him so very truly thy Richard to command. I prophesy that, Richard vanished, his glad ghost shall yet watch over thee till at the last this murder shall out—then shall he reappear to clasp, to clutch and seize thee to his heart and then—how say you, Helen?"

"Nay prophet, speak thou!" she murmured.

But, even as she uttered the words, a distant clock chimed four . . . from the dense leafage above them a rousing bird uttered a hoarse croak and, glancing up and around, she saw all things shrouded in an opalescent haze.

"Richard," she whispered in sudden awe. "Oh, Richard, tis the day-spring, dawn is upon us!"

"As I did prophesy!" he nodded. "And thou'rt not cold . . . thy feet?" he enquired anxiously.

"No, no, but what o' thyself? You must away now—this very moment—come!" so saying she rose so he did likewise.

"Here have we sat the night through," sighed he, "nor have I presumed to kiss thee once!"

"Indeed but you have, sir—my hands—both of them!"

Viscount Brocklehurst, elaborate as to detail, superlative as to adjectives, had described his vicious assault
upon the dead man—" with a whip, demme, sirs."

Captain Despard deposed briefly as to the impending duel. Mr. Trumpington, sighing and soulful, had
admitted such duel could end but in the wounding or
death of the accused, Sir Richard. Tom Pitt, quiet
and convincing, had told how, at about the fatal hour,
he had chanced to see Sir Richard gallop his horse
very furiously out of the wood, flourishing a pistol in
his hand. Then followed evidence as to the finding
of Sir Richard's blood-stained cloak near the scene of
the crime; whereafter the coroner summed up and
the jury, without retiring, had pronounced their verdict:

"Wilful murder 'gainst Sir Richard Gyfford of
Weare, baronet."

"And zounds!" muttered Sir Richard, shaking solemn
head at the candle, "never sounded man more guilty
rogue than I! But ha, Tom . . . Tom Pitt—you
must clap a pistol in my fist to damn me beyond
redemption—I wonder why? Faith, we must look
into this, and soon, Tom, soon!"

It was growing late, and yet, judging by the stir
and bustle all around his hiding-place, the inn was
still thronged. . . . Feet pattered to and fro, boards
creaked, and upon the air was an inarticulate, never-
ceasing babblement of voices amongst which he thought,
once or twice, to distinguish the pompous, leisured tones
of Sir John Parret and Viscount Brocklehurst's high-
pitched, giggling laugh. All about him were men who
talked of him, men who, believing him cowardly murderer, were eager to seize and drag him to a shameful
doom—more especially Viscount Brocklehurst and Tom
Pitt, judging from their testimony. And wherefore?
The one had been Julian's familiar friend, the other,
his servant. Now wherefore should these twain strive
so desperately by their evidence to prove him murderer?
. . . Then, there was his cloak, found in the wood
and smeared with blood. How came it there? If

Helen had spoken truly, a man had worn it that evening in the lane, a man who had mimicked his own trick of whistling between his teeth—hence a man who must know him very well! And yet, if Helen's tale prove very truth, what of Julian's dying words regarding the cat's-eye?

Long sat Sir Richard staring at the flame of his solitary candle beneath brows knit in a painful concentration of thought, seeking an answer and finding none, until he was roused suddenly by a gentle yet persistent scratching sound.

Up he got and taking one of the pistols that lay to hand, he crossed to the door, drew the bolts gently, set wide the stout oak and in stepped the landlord, John Bly, bearing a tray covered with snowy napkin.

"Your supper, sir!" he announced.

"And 'tis vastly welcome, John. Pray, sit down."

"Cold beef, sir, with a sallet and a pint o' strong ale," said landlord John and, setting down the tray, jerked thumb towards the judas in the corner. "You heered arl the evidence, Sir Richard?"

"Every word, John. Faith, I've heard myself proved so absolute a murderer that I blame none for so believing me." Here Sir Richard fell to his supper with hearty appetite.

"Sir," enquired John, staring at the candle flame with troubled eyes, "did ye chance to notice this here Titus Oldcraft at the inquest, 'e were settin' along o' Sir John Parret?"

"Ay, a cunning looking fellow, John."

"Ah, 'e be all o' that, sir, and mighty overbearin'—and his comrades the same. And wot's more, I've sent Pen over to her aunts at Wilmington to be out o' the way of 'em."

"How many are they?"

"There's three besides him. And, sir, drink they can—and do."

"So much the better. Do they lodge here?"

"All on 'em, worse luck, sir."

"So here," said Sir Richard, setting down half-emptied tankard, "here under one roof we have Viscount

CHAPTER XXV

WHICH IS CHAPTER SUGGESTIVE OF MANY THINGS

"So n-never, ' sobbed Angela, meekly tearful, "never now shall I wed, the dream is past! L-love shall be a stranger to me all my lonesome days! For, oh my Helen, this p-poor heart is quite broke, s-shattered, my dearest, beyond repair! The vision is faded, the dream is o'er. Oh I am the f-forlornest creature, the w-woefullest wretch alive and shall never, never love more, ah never again, my dear one, never, nevermore!"

"And so," nodded my lady, setting determined chin, 'I have quite decided to make you the Marchioness of Merivale.'

"But—but Helen, dear heart, don't I tell thee——"

"Nay, 'tis I am telling thee, my poor child. If thou'rt not a happy wife and marchioness within the year, well—a dog bite me! And now of your late most detestable lordling lover. Tell me all, confess everything, my poor Injured Sweetness, how you contrived to—to lose the wretch?"

"Alas, my Helen, 'twas in a bower, the moon was rising, my mother had but just left us, and 'twas all so sighfully romantic, and the roses, and the jasmine, and his hand clasping mine, and my poor heart so beat, and the roses so fragrant, and my soul so . . . so uplift, and life and the world so sweetly beautiful that tell him I had to——"

"Heavens, child! Tell him what? How much? And how, Angela, how?"

"'Eustace,' sighed I, 'now must I humbly to thee confess——'"

"Oh, thou Innocent—Idiot! Never confess and, above all, never to a man, good lack! And never humbly! Nay but, say on."

"Nay, Helen, I—I——."

"Tush! 'Confess, says you to your superior male wretch—well?"

"C—confess," repeated Angela with small, meek sob, "'that this h-heart, now thine, was once another's, a heart all confiding but——'"

"Ah!" cried my lady with the utmost ferocity. "Now could I shake the very heart and soul o' thee!"

"D-don't, D-dearest," wailed Angela, "or I shall w-weep."

"Go on, thou Deceitful-Innocence, what comes after thy 'heart all confiding, but'?"

"Nay, Helen, you put me out. . . . I—I forget, only I t-told him all."

"All, miss, all? There was nought to tell told properly. What more did you 'confess' to your high, pragmatic fool—what more o' your silly heart? Speak or I'll slap thee!"

"Why then, dear Helen, ah, reproach me not! I told him twas a heart torn by another's cruel fingers, trampled by another's merciless feet, an altar desecrate, a——"

"A flapdragon!' exclaimed my lady.

"Oh—Helen!" wailed Angela louder than before.

"And oh, thou—thou Puling Perversity! 'Tis small wonder the poor fool fled thee like the plague—such talk of 'trampled hearts' and 'altars desecrate' should fright any prospective spouse—Oh Gemini! 'Tis like enough he accounts thee a walking Depravity—Lais, Thais, Phryne and Messalina, all in one. Oh, gracious, merciful goodness—why must you so malign yourself to the masculine wretch?"

"Nay, oh, my love, I but said to him: "'Eustace——'"

"A hateful name—so hissy!" quoth my lady.

"Nay, Helen, 'tis b-beautiful name sweetly romantic! 'Tis name to sigh forth in l-leafy bower to the dying moon, while jasmine and honeysuckle twining breathe——"

"Shush!" exclaimed my lady, whereupon Angela raised drooping head and opening dove-like eyes, actually bridled.

So came they into the house; and aloft, shut within my lady's bed-chamber, fell to work. And who shall say what cunning arts were there employed, what bathings, pattings, dabbings and anointings, what waters, creams, essences, lotions and powders? Faith, not I!

Howbeit, some half-hour later, the Marquis, making his profoundest reverence to this bewitching twain (each so much the other's opposite), opened his languid eyes rather wider than usual in eager endeavour to take in all the radiant loveliness of this slimly elegant creature whose dainty, small nose was so altogether bewitching, so perfect in its shape, so exquisite in contour and, as to hue, might have been a little work of art delicately carved on alabaster.

" I . . . ah! . . . vow 'n protest, m'dam, y'ı truly humble, 'bedient t' command!" murmured the Marquis, transfixed (as it were) by this small, delicious nose.

" Oh, my lord . . . indeed!" a blush, a little gasp and down sinks Mistress Demureness, down and yet down, amid billowing silken folds, in the deepest and most graceful of curtseys.

" Um . . . ah! . . ." stammers the Marquis, still transfixed, "'pon my soul . . . that is . . . the day, madam . . . very warm!"

" Truly, sir, 'tis very warm."

" So . . . so . . . hot, madam, that is to say . . . the sun——"

" Truly, sir, 'tis very sunny."

" Then come we into the shade," laughed my lady, " 'neath the cherry tree . . . and, good lack, let us earnestly strive to talk o' better things than the weather! Thus, my dear Ned—and I felicitate thee on thy so sturdy name, Ned—this Angela o' mine is creature so bitter set 'gainst all man-kind, so disdainful o' love and scornful o' matrimony that she contemplates a nunnery —hush, my love!"

" But, Helen!"

" Peace, child! A nunnery, Ned!"

" Heaven forbid!" quoth the Marquis.

"Nay, but a nunnery is her passion, Ned—to sink, to shrink and shrivel into sere and yellow leaf—I mean an old hag."

"Faith, now I . . . I protest 'tis monstrous!" gasped the Marquis.

"Why, so say I, dear Ned, but she, this Angela, though nothing large and seeming so meek—note you her soft, sweet eyes, Ned, and her nose—her little pretty, dainty tender nose—you remark it?"

"I . . . indeed how may I help so doing, Helen? I vow 'twill haunt me!"

"Oh, Helen! Oh, pray!" twittered Angela, hiding behind her fan.

"Then know and take heed, Ned, that despite her nose and all her seeming gentleness she hath will like iron!"

"Nay, Helen . . .! Oh, my lord, prithee heed her not!"

"She is set in her determination, Ned, like adamantine crag, fierce for her nunnery as a gorgon. Alas, nought is there may save her from herself and immolation except——"

"What, madam, what?"

"Except Eros transfix her stony heart or—Oh plagues and scorpions—there is that odious Brocklehurst! Let me hide!"

But the Viscount had seen them, and forthwith minced across the wide lawn, himself a dazzling vision in sky-blue and silver. So perforce they bowed, all four, they curtseyed, they smiled and simpered, while the gentlemen flourished their hats at each other, though to be sure the Marquis seemed somewhat grim and stiff in the back.

"Madam," said the Viscount, proffering slim hand, "shall we walk?" My lady hesitated but, observing Angela's shy-sweet eyes and the unusually wide-awake air of the Marquis, she placed two white fingers within the Viscount's eager arm and moved away with him along the yew-shaded walk, though with an evident reluctance.

"Helen," said he in his quick, nervous manner, "it seems your aunt, the Duchess, gives a rout . . . a fête, next week."

"To honour her birthday. Well, sir?"

"There will be dancing?"

"'Tis very like."

"Then wilt promise . . . promise here and now to step the last minuet with me, wilt promise, Helen?"

"Why should I?"

"Because," he answered, stooping passionate mouth towards the glossy tress above her ear, "I . . . I adore thee!"

"Viscount," sighed she, wearily, "so you said— yesterday, was it?"

"So shall I say to-morrow and the day after and for ever. Well, madam, well?"

"Nay, 'tis regrettable waste o' breath."

"Helen, I've adored since first I met thee."

"Then would you'd met another!"

"Ah, do not—no, do not flout me, you were wiser not. When, when wilt marry me?"

"Never."

"Is this . . . this your answer?"

"As it hath been and ever will be, sir."

"Never, Helen?"

"Never, Viscount!"

His brows twitched petulantly, and he smote viciously at a hovering butterfly with his walking-cane.

"Howbeit, yet I do adore thee, Helen!"

"Heigho!" sighed she, "we find the man becomes monotonous."

"What o' this—this country squire, this Gyfford?" he demanded in sudden, breathless fashion.

My lady yawned behind a finger.

"Who, sir?"

"Gyfford, Richard Gyfford, the proclaimed murderer! Hath he found favour in your eyes—ha, is this so, Helen? Or—or is it—Despard? Which? Which?"

"And now," sighed my lady, lifting serene gaze to the blue serenity above, "we will retire, for the man becometh an odious impertinent!"

"Forgive . . . forgive . . . pity me!" he pleaded, but through shut teeth. "Truly I am ever your most obedient servant, your most devoted humble——"

"And tattle of me with my servants!" she retorted disdainfully.

"Because I . . . I worship thee!"

"Such worship is degrading, sir," said she, and stopped so that he stopped also, and, reading the bitter scorn in her look, he abased his own, and stood thrusting nervously with his cane at a strip of torn paper lying conspicuous beneath the neat hedge.

"I . . . I love thee so desperately," he stammered, "and thou . . . thou'rt so aloof, so cold, so——"

She heard the soft hiss of his breath, saw his staring eyes dilate and, following his gaze, beheld a piece of torn paper, read thereon two words in straggling scrawl, then he had snatched it up.

"Show me!" said my lady, stretching out imperious hand; slowly, almost unwillingly he gave it to her; this:

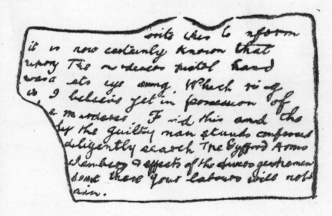

"Strange!" murmured Helen, glancing vaguely round about. "How came this here, I wonder?"

"A . . . cat's-eye ring!" muttered the Viscount glaring about him also.

"It was my ring!" said she, thoughtfully.

"But you . . . you gave it to Gyfford, eh, madam?"

"Never!"

"Why then . . . 'tis evident . . . 'tis very evident he found it!"

"Nay, 'twas the murderer found it."

"And is he not the murderer proclaimed?"

"True," nodded my lady, staring at the paper again, "proclaimed but not proved."

Now at this moment was a tuneless whistling, and down one of the paths came a man trundling a wheelbarrow, a tall, gipsy-seeming fellow to whom my lady beckoned and, crumpling up the paper, tossed it into the barrow; then, hearing the Viscount's exclamation of pettish anger, she turned and saw Captain Despard's tall stately figure approaching.

"Ah, madam," said he in his strangely musical voice, "I protest thou'rt Summer's very incarnation, radiant as this so glorious morning—by reason o' which I find pleasure—even in Brocklehurst's scowl o' welcome."

My lady laughed, the Viscount muttered inaudibly, and thrust his cane into the soft turf as it had been sword into the bosom of an enemy.

"And I come a beggar," continued the Captain, "a humble suppliant suing o' thee the first gavotte and last minuet on Thursday next!"

"Impossible, George!" cried the Viscount fretfully. "'Twas I asked first . . . first, I tell ye."

"Ah, but then," said the Captain gently, "if you asked first, I plead—now!"

"And, o' my conscience," smiled my lady, glancing from one to the other, "'twixt your demanding and your pleading should be no choice for person o' spirit, yet he shall dance with me who greets me first o' Thursday."

CHAPTER XXVI

IT was evening, and Master Titus Oldcraft swore at his jaded horse as he clattered into the yard of the Gyfford Arms and, getting stiffly from the saddle, turned to swear at his two dusty fellows who came clattering after him, and, espying a tall, gipsy-seeming fellow who chanced to be gaping at all and sundry over the half door of a nearby stable, Master Titus cursed him likewise.

"And there's for ye, clod!" quoth he. "Now come and take my beast, and see ye rub him down well—d'ye hear?"

"Aw!" said the country fellow, and goggled; whereupon Master Oldcraft cursed him more bitterly than ever:

"What, ye damned doddipoll, ye curst numps? Come and take my horse or——"

At this moment Viscount Brocklehurst rode into the yard, and Titus, having the very greatest respect for "the Quality" at any and all times, instantly checked his furious tirade and, taking off dusty hat, bowed his long, dusty person with the utmost deference.

"My lord," said he, while his men proceeded to stable the horses. "Your lordship's very obedient, I trust I see your lordship well?"

The Viscount nodded sulkily, and rode on across the wide yard, but having dismounted he stood a moment eyeing the dusty Oldcraft with eyes furtive yet keen; then, as the law-officer met this calculating look, he beckoned with the whip, an imperious gesture which Oldcraft hastened to obey.

"You're the tipstaff fellow, a'nt you?" enquired the Viscount, his gaze on Oldcraft's dusty boots. "From London . . . the catchpoll—thieves and murderers, eh?"

"Very humbly at your service, my lord!"

"No, no, damme, not mine—not mine, rat me!" cried the Viscount peevishly. "You're after Mr. Gyfford's murderer, a'nt you?"

"Ay, my lord, I am. All day and every day I'm after him, ah, and night, too, my lord, if necessary. Titus Oldcraft don't shirk his duty, my lord, zealous is Titus, sir, and——"

"Well, well—how's your luck?"

"Bad, my lord, bad I must confess," sighed Oldcraft, shaking his lank head. "I've no luck so far, but I'm on his track, my lord and——"

"Are ye so—are ye, now?"

"Indeed, my lord—though 'tis very evident the country folk hereabouts are aiding him, my lord."

"Ha, d'ye think so?"

"My lord, I'm convinced of it. They're aiding and abetting him, my lord, comforting, sustaining, ah, and warning him, my lord. This very morning word comes of him being at Litlington, so to Litlington we go, only to learn he's gone on to Seaford, so there go we, and hear he's just rid off to Brighthelmston, so thither we gallop and plaguy hot, my lord, but——"

"Pish!" cried the Viscount pettishly. "Y'do but chase a shadow! The devil, y'must seek him nearer home, man!"

"Does y'lordship mean his house of Weare?"

"Ay, or thereabouts—thereabouts!" nodded the Viscount. "But then are ye sure—quite sure the murderer is Sir Richard Gyfford, are ye so assured, so certain, I say?"

"Who else, my lord?"

"Ay, let me perish but that's the question—who? For mark, I say mark this—the dead man had other enemies a-plenty, 'tis said! And then what's all this I'm hearing of a cat's-eye ring, eh—eh?"

"My lord, I've heard no mention o' such."

"Not . . . not heard on't? Oh, sink me! Not heard? Why, Lord, man, 'tis rumour flying broadcast. 'Tis said the murderer wore a ring set with a cat's-eye stone. 'Tis whispered everywhere and you have not heard—are y'deaf?   Oh, smite me dumb!   Are y'blind?"

"Neither one nor t'other, my lord, but——"

"Can ye read, eh? If y'can read—look at this. Look at . . . ha, where is the curst thing, where?"

Thrusting sudden hand into the pocket of his flower-embroidered waistcoat the Viscount fumbled there impatiently, and presently drew thence a crumpled paper, smoothed it, glanced at it and thrust it into Master Oldcraft's ready hand; quoth he:

"Read—read that and say what you think on't. Read it out." So Master Oldcraft read aloud as follows:

"'Write this to inform you it is now certainly known that upon the murderer's pistol-hand was a cat's-eye ring. Which ring is yet in possession of murderer. Find this and the . . . the guilty man stands confessed. Diligently search the Gyfford Arms . . . chambers and effects of the divers gentlemen . . . dent there . . . your labours will not be . . . vain.'"

"Well?" demanded the Viscount, while Oldcraft stared at this torn paper, turning it this way and that. "Well?"

"Very well, my lord, ay, passing well—unless——"

"Unless what, man, what?"

"Unless it be a hum, my lord, a hoax!"

"Tush!" exclaimed the Viscount, and turned away in sudden fierce petulance.

"My lord, whence had ye this?"

"'Twas picked up in the garden at the Moat House. But what matter if it be a hoax?"

"And how," said Oldcraft, frowning at the letter, "how should it come there, my lord?"

"'Sdeath, man, how should I know? There 'twas found and there it is, hoax or no."

"Who found it, my lord?"

"I did. Now tear it up and be done with it."

"My lord. I'll keep it if I may."

"What, a hoax, a hum? Nay, tear it up."

"Why it may be no hoax, my lord. Howbeit, wi your lordship's kind permission I'll keep it——"

G I

"Why, then, keep it, man, keep it. Act on it or do what ye will wi' the curst thing. I'm well rid on 't."

"Act on it?" repeated Oldcraft. "Doth your lordship mean search the inn, the apartments o' you gentlemen?"

"Do as y'will, fellow, all's one to me," and the Viscount turned to be gone.

"Pray, my lord, how many gentlemen lodge here at present?"

"You should know this," retorted the Viscount, over his shoulder.

"Why, my lord, so I do. There was my Lord Carberry, but he's gone back to London. There's Mr. Trumpington, but he's away—which leaves Captain Despard and——"

"Myself!" nodded the Viscount.

"Very true, my lord. As to this cat's-eye ring now —hath your lordship any suspicions, any——"

"Gad—no, not I! Damme, I'm no tipstaff, so——" Here, chancing to catch sight of the country fellow goggling at him over the half-door, Viscount Brockle-hurst stopped to scowl and point at him with his whip:

"Ha, damme, will y'stare at your betters, rascal, will ye peep, will ye pry?"

"Ar!" quoth the fellow and, knuckling an eyebrow, he chuckled.

"Let me die," exclaimed the Viscount peevishly, "rot me! What . . . who—who the devil is he?"

"A half-wit, I judge, sir," answered Master Oldcraft also scowling at the fellow in question, "a natural by his looks, my lord. Now concerning this——"

"A hang-dog rogue!" quoth the Viscount, turning on his heel.

"But as to this cat's-eye ring, my lord," persisted Master Titus, following him, "to search this inn I must have a warrant."

"Well, sir John Parret is a justice——"

"True, my lord, but Sir John is away at Lewes and——"

"Tush!" exclaimed the Viscount, and strode away into the house, whither, after momentary hesitation, Master Oldcraft ventured to follow him.

And so, quiet descended upon the inn-yard, a drowsy stillness with nothing to hear save the soft cooing of pigeons, the snort of a horse, the cluck of hens and the murmur of voices from the adjacent taproom.

The country fellow, brawny arms crossed upon the half-door, stared up at the wheeling pigeons, down at the ever-busy hens then, roused by a jeering laugh, glanced round and beheld Master Oldcraft's two men watching him, sharp-faced Londoners they, with lofty contempt for the country and all things bucolic.

"Rot me!" cried one, nudging his fellow. "Rot me, but 'tis Chawbacon Jack! Wot's to do, Sharp-shins, wot's your lay?"

"Fishing!" answered the country fellow, and chuckled.

CHAPTER XXVII

GIVETH SOME DESCRIPTION OF THE ODD MAN

IT was a hot morning, very slumberous and still; a bird chirped drowsily from shady eaves, an errant cow, standing knee-deep in adjacent horse-pond, flicked languid tail, blinking sleepily, and a butterfly, hovering on gaudy wings, fluttered and wheeled, erratic and uncertain, up and down, to and fro until, as if suddenly making up its small mind, it alighted upon the hat of a country fellow who sprawled upon one of the broad, hospitable settles before the Gyfford Arms; a stalwart, loose-limbed fellow in patched and stained smock-frock, his gaitered legs and heavy boots dusty with travel. Motionless sat he, long legs out-stretched, brown hands crossed upon stout ash stick, head bowed, blinking drowsily at the drowsy cow while the butterfly swayed gorgeous wings to the genial sun.

Upon the wide green a duck quacked suddenly, from open doors and lattices floated pleasant, homely sounds —a rattle of crockery, the vague, infrequent murmur of voices, a cow lowed softly from distant byre.

Then, with jingle of spurs, firm and masterful of tread, Captain Despard stepped from the inn, himself as gorgeous as the butterfly upon the dusty country-man's hat.

"Fellow!"

The butterfly took wing as the countryman raised drowsy head, showing a dark, gipsy-seeming face, lit by a pair of eyes surprisingly keen.

"Fellow," said the Captain, in his pleasant voice, "would you earn a pint or so?"

"Ar!" nodded the countryman, knuckling an eye-brow.

"Then see here!" and the Captain held out a hat, a gold-laced and be-feathered confection more magnificent even than that which crowned his own stately splendour. "Go, toss me this thing into the horse-pond, my man."

The countryman stared, rose and taking this thing of splendour, clumped stolidly away forthwith and reaching the pond, pitched the hat therein and shambled back to where Captain Despard waited astride his impatient sorrel.

"Good lad!" he nodded, dropped the man a silver coin, touched spur to his horse's glossy flank and cantered gallantly away.

The countryman was still gaping at the coin in his palm when from certain open casement of the inn issued a voice in high-pitched, querulous complaint:

"My hat, Tom, where a plague is't? What ha' ye done with the curst thing—what?"

"My lord, you had it," began another voice, instantly silenced by a volley of peevish oaths:

"Ha, 'pon my perishing soul, he's away! Despard's off I tell ye! Oh curse it, my hat—where is it in the fiend's name—where?"

"My lord, I gave it to you, I——"

"Well, and now 'tis vanished. Find it, fool, find it! I must be gone, and how the devil may I venture forth and no hat? And Despard on his way! My hat . . . demme, my hat—this instant!"

"Indeed, my lord, 'tis not here. . . . But your lordship hath other hats a-plenty."

"Other hats, fool? Why curse it, an't I dressed for my new French hat wi' the feathered trimming?"

"Alas, my lord, 'tis quite gone."

"A thousand devils! The thing can't ha' flown or run away."

"But perchance 'tis fallen out o' the window, my lord."

"Ha—the window!"

A hurry of feet, a clink of spurs, and Viscount Brocklehurst, speeding out of the doorway, collided with the countryman going in.

"Fifty thousand fiends!" snarled the Viscount, straightening his lofty periwig deranged by the impact, "who are you? What the devil d'ye mean? Where are ye trampling, clown?"

The countryman merely gaped, and touched stick to the brim of his shapeless headgear.

"Where are ye coming to, clod?"

"Tap, zur . . . ale, zur!"

"Plague on ye for clumsy oaf!"

"Ay, zur!"

"Tell me, have ye seen a hat?"

"Ay, zur."

"Well, well—where is it, fool?"

"'Oss-pond, zur."

"Eh—eh?" gasped the Viscount, staring his amazement. "I' the horse-pond, d'ye say? How came it there?"

"I throwed it in, zur."

"What you . . . you!" The gentleman raised his horsewhip to strike, the yokel, his ash stick to parry; and so stood they for a moment.

"Damned villain, why did ye throw my hat in the pond?"

"Becos t'other gen'leman bid me to't."

"Ha—did he so, curse him! Demme, but he shall pay for this! What, Tom, Tom, I say, bring me a hat —any hat, d'ye hear? . . . Landlord, my horse! Why, who a plague are all these? Am I a demd raree-show? Stir—hustle—off, I say!" raved the agitated gentleman, whip a-flourish, for a small crowd had gathered, curious villagers, ostlers and tapsters from the inn while, at divers lattices, mob-capped waiting-maids peeped and giggled; but now, meeting the Viscount's baleful glare, they incontinent vanished, one and all, with the exception of the countryman, who sat blinking sleepily again at nothing in particular. And now appeared Tom Pitt, hat in one hand, brush in the other.

"My lord," he began, "this, I venture to think——"

The Viscount snatched the hat, clapped it on, and beckoning Pitt aside, seemed to give certain orders in fierce whispers, which Pitt acknowledged with repeated bendings of obsequious back. Then, the Viscount's horse being led forth, my lord mounted and, calling down curses on all and sundry, galloped furiously away.

So the village sank to dreamy hush again, a slumberous quietude with a soft cooing of pigeons from adjacent stables, the cluck of busy hens.

And, after some while, Tom Pitt reappeared, soft treading despite heavy, spurred boots, but on his way to the inn-yard, paused a moment to stare with his narrow furtive eyes at the somnolent countryman asprawl on the weatherworn settle.

" You're a stranger hereabouts, eh, friend? " he questioned. The countryman snored gently, whereupon Tom Pitt stooped to peer under the wide-eaved hat, but seeing no more than a dark, sunburned cheek, ventured to poke the sleeper gently with his whip.

" A stranger, eh? " he repeated.

The man stirred, muttering sleepily.

" Romany . . . Gorgio . . . chal, my chavo——"

" Aha, a gipsy! " quoth Pitt, and betook himself to the stables whence he issued presently on horseback, and trotted away while from the shadow of shapeless hat the countryman watched him out of sight with eyes remarkably keen and wideawake. He was apparently dozing again, however, when once more he was disturbed, this time by the drumming of hoofs, the snort of a horse and a distressful voice:

" Oho—you! You theer on t' bench, come 'ee and 'old t'mare afore she pulls out me arms b'the roots! "

Upon the green a magnificent animal pranced, glossy of coat, rolling of eye, blood and breeding in every line of her shapeliness as she tossed proud head and reared coquettishly, jerking at the halter whereto clung a little, old man whose booted legs now waved in air, now planted themselves desperately on mother earth only to be plucked thence again—but a very determined little old man who clung on stoutly, none the less. Up sprang the countryman, and running forward, gripped the rearing animal by the head-stall with one powerful hand, soothing her with the other.

"Eh, lad,' gasped old Ben, mopping perspiring brow, "you be useter 'osses, I can see. Gentle 'er, lad, gentle 'er, the Witch aren't got no vice, she be only a bit skittish-loike 's marnin. But Lordy, me old bones be arl shook up, lad. Ave 'ee got 'er safe?"

"Ar!" growled the countryman, and as he spoke, the mare, whinneying softly, dropped to all four feet, arched shapely neck to that caressing hand, and became as coyly demure as such high-bred lady could be.

"Cast 'er shoe she did 's marnin," old Ben explained, "and I be tekkin' 'er to Joel Bim, ye can see 'is smiddy 'crost the green yonder. Lord, I be that dry—yonder, jest ayont them trees, du 'ee see?"

"Ar!" nodded the countryman.

"And Lord I du be that dry, lad!" sighed old Ben, "an' me innards arl of a quake loike. D'appen now as you'd take the mare to the smithy for I and leave 'er wi' Joel. I'll 'ave a pint waitin' for 'ee. Wot du 'ee say now?'

"Ar!" quoth the fellow, and led the now gentle Witch away forthwith; returning presently he found Ben deep in converse with landlord John and frothing tankards on the rustic table.

"'Ere be thy ale, lad," cried the old man, "drink 'earty! . . . and as I tell 'ee, John, there be bad blood atwixt 'em, I seed it, quick as a flash, and the Duchess seed it and kep' 'em apart! And arl for love o' my lady tu, I rackon, shouldn't wonder if they don't fit a dool."

The countryman took up his ale, nodded to each and, having drunk deep, seated himself at the extreme end of the long settle.

"But wot be the matter with 'ee, John? So glumbersome 'ee do look—wot be matter?"

John glanced up and around uneasily, shook his head and softly closed the lattice behind them.

"Matter enough, Ben," he sighed.

"But trade's a flourishin' beant it, John? Wot wi' th' inkwest and comp'ny and quality from Lonnon, business should be proime, John.'

"Business," sighed the landlord, seating himself beside the old man and shaking head despondently, "business was never better, Ben. But all's amiss wi' me since "—and here John lowered his voice in awesome manner, "since—he come! I be watched, Ben, watched constant, first 'twas Pitt and now—him!"

"Oh—oo?" enquired old Ben, staring.

"Titus Oldcraft!" murmured John, adding like an after-thought, "dang him!"

"Ay, but oo's him?"

"Why this catchpoll from London, Ben, the biggest thief-taker of 'em all next to Jonathan Wild, and as big a rogue!"

"Oho—'im?" exclaimed old Ben, staring at John who nodded gloomily, and both of them wholly unaware that the lattice behind them was opening slowly inch by inch, though the countryman in the act of taking up his tankard, grasped his ash stick instead.

"Come down about this yer murder, eh, John—but why doth he watch thee, lad—eh?"

John sighed deeper than ever and shook his head.

"Du 'ee think as 'e'll catch the guilty party, John?"

"I dunno, Ben, but—he'll ketch somebody or other and get the fact swore to 'em, I'll warrant. Titus allus does, Titus won't go back empty-'anded. Titus won't fail, no—he'll tak' good care as somebody swings, guilty or no!"

"Love us!" exclaimed old Ben. "Then nobody beant safe from 'ee?"

"Nary a soul, Ben."

"Du 'ee think 'twere Sir Richard as done it, John?'

"No, I don't!" answered the landlord, stoutly.

"Ah!" nodded Ben. "No more du my leddies at the Moat 'ouse and—wot's more, no more don't I, 'spite o' the inkwest an' Sir John Parret an' arl. Dannel th'inkwest, I says—ah, an' him into the bargain!"

"Ye see, Ben, Sir John's got his eye on the land. If Sir Richard was took and topped, and him the last o' the Gyffords, the Manor o' Weare would come into the market.

"Ay, ay," nodded Ben, "but, b'the pyx, S'Richard beant hung yet, seein' as 'e beant nowise took."

"And, Ben, he aren't like to be if I knows aught—not 'im!"

"Eh, John, eh—do 'ee mean—?"

The landlord shook his head, glancing warningly at the slumberous countryman, and rose.

"Well, well, I'll get back t' my kitchen," said he, while forth of the softly-opening lattice behind him crept a long, lean hand at the end of a prodigiously long, lank arm, a hand that hovered in the air above him with fingers crooked talon-like.

"Wilt drink a drop more o' my home-brewed for friendship's sake, Ben?"

"Ay, and thankee koindly, John, I'm sure."

So Landlord John took up the empty tankard but, in that moment the clutching hand had clenched itself upon his shoulder. . . . The tankard fell with a clatter, and, uttering a strangled cry, John spun round and beheld a face out-thrust from the open lattice, a lean visage, very small as to eyes, which blinked and glittered 'neath great jut of brow, and very large as to jowl, a pallid face framed and topped by the curls of a brown riding-bob.

"How then, Master Bly," said the face, between lips upcurling in slow smile, "you han't forgot such gripe? The hand o' the Law, Master Bly, look at it—ah, look! Here's hand as, when it fastens, never lets go! And hearkee, Master Bly, 'tis hand as, soon or late, is a-going to get gripe on Gyfford o' Weare. Now belike you may know just where this murderous gentleman hath gone to earth—hey?"

"Not I, Master Oldcraft," answered John, once more his stolid self.

"Why then, belike ye may know o' one as doth know—hey?"

"Not I, Master Oldcraft."

"Nay but, honest Master Bly," said Titus Oldcraft smiling broader than ever but with eyes fiercely intent, "says you a moment since, 'he,' meaning Sir Richard Gyfford, 'an't likely to be taken if you know aught o' the matter.' These be your very words, good Master Bly, so now I ask you, and take heed how ye answer me, what do you know of it? Come now!"

John picked up the fallen tankard, glanced at it, looked at his questioner and shook his head:

"Nothing!" said he.

"So?" smiled Titus. "Why then belike we can find means to stir your memory, soon or late. Meanwhile, you may bring me a bottle of Geneva."

Abruptly John turned and entered the inn, and the face as suddenly vanished from the window, whereupon old Ben drew a long breath.

"Lordy—Lord!" he quavered, turning to the countryman in staring consternation. "Did ye 'ear 'im, friend, did ye see? Poor John! Dannel me if ever I see a chap wi' such f'rocious ways as this 'ere Oldcraft—and smile 'e do! Dunno but I rackon 'tis toime I went arter the mare. No more ale for I wi' the loikes o'—Lorramighty!" he gasped for, chancing to turn, he beheld that same evil-looking hand poised in the air above him—but, even then, down upon this clawing hand whizzed a stout ash stick. . . . An inarticulate howl of pain and anger, a clatter of passionate feet and out of the inn leapt Titus Oldcraft flourishing a horsewhip, a bony man, very tall, very arrogant and, just now, breathless with furious amazement:

"Which . . . who, who was it?" he panted. "Which o' ye dared strike Titus? Who . . . who was it?"

"Me!" answered the countryman, stabbing himself in the chest with sun-burned thumb. "Come—no pickin' o' pockets 'ere! No thievery—come!"

"Thie—thievery," spluttered Titus, "ye curst, besotted bumpkin—thievery?"

"Ar!" nodded the countryman, "see y'r at it—caught 'ee I did—pick-pocketin'——"

"Why ye drunken rascal, I'm an officer o' the law, Titus, Titus Oldcraft, that's me!"

"Gammon!" retorted the countryman. "I see ye——"

His sleepy voice was drowned in a torrent of fierce abuse and foul invective insomuch that, once again, the drowsing village roused—faces peeped and peered from lattice and open doorway; perceiving which, the countryman arose, stick a-flourish:

"Oho, folks!" cried he hoarsely. "Oho, neighbours, lookee—here be a thief caught in th'act, a-pickin' o' pockets and yonder be th' 'orsepond! Come, let's heave one in t'other!"

The faces multiplied, from inn-yard and taproom hurried divers burly fellows, while from his smithy across the green, strode mighty Joel Bim, swinging ponderous hammer. Titus Oldcraft looked, scowled and, muttering fierce threats and blasting imprecations, incontinent betook himself within doors.

"Aha—oho!" chucked old Ben, digging the smith in brawny ribs, "wot do 'ee think o' that, Joel? Dog bite me ef I don't buy this young chap another pint! The way 'e clouted yon Titus Oldcraft 'crost the knuckles! Dannel me ef I don't mak' it a quart! Wot do 'ee say, young chap?"

The countryman showed a row of white teeth and shook sleepy head.

"Lord!" exclaimed Ben. "No ale—then wot du ee want?"

"A job."

"Wot can 'ee du?"

"Most things."

"Well, you'm tidy 'andy wi' osses, I know."

"Ar."

"Wot more?"

"Dig."

"You be a stranger 'ereabouts, eh?"

"Ar."

"Where be come from?"

"Pease Pottage."

"That be a goodish way from 'ere."

"Ar."

"Wot be thy name, lad?"

"Dick."

"He beant much of a talker, eh, Joel?"

The sturdy blacksmith surveyed the countryman's good-natured, vacant-seeming face and tapped himself on grimy forehead with grimy finger:

"A bit weakish-loike up 'ere, Ben," he suggested, "A bit looney-ish, eh?"

"Well, I dunno, Joel. I rackon 'e beant sich a doddlish fule as 'e looks. 'Ows'ever, Dick, go along wi' me, 'tis likely I'll find a job for 'ee over to the Moat 'ouse. Gurt company there to-day . . . all the quality. Be the mare shod, Joel?"

"And waitin', Ben."

"Why then, you Dick, come thy ways, for I've took to 'ee, so come along o' Ben."

Obediently the countryman arose and presently set off in company with the mare who pranced, and old Ben who talked and chattered, until they came within sight of the Moat House stables; here the old man paused.

"Dick," he enquired, "dost believe in Ghost-es, lad, speckitaturs an' sich?"

The countryman closed one eye and nodded.

"Now an' then," he answered.

"Well, I dunno," said Ben, shaking his head, "but our Jarge do swear as 'e seed one t'other night as flittered an' skittered i' the garden, but—I dunno. Though there be chaps do swear they've seed a friar all bloody a-moanin' and groanin' over Deepdene way, along by the gibbet—but I dunno! Be 'ee married, Dick?"

"Naw."

"Then watch out for Betty, my leddy's maid, a rare caution she be and, though a bit thick p'raps, you'm a likely chap. And 'ere we be. Bide 'ee 'ere whiles I litters the mare." So off went old Ben into the stables busying himself to the Witch's comfort with the assistance of George, the under-groom.

"Jarge," quoth he, "I got a chap outside, a stranger, a furriner from Pease Pottage way."

"Oh?" said George, fondling his right whisker.

"Ay, thought as 'e might give us an 'and wi' the garden, mebbe."

"Ah!" said George, caressing his left whisker.

"And Jarge, though a bit softish-loike, 'e beant sich a gurt fule as 'e seems, so doant come naun o' y'r trickses wi' un."

"Wheer is 'e, Ben?"

"Outside i' the yard."

George thrust his whiskers over the half-door and peered right and left.

"Beant no chap nowheers as I can see, old un," said he; so forth of the stable stepped old Ben to stand and gaze round about and scratch his white head.

"Well . . . dog bite me!" he exclaimed, for Dick, the countryman, had vanished.

CHAPTER XXVIII

MADAME LA DUCHESSE had given a garden-fête, for it was her birthday. Consequently the Moat House lawns were gay with colour silks, and satins, velvets and brocades, where gorgeous coats and silk gowns bowed and curtseyed each to each while their wearers smiled and ogled, lisped and languished; fans waved with a gracious languor, be-laced handkerchiefs wafted the sunny air, snuff-boxes clicked; for to-day, being an occasion, the whole county was here to pay due homage to Rank, Wealth and Beauty.

So the County paced, minced, or ambled to and fro across the velvety sward; it sat or stood beneath shady tree or clipped hedge, it chattered, laughed and sighed while Rank, typified by the Duchess, sat throned in state beneath her cherry-tree, what time Wealth and Beauty, in the shapely person of my lady Helen, paced languidly beside my lord Viscount Brocklehurst whose high-bridged nose stooped, ever and anon, so near her blooming cheek and whose eager, full-lipped mouth spoke soft, quick words whereto she responded by vague, faint smiles or shakes of her handsome head; from these twain the Duchess's keen glance roved to the tall figure of Captain Despard who, listening to Sir John Parret's gorgeous lady, contrived to keep his dark gaze ever upon my lady Helen.

Now, remote from all this babbling splendour yet within eye and ear-shot, a dark-avised country-fellow laboured in the herb-garden, which industrious rustic straightened his back, now and then, to wipe moist brow and stare at all this perambulating magnificence through a gap in the intervening hedge.

And the County, male and female, having assured each other that "'twas insufferable hot," chattered of the late Julian Gyfford, his murder, the inquest, and "that blood-guilty wretch," Sir Richard—and forthwith shuddered, and shivered, looked grim or looked knowing, and agreed that the sooner he was taken and made a dreadful ensample and object lesson to like-minded murderous villains the better for the world in general and the County in particular; so said all save the Duchess who talked, now, with the portly, rosy-faced cleric on her right, now with the shriveled, hook-nosed old warrior on her left, and watched the company meanwhile, more particularly Helen and the Viscount, and beckoned to Captain Despard, all at once and the same time. Quoth she:

"Tell me now, me dear Bishop, why are ye all so vastly uncharitable to the poor gentleman?"

THE BISHOP: Uncharitable, madam? Ahem! To a murderer?

THE DUCHESS: He is not proved so—and suspicion is not proof—eh, General?

THE GENERAL: (*snuffing*) Brrh! Man shouldn't get himself suspected, ma'm.

THE BISHOP: Alas, madam, as we sow, so must we reap.

THE DUCHESS: Och t'be shure, sir—with other folks' assistance.

THE BISHOP: But Sir Richard Gyfford was a—ahem— a notorious consorter with persons of ill-repute.

THE GENERAL: Thieves, ma'm, smugglers, poachers— bah! Draggle-tail gipsies.

THE BISHOP: An absolute wine-bibber, madam, with no respect for laws human or—divine!

THE GENERAL: Nay, b'heaven, he—he—brrump!—en- couraged poaching!

THE BISHOP: Moreover, dear madam, report hath it that he was also a——

THE GENERAL: Toss-pot, ma'm. Aha, and one o' these macaroni highwaymen—ay, Captain Archer himself, like enough.

THE DUCHESS: Ah, shure now ye paint his weaknesses at their strongest. How say you, Captain Despard?

THE CAPTAIN: (*bowing*) That to some women a man's very weakness may prove his strength. As for Sir Richard Gyfford I heartily commiserate his misfortunes.

THE GENERAL: (*snuffing and fierce*) Pishah! Misfortunes, sir, misfortunes, d'ye say?

THE CAPTAIN: (*bowing*) Indeed, General. Sure 'tis sad misfortune to be so bitterly misjudged, so unjustly condemned.

THE GENERAL: (*gasping*) Unjustly, sir . . um . . . Broumph! (*Chokes and strides away, sneezing.*)

THE BISHOP: (*amazed yet placid*) Can it be that you believe the accused gentleman guiltless, sir?

THE CAPTAIN: As you, sir, or—even I.

THE BISHOP: Then, my very dear sir, I pray your faith may be justified. (*Bows, smiles and moves gently away.*)

THE DUCHESS: (*proffering snuff-box*) Captain, me dear.

THE CAPTAIN: (*Bows, snuffs, and returns box with profound obeisance.*) Ah, madam, I protest you do me too much honour.

THE DUCHESS: 'To some women a man's very weakness is his strength,' says you and, ah, shure ye read me right. A friend o' Richard's is a friend o' mine. Sit ye here beside me.

THE CAPTAIN: (*complying*) I fear I cannot lay claim to Sir Richard's friendship.

THE DUCHESS: Y'acted the part t'other morning in regard to that cloak, and again to-day. But tell me, what ails Brocklehurst? Such ferocity o' gloom!

THE CAPTAIN: (*smiling*) Who shall say, madam? Perchance his breakfast disagreed with him.

THE DUCHESS: Y'watch him, I think? See how close he bends to murmur in Helen's pretty ear!

THE CAPTAIN: And how she frowns and turns away!

THE DUCHESS: And you smile, sir.

THE CAPTAIN: And laud her judgment, madam.

THE DUCHESS: But is he not the friend you honour?
THE CAPTAIN: Say rather, the rival I pity.
THE DUCHESS: Think ye his suit so hopeless, then?
THE CAPTAIN: Perfectly, madam, for am I not his rival?
THE DUCHESS: D'you esteem yourself wooer so irresistible?
THE CAPTAIN: 'Tis so my constant hope and prayer.

"I wonder?" said the Duchess viewing his handsome person and indomitable look with wistful appraisement.

"And I—hope!" he answered gazing away towards Helen's distant figure. And then Sir John Parret puffed up to them, being a little incommoded by the heat of the day.

"Lud, Sir John," nodded the Duchess as he bowed, "ye look a throifle warrm, me dear soul, but faith, 'tis hot weather for hunting."

"Hunting, ma'm?"

"Chasing elusive murderers, Sir John. Have ye anny success now, anny news?"

"Affairs promise, madam," puffed Sir John, handkerchief a-flutter, "to-morrow, to-day even, ye may hear of his—hum—his capture. The county folk would seem highly zealous and eager to aid us, information of his whereabouts comes in on all hands. His every move is watched, ma'm, he is dogged, he shall not long go untaken. And what's more, madam—ha, I say moreover, my lady,—hum——"

"Nay, me dear man, abate your humming and speak like an obleeging Christian soul, do."

"Why then, my lady, tis now known that the murderer wore a—ha—a . . . Lord, 'tis very warm!"

"The saints teach me patience! A what, sir, what?"

"A cat's-eye ring, ma'm."

"Aha, and what then?"

"Why, ma'm, 'tis at once apparent that we have but to—hum—to find this same ring and—ha—our case is brought to successful issue."

"Ay shure, Sir John, always supposing this ring has the murderer safe inside it! Ah, me dear Captain, very well, ye may go, ye may leave me and—follow your eyes."

So the Captain rose, bowed and went; and whither should his eager yet leisured feet bear him but in the one and only direction, and though often he paused on his way for a word here or a bow there, his keen gaze seldom left that shady walk where Helen paced beside her eager, quick-gesturing companion.

"So . . . so you persist?" demanded the Viscount, breathlessly. Helen moved on beside him in contemptuous silence. "Is it . . . is it because you . . . love another?"

My lady turned and swept him with proud glance from sparkling shoebuckles to glossy periwig—and beneath this look his pale cheeks glowed, his heavy eyelids drooped, between parting lips was a glimmer of sharp teeth; then, hissing from that writhen mouth came a sibilant hurry of speech:

"Stint . . . stint your lofty pride, madam,—'tis well known you ride out o' nights to keep tryst with . . . a murderer!"

Helen gasped, and turning, stood appalled, so fearful was the change in him; lips back-drawn from gnashing teeth, eyes that burned with demoniac glare; here indeed and indeed was no "mincing clothes-horse," but a something wholly new in her experience and therefore terrible. . . .

Then, stepping back suddenly, he bowed and reached forth hands tremulous and supplicating:

"Forgive . . .! Forgive!" he stammered. "Pardon . . . forget my rash words. Pity me, Helen, pity me for when a man loves as I——"

But, even as he spoke, she turned and left him, left him shaken as with an ague fit, but staring after her with eyes baleful as ever.

"Good lack!" quoth my lady within herself, "as if a butterfly had snapped at me!" And she tried to laugh even while her flesh crept with sudden, strange, unaccountable dread; thus when she found the Captain walking beside her, his assured air and pleasant voice were alike, for once, unfeignedly welcome.

"Our Brocklehurst," said he smiling, "shows something peevish, and 'tis possible I am to blame."

"You?" she questioned wondering. "Pray, how?"

"His hat. I paid a yokel to fling it into a horse-pond."

"Oh? Why?" she enquired, her eyes very joyous.

"Thereby to win of you the first and last dance, since 'twas I did greet thee first, Helen. Wherefore the pettish fellow angered you, I think, which pleases me."

"He is—insufferable!" cried my lady.

"And I think, dangerous, Helen, a creature of wild, ungoverned passions. And this also pleases me."

"And wherefore?"

"Because to protect you from such dangers will be my supreme and constant joy."

They had reached the end of the walk, and now paused hard by the rustic arbour.

"But," said she, glancing back at the ever-moving company beyond the screening hedge, "how if I refuse such protection?"

"You cannot," he answered gently, "for I have made for you an armour of my love. A shield shall guard thee night and day, so long as I draw breath. . . . Nay, hear me, Helen, for dost know I love thee, my eyes have spoke it since first they looked on thee. But thou'rt rich! What then, wert thou a beggar I'd worship thee in thy rags. Thou'rt become my inspiration to live for, die for—ay, I'd toss away my life, my very soul for thy sake and joy to do it. Helen, Helen, whatever in me is good I'll cherish for thy sake, ah, so cherish that I may grow to thy love. . . . Couldst thou but learn to love me then life were joy and I a god . . . Helen?" His voice shook, his cheek glowed, his long-lashed eyes held hers; and seeing him so deeply moved, she stood a moment speechless. . . . And then, from somewhere nearby came a tuneless and doleful whistling.

"Captain Despard," said she very kindly, "I am sensible that you would honour me because I do believe you sincere, but I——"

"Nay, Helen—wait!" he pleaded. "Do not slay

my hope so soon. Wait . . . know me better . . . give me time, and though I am not overly patient yet for thy sake I——" The whistling came nearer; Captain Despard frowned, fell silent and glanced angrily about; then, sighing her relief, Helen turned and sped away. Hardly was she gone than a fierce hand clutched the Captain's arm and he beheld the contorted features of Viscount Brocklehurst.

"Damned—damned traitor!' he panted. "I—I heard——"

"So?" nodded the Captain. "Prying were you? Eavesdropping, eh?"

"Curse your double-dealing!" exclaimed the Viscount wildly. "So now you'll—you'll protect her, will ye—and against me, will ye?"

"Never doubt it, Viscount."

"Then by God, Despard, I—I'll see ye in fetters, ha, let me perish but I'll——"

"Tush, man, don't bluster! And mark this—attempt your damnable plot against her at your peril!"

"My plot—mine?" cried the Viscount, shaking the arm he clutched in a very paroxysm of fury. "Mine I'ye say, why damme, 'twas you suggested it!"

"Well, I now forbid it."

"What, you forbid it—you?"

"I—myself!" answered the Captain soft-voiced, but he struck that clutching hand away so viciously that the Viscount staggered, though his wide gaze never left the Captain's placid face, and when next he spoke it was in strange, whispering voice:

"By . . . by God, I see it now! You . . . you want her for yourself . . . is that it?"

"That," nodded the Captain, "is precisely it."

"You . . . you grow desperate reckless, Despard!"

"How so?"

"Nay, sure you take my meaning, Despard?"

"Not I."

"Why then I mean . . . that I know . . . what Julian knew."

"Ah?" murmured the Captain. "And Julian—is dead!" For a long moment they stood staring eye to eye and utterly motionless, then slowly Viscount Brocklehurst recoiled until he was stayed by the side of the arbour. . . . Suddenly from the adjacent lawn came the plaintive wail of fiddles tuning, the silvery ripple of flute and oboe.

"So ho, the music is here," smiled the Captain, shooting his ruffles. "Come, my lord, and you shall see her tread this first measure—with me."

So saying, Captain Despard strolled away, but the Viscount leaned there against the arbour, his eyes closed as if he were faint. . . . Borne to him on the warm, stilly air came the ceaseless murmur and stir of the company, voices loud and soft, laughter, snatches of talk; then someone nearby began to whistle dolefully, and, opening his eyes, the Viscount beheld the broad back of a gardener bowed to his labour and, staring at this back, became aware that the company had grown strangely quiet, the chatter and laughing babblement seemed hushed all at once. The Viscount, therefore, glanced towards the crowded lawns and saw the fine company draw apart to make way for the lank, grim figure of Master Titus Oldcraft, a carrion crow among so many peacocks.

Now at sight of this sinister figure Viscount Brocklehurst's pale cheek flushed, his eye brightened, and he started forward so suddenly that he collided with the gardener, but, muttering a fierce imprecation, the Viscount pushed him aside and hastened to join the silent and curious company now grouped about Master Oldcraft who, taking off his hat bowed right and left repeatedly until none stirred; then spake he in voice authoritative yet highly respectful.

"Sir John Parret, my lords, ladies and gentlemen, as an officer o' the law, extreme zealous in his duty by day and by night, I humbly crave your gracious leaves and beg forgiveness for this intrusion. Sir John, my lords, ladies and gentlemen, have I your permission to ask a question o' this so highly distinguished company?"

"Yes! Yes!" cried The County, male and female.

"Master Oldcraft," quoth Sir John Parret with grandiloquent gesture, "in such company as this you

may—hum—you may rest assured the Law is para-
mount. You have our permission to speak. Say on!"

"Then," said Master Titus, looking round upon the
eager and expectant company, and making the very
utmost of the occasion, " Sir John, my lords, ladies and
gentlemen, by reason of devotion to duty, of zeal
unremitting and dogged determination we ha' lately
discovered that the malefactor wanted for the late
heinous crime o' murder bore upon his hand . . . a
cat's-eye ring, that is to say a ring set with a cat's-eye
stone. Therefore I, as chief officer hereabouts and
representative o' the law, set about a-seeking o' this
same ring and——" here Master Oldcraft paused to
glance round upon his so attentive auditory, nodded
portentously and held up his clenched right hand;
quoth he:

"Sir John, my lords, ladies and gentlemen, with
this happy and fort'nate result!" Master Oldcraft
opened his hairy fingers. The County craned forward
its individual heads and beheld upon Oldcraft's broad
palm a slim, gold circlet whence the cat's-eye stone
seemed to glare at them, each and every; whereat
rose a whisper, a hum, a buzz of excited comment,
instantly hushed as Master Oldcraft continued:

"My lords, ladies and gentlemen, now is there ever
a gentleman present as claims knowledge o' this ring?"

Silence, deep and breathless, while eye questioned
eye.

"How, no one, sirs?" persisted Master Oldcraft.
"Doth no gentleman here dare claim knowledge of
it?"

Silence, awkward, irksome and growing ever more
so.

"Why then, my lords, ladies and gentlemen, as
zealous officer o' the law it now behoveth me to speak
and say precisely where I found this deadly evidence.
Ladies and gentlemen, I and my fellows have beat
up and down the country, searched every town and
village 'twixt here and the coast, but—yesterday I
turned my attention to this village—to the Gyfford
Arms. I hunted high and I hunted low, and at last

my determination was rewarded and I found this ring in—a gentleman's bed-chamber, stowed away in—a gentleman's valise! Ladies and gentlemen, 'twas hid away in the valise of—Captain Despard!"

Ensued another painful silence whelmed, all at once, in wordy clamour: amazement, disbelief, derision, conjecture—all tongues were busy, it seemed; only Captain Despard was mute, gazing down upon the cat's-eye ring where it twinkled on Titus Oldcraft's open palm.

At last Sir John's dominant voice stilled the hubbub and he turned upon the silent Captain.

"Sir," said he, glancing from the Captain's serene face to Master Oldcraft's watchful, eager eyes, "here, perchance, is some odd—hum—some odd coincidence that you can explain, if so—pray speak, sir."

Captain Despard smiled and reached out his hand:

"May I see this ring more nearly?" he enquired.

Master Oldcraft hesitated, but at stealthy nod from Sir John he placed the ring upon the Captain's open hand.

"Now, sir," questioned Sir John, watching the Captain's imperturbable features, "ha' you ever seen this ring ere now?"

"Why, yes, I fancy I have, Sir John."

"Aha, and where sir, where?"

"That, sir, I do not feel called upon to say."

"But the law calls upon you," cried Sir John, indignantly. "I call upon you."

"Then, my dear Sir John, spare your breath."

"Why then, Captain Despard, and pray take note 'tis mighty serious business this, perhaps you will be so obliging to tell us how it came hid in your valise."

"Ah, Sir John, this I propose to discover at the very earliest opportunity," smiled the Captain though, for a moment, his eyes glared. "Meantime you tell me this ring was actually upon the murderer's hand, officer?"

"Indeed, sir!" nodded Master Oldcraft. "'Twas on the villain's deadly pistol-hand, sir."

"Why then—see now!" said the Captain. "Your murderer's hand was something smaller than mine, 'twould seem—lookee!" And holding up his right hand Captain Despard showed the ring perched upon the tip of his little finger. "Alack!" sighed he, "my poor hand is larger, grosser than methought." So saying, he laughed gently and tossed the ring at Master Oldcraft who, contriving to catch it, with an effort, thereafter stood mumchance scowling down at this cat's-eye ring much as if it had bitten him.

Then Helen spoke:

"Captain Despard," said she, reaching him her hand, "the musicians are ready, and I step this first gavotte with you."

H

CHAPTER XXIX

DESCRIBETH A NIGHT OF INCIDENT

SIR RICHARD, seated in the secret chamber, glanced at the sturdy landlord's troubled face:

"I'm back again, John, though not for long," said he softly.

"And I be glad to see 'ee, sir," answered John, in the same hushed tone. "You've heered the noos, sir?"

"'Tis why I'm here. How did it happen?"

"Why, sir, I dunno. But then, ecod sir, there be so much 'appening lately, do 'ee see."

"Captain Despard is hurt, eh, John?"

"Broke 'is arm, sir, and all shook up, so Doctor Samson tells me. 'Bout a hour agone, 'twould be, as the pore gen'leman trips and falls downstairs—and him nowise drunk, sir—which, if strange, be gospel true, Sir Richard, as I can testify on oath, sir."

"Hum!" murmured Sir Richard, staring at the candle-flame. "Had he quarrelled . . . with Viscount Brocklehurst, by any chance?"

"Well, no, sir—though, now you mention it, I do believe as 'e meant to. For, sir, early this evening he comes galloping into the yard and spying o' me, 'John,' says he, soft-like, yet looking mighty grim, 'John,' says he, 'is the Viscount indoors yet?' 'No sir,' says I. 'Why then,' says he, giving his 'oss to one o' the stable lads, 'let me know the moment he arrives, the very instant, mind,' says he, and walks off very slow and thoughtful-like, and then, sir, I see him stop and ease his sword in the scabbard; and this and his quiet deadly look sets me a-thinking, d'ye see."

"But, John, Viscount Brocklehurst left the Duchess's rout before the dancing began—hours ago."

"True enough, sir, and back he comes here, surely, him and that Titus Oldcraft, and mighty familiar together too! Calls for a bottle o' my best he do and they sits talking and drinking for a hour or more. Then his lordship calls for his man, Tom Pitt, but Tom's away, as I tell him, so his lordship curses and goes out a-walking."

"And when did he return?"

"'Bout ten minutes arter the Captain had went upstairs, sir—ah, and a precious rumpus and to-do he made."

"What, d'ye mean he shouted, John?"

"Ay, sir, he shouted for Tom Pitt, and Tom still away."

"And 'twas about then that the Captain fell, eh, John?"

"That very moment, sir—for I were just tellin' his lordship as Tom wasn't in, when he heered the Captain above stairs—or leastways his futsteps and then a muffled sort o' cry and down he come, sir, crashing 'ead-first and lay all still and bloody, ah, so still, sir, that I thought he'd broke his neck, but 'twere only 'is arm, so Doctor Samson says."

"Then what did the Viscount, John, what said he?"

"Sir, 'e runs to aid me lift the unfortunate gen'leman and 'By God e's dead!' says 'e."

"And where," enquired Sir Richard, frowning thoughtfully at the candle-flame, "where was Master Oldcraft meanwhile?"

"I dunno, sir—but arter a bit 'e comes running downstairs. So we sends a lad galloping for Doctor Samson and——"

But at this moment Sir Richard held up arresting finger and, rising hastily, crossed softly to the iudas in the corner.

. . . Master Oldcraft bowed and, obedient to the Viscount's gesture, sat down at the table and helped himself to a glass of wine:

"Long life, my lord," said he, lifting his glass and surveying his noble companion with wide-lipped smile, "I do hope your lordship is not too much affected by Captain D's sad mishap. Alas, my lord, accidents will happen and——"

"Ay, but," retorted the Viscount with fretful gesture, "'tis merely his arm, man, his arm!"

"Why i'faith, my lord, it might ha' been . . . worse! The Captain is very singularly fort'nate. But y'r lor'ship must allow that a gentleman with his arm broke can trouble nobody till it be sound again."

"Ay, true—true enough!" nodded the Viscount.

"And now, my lord, of t'other matter, the business you spoke of this afternoon?"

"Don't shout, man—damme, don't shout!" said the Viscount and, glancing swiftly at door and window, he leaned across the table and spoke in gabbling whisper, while Oldcraft leaned across the table to listen, his crafty eyes half-shut yet very keenly watchful. Thus spoke the Viscount in rapid, hissing undertone awhile, then Oldcraft questioned him, whispering also:

". . . plans all laid—eh, my lord? . . . trustworthy fellows? . . . yet I must . . . being officer o' the law——"

"Damme," cried the Viscount peevishly, "'tis why I'm willing to . . . in reason."

"Ah, my lord," murmured Oldcraft, opening his watchful eyes, "but what d'ye call 'reason'?"

"I'll pay . . ." the Viscount leaned nearer and whispered more softly than ever . . . "have her safely aboard!"

"Very handsome, my lord!" nodded Oldcraft, licking his lips. "Y'r lordship is generous . . . as I ha' proved already."

"Well, well? D'ye agree, man—is it yes?"

"Yes, my lord, heartily—on a condition."

"Eh, condition? What condition?"

Master Oldcraft rose and crossing softly to an oak press in adjacent corner, came back bearing pen, ink, and paper, beholding which the Viscount swore. Master Oldcraft bowed:

"As merest matter o' business, my lord," said he in gentle, wheedling tones, and setting the paper before the Viscount, dipped quill in ink and tendered it to him. The Viscount hesitated, frowned, muttered and finally, snatching the pen, wrote what was required, whereupon Master Oldcraft took up the paper, sanded it carefully, read it through, and folded it into a large pocket-book which he stowed away in the bosom of his long, flapped waist-coat.

"Merely, my lord, as a matter o'——" he checked suddenly as, with loud, perfunctory rap, Doctor Samson entered, beaming and rubbing his hands.

"He'll do, sir," nodded the doctor cheerily, "our gentleman under the circumstances, is admirably well."

"Eh? Well . . . well dy'e say, sir?" queried the Viscount.

"Blooded, splinted and strapped, my lord, our gentleman is comfortable, sirs, is cosy as, not to put too fine a point on't, a bug, gentlemen, in a rug, sirs."

"But his arm, Doctor?" questioned Oldcraft, "an't it broke?"

"'Tis no great matter, sir," beamed the little doctor, "a simple fracture of the ulna. I'll have the Captain on his legs again in less than no time. So pray do not suffer yourself to worry for him unduly, my lord."

The Viscount rose with a jerk and turned towards the door, but there the doctor intercepted him.

"My lord, I must ask you not to visit him to-night, he must not be disturbed, as his friend, sir, you will temper your natural anxiety and permit him to sleep, sir, to snooze, to, in short, my lord, to slumber."

The Viscount nodded, muttered and went out clapping the door behind him.

"Hum!" quoth the doctor and took a pinch of snuff. "His lordship would seem put out. . . . But pray, sir, what is your business with me?"

"Well, Doctor," answered Oldcraft with his wide-lipped smile, "I'm an officer o' the law."

"I'm aware on't, sir."

"Then as such, Doctor, I ask ye to sit down and answer me a question or so. . . . You attended Mr. Julian Gyfford in his illness, I understand."

"I did, sir. And an ill patient I found him in every sense."

"How so, pray, Doctor?"

"A rebel, sir, very wild and extreme unmanageable!" answered Doctor Samson, shaking his head. "He was wild as a boy, I mind—a headstrong imp! Latterly he disobeyed my instructions, with the very natural result that his wound suppurated, he fell into a low fever, lost strength and suffered from ill dreams, hallucinations amounting in the end to a positive dementia, sir."

"Ha!" nodded Oldcraft. "And you were with him on the day o' the murder, Doctor, how was he then?"

"Strange, sir, very odd—remarkably so! And small wonder indeed, for he rose from a sick-bed, insisted on't—went forth into the air from a close chamber—out, sir—out into the open air! Oh, madness! The marvel is that he didn't fall dead on the spot! And, on top of't all, he must go a-walking and—mark you, in the open air! A most desperate, headstrong gentleman, sir, a hopeless subject for any man o' medicine——"

"'Twould seem so, Doctor. And he was strange and odd, says you. Pray how, sir?"

"Well, he was highly feverish—and no wonder, a flux o' humours to the head! His speech was rapid, his looks wild—'twas as if he thought—as though he expected to, in short, to die!"

"Ah!" murmured Oldcraft. "Expected to die—yes. Said he as much, Doctor?"

"No, no, 'twas but his general demeanour."

"In your evidence, Doctor, you deposed that you left him at the stile leading into Fallowdene Wood. Now did he say aught of importance, give you any message—ha?"

"Nothing, sir, nothing of any reasonable sense . . . and yet—hum!"

"And yet, Doctor—what, pray?"

"Well, he left with me his pistol as a gift for his cousin, Sir Richard."

"As a . . . gift to him, Doctor?"

"As a gift, sir."

"Said he anything?"

"Words, sir, mere idle words," answered Doctor Samson, shaking his head. "'Give this,' says he, 'to

Cousin Richard and bid him know "There's more in it
than meets the eye"'—or some such nonsense."

"Have ye this same pistol, Doctor?"

"Sir, I have."

"Then, as an officer o' the law I must charge ye to
deliver the same up to me."

"Why so I would sir, but I pledged myself to give
it to Sir Richard—himself only and——"

"'Tis no matter, Doctor. Sir Richard being the
suspected party, 'tis now your very duty to deliver
this pistol up to an officer o' the law."

"Then so I will, sir," said Doctor Samson, rising,
"and mighty glad to be rid on't, I vow. Come with
me and you shall have it at once."

"I'll call at your house for it, sir—say ten o'clock
to-night, sharp."

"Why, very well, sir. And while we are on the
subject, I take occasion to aver that Sir Richard
is no more concerned in this murderous business
than I am."

. . . "John," said Sir Richard, gazing thoughtfully
at the candle-flame again, "what time do you expect
Black Nick, to-night?"

"Lord love ye, sir,' chuckled the landlord, winking,
"Nick were 'ere an hour agone, ah, more!"

"Eh—here already, d'ye say?"

"Leastways—in the cellarage, sir."

"The audacious rascal!" exclaimed Sir Richard, and
chuckled also.

"Hor—dacious be the only word for 'im, sir."

"And i'Gad, nothing could be more opportune!"
exclaimed Sir Richard, getting nimbly afoot. "I must
have word with him."

"Then, sir, tak' care as nobody spies ye."

"What matter, John? You forget."

"Ay, by goles, sir! I do be gettin' that used to 'ee,
nodded John, opening the door cautiously to peer and
listen. "Coast be clear, sir!" he whispered.

So down the narrow stair they crept and along dim-
lit passages they sped stealthily, turning unexpected
corners, across unlighted chambers, down sudden

"The empty vapourings of a fevered brain, sir!" he pronounced. "The wild fantastical out-pouring of an intelligence all distraught!"

Master Oldcraft stared anew at these written words, scowled at them, cursed them beneath his breath yet very heartily, then, folding up the paper set it away in his large pocket-book, thrust the pistol into his girdle and took up his hat, and so Doctor Samson presently lighted him to the door.

Now it was a dark night, for the moon was not yet up, and thus, as Master Oldcraft took his way along the shady lane how should he see or be aware of the dim, stealthy shapes that crept after him, that closed upon him so silently—nearer . . . nearer yet. . . .

CHAPTER XXX

TELLETH OF THE MORNING AFTER

AURORA of the rosy fingers waking, smiled—and lo, it was the spring of day! A soft and fragrant dawn, all pink and golden, whose tender glory mellowed hoary church-tower, twinkled and glowed in the many bright lattices of the Gyfford Arms and upon the face of him who stood yawning sleepily in the stable-yard, that same gipsy-seeming fellow who answered to the name of Dick Fullalove.

These being the days of early-rising, the village already showed signs of wakefulness; from divers chimneys blue smoke curled lazily, cocks were crowing cheerily, a dog commenced a joyous barking, from cottage-well came the clank of bucket and chain, and the man in the stable-yard having yawned once, yawned again, stretching long arms luxuriously but, all at once, his white teeth shut with a snap and he stared away across the village green where, hard beside the churchyard wall stood the parish stocks—for there, with long legs fast shut within this instrument of shame, sat a prisoner, a very strange-seeming object, his upper parts hidden from sight by an enveloping sack.

So the man Fullalove, cutting short his yawn, stared as one amazed, shambled over to the stocks and stood there—goggling:

" Hul-loa!" quoth he, at last, whereupon issued an answering bleat from the pinioned, sack-shrouded form.

" Eh?" enquired Fullalove, coming a step nearer, " Wot say?"

" Lemme . . . out!" gasped a strangled voice.

" Oh!" exclaimed Fullalove, rasping unshaven chin. " Why?"

The prisoner vented muffled, though fierce, imprecations and threats:

"Loose me, d'ye hear? Are ye there, fool?"

"Ar!" said Fullalove. "'Ere I be, leastways I beant nowheres else, I rackon."

"Then—let me out!"

"'Ow?" enquired Fullalove and scratched his ear, then turned as Joel Bim, the blacksmith, came striding across the green.

"Love us!" exclaimed the blacksmith. "Oo be this?"

"Ar!" nodded Fullalove. "Oo indeed?"

"Rackon I knows them legs," quoth the blacksmith.

"Pretty long 'uns!" nodded Fullalove.

"But if," said the blacksmith, scratching puzzled head, "if so be it do be 'im as I thinks it be—'ow did 'e come into they stocks?"

"Ar!" nodded Fullalove. "'Ow?"

"'Ad us better take a look at 'im, do 'ee think?" enquired Joel staring hard at the writhing, shrouded form. Having pondered which question, Fullalove nodded and, while the prisoner uttered stifled curses, proceeded to unknot constricting rope and, lugging off the sack, discovered the passion-contorted features of Master Titus Oldcraft.

"Love us all!" ejaculated the blacksmith, while Oldcraft, wrenching open coat and waistcoat drew thence large pocket-book, opened it, glanced through its contents and cursed more vehemently than ever:

"Robbed!" cried he. "The villains robbed me!"

"Oo?" demanded the smith. "When, maister, and wheer? And Lord! 'Owever did ee get into they stocks?"

Oldcraft merely swore, bidding them let him out.

"Ay, but," demurred the cautious Joel, "oo put 'ee in?"

"Two rogues, two damned villains . . . and robbed me!"

"Pick-pocketin'!" nodded Fullalove.

"Ay, but wot like rogues was they?" questioned Joel.

"How should I know!" snarled Oldcraft. "They were masked, fool, masked!"

Now at this moment, forth of the inn stepped Tom Pitt, beholding whom, Oldcraft called and beckoned, whereat Tom Pitt hastened up, his narrow eyes much wider than their wont for sheer amazement.

"Why, Mr. Oldcraft!" he exclaimed, "whatever——?'

"Tush!" cried Oldcraft. "Call your master, rouse my lord Brocklehurst . . . these gaping clods 'll keep me here all day, dammem! Fetch the Viscount—say I'm robbed—important papers—go!"

So away sped Pitt leaving Oldcraft to curse and fume and fret while Joel Bim scratched his head and stared at Dick Fullalove, who rasped his chin and gaped at Joel Bim.

"Robbed!" nodded Joel. "And if you was to up and ax me, I should tell 'ee as I specks them theer 'ighwaymen's been at their tricks."

"Ar!" nodded Fullalove. "Pick-pocketin'!"

"The key!" snarled Oldcraft, jerking his prisoned legs impatiently. "Don't stand there like two damned posts—look for the key!"

"Ay, but wheer?" enquired the smith. "Tell me wheer to look and us'll look, 'earty an' willin'——"

"Look anywhere—everywhere!" cried Oldcraft. "Oh damme, here's a guinea to the man as gets me out!" and plucking forth a coin he held it up.

"A guinea, by goles!" said the smith. "Lookee now, I might get 'ee out wi' 'ammer and chisel or . . . why, dannel me if key beant i' the padlock—staring we in the face arl this time!"

"Then unlock me!"

"Guinea first, maister!"

So Oldcraft tossed him the guinea and a curse with it, whereupon Joel rubbed the coin, stared at it and nodded to Fullalove. "Here be 'alf for thee, lad," said he and proceeded to unlock and free the prisoner who, staying for no word of thanks, hastened across to the inn as speedily as cramped limbs would serve him, and followed by Fullalove yawning again and stretching as he went. Oldcraft was still some yards from the inn door when forth thereof stepped Viscount Brocklehurst in silken dressing-robe and tasselled nightcap.

"What now?" cried he in voice shrill and querulous. "What's this I hear? Sit ye down man here—here beside me on this bench, sit i' the devil's name and tell me what's to do?"

"Last night, my lord," answered Oldcraft, sinking wearily upon the settle, "I was waylaid outside the Doctor's house. I was trepanned and scurvily used, choked, my lord, nigh strangled, trussed, tied, clapped i' the stocks and—robbed."

"Ha, your purse, your watch?'

"No, my lord, all the villains got off wi' was the cat's-eye ring and——" here Master Oldcraft sunk his voice to a whisper.

"'Sdeath!" cried the Viscount recoiling. "Are ye sure?"

"Alas, my lord, 'tis clean gone, and with this another paper as I found last night i' the barrel of the late Mr. Julian Gyfford's pistol—good God, my lord, what—what is't?" he exclaimed; for, uttering a hoarse cry, Viscount Brocklehurst leapt up as if he had been stabbed.

"Death and hell!" cried he. "Julian's pistol? Are ye sure?"

"So Doctor Samson tells me, my lord. And here is the pistol, I had it from the Doctor last night, and the rascally thieves must ha' overlooked same, howbeit— here 'tis!" And Master Oldcraft laid the pistol on the rustic table.

"The . . . the pistol!" gasped the Viscount, staring at the weapon with a strange, wide-eyed intensity.

"You recognise it for Mr. Gyfford's property, my lord?"

"And you say," said the Viscount, his devouring gaze still upon the pistol, "you say there was a . . . a paper hid in't . . . writing . . .?"

"Ay, my lord, writing as I could make no sense of nor the doctor either, for that matter."

"The pistol!" murmured the Viscount. "'Twas in the pistol!"

"Rolled up, my lord," nodded Oldcraft, "in the barrel o' same!"

"Ha—confusion!" cried the Viscount suddenly, and catching up the weapon hurled it from him so violently that the clatter of its fall roused the somnolent Fullalove who lolled on the adjacent settle.

"And what of this paper? Where is it?" demanded the Viscount as Oldcraft stooped and picked up the pistol. "And you read it, man, you read it through—what did it say—what?"

"Nought as I could understand, my lord, nor the doctor neether."

"And you lost this paper—you lost it—ha?"

"No, my lord, 'twas stole from me."

"So then you shall tell me what was writ.'

"Words, my lord, words a-plenty, too many to bear in mind, wild words as made no sense——" Here Master Oldcraft gasped in his turn, for the Viscount was shaking him in fierce gripe:

"Speak I say!" cried he. "Tell me what you saw—speak, fool!"

"Why my lord . . . indeed . . . if your lordship will give me time to think!"

"To whom was it written?"

"To his cousin, my lord, to his cousin, Sir Richard."

"Did it mention any names?"

"None, my lord, none but Sir Richard's. But, indeed, 'twas mad letter full o' devils and death and the like."

"But why," cried the Viscount with passionate gesture, "why should these thieves steal your papers only—why? What manner o' rogues were they?"

"Ah, my lord, 'twas dark and they went masked, and——"

"How many were they?"

"Two, my lord."

"Ha, but two, d'ye say—two only and you armed!"

"True enough, sir," answered Oldcraft sullenly, "but they were devilish quick, they had me nigh strangled afore I could so much as cry out, dexterous rogues I'll warrant me! And yet, my lord, though

so in my spirit I do kiss thee a long Good night,
Cousin Rick, and now fare thee well."

Many times Sir Richard conned these hastily-scribbled
words beneath brows close-knit in troubled perplexity;
finally, taking pen and ink and paper, he made of this
so urgent message a copy, word for word, which done,
he folded and thrust it into an inner pocket of the
silver-braided riding-coat that draped his chair-back;
then, extinguishing the candle, he groped to the door,
listened a moment, and went softly down the secret stair.

Now after some while it chanced that my lady Helen,
busied thus early among her roses, scissors in hand,
basket on rounded arm, heard a soft, melodious whistle,
and glancing round beheld a broad back stooped laboriously in the distant kitchen-garden; thus, as she snipped
the fragrant, dewy blooms laying each in her basket
with loving care, she glanced now and then towards
that busy figure and so, presently caught him watching
her beneath the crook of his elbow. Whereat she
frowned, and turning disdainful back, saw the Duchess
waving to her from the terrace and hastened forward
to aid her down the steps.

"Aunt," said she, "pray look yonder! Who is
he? Who is the male creature haunts the garden o'
late?"

The Duchess looked.

"Shure now, child, and isn't ut the gardener man,"
she answered, "the odd man that Ben found t'other
day."

"Was 't you engaged him, Aunt?"

"Who else, me dear soul? And see how well he
does—not a leaf out o' place, the hedges so trim and
the walks so tidy!"

"Well, but he—stares at me, Aunt."

"Och, the villain!"

"Persistently."

"But then, mavourneen, they do say he's but half-
witted."

"Oh, madam, and indeed!" said Helen, and severed
another rose with vicious snap of her scissors. "Then

suffer me to tell you that twice I've caught him gossiping with Betty, that she-viper!"

"Gossiping, d'ye say, Helen? Shure now and this reminds me! Ye've heard o' poor Captain Despard?"

"No, Aunt. What of him? And wherefore 'poor'?"

"The misfortunate gentleman pitched downstairs last night and broke the arm of him."

"Then he was probably drunk, Aunt."

"Well, and shall this dry up the fount o' sympathy for the suffering soul of him?"

"Aunt, I detest a sot."

"Indeed, miss? Now I protest ye astonish and astound me beyond expression."

"However," sighed Helen, busy with her scissors again, "'tis to be supposed I shall ride over to enquire after the miserable creature and leave a posy for him, mayhap."

"And troth, my lady, he should thank his stars and every saint in the calendar for such extreme and gracious condescension!"

"Indeed, my dearest aunt, I think he should!" nodded my lady serenely. "And yonder cometh Angela, and in that frightful old taffety!"

"And mighty sweet she's looking!"

"And extreme hoydenish!" nodded my lady. "And to-day she must be elegant, for this morning the Marquis waits on us, and I intend to marry 'em within the month."

"Och, shure, me gentle soul, 'tis a little providence in petticoats ye'll be entoirely and no mere mortal if ye don't take care."

"Lud, Aunt!" exclaimed my lady, opening her eyes and arching slender brows. "Now whatever in wonder's name can you——"

"'Tis Fortune's pampered pet y'are, me child, and 'tis a dose o' suffering ye need to make ye human, a taste o' terror to make ye womanly and tumble ye down from your towering pedestal o' self-esteem. Then maybe Love shall stoop and pick ye up again!" So saying the Duchess nodded, snorted, and hobbled away before my lady might find adequate retort.

arrested, scissors agape, staring at a small, folded paper which was securely impaled upon two thorns in the very midst of the rosebush; having eyed this paper for a long moment, she detached it carefully, opened it, and read these words scrawled thereon in bold characters:

"This midnight. R.
"Come down lest I climb up.
"N.B. Neither ride nor walk abroad."

Having read, she twiddled the paper in her fingers, crumpled it angrily, tossed it away contemptuously, snipped off two roses, glanced furtively round about and, stooping swiftly, caught up the paper and thrust it, a crumpled ball, beneath the fragrant laces of her bosom; and then, hearing a silvery jingle, glanced up and saw Viscount Brocklehurst approaching, booted and spurred for the road. He bared his head, he bowed and stood gazing upon her with eyes aglow, a look so persistent that she, being greatly aware of that crumpled paper ball tickling in its downy nest, flushed beneath his ardent scrutiny:

"Well, sir?" she demanded at last.

He started, drew a deep breath and flung out eager hand:

"Ah, Helen, I . . . I vow," said he in his quick, breathless manner, "you do grow ever the more beautiful. You madden me . . . bewitch me! Each day doth but make thee more lovely!"

"And you, my lord, the more fulsome!"

"Oh, Helen, wert thou but gentle as thy looks!"

"Nay, sir, then my looks belie me for to day I am savagely fierce."

"Not—I trust not with me, Helen?"

"With all the world, sir. . . . But I think you bring us news of Captain Despard's mishap?"

"Mishap?" repeated the Viscount, fumbling with his riding-whip. "Ay, to be sure he took a tumble . . . down the stairs, but——"

"And broke his arm, sir, we hear?"

"Something o' that. But, Helen, I——"

"How did it chance?"

"Why, I scarce know. He tripped—caught his spur,
or some such. . . . But, Helen, I . . . I am come
to beg you ride out with me . . . a gallop on the
Down. 'Tis . . . 'tis joyous morning. Come now I
pray let us go if . . . if only for an hour . . . go
with me, I do entreat."

My lady, arranging the flowers in her basket, glanced
curiously at the speaker, surprised and repelled by
the odd, repressed eagerness of his manner, for his
voice was hoarse, his burning eyes glanced up, glanced
down, his thin nostrils quivered, his slim hands seemed
even more restless than usual. "You—you'll ride
with me, Helen—come?"

"Nay, sir, to-day I'm in no mood for a gallop," she
answered lightly.

"Then so be it—we'll walk. Let us walk, Helen,
there is the charmingest prospect I can show you
from the Down, across Pevensey level to the sea. Come,
prithee, let us walk."

"Oh, my lord, 'twill prove too hot a day for walking."

"Why then, a chaise . . . 'twill be pure! There
is a chaise at the inn and——"

"My gratitude, sir," she laughed, "but to-day I
. . . I shall stay among my roses."

"Roses!" he muttered, and, with stifled exclamation,
swung on his heel, took three paces, came back swiftly
and spoke in gasping whisper.

"Helen, I love thee and . . . no man shall ever
come betwixt us, I swear it—ay, on my life, my very
soul! But to-day must I leave thee . . . business of
moment calls me hence to . . . to town. But I
shall come back. Oh I shall return, for, Helen, I
leave my thoughts, my very heart with thee. . . ."

"Then, my lord, I beg you'll take 'em with you."

"What, d'ye mock me, madam . . . will ye
flout——?"

But at this moment, and with portentous rustle of
voluminous skirts, the Duchess descended upon them:

"Ah, me dear Viscount," quoth she, all in a breath,
"the top o' the morning to ye now, and tell me arl

"To be sure!" nodded Helen. "He called here the other day."

"So 'e did, ma'm—well, this marnin' as ever was" —here old Ben chuckled—"this 'ere very marnin', my leddy"—here Ben laughed till he gasped—"they finds this Maister Oldcraft . . . fast i' the stocks . . . tied up in—a sack! Oho, aha!" Here old Ben choked.

"In the stocks?" cried Helen, clapping hands joyously. "'Tis an odious man!" Here she laughed also.

"Ar, ma'm," gasped Ben in wailing merriment, "and 'e'd been . . . in they stocks . . . arl night long! Aha—oho!"

"But, Ben, how came he there? Who did it?"

"Why, ma'm, 'tis wot nobody doant seem nowise to know, nohow. Theer be fules do say 'twas footpads, thieves an' 'ighwaymen, an' some says 'twere ghostesses, but me an' Joel Bim be pretty sartain-sure 'twas pharysees!"

"Pray, what are they?"

"Liddle bits o' chaps, ma'm, small folk as works their tricksies whiles us-loikes sleeps o' nights, mischievious liddle fellows they be—like willy-wipsies an' sich, though 'tis fairies as some du name 'em."

"So you think the fairies tricked Mr. Oldcraft?"

"Ar, ma'm. Though ef you was tu say 'twas pixies I shouldn't go for to argle-bargle about it, no."

"Was the detestable man hurt, Ben?"

"No, ma'm, 'e weren't nowise teched—no blood nor wounds no nowt o' that—though Joel Bim, as 'elped to foind 'im, du tell me as Muster Oldcraft stank pretty strong o' brimstone!"

"Horrors, Ben!"

"'Orrers be the word, ma'm! There be things 'apping 'ere o' nights as didn't nowise ought! F' instance, theer be th'owd haanted mill—full of 'orrers every night, it be! I seen loights theer, more nor once, an' Jarge du ha' seed 'em tu—gashly loights!"

"How so, Ben?"

"Well, they flitters 'ere, my leddy, an' they flitters theer—they skips, ma'm, and they likewise dances.

And ye see, nobody don't never go nor venter a-nigh
the plaace, day or night."

"Ax-cuse me, Ben!" said George, appearing suddenly
and blushing through his ferocious whiskers, "but I
see Mr. Pitt theer t'other arternoon, along o' one o'
the gen'lemen."

"Pitt?" repeated my lady. "Why then, George,
was the gentleman Viscount Brocklehurst?"

"Ay, my leddy, it were so, ma'm."

"And what did they there, George?"

"I dunno, my lady, the Vi-count see me, ma'm, an'
ordered me off, my lady!"

"That'll du, lad!" cried old Ben shrilly. "That'll
du, Jarge! Get 'ee back to thy burnishin'. I'll talk
tu my leddy arl she wants. Lord love y'r bootiful
eyes, ma'm, theer be nobody can't tell 'ee more 'bout
ghostesses an' goblings than me! And right busy
they've been o' late. I meets old Truffeni Camlo
t'other day, as be a Wise Woman and summat of a
witch they du say—and 'Truffeni, ma'm,' says I,
'theer be so much a-goin' on a nights, such strange
things,' I says, 'as it du seem loike 'twas a curse on the
village,' I says. 'Ah, an' so it be,' says she, openin'
'er big eyes at me, wherefore, ma'm, I crosses my fingers
quick, y'may be sure, lest she throwed a spell on me,
and then Old Truffeni tells me 'tis a curse, sure-ly, as
wunt be took off till justice be done, an' Sir Richard
Gyfford proved innercent. . . . And talkin' o'
S'Richard—I seen 'im t'other noight!'

"Oh?" said Helen, softly questioning, "where,
Ben?"

"In the sunk garden, ma'm, a-starin' at the chimbleys,
my leddy."

Helen raised hand to rounded bosom and was immediately aware of that tickling ball of crumpled paper:

"At midnight!" she murmured.

"Why no, ma'm, it were just gone ten o'clock b'the
church clock."

"And he was staring, you say, at——?"

"The Moat 'Ouse chimbleys, ma'm. Leastways if
'tweren't 'im 'twere 'is phantom, for when I calls out

"Happy creature!" murmured the Captain. "Fortunate wight! Your friend! Would you have done as much for any other, for me, Helen? For . . . Brocklehurst?"

My lady, being upon her feet, turned her back in haughty petulance, and swept towards the door even as the odd man slouched by, pitchfork on shoulder.

"Pray, Helen,' sighed the Captain, still fanning himself gently with his hat, "would you do for any other what you are doing—for him?"

With her hand upon the door Helen turned, viewing the speaker in wide-eyed amazement.

"I detest riddles, sir," said she loftily. "You must speak plainer."

"Plainer? Is it needful?" he questioned gently, but watching her with sudden, keen scrutiny. "Yes, upon my life, I do believe it is! Then . . . and yet, Helen, can it be possible you are unaware—that you have no suspicion——"

And then, with wild clatter of hoofs the Marquis galloped into the stable-yard and, espying Helen, reined up his snorting bay all in a moment.

"Alas, Helen—Richard's taken!" he cried. "I met that fellow Oldcraft on the road who tells me they ha' the poor f'low fast by th' heels at last!"

"Ah!" breathed my lady and, though the exclamation was scarce more than whisper, she leaned heavily across the half-door, crushing the harsh edges of that ball of crumpled paper into her tender flesh yet feeling it no whit.

"What can be done?" she questioned breathlessly. "Ned, what can we do? Do something, Ned!"

"Ay, faith!" cried the Marquis, wheeling his eager animal, "I ride now to comfort the poor soul."

"One moment, my lord!" said Captain Despard. "Pray when was he taken, and where?"

"Last night, sir, so Oldcraft tells me, at a small place hard by Newhaven."

"Then, my lord, either this information is false or Sir Richard hath since escaped."

"How, sir . . . ha 'scaped? Pray wha' d'ye mean?"

"I mean, Marquis, that he is free as you or I!"

"Free, sir, free? How d'ye know this, sir?"

"My lord, I saw him—not ten minutes ago."

"Where, sir—where?" cried the Marquis, glancing about eagerly. "Ten minutes, say you? Then b'gad, he can't be far! Pray tell us!"

"No, my lord," answered the Captain, smiling, "since I have surprised this gentleman's secret, you must suffer me to keep it secret still."

Then she slipped on her shoes, wrapped herself in hooded cloak, and, opening the bedroom door, stole softly downstairs.

She found him awaiting her on the terrace, but neither uttered a word until they had reached the cherry-tree. But, having come thus far, and safe from all eyes and ears, my lady halted and, feeling the burning need of vindicating herself, turned and fronted him, chin aloft:

"Such shameless, such detestable audacity!" she exclaimed. He merely took off his hat and bowed. "Never—ah never in all my days have I suffered such outrage, such abhorrent disrespect!" Sir Richard immediately bowed again, whereupon, finding him thus mute, she stood silent also, viewing him in the dimness with the utmost indignation, while he regarded her, head bowed and hat in hand. And thus stood they some while.

"Well?" she demanded at last. "Since I'm here, sir, pray what now?"

"First," he answered. "I am humbly grateful."

"Grateful?" she repeated. "Grateful indeed!"

"Indeed, ma'm, purely grateful."

"Heaven love me!" she cried. "You outrage my midnight privacy, you snatch me from my bed——"

"Fie—no, ma'm, I protest!"

"You drag me abroad at this unholy hour and tell me—you are grateful, forsooth!"

"Yet, forsooth, ma'm, grateful am I indeed that you are here in answer to my humble prayer."

"Prayer, sir—humble prayer, indeed? And you . . . clambering to my chamber-window!"

"But then I clambered very silently, ma'm, and with the very utmost reverence."

His voice sounded solemn as usual and yet——

"Oh will you laugh?" cried she, in swift anger. "'Fore heaven your assurance is hateful as your audacity, I'll leave you, sir." But when she would have done so, he caught her cloak and, turning upon him, she saw his face bent close in the dimness with lips and eyes very grave indeed:

"Ah, my lady Petulance!" said he, gently. "Go an you will, though I had counted on your aid, your friendship to-night. . . . But first, since I may not be always near—be warned, madam—neither walk nor ride abroad after sunset, and never alone."

"And wherefore not?" she retorted. "What is this mystery? How am I threatened? How am I affected, pray? 'Gainst whom do you warn me and what?" Here for a moment he stood mute, peering at her with troubled eyes:

"I' faith," said he, passing hand across brow with a weary gesture, "'tis what I cannot tell you for lack o' proof. . . . Ah, by heaven, had I but one vestige of real proof! . . . Howbeit, I do believe some danger threatens, and a danger very real, so—pray be warned."

"But of whom? Of what?" she repeated, leaning nearer. "Can you not tell me or will you not?"

"Would I might indeed, Helen, but——"

"But!" cried she, derisively. "Oh 'tis folly!—you write me warning by day, you speak me warning by night, yet with all your warning when I question you can but shake your head and—sigh!"

"Alack, 'tis true enough!" he answered, and sighed again. "And yet, ma'm, spite your peevish humours and petulant impatience, I beg you'll heed my warning nevertheless. . . . And now—Good-night t'ye, ma'm. I wish you happy dreams." So saying, he bowed and strode off so suddenly that my lady caught her breath and stood looking after him in frowning dismay; then she gathered up her petticoats and began to run, looking neither left nor right and thus nearly tumbled over him where he stood waiting beyond tall yew hedge.

"I hoped you'd follow," said he, reaching out a hand to steady her.

"Oh, then . . . you expected . . . I should?" she panted and with as much dignity as circumstances allowed.

"I merely . . . hoped," he answered gravely.

"And am I . . . such petulant creature?"

"Only—now and then."

"And . . . peevish?"

"But only—when not petulant."

"Oh, sir, my very humblest, most grateful thanks!" said she, sinking before him in profound curtsey; then he heard her laugh. "And yet," said she, walking on beside him, "I am to believe you had counted upon this peevish, petulant creature's aid and friendship?"

"I had," he answered.

"But—are we friends, sir?"

"Are we not, ma'm?"

"Indeed, Richard, I hardly know. You are become so strange o' late, so detestably mysterious! And, pray, is it the act of a friend to vanish utterly—and never a word?"

"At least, Helen, 'tis discreet if he happen to be hunted as a murderer."

"So then you do not trust me!" sighed she, reproachfully.

"Infinitely!" he answered.

"Yet you do not confide in me—you tell me nothing!"

"What would you know?"

"As your friend I would know what you have been doing since you vanished."

"Using my eyes and ears," he answered a little wearily, "taxing my poor wits to the proving of one, Richard Gyfford, his innocence. I've hunted the hunters—though with small success so far."

"Then—if I am your friend, Richard, confide in me yet more—confess where you lay hid this morning at precisely eleven o'clock."

"Wherefore this particular hour?" he enquired, slackening pace the better to peer at her in the starlit dusk.

"Because 'twas then, or thereabouts that Ned—your friend the Marquis, galloped into the stableyard with report of your capture."

"S'life!" sighed he. "Report hath it seems been capturing me daily somewhere or other. Well, ma'm?"

"Well, sir, the Marquis was for riding to your aid and comfort instantly but Captain Despard assured him such report was false because he himself had seen you that very morning and not ten minutes since."

Sir Richard halted suddenly, and stood rubbing his chin like one very much at a loss:

"Faith now, I suspected as much!" he murmured. "And yet, egad, his eyes must be mighty sharp!"

"Richard, where were you hiding, that is the question?"

"Nay, Helen, the question rather is—how soon will the fellow betray me?"

"Lud, sir, why must you doubt him? Captain Despard is a gentleman, a man of honour!"

"Ay, but then—so is Sir John Parret, ma'm—so is my lord Viscount Brocklehurst, and Magnus and Threep—these be all worthy gentlemen and esteemed men of honour, and yet they'd give me but short shrift. But the Captain? Ha, 'tis very awkward complication!"

"Nay, stint your apprehensions, sir, none knows but Captain Despard, and you may trust to his honour."

"You think so, ma'm? I wonder!"

"And I am assured of't."

"And, i'faith, you are warm in his defence, ma'm."

"Because in my mind I once did him cruel wrong and great injustice, sir!"

"Hum!" quoth Sir Richard.

"Never hum at me, sir!" she cried in sudden anger. "And moreover the word 'ma'm' is rustically boorish!"

"Why, I am but a rustical soul," he answered.

"Howbeit, Sir Humility, if you will not name my name, name me not 'ma'm.'"

"Lady, forgive me," he murmured humbly.

"A flapdragon!" quoth she, and they walked some while and never a word between them; at last:

"Well, Richard," said she, "I yet wait your answer—where was it you lay hid this morning?"

"Faith, Helen, 'twere hard to say, for I flit hither and yon like a very ghost. I am here and there, my lurking places are many. Go with me a small distance farther and I'll show you one."

For by this time they had crossed the wide kitchen garden, and now Helen paused at a flight of stone steps mossy and age-worn.

"Why 'tis the sunk garden!" said she, peering into the dimness below. "A dreary, desolate place."

"True," he answered. "Once, ages ago, this was the moat.'

"To be sure, Richard, you should know these gardens well."

"I do," he nodded, "every stick and stone, for you see as a boy I used to play here with my cousin Julian. And 'tis by reason of him I seek your aid, Helen, to read a letter, the last he ever wrote. 'Tis strange letter, and I would beg you set your woman's wit to resolve the meaning on't . . . so, wilt go with me, Helen?"

"Ay, Richard, I will," she answered kindly, "but whither wouldst take me?"

"To a place where I may light a lantern safe from all chance observation. And now . . . this stair is somewhat treacherous . . . wilt give me thy hand?"

Mutely she obeyed him and, hand in hand, they descended these crumbling steps into a dusk that gloomed more dark, here below.

"Nay, leave me thy hand awhile," said he gently. "I'll give it back so soon as I may but 'tis rough hereabouts."

"And very dark!" she murmured, as they followed vague and bush-grown walks.

"Dark, and a late moon," he answered, "and should be a right proper night for ghosts!"

"Oh, Gemini!" she exclaimed. "Why mention such horrors, Richard?"

"But thou'rt never afraid, Helen—thou!"

"Assuredly not!" she answered resolutely. "Not I . . . no! . . . Yet I might be!" Here her hand snugged itself a little closer in his.

"Hast ever seen a ghost, Helen?"

"No, nor wish to . . . if such there be. Have you?"

"Ay. I've thought to see several o'late."

"Oh, Richard!"

"But dost not believe in such idle folly—thou?"

"Nay . . . indeed no . . . not when the sun shines!"

"Neither do I, Helen. Nay, here's no reason to loose my hand yet."

"Folly!" said she, though not very angrily, and yet slipped her fingers free none the less. "So, sir, having seen ghosts you disbelieve in them?"

"Heartily, my lady, for though these phantoms flitted vastly ghost-like I yet proved 'em too purposeful and over solid"—here, going astray in the gloom, she stumbled and he took her hand again. "And here is one o'my divers hiding-places!" As he spoke he pointed to a seeming wall thick-grown with ancient ivy and shut off by a tangle of dim-seen weeds and bushes.

"Watch now!" Going in amid these bushes he parted the dense ivy discovering a low and narrow arch that opened upon an echoing blackness.

"What horrid place is this?" she whispered.

"It was a culvert once that fed the moat."

"'Tis dreadful place, Richard!"

"Not so, though 'tis something dark. Wilt venture in with me, Helen?"

"Oh, surely!"

Now at this she felt his fingers tighten upon hers for a moment, then they stepped out of the starry dusk into a pitchy darkness, between narrow walls that echoed strangely as they went.

"Bide you here a moment," said he, and loosed her.

"What would you, Richard?" she whispered.

"Light the lantern."

Standing in this awful darkness she waited while Richard struck flint and steel and lighted the lantern, whose welcome beam showed crumbling walls and vaulted roof; it showed her also Sir Richard's face, very worn and haggard, though his lips were smiling and his eyes bright and glad.

"Upon my soul," said he gently, "friendship such as thine is rare and lovely thing, my lady."

Then, taking a cloak from some shadowy niche, he spread it against the wall and invited her to be seated; so down she sank. And now, seated opposite to her, the lamp on the ground between them, Sir Richard

drew from his breast a large and somewhat clumsy
wallet and, taking thence a folded paper, placed it
in her hand.

"Thou'rt pale, Richard," said she never glancing at
the letter, "so very pale!"

"Why then," he answered, smiling a little wearily,
"'tis very well, for I have been playing ghost, and
these are pallid things, or should be. But read Julian's
letter, see an you can make——"

He started suddenly, the words died on his lips as,
from the outside world, stole a soft, leafy stirring;
now, beholding the sudden, fierce intentness of his
look, and how his fingers had clenched themselves
upon his sword, it seemed as if some dire change was
wrought in him even as she watched—it was growing
in his scowling brow, waking in his glaring eyes, in
the grim ferocity of mouth and jaw, in the purposeful
hand that griped and griped upon his sword: thus
she stared on him amazed, and cold with growing
dread of that which, long banished from her thoughts,
she feared now to think on:

"'Twas . . . 'twas but the wind!" she whispered.

"But there is no wind!" he answered, and now the
very tones of his voice seemed altered; as he spoke
he was afoot, and had vanished, creeping with never
a sound—even as might creep Murder; and she was
staring after him in a dreadful dismay. And presently
when he came creeping back, she saw the glitter of
his naked sword, and shrank instinctively.

"You were right," he nodded, sitting down again,
"a wind is rising."

"But . . . why draw your sword?"

"A fugitive's instinct!" he answered, laughing a
little oddly as he met her look. "Also I've slept little
o'late."

"Richard," said she gently, "pray tell me—what is
it you fear?"

"Capture!" he answered. "For aught I know
Despard, who sees so much, may be aware o' this
haunt of mine, may be on his road hither at this very
moment, and the tipstaffs with him!'

"Nay, Captain Despard is to be trusted, I vow to thee, Richard. Why but this very morning when we questioned him, Ned and I, he declared that since he had surprised thy secret he would keep it secret still."

"Ay, but then others, my lady, others may question him to very different effect—and——"

"Not so!" cried she, and up went her imperious head. "Never! Your suspicions of this gentleman are unworthy, sir!"

"Yet natural, madam.'

"Captain Despard, I repeat, is a man of honour."

"Very well, ma'm—then may I suggest you read the letter and be done with it?"

My lady frowned at the speaker, frowned at the letter as if she'd a mind to tear it up, and, finally unfolding it, stooped to the lantern, but having read, glanced up with eyes of questioning wonder:

"Here is some mistake!" said she and forthwith read aloud, as follows:

"'Upon the day I come to my desire and am master of the fortune specified, I promise to pay Titus Oldcraft Five Hundred Guineas.

BROCKLEHURST.'"

"Ay, faith, here's mistake indeed," nodded Sir Richard, and, taking the paper from her, he folded it up and sat twiddling it absently between his restless fingers.

"'Tis strange," said she, staring at his grim-smiling face, "strange and very odd, Richard!"

"Cometh o' pick-pocketing!" he murmured, nodding at the candle-flame. And as he sat thus, chin on breast, sombre gaze abstracted, the glittering sword across his knees, once again the ominous change in him smote her and once again all those dark forebodings and suspicions, those half-formed fearful doubts that had haunted her upon a time, grew ever the stronger, the more intensified until they found sudden utterance at last:

11

" Indeed but you . . . are greatly . . . greatly changed ! "

Without lifting bowed head he glanced up at her beneath drawn brows :

" 'Tis like enough," he answered gently. " And would you reproach me therefor? "

" Nay, Richard, here is no reproach, for am I not thy friend . . . more so to-night than ever, as I do think."

" Then, good my friend, here now is Julian's letter." and he set an unfolded paper before her, " resolve me the meaning of it an you may."

So she took up the letter; and now as she read, he sat watching her lovely, intent face a little anxiously, tapping the bulbous wallet nervously upon his knee.

" Oh, wonderful ! " she exclaimed suddenly, glancing up at him bright-eyed.

" How so ? "

" Why, see you not, this of itself might prove your nnocence ! "

" Not mine," he answered bitterly, " never mine, Helen, t'will need more than this to convince the accusers of Gyfford o' Weare—they must ha' proof absolute and manifest for such as I."

" Richard . . .! Oh Richard !" said she breathlessly, and leaning forward, viewed him with strange, half-fearful intensity, " if . . . if you are . . . truly innocent, why fear to face your accusers boldly? Oh why? "

" Because," he answered, meeting the searching look with his sombre eyes, " because such boldness would be arrant folly."

" Yet would it be the nobler course ! " she retorted. " 'Twould be the braver way. . . . Oh, 'twould be heroic ! "

" Howbeit, ma'm," said he sullenly, " just now I had sooner be a craven at large than a hero in cage and fetters."

" What matter," cried she. " Ah, what matter a cage or fetters to Conscious Innocence ? "

"Why, faith, madam, I should say these would matter more than to Conscious Guilt. And egad, a caged hero not only seems the most helpless o' fools, but will probably hang as such—the which should be sorry end for any heroical ass and mighty uncomfortable, to my poor thinking."

My lady bit rosy nether lip, arched disdainful eyebrows, twitched shoulder contemptuous and shook her head:

"Alas!" sighed she, "we live in sorry times—the race of heroes is dead, 'twould seem!" Having said which she bent to study the letter again, and then— Sir Richard chuckled, not loudly, and somewhat hoarsely, to be sure—still—he chuckled. My lady started as if she had been stung, and flashed him a look of such furious indignation as went far beyond all speech; yet she spoke, none the less, and without an instant's hesitation:

"Oh laugh! laugh! Sir Richard. Mock, sneer, jibe as you will, sir, but if—if you be not guilty indeed, then Innocence, like an armour, should clothe you 'gainst all dangers and aspersions! If—I say, sir, if you are truly innocent, if guiltless in word and deed, then why—why must you hide thus and cower so contemptibly in corners?—why, sir, why?"

"Nay, if, ma'm, if?" sighed he, shaking head at her reproachfully. "You speak me a many 'ifs' and with each do question my integrity! If I am truly innocent—if I am not guilty. Oh 'sbud, madam, are ye not assured o' this—even yet?"

"Then tell me, sir, tell me why you thus cower and creep in corners so shamefully? 'Tis not to protect me, to draw suspicions from me, there is no need o' this as you do know passing well. So why must you hide, sir, and skulk?"

"To the less noble purpose of protecting my unworthy self!" he answered, bowing with an airy flourish of the wallet, and lo—forth of it leapt small, bright object that gleamed and fell into her lap . . . and, beholding what thing this was, she uttered a gasp of horror for there, staring up at her, lay the cat's-eye ring.

"Heaven's mercy!" she whispered. "Look. . . . Oh, Richard. . . ."

"Your cat's-eye ring, Helen," said he quietly, but smiling grimly at what he read in her look, "'twould come back to you, it seems."

"No!" she cried, shuddering violently. "No. Take it away . . . take the hateful thing away."

Smiling still, he picked up the ring and slipped it upon his little finger. "It fits snugly, ma'm!" said he and laughed.

Now at this, she rose and stood leaning against the wall.

"Why . . . show me?" she questioned faintly.

"To set an edge to your suspicions, belike."

"But, oh, Richard, you . . . you will deny——"

"Nothing!" he answered bitterly, and drawing Julian's letter from her nerveless fingers, folded it carefully away. "So here, madam, will be an end to your friendship, I take it. And now——"

"Friendship?" she repeated. "Friendship such as mine knoweth no end, thou poor, blind soul!"

"Would you then befriend one you deem a murderer?"

"Richard," she murmured, "if Julian is dead by your act, I am persuaded he died in fair fight."

"Fair fight, say you, and he an invalid?" Here, once again Sir Richard laughed and more bitterly than ever. "Oh, lady, accept my thanks, but I will not have you condone my sins to yourself or to others. I am— what I am! And now suffer me to escort you back to the house." So saying, he rose, stooped for the lantern and thus remained, smitten motionless, for in the dimness all about them rang a fearful, long-drawn cry that rose to a shuddering wail inexpressibly dreadful to hear.

CHAPTER XXXIV

TELLETH OF ONE DEAD THAT WALKED

SIR RICHARD drew a deep breath and, as he turned, my lady saw the glitter of his sword; so for a long moment stood they motionless, staring on each other in a fearful suspense.

"Somebody . . . is dead!" she whispered at last. "Oh what . . . what horror lieth yonder?"

"That I must learn," he answered, peering into the darkness whence that terrible sound had come. "Will you wait here with the lantern or go with me in the dark?"

For answer she slipped a tremulous hand in his, and so, with never a word, began to follow whither he led; into a gloom between rugged, narrow walls; into an ever-growing blackness full of stealthy sounds that were the echo of their going; into a blinding darkness where, since her eyes were useless, she closed them against the horror, but clung the faster to that strong, sure hand that guided her unfaltering until—came a gentle wind touching her brow like a caress, and opening her eyes she saw the loom of Sir Richard's be-wigged head against the stars. And then they were forth of this place of darkness, grass under foot, overhead the wide expanse of heaven luminous with a rising moon whose silvery splendour was putting out the stars.

Helen sighed and looked around; trees she saw, with the dark and sullen waters of a pool, while hard by this, gaunt and forbidding, loomed the ancient mill, its broken roof a jagged outline against the rising moon.

"The old mill!" she whispered. "They say 'tis haunted!"

"And well they may!" he answered, whispering also.

"Are we going inside, Richard?"

"That is the question!" he answered glancing from the forbidding ruin to her pale face, with troubled eyes. "I think you were wiser to wait here whiles I——"

"No, Richard, I am nothing wise to-night—where you go there go I."

"Nay, Helen, consider! Who knows what may lie yonder, waiting to be found?"

"No matter," she whispered, nodding determined head. "I am resolved. So let us go on."

"Art not afraid?"

"Yes!" she answered shivering. "So let us see— what is to see."

"Thou courageous soul!" he murmured. "Come then!"

So, side by side, they crept across the grass until they were in the shadow of mossy wall then, turning a sharp corner, they halted suddenly for, from jagged hole that once had been a window, poured a beam of yellow light.

Approaching stealthily they peered in but saw, at first, only bare floor and discoloured walls lit by a lantern; then was a soft strange whimper of sound and, looking whence this came, they espied something huddled in remote corner—the form of one who crouched upon his knees, whimpering faintly ever and anon, with head clasped between griping hands—a drawn face, in whose pallor two eyes glared dreadfully towards the open doorway.

Now beholding who this creature was, Sir Richard backed away and stood a moment considering.

"Oh what is it?" she whispered. "What will you do?"

"I must question him, Helen. . . . And yet he must not see you. I pray you, follow me."

Mutely she obeyed, and he brought her to shady niche screened by the warped skeleton of the great water-wheel. "Bide you here till I return!"

"Then keep me not over long," she pleaded.

"Nay, this I promise!" he whispered. "Only wait and fear nothing." Then he stole away, keeping ever in the shadow, and so came to the yawning doorway, paused a moment to listen, and stepped into the mill, sword advanced in ready hand; the dim figure never moved, so he advanced and bent above this crouched and whimpering misery.

"What, Tom," said he, "why, Tom Pitt, how now? What ails ye, man?"

But Tom Pitt neither spoke nor turned his glaring eyes from the one direction, only he whimpered again.

"'Sdeath, man—speak!" cried Sir Richard, and tapped him lightly with his sword; then, but with eyes still fixed in their awful stare, Tom Pitt slowly raised one arm and pointed with shaking finger:

"There!" he gasped. "'Twas there I saw him . . . him that is dead, yet walks . . . him that was murdered and cannot rest . . . him that is buried and yet flits abroad. . . . Mr. Julian! . . . I saw him yonder . . . he stood and looked on me all bloody with murder."

"Ay, and who—who killed him, Tom?"

"'Twas not me. . . . Ah, not me! And yet he . . . pointed at me . . . but—ah, 'twas not me as did it!"

"Who then, Tom—speak!"

"No . . . no . . . I cannot . . . I don't know ——"

"Why, then you guess, Tom, you guess. Who was it—answer me! Listen then—was it——"

The words were lost in sudden hoarse cry:

"Look. . . . Oh, God—he comes again!"

Sir Richard turned about and instinctively recoiled —for, beyond the open doorway stood an awful cloaked shape, in familiar green velvet riding-coat, topped by a face, ghastly, blood-bedabbled, half hidden in the flowing, auburn curls of great periwig, a face that seemed vaguely luminous, horrible with corruption. . . . For a breathless moment it leered askance on them, blasting the very night with horror, and then—was gone.

Sir Richard leaned back against the wall and, closing his eyes, lifted hand to clammy brow . . .

A moment's deathly stillness, then—uttering a broken, inarticulate cry, Tom Pitt leapt to his feet, laughed, sobbed and rushing to the window, clambered through and away. Next moment Sir Richard was outside, glancing wildly here and there but, though by now the moon's level beams were bright about him, he saw no more than sombre trees and placid, sullen pool; so, sheathing sword, he hastened back to Helen.

"Did you hear . . . see . . . aught?" he questioned.

"I heard the murmur of your voice, Richard. I heard the man Pitt groaning. I saw him come leaping from the window, yonder——"

"Did he spy you, Helen?"

"Nay, he fled like a wild thing. What ailed him, Richard?"

"Ghosts, Helen, and an uneasy conscience, mayhap. But come you home, the hour grows late."

"What matter for that, Richard? Since we are here, let us seek your cousin's hidden message."

"Nay but," he answered, glancing furtively round about, "dawn is none so far——"

"So much the better," she answered serenely, "at such dead hour none are like to disturb us."

So, with keen eyes watching furtive as they went, he brought her into the mill; and here seated, the lantern placed conveniently, my lady set herself to puzzle out Julian Gyfford's last message.

"'Opposite the day?'" sighed she, conning the directions beneath wrinkled brows. "Now what should this be, think you?"

"What other than 'night'," he answered, watchful glance upon the open doorway, ears straining for stealthy sounds.

"'Night?'" she repeated dubiously. "'Tis likely . . . and yet . . . no, it scarce can mean night— listen:—'Tis written thus: 'Opposite the day, the sixteen from going out and in, the fifteen from that which bears you up!' So runs your riddle.'"

"And sounds mere folly!" he answered.

"Opposite the day!" she murmured and her abstracted

gaze roved from the written words to the beams overhead, to discoloured walls, to the jagged hole that
once had been a window—and: "Richard!" she exclaimed, "look now,—where may one see the day but
by the window? The window, Richard—your riddle
begins: Opposite the window!"

"Faith, now——" he began but she cut him short.

"'The sixteen from going out and in'! Now, how
may one do so but by a door? The door, Richard."

"Ay, so I think, thus much I had——"

"The sixteen from the door, Richard!"

"Ay, but sixteen—what?"

"Paces, Richard—try paces. Opposite the window,
sixteen from the door!"

"Nay, it can never be paces," he answered, measur-
ing the floor space with his eye. "Let us count the
floor-boards. . . . No, we're out again, for on this side
but ten and on t'other, scarce six."

"Why then, the bricks, Richard, try the bricks."

So, from the door he numbered the bricks of the
wall until he had counted sixteen.

"Well?" cried Helen watching him, flushed and
eager. "What do you find?'

"Alas, Helen, nought but the veriest brick."

"Wait, Richard! Now count fifteen from 'that
which bears us up.' And that must be——"

"Ha—the floor!" he nodded.

"Oh, sir!" she exclaimed, throwing up hands and
eyes, "now I protest you amaze me! Such nimble
wit! Such instant—Lud! What have you found?"

"The fifteenth brick!" he answered and speaking,
lifted it from the wall.

"And the secret message—is it there—is it there?
Oh, Richard!" she whispered as from the cavity where
this brick had lain he drew a folded slip of paper; for
a moment he eyed it beneath drawn brows then, smoothing it out, bent to the light and began to read aloud,
as follows:

"'My dear Richard,
    'I have been killed——'"

"Well?" she cried in breathless impatience, for he had stopped all at once. "Oh, will you not read?"

"Ay, but not now," he answered, glaring fearfully towards the open doorway.

"Why not?" she demanded. "Wherefore keep me in suspense? Why, what now——?"

"Pray hush!" he whispered. "Do you hear anything—hark!"

Borne to them on the soft night wind stole a vague sound that as they listened grew rapidly louder and nearer. Sir Richard thrust the paper into pocket and drew his sword:

"Put out the lantern!" he whispered. "So! . . . Now stand back—back to the wall!"

Footsteps in the night outside, hurried footsteps that checked suddenly as if unsure. . . . An interval of silence . . . the pant of hurried breathing and then a hushed voice spoke:

"Here's no light. . . . They're away, ma'm, thank God!"

Next moment Sir Richard was in the doorway hand outstretched:

"Greg!" said he. "Lord love you, man!"

"Quick, sir!" whispered Gregory. "Begone wi' dame Truffeni—quick! Tom Pitt's gone mad and roused the village—swears he's seen Mr. Julian—ah, and you, too, sir. The hunt'll be up after ye by this. . . . Oldcraft and——"

"Zounds!" exclaimed Sir Richard, sheathing sword. "Say no more, Greg, for here must I incontinent to earth . . . but . . . I'm not alone, Greg, and——"

"Ay, ay, I'll see my lady safe within doors, sir, only begone"—here Gregory pulled off his hat as Helen stepped into the moon's waning light.

"What's to do, Richard?" she enquired, glancing about, anxiously, while Gregory went aside, leaving them together.

"The hunt is up," he answered, with haggard smile. "So must you home—Gregory shall see you safe. And now farewell, and pray think your kindest of me despite your so determined friendship."

"How despite it?"

'Faith, ma'm, your friendship is based only on your belief in my guilt, it seems. Ah, well, get thee home to bed and my gratitude with thee——''

"And you, Richard?"

"'Slife, in fashion unheroical I must needs creep, crawl and hide again." Here, before he knew it, his hand was caught and held fast between her soft, warm palms:

"Why then," said she laughing, but somewhat unsteadily, "creep swiftly, Richard, crawl fast and . . . and I pray God keep thee in His mercy!" Then she called to the anxious Gregory and giving him her hand, sped away.

"Should ha' kissed her, my chavo!" said a soft voice, and, glancing round, Sir Richard espied a tall, hooded shape beckoning from the leafy shadows hard by.

"Ay, Truffeni,' said he, hastening towards her, "now bless thee, good mother, right trusty friend."

"Still, my chavo should ha' kissed her."

"Nay," he answered as they went on together through a rustling gloom, "in her soul she suspects me—even yet!"

"And implores God's care on thee!"

"Women be strange creatures, Truffeni."

"Men be such children, oh, man!"

"Whither go we, good dame?"

"Where you shall sleep safe, for by your look sleep's your need."

"I' faith, and that's true enough!" he sighed. "Also this hath proved a night o' disappointments . . . That she should doubt me yet! . . . Moreover, dame, though I have Cousin Julian's hidden message it is nothing to my purpose."

"So you found it, my Gorgio rye! In the Mill?"

"With my lady's aid. 'Twas behind a brick, the sixteenth on the right hand going in, the fifteenth from the floor. But 'twas all labour in vain."

After this they journeyed in silence, for Sir Richard, oppressed by gloomy thought, distressed for lack of

sleep, stumbled blindly on, careless of direction, following silently whither the old strange gipsy led, through
shine and shadow, by trackless ways ever deeper into
the wilderness until at last they reached a little glade
full of the moon's tender radiance. Here old Truffeni
halted suddenly, to point with her staff to where lay
certain twigs disposed in an artful disorder.

"Lookee, sir," said she, "'tis the Romany's patrin
and says 'beware!' So bide ye here. I'll go look and
listen. If ye hear an owl cry, steal into the shadows
yonder and wait."

"As you will, ma'm!" he nodded, clasping hand to
aching forehead and next moment was alone.

The moon, high risen, shone in glory, and Sir Richard,
sinking down with his back against a tree, blinked up
at her vacantly for a while. And presently as he sat
thus the leaves opposite parted with scarce a rustle
and a dark and hairy visage peered forth at him.

Sir Richard roused suddenly and sat up, the hairy
head nodded and spoke in hushed tones:

"Where's Herself, brother?"

"D'ye mean Truffeni—Mrs. Camlo?"

"Brother, I does."

"She went aside to look and listen."

"Ay, then she sees my patrin, my warning—there
was footsteps i' the lane."

"Is your name Wentzelow?" enquired Sir Richard,
heedful of the man's thick curling black hair and whiskers
that grew to the very eyes of him. "Wentzelow of the
Hearnes?"

"The same, brother."

"Then stand forth, man, for though I've heard of
you frequently, I never clapped eyes on you ere now."

"No, but I sees you often, brother, when I comes
and goes."

"And how is my small friend, Shuri?"

"Fresh as a flower, brother, as a sparkle o' doo!"
So saying Wentzelow stepped into the clearing, a long,
slim man who moved with hardly a sound. "And
lookee, S'Richard," said he in the same cautious tones,
"six brace o' birds I has off 'n Sir John Parret's land

las' night, and more to come. Ye see he has our Shuri whipped three months agone, him and Mus' Battleby, and I don't forget, the Romany never forgets! So I shall whip Mus' Battleby one day and—whisht, here comes Herself!"

Sure enough a few moments later old Truffeni appeared, and questioned Wentzelow in the strange soft gipsy tongue; and when they had talked thus awhile, she turned to Sir Richard:

"We o' the Poor Folk has eyes and ears and uses 'em, sir. Tell him, Wentzelow."

"Well, brother, 's arternoon the Viscount gen'leman leaves the 'Gyfford' and sets out for Lonnon, takes the Lonnon road, 'e do—leastways 'is chaise do, but himself doubles back to Seaford and there he lays at the 'Anchor.' And wot's more, he's seen a-talkin' wi' Jonas Skag and two other rogue-lads. And wot's more again, this same Jonas and two rogues ; now a-laying at the 'Black 'Oss' in the village. A l for why, brother?"

"Mischief," nodded Sir Richa l, getting to his feet, "but what?"

"Well, brother, I knows as Cap'n Sharkey Nye and the rest o' they 'free-traders' don't nowise trust Jonas, and has throwed him out, so Jonas have took up wi' Pete Legrand, a Frenchee as runs his lugger over to Birling Gap, frequent."

"Ha!" exclaimed Sir Richard, filled with a sudden anxiety. "So here's why you gave me warning, Truffeni! S'death, I must stir, it seems, I must to work!"

"Ay, let us be stirring, my chavo, for ye must sleep, and sleep thou shalt. Come with us."

"Sleep?" repeated Sir Richard, shaking heavy head. "Not so, friend, for whiles I sleep——"

"Shalt find new strength for mind and body. So come, Sir Richard, you must sleep this night. Lead on, Wentzelow!"

So, in the end, blinking and stumbling with weari ness, Sir Richard followed whither he was led.

The camp fire gave forth a comfortable, drowsy heat, the little shadowy tent hard by looked cosy and inviting, but Sir Richard, shaking resolute head, seated himself beside old Truffeni and drew a crumpled paper from his pocket.

"My thanks, kind friend," sighed he wearily, "but though I yearn for sleep I could not until you have heard this. So, Truffeni, hearken and counsel me."

And bending to the firelight he read aloud as follows:

"'My dear Richard,
        'I have been killed by three or one of three, for the following reasons, to wit:
    '1. By Tom Pitt (possibly) because I know him for convict returned from transportation.
    '2. Captain Despard (possibly) because I hold proofs that he was once the notorious highwayman and malefactor Captain Archer sometimes called Captain Midnight.
    '3. Viscount Brocklehurst (probably) because I have his signed confession to the killing of young Allison, whose untimely decease was put off on you, Dick. The proofs of all this I have hid in the third volume of Montaigne's Essays in the library at Weare. Use them, an you will, to avenge thy forlorn and remorseful cousin
                        'JULIAN.'

"So there it is!" sighed Sir Richard despondently. "And doth advantage my case no whit, for though I prove the Viscount guilty of killing Mr. Allison, here is no proof that I did not kill my cousin Julian."

"Then," said the old gipsy, nodding at the fire, "then must we force proof."

"Ay, but," questioned Sir Richard, blinking heavy eyelids and drooping with fatigue and dejection, "how, Truffeni, tell me how?"

"My chavo," she answered, leaning to touch his bowed shoulder, "why doth a dead man walk?"

"Ah!" he exclaimed. "You . . . mean——?"

"That we must bait a trap, set a snare to wring truth from tongue unwilling. The dead shall not walk in vain—ah, no! We must spread a net—to-morrow

I will show thee how—but now go and get thee to sleep."

"No, no!" he answered rising, "whatever it be, I'll do't now, Truffeni, who knoweth what to-morrow's dawn may bring?"

So Truffeni, rising also, brought him into a tent set somewhat apart and larger than the others; here seating him at small table she set pens, ink and paper before him.

"Now write as I bid ye, and as much like your cousin Mr. Julian's hand as maybe," she commanded, and he wrote this at her dictation:

"Dear Richard,
        "You shall find the sealed packet of my secret papers relating to Brocklehurst behind the midmost joist in the Moat House Garden,

                                        "JULIAN."

"Nay, but," said Sir Richard, blinking sleepily from this to old Truffeni's hawk-like features, "think ye this shall draw him?"

"I'll warrant me!"

"And how then?"

"He shall there find that he doth not expect—aha, that which shall ope his lips ere he know it and drag thence the truth despite himself, and here shall Guilt accuse itself for all to hear who will."

"On my life!" murmured Sir Richard, his throbbing head between his hands, "'tis desperate, 'tis wild plan and yet—may succeed——"

"It shall!" Now looking into her great black eyes so keen and fiercely bright, he shivered suddenly; and then Wentzelow appeared grasping a long musket, and spoke whispering in the Romany. Truffeni held up a finger for silence, and hearkening thus, they heard a voice afar that chanted snatches of psalmody in dreadful, hoarse gasps, that wailed and shouted, drawing ever nearer; and as they stepped out of the tent Sir Richard heard the click of Wentzelow's musket as he cocked it. . . . For a long moment they stood,

motionless all three, then the underbrush was burst
asunder and a wild figure leapt into the fire-light—
hatless, wigless, without coat or waistcoat. . . .
Instantly the camp was all astir, faces peered, voices
whispered, knives gleamed; but Truffeni clapped her
hands, spoke three or four words, gestured imperiously
and the whispers were hushed, the faces glimmered
and vanished.

Sir Richard, blinking at the awful figure beyond
the fire, saw a small, haggard face topped by a stubble
of white hair, saw arms wild tossed, one swathed in
a bloody clout.

"Vengeance!" cried a shrill voice. "Blood!" And
then in gentler tone: "Brethren, 'tis writ ' Inasmuch
as ye did it unto one o' the least o' these ' . . . but,
sirs, he was my father, a man guiltless and innocent,
and they hanged him by perjury . . . a man o'
God! . . . They choked him on a gallows. . . . I
saw that innocent, white head jerk i' the cruel noose
till death stilled it at last. . . . Ah, God o' Vengeance,
'twas my loved and honoured father. . . . Titus
Oldcraft took him and swore his life away. . . .
Jonathan Wild pouched the blood-money. . . . Oh,
Perjury! Titus and Jonathan . . . but Titus first,
and when he lieth dead I'll mark him i' the brow like
Cain. . . . But, brethren, dearly beloved, how idle a
thing is grief—even mine! For high in heaven is a
bright angel whose poor body rotted long ago . . .
but he was my father and I watched him die on Tyburn
Tree, and I, his son, a child forlorn . . . but now is
the time at hand. . . . Vengeance . . . ! Blood . . . !"
And then a lithe, masked man sprang into the fire-
glow to clasp this distraught figure in comforting arm:

"Nay, now . . . nay, Rob, easy, lad! Comfort ye
—there's none but friends and good pals here."

"But Oldcraft lives . . . lives . . . and killed my
father! And, Oh, Brethren, bethink ye how—' Like as
a father pitieth his children so the Lord pitieth them
that call upon Him——' so now call I . . . pity me,
Lord . . . that I may 'bathe my footsteps in his
blood.' . . ."

"So-ho, Rob, so-ho!" murmured Nick, patting the other's tear-wet cheek. "Easy, lad! . . . Lord, Mrs. Camlo, ma'm, poor Rob's been a wild man all night, and me a-watchin' of 'ee, but no sooner do I close my peepers than 'e's up and away, ma'm. 'Tis beyond me, he is, so—if so be, ma'm, you could spellbind him, ma'm, or aught o' that natur', I'd be mighty grateful."

Old Truffeni, approaching the sick man, caught his restless hands, looking into his eyes.

"'Tis the fever, Nick," said she. "Bring him hither." Muttering and weeping, this small, grey-haired man, whose name was a terror, tottered abjectly into the tent.

"Brother," said Wentzelow, leaning upon his long musket, "'tis a sick man he looks, and 'tis sick man 'e be, and yet I wouldn't be in Titus Oldcraft's shoes for a fortun'."

Sir Richard shivered, and, drawing stool to the fire, sat down and crouched in the warmth.

"Ah!" quoth Wentzelow, also approaching the genial fire, "'tis the death hour—I smells the dawn, brother, and there be many a one as lays a-dying at this moment."

"Well, but death, friend Wentzelow, is none so ill if it be quick and sure."

"Mebbe, brother, mebbe, but—I wouldn't be in Titus Oldcraft's shoes—no, not for three fortun's!"

CHAPTER XXXV

GIVETH PARTICULARS OF ONE DAY—MORNING

AWAKING untimely from dreamless and much-needed sleep, Helen sighed, and lay awhile blinking at the sunbeam that shot an inquisitive ray between her bed-curtains; then, covering her eyes against dazzle with rounded arm, she stretched luxurious limbs between the cool sheets, and had composed herself to slumber anew when she was roused again by sudden, stifled sob and opened her unwilling eyes once more.

Betty was weeping, crouched in chair beside the lattice she wept copiously; her buxom face showed all blubbered with her woe, tears hopped from rounded cheeks, they trickled down her shapely nose to splash upon the dainty, ruffled garment she had been sewing at.

My lady, finding herself wideawake and thus cheated of her so desired rest, started up and, clenching fist, pounded her pillow resoundingly:

"Crocodile!" cried she, whereat Betty, jumping violently, sobbed louder than ever. "Snake, will ye sob? Asp, adder, venomous toad—wilt weep and rob me of my needed rest?"

"Oh, m-ma'm!" sobbed Betty. 'Oh, d-dearest my l-lady——"

"Don't dare 'dear-my-lady' me, thou sniffing serpent . . . dropping your alligator tears all over my latest shift, too!"

"But—ah, my lady—my poor heart is breakin' all along o' Mr. Pitt. . . . And desprit frighted I be, all along o' Mr. O-Oldcraft——"

"Wench—what d'ye mean?" demanded my lady, sitting up among her tumbled pillows.

"He—he's left me, ma'm, he's gone—flowed away and——"

"Who has? Which?"

For answer Betty rose, curtseyed, wiped her eyes and proffered a tear-sodden missive, a blotched and crumpled sheet of paper whereon my lady read these words, scrawled, it seemed, in desperate haste:

"Dear Betty forever fare well Tis ended and I distraught for I saw him last night a gory specktackle Mr. Julian tho' dead walks all bloody of a night crying for vengeance and it is beyond me to bear that am an innocent party. Sir Richard was there also and see the awesome sperrit and if ever a guilty face was his was. And blood upon the face Mr. Julian's horrible to see and pointed at me tho' innocent as babe. So if they question and ask you who done it you may swear not me but Sir Richard was the fatal hand and cannot deny same. I suspected and now am sure. as this is the last word to thee Bet now and ever and fare well to thy

"POOR TOM."

"And good riddance, too!" nodded my lady, tossing down the letter. "So here, minx, here's the reward for peeping and prying! This wicked man teaches you treachery to your poor mistress, makes you try to betray me and now runs off and leaves you—which is the best service he could ha' done you."

"Oh, but, ma'm, I'll vow I never betrayed nobody. Oh, never! I only did as he bade me and all—all for your ladyship's happiness——"

"My happiness, girl! How, pray?"

"Oh, ma'm, he—he adores the very shoes you walks in, the dust you treads in—he——"

"Who, creature, who?"

"My lord, ma'm, the Viscount Brockle——"

"That mincing fool!"

"Oh, my lady, but he dotes——"

"Baggage, fie! Hold that impertinent tongue! . . . And now, since you've murdered sleep, I'll be dressed. Bid Mary to me."

"Mary? Oh, but I—I be your ladyship's true maid and——"

"A base, designing, sly, creeping reptile!"

"Nay—oh, ma'm! Ah, my lady, I never meant thee any harm. . . . I thought 'twas all for thy happiness —you an' my lord . . . wedlock, ma'm . . . happiness and—Oh, my lady, pray be kind to poor, heartbroke me as truly loves thee . . . on my bended knees——"

"Indeed," sighed my lady, softened by Betty's very evident sincerity. "I begin to think you more simple than wicked, and so must needs forgive thee—one o' these days, but now—bid Mary to me."

And so, after some while, my lady descended to her solitary breakfast, drinking little and eating less; and presently going forth into the pleasant garden there found the Duchess basking placidly in her favourite elbow-chair beneath the cherry-tree.

"Well, me dear?"

"No, Aunt—everything is most hateful and most especially—myself."

"And, b'the powers, Nell, ye're pallid as a candle!"

"And feel like a farthing dip in a gale o' wind!"

"Me poor, tender bird!"

"Nay, Aunt, this bird hath beak and talons!"

"Me gentle lamb!"

"With teeth and claws, Aunt!"

"And is that the way of it, then? A megrim— a fit o' the vapours!"

"Ah, 'tis poor, paltry, miserable, hateful world, Aunt!"

"Is he, me dear soul?"

Helen checked a sigh to stare:

"Is who—what?" she demanded.

"Richard."

"And what of him, pray?"

"Doth he so trouble ye, me poor, love-sick wretch?"

Helen sighed, flushed and then, sinking into vacant chair, turned to frown:

"Love-sick?" she repeated with disdainful shiver. "I shall never stoop to love any male creature!"

"Ah—so he didn't kiss ye then last night—the blind omadhaun that he is?"

"Kiss me, Aunt? Heavens, madam, no indeed! Such question affronts me! I suffer no man's kisses, the mere idea is abhorrent! Indeed, Aunt, you are sometimes——"

Helen paused and turned with sudden, breathless question, "But . . . but how know you of last night?"

"Faith, me child, didn't I watch ye creep off to him?"

"Madam, I never creep!"

"Why then, shall we say—I watched ye slink, Helen."

"Oh, what you will, madam. Howbeit, since it seems you thus pry upon my actions, you shall know I . . . accompanied Sir Richard to the Old Mill, last night, in quest of letter there hid for him by his cousin, Mr. Julian."

"Aha? And did ye find it?"

"I—found it."

"Och, and did ye so? Well, well—what of't?"

"As I say, Aunt, 'twas I found it!" . . . Here my lady yawned as provokingly as possible, whereupon the Duchess had recourse to her snuff-box.

"And you say, me dear love, 'twas yourself found it?"

"'Twas I, dear Aunt!" Here my lady hummed a snatch of song, very soft and sweet.

"Ah, shure, me dear angel," sighed the Duchess gently, "there's times I yearn for the days ye could go so easily across me knee!"

"Oh, madam!" shuddered my lady, "you become merely shocking!"

"Ah-h-h!" murmured the Duchess, "and 'tis shocking ye I'd be, miss, were ye of handier size!"

"Fie, madam!" sighed Helen, rising. "I'll go walk among my roses."

"But 'tis no billet-doux ye'll find in 'em this morning, me gentle soul!"

"How . . .?" breathed Helen, opening her eyes. "What. . . . Oh, what know you of such . . .?"

"Why 'tis mighty fine morning!" nodded the Duchess. "Which reminds me—did ye see this terrible spectre last night, Helen?"

"Nay, what spectre, Aunt? And pray how——"

"Och, shure now, phwat but this same ghost every-body's so full of, the same as sent the rogue Pitt into raving panic—the spirit o' Julian Gyfford. 'Tis the talk o' the village, so Ben tells me. Angela's away there to gather news."

"Julian's ghost! So this was why Pitt fled? Oh, horrible! But, Aunt, you never credit such tales—you don't believe in ghosts surely?"

"Well, no, me dear—not this morning. But then this is the morning, and if ghosts walk, indeed, or phantoms flit by day, the sun puts the poor things out —so, who knows but there may be spirits and goblins all about us at this very moment. And this being Julian's ghost may—hum!"

"May what, Aunt? Pray what?"

"Well, me dear, being Julian's ghost, I think——"

"What—oh what, pray?"

"That I'll go walk among me vegetables!"

"Oh!" exclaimed Helen, stamping petulant foot. "Go, madam, but methinks you'll walk alone, for what's become o' your jobbing gardener—the odd man?"

"Faith, 'tis wondering I am."

"So am I, madam my aunt—wondering how you should stoop to familiar talk with such as he—a mere, rustical boor——"

"Ha?" quoth the Duchess.

"A rude, half-witted creature."

"Hum!" murmured the Duchess. "And yet ye've got things in your head that look like eyes!"

My lady merely raised her brows and turned away.

"A bat!" chuckled the Duchess. "A mole!"

AFTERNOON

The Marquis of Merivale, a splendid yet solitary figure, sat beneath the cherry-tree and bored small holes in the turf with the ferrule of his cane very per-tinaciously what time he murmured fitful curses, and glanced very frequently towards the house with a certain nervous impatience.

Meanwhile in shady parlour on cushioned settle far removed from the windows, crouched Angela flushed and softly rebellious while Helen, standing at the casement, glanced from her dainty loveliness to the distant figure of the Marquis.

"Weep!" commanded my lady between white teeth. "Weep, miss, I say, be tearful—this instant!"

"I'll not!" answered Angela, meekly resolute.

"And I say you must and shall!"

"But, lud, Helen, I don't want to weep! Why should I weep?"

"Because the occasion demands it."

"What occasion?"

"Weep, little fool!" cried my lady, with the utmost ferocity. "Sob, simpleton, sob or I'll tear thy hair!"

"Oh, Helen—why art so strange, so cruel harsh to thy poor friend?"

"Because I'm out o' tune with Nature."

"And why vent it on poor me?"

"I lack for sleep.'

"'Tis none of my fault, Helen! And thy look so fierce —nay, I'll leave thee!" And up sprang Angela, but scarce was she afoot than my lady's forceful hand whirled her down again.

"Oh!" gasped Angela, beginning to sob, "t—thou'rt hateful . . . a cruel c—cat!"

"I know it, miss!" sighed Helen. "But better a cat than mouse that can merely squeak and scutter! And now—now will you weep?"

"How may I he—help it and thou so harsh and——"

"Good!" nodded my lady. "Then do thy weeping here, nor stir lest I work thee injury! Bide ye here till I return—you hear me?"

"Yes—but—oh, Helen, w—why art so strange—so hatefully——"

But Helen was gone; forth and away she went hurrying yet gracious. . . .

"Ah, Ned!" sighed she, returning the somewhat gloomy salutation of the Marquis. "You expected my poor, sweet Angela—confess!"

"Why, as to that, Helen, I—b'gad I did, but——"

"Alas, Ned, I left the gentle soul dissolved in piteous tears—such grief!"

"Eh—tears? Grief? Goo' God, but——"

"Indeed such woe! The gentle creature is still breaking her tender heart for love."

"No? Oh! Is she though? Ha, plague on't!" sighed the Marquis, dismally. "I—rat me but I thought that 'ffair was over a month since."

"So did I, Ned," said my lady, sighing also.

"Ha!" exclaimed the Marquis, stabbing another hole viciously into the turf. "Then perdition seize the f'low!"

"Hush, sir! Curse not lest thy curse cometh home to roost."

"But, burn me, Helen, this f'low Althorp is but the veriest fribble! By heaven, were he a man I'd have him out 'n' settle th' matter comfortably so, but Althorp is a——"

"'Tis not for my lord Althorp my poor gentle dove is languishing her soul away, Ned."

"Eh? No? Not? Not Althorp?'

"No, Ned!'

"Why then . . . a God's name, in a word—who?"

"Thy Angela pines for one who, though a poor-spirited, shill-I, shall-I, dare-I-venture me, backward creature, is yet the creature of her darling choice."

"And can she truly love such fool?" he groaned.

"Most truly, Ned."

"And the fool so—so curst backward?'

"Oh, Ned, 'tis creature blind as bat, deaf as owl!"

"Then damn the fool!"

"Hush thee, Ned! For, though indeed such blind and backward fool, the fool loves her most truly as I think. He waits on her, he sighs, ogles, languishes so desperately he will sometimes sit a-stabbing of little holes in the turf——"

"Eh?" cried the Marquis, and dropped his cane.

"What, Ned?"

"F' th' love o' heaven what—whom d'ye mean?'

"Ned, Ned!'

"How? Why . . . ye powers above! Can it be
that she cares for me?"

"Devotedly, Ned! She weeps her loving heart out
even now . . . in the parlour, Ned."

He sprang to his feet and glanced eagerly towards
the house.

"In . . . in the parlour?" he quavered.

"Unless she hath dissolved away in tearful woe,
Ned."

"Helen . . . God bless thee!" said he, and strode
off. . . . And thus he presently beheld a small,
desolate figure outstretched upon the settle, slim, yet
still solid enough despite her tears.

"Madam!" said he, and stepped lightly through the
window. Angela started, and glancing up at him over
rounded shoulder, discovered a sweet, tear-wet face.

"Angela?" he murmured and leaned reverently above
her; at this, she stole another look and, sobbing, smiled.

"Dear heart!" he whispered and took her in his
arms. . . .

Beholding all of which my lady Helen sighed for
very sympathy and, turning away, wandered aimless
across the wide lawn, and thus espied a rough-looking
man watching her who, now approaching, pulled off
weather-beaten hat, knuckled an eye-brow, and gave
her a sealed letter; then staying for no question, grinned
and hurried away. So, breaking the seal, she unfolded
the letter and saw this:

"MADAM,

"Having discovered certain property of
yours (personal) at the Old Mill, left by yr. ladyship
in yr. ladyship's hurried flight therefrom last night,
T.O. begs to inform yr. ladyship same shall be returned
and no questions asked if yr. ladyship will call for
same at the Gyfford Arms to-day at sunset. Come
alone, and do not fail or it may lead to an unpleasant
notoriety which wd. sensibly affect yr. ladyship's
honour and grieve

"Yr. ladyship's humble obdt. servt.
"T. OLDCRAFT."

K

Twice she read this through in an ever-growing wonder and unease, then frowned towards the west, already glorious with sunset. Thus stood she awhile like one between two minds; finally she hurried into the house and presently came forth, almost furtively, and draped in hooded cloak.

EVENING

Upon a stile deep-set in leafy hedge and over-shadowed by gnarled tree, sat two men, black-avised fellows, whose growling speech, like their rough garments, smacked of ships and the sea.

"Sunset, Jonas!" said one, a squat, red-faced man, getting to his feet and leaning to peer down the lane. "Sunset, Jonas, and she be nigh doo, I rackon!"

"An' my bottle's out!" growled his companion, a lank fellow whose sullen eyes were close-set beneath scowling brow. "My rum be all gone, so gi'e 's a suck o' yourn."

"Avast, Jonas, belay now! She'll be a-heavin' into sight if she'm a-comin'—so get 'ee down and stand by wi' the cloak, 'twunt do to let 'er squeak."

"She ain't a-goin' to do no squeakin' once I gets my 'ands on 'er, Will, not she!"

"Well, I wishes it were darker, Jonas—it be too cursed light for such-like job."

"Well, it ain't my fault, is it? Don't go a-blamin me!"

"No more I ain't, Jonas. . . . But wot's become o' that gipsy-lookin' cove, eh?"

"Wot cove?"

"Why 'im as was a-standin' off and on in our wake.'

"'Ow should I know?"

"Do 'ee think 'e were follerin' us, Jonas?"

"No, I don't."

"Well, but s'pose 'e were?"

"Can ye see any sign of 'im?"

"Why no, I can't, but——"

"Then shut your meat-trap an' use your years!"

So, the better to listen, they stood mute in that place of deepening shadows, viciously alert, like the predatory animals they were, while from dry ditch at no great distance, a pair of keen eyes watched them through tangled wisps of gipsy-black hair.

"Futsteps!" whispered the squat man, suddenly snatching up a coil of small-cord and peering down the darkening lane.

"I 'ears 'em!" nodded Jonas, gathering up a heavy boat cloak.

"'Tis our party, Jonas—stand by!"

"Well, so I be!" whispered Jonas.

A quick, light tread of feet coming rapidly nearer . . . nearer yet . . . the two human animals crouched to leap. . . . Thus, in the shadow of that gnarled tree, my lady Helen found herself suddenly confronted by two vague yet menacing shapes and, reading the dreadful threat of them, turned to fly, but fierce arms imprisoned her; she strove to scream but a brutal hand choked her—then the heavy cloak smothered, blinded, stifled her, a deftly-knotted cord pinioned her struggling limbs, biting cruelly into the tender flesh of her. . . .

A gasping oath and she was down, rolling helpless in the dust yet with a consciousness of desperate strife above and all about her—a sound of blows, trampling feet, breathless cries and imprecations, a wild hurly-burly suddenly ended. Then my lady felt herself seized in strong hands, swung aloft in powerful arms—but now what with shame, dread, and the swift horror of it all—for the first time in her life my lady Helen, actually and truly, swooned away like the merest, ordinary female.

When her eyes opened again she saw the gnarled tree yet above her and, between this and herself, a face framed in curly black hair.

"Who . . . Oh God! Who is it?" she gasped.

"Only me. . . . Fullalove, ma'm. . . . Dick."

"Oh, thank God . . . then I'm safe?"

"Ar!"

"But . . . those men! Are they gone?"

"Ar!"

"What . . . oh, what did it mean?"

"Pickpocketin'!"

"No—here was more . . . more than robbery! Are they quite—quite gone?"

"Ar!"

"Then . . . oh 'twas you drove them off! 'Twas you saved me from——"

Hoofs upon the road approaching at brisk canter, a horseman who sang happily. . . .

"Ned!" cried my lady. "Oh, Ned!"

An exclamation of startled surprise, a furious oath and down leapt the Marquis and had pinned Fullalove by the collar, all in a moment.

"Aha—dog!" snarled the Marquis, and whirled his riding-whip.

"No!" cried Helen, rising to her knees. "Stop, Ned, stop!"

"Eh?" gasped he in amazement. "Is't you, Helen. Oh sink me, what's this mean?"

"Two men, Ned. . . . They attacked me! They choked me! They bound me! This brave, good fellow drove them off . . . he saved me . . . saved me from—Oh, Ned!" And Helen shuddered violently and covered her face.

"Split me!" exclaimed the Marquis and, loosing the "good fellow" in question, gave all his attention to comforting Helen.

"There, there, dear soul!" said he, clasping a protecting arm about her shivering form. "God love you there's nought to fear now—and the devil's in't tha I came not sooner! Don't tremble, my dear, all' well! The rogues are quite gone—alas. . . . Ha, 'ti curst fortune I should ha' missed 'em! So, Helen take comfort I'm here . . . would to the bottom o my soul I'd only been sooner! What like were th rascals?"

" 'Twas too dark to see."

" Devil take 'em!"

" Indeed, but you needn't squeeze me any more Ned."

" Canst stand, m'dear? "

" If you'll but suffer me."

" Canst walk or shall I set thee on my Silver-heels? "

" I'll walk, 'twill do me good."

" Then take my arm—so! Now tell me all that befell—did the villains rob you? "

" No," she said, shivering again, " they meant not robbery, Ned."

" Ha—d'ye mean—— "

" No matter. Talk we of sweeter subject . . . tell me of thy Angela."

" Angela? " he sighed. " By heaven she's a saint, Helen, ay, 'pon my soul a very angel, too purely good for such earthly creature as I."

" An extreme proper sentiment, Ned. Cherish it, I beg, for truly Angela is all sweetness from pretty head to dainty toe and I'm . . . Oh lud!"

" Eh? Oh? What now, Helen? "

My lady stopped to turn and look back.

" Fullalove! He fought for me—I saw blood on his face! He saved me from—from what I scarce dare think on and—Oh, Ned, I never spoke him one word of thanks!"

" Eh—the gardener f'low? Why 'tis no matter, my dear. I'll see he's sufficiently rewarded—ay, I will, b'gad! So come, let's on and I'll tell you more o' my Angela—how she looked when I—— "

" You'll also tell him my gratitude, Ned? "

" Him? Oh, the gardener f'low? Ay, ay, I will so. But speakin' o' gratitude, Helen, lemme die but my gratitude t'you is boundless—positively, for d'ye see, I've worshipped Angela ever since I first. . . ."

So Helen came safely home with Angela's name sounding in her ears repeatedly, but before her mental vision a face marked with blood, grim-smiling, shadowy, framed in curly, gipsy-black hair, a face that, stirring memory, was to follow her to bed and haunt her slumbers.

CHAPTER XXXVI

WHICH HINTS OF DANGERS IMPENDING

CAPTAIN DESPARD had manifested an unwonted restlessness all day. He had paid his accustomed devoirs to the ladies at the Moat House yet, even there, his usual serenity had seemed somewhat ruffled; returning to the village he had paced the green with expectant gaze upon the dusty high road; he had taken his glass sitting on the bench before the inn, himself a mark for the worshipful salutations of the rustics, and even while drinking, his glance had wandered, in the same direction. Later, aloft in the seclusion of his pleasant chamber, he had lolled in the open window, a splendid, idle-seeming personage yet with eyes still keenly alert and watchful.

Thus when, towards sunset, Mr. Titus Oldcraft rode up to the inn and, dismounting, paused to shake much dust from his coat-skirts, he beheld the Captain's comely, be-wigged head leaning forth of the lattice above.

Mr. Oldcraft bowed; Captain Despard merely beckoned with languid finger but, obedient to that mute summons, Mr. Oldcraft betook himself upstairs forthwith.

"You dispatched your mission?" enquired the Captain from elbow-chair.

"Fully and completely, sir."

"You bring me a message—a letter, perhaps?"

"Sir, I do," answered Mr. Oldcraft, glancing towards the nearest chair.

"Then," said the Captain, pointedly ignoring this look, "suppose you deliver it?"

"All in due time, sir!" answered Oldcraft, thrusting hand into the breast of his dusty coat and surveying

286

the speaker with narrow eyes half-shut. "But first may I venture to remind you as there was promised a small honorarium, a mere——"

"A bribe, Mr. Oldcraft, of twenty guineas."

"No, Captain, a fee for—value received."

"I promised you twenty guineas to carry me a letter to Viscount Brocklehurst since I knew not where to find him."

"Just so, sir. Well?"

Captain Despard tossed a purse upon the table:

"You will find the specified sum there."

Master Oldcraft, having very deliberately assured himself of this fact, drew forth a letter and gave it to the Captain who broke the seal, glanced at it and nodded towards the door:

"You may now leave me," said he.

Mr. Oldcraft scowled, hesitated, but meeting the Captain's wide stare, clapped on his hat, a little aggressively, squared his shoulders, a little defiantly, but took himself away without a word. Then the Captain read the brief missive, smiled and rang the bell.

"Pray, child," said he to the trim maid who presently appeared in answer, "desire landlord John to step here."

The maid curtseyed and, vanishing, was duly replaced by the stolid John.

"Landlord, you can read, I believe?"

"Ay, sure-ly, sir."

"Then read me this letter—read it aloud."

So John took the letter and, clearing his throat, read forth as follows:

"'I fear no man breathing, least of any yourself. I will meet you to-night, about ten o'clock at the Old Mill. We can settle our business by lantern-light.

'B.'"

"D'ye know the hand, landlord John?"

"No, sir, I don't."

"'Tis letter writ by my lord Viscount Brocklehurst."

" But he be in Lonnon, sure-ly, sir?"

" However, he will be hereabouts to-night. Do you gather the purport—the meaning of this letter?"

" Well, sir, I do and I don't."

" It means his lordship and I are to fight a duel."

" Lord love us——"

"And I will ask you, friend John, to see none gets wind o' this—yourself will be extreme secret. Have I your promise?"

"You have, sir. . . . But, sir—your bad arm?"

"Why, yes," murmured the Captain, glancing down at sling and splint, "'tis probable he counts on this, yet it shall not prevent me killing him, I hope—and believe. But listen, my good John, and pray heed me well! We meet at ten o'clock. Now should I return not—say by midnight, then you will pray send in quest o' me. Should I be dead on the place by sword or bullet why 'tis very well. But—should I have vanished, friend John, then shall you search the Old Mill for me, ay—every nook and corner, you shall drag that ghastly pool, you shall quest amid the underbrush. Should my corpse be found in either place— why then, friend John, you will surely know my murderer, this letter shall be sufficient proof. So this letter you will take charge of and guard carefully."

"Why . . . so I will, sir," answered John, shaking troubled head. "But Lord, it do sound mighty bloody business, your honour."

"And 'twill prove so, I trust," murmured the Captain with his pleasant smile. "And now, friend John, pray have up a bottle of your best and we will crack it socially together."

The wine having duly made its appearance and ushered to the table with the reverent formality such vintage demanded, Captain Despard invited John to be seated, and himself filled the glasses ; quoth he, daintily sipping :

"It does you credit, landlord !'

"Sir," answered solemn John, also sipping, "'tis joy to know such is truly appreciated."

"Also, friend John, you have a cosy house here, very snug and very old, I take it?"

"Ay, sir, 'tis pretty old."

"And consequently," murmured the Captain, "creaks damnably o' nights!"

"Creaks, sir?" repeated John, staring very hard at the wine in his glass. "Do it, sir? Well, old places gets an 'abit—like, d'ye see."

"Also, I've fancied sometimes to hear a whisper of creeping footsteps."

"Futsteps, sir?" repeated John, his gaze still fixed. "Lord, now think o' that!"

"Perchance the old place is haunted, eh, landlord?"

"Well, sir," answered John, ponderously, "I ain't never nowise see nothing o' no ghost myself, but—seeing as the place be so old——" Here, meeting John's stolid gaze at last, the Captain laughed softly.

"Neither have I," said he, "perhaps because I've never troubled to look. Do you credit ghosts?"

"Well, sir, I do and I don't—but I wouldn't go a-nigh th'owd mill arter dark—specially not, arter wot Tom Pitt see there last night."

"The shade of Mr. Julian Gyfford, I believe?"

"That same, sir . . . all afire wi' brimstone and likewise bloody!"

"I'm wondering what should take Pitt there at such hour?"

"I dunno, sir, nor I don't want—Mr. Pitt's a chap as keeps hisself to hisself, which be no loss to nobody, and since he be gone—so much the better, says I."

The bottle being out at last, John bowed himself out also, and straightway hied him along certain narrow passages and up secret stair to small, windowless chamber where one sat writing busily by light of a candle.

"Why—how now, John?"

"Lord love you, Sir Richard, such desprit, bloody business!" quoth John, and placing the letter on the table, recounted the whole matter.

"Hum!" murmured Sir Richard, nibbling the feather of his pen. "And no one to second him! 'Tis most irregular!"

"Why so thinks I, sir."

"And devilish dangerous! This must be looked to, John."

"Ay, so think I, your honour. But the Cap'n's mighty high and determined, and not easy crossed."

"There's evil waiting at the Old Mill to-night, John."

"Sure as we'm born, sir! Ghosts, your honour, phantoms and—worse!"

"Ay, there's death, John! So we must needs find the gentleman a second of sorts, come what may."

"What, sir, d'ye mean as you——?"

"Ay, verily!" nodded Sir Richard, folding up the letter. "So take you this and hold it safe."

"But, sir—your honour, how if you be seen?"

"I must risk it—nay, begone man and let me write —faith, here's a packet, 'tis for Madame the Duchess at the Moat House, John; you'll see it reaches her to-morrow morning by a sure hand."

"Ay I will, sir, but——"

"Then off with you, but warn me the instant Captain Despard sets out to-night."

CHAPTER XXXVII

AND thus it befell that, as the church clock chimed the three quarters, Captain Despard went a-walking. He sauntered across the deserted village green, he paced leisurely along the glimmering high-road, to all seeming a gentleman very much at ease taking the balmy air. But, reaching a certain stile, he paused and glanced about swiftly, keenly, in manner almost furtive.

It was a warm night of a brooding stillness wherein sounds carried far, also, though the moon was not yet risen, the stars made a dusk wherein the eye visioned objects with a strange clarity.

So the Captain stood awhile, motionless and very alert, glancing stealthily about him and listening with straining ears, but saw no movement and heard no sound, all Nature, like the village itself, seemed hushed in kindly sleep. And so, lightly, swiftly, despite injured arm, he vaulted the stile and instantly became, as it were, another man, for now he went at speed, crouched and purposeful, often pausing to listen again and glance about him. Thus came he to a place of bosky thickets where the night lay blacker, beyond which loomed the grim and jagged outline of the Old Mill.

With the same extremity of caution he turned aside amid these thickets and so crept where he might behold this dreary ruin, and that deep, dark, silent pool beyond, and this it was, rather than the mill itself, that held his gaze, that seemed to draw him on, luring his slow, soft-treading feet until he was standing where he might gaze down upon the black and awesome mystery of these silent waters. For some while he stood thus,

utterly motionless, like one rapt and spell-bound, then
—from the inner darkness of the mill stole a faint
rustle of stealthy movement—thither turned he instantly, tense, peering, hand on sword-hilt, waiting,
watching; at last he spoke:

"If you are there, my lord, come out and——"

From the imminent shadows behind him leapt two
dim forms with arms aloft, merciless arms that fell
only to rise again. . . .

Captain Despard reeled blindly, uttered a groan and,
swaying aside, plunged over and down—down into the
black horror, the hungry deeps of that sombre pool.
. . . Upon the bank crouched two who peered at
these waters that swirled, rippled, lapped sleepily and,
growing placid again, showed nothing to mar their
death-like serenity—save bubbles that rose and vanished—rose and vanished. . . .

A long, breathless moment and then, as if by common
consent the watchers turned from the ghastly silence
of that murderous pool and fled in headlong career,
bursting wildly through tangled undergrowth—but, even
while the sound of their flight yet filled the air, these
sullen waters echoed to a second hollow plunge. . . .
Came silence again, a dreadful stillness, then, upon this
deadly hush rose a splashing, a hoarse, distressful
gasping. . . .

And, after some while, above the grassy verge rose
a desperate hand that clutched and clawed until it
had secured firm hold and up—up from these merciless
waters struggled a dripping, gasping shape that dragged
behind it a heavy burden—up and up, painfully,
laboriously, groaning in an agony of effort.

And there, beneath the scowling ruin of the ancient
mill, began a bitter contest between Death and Life,
a battle that raged, grimly unremitting, while the odds
swung back and forth, to and fro, until at last was a
faint sigh, a choking gasp, a groan.

Thus then, outstretched upon mossy turf, battered
and all but drowned, Captain Despard came back to
life and, opening vague eyes, stared up at a pale, glimmering face bent above him, a very strange face whose

draggled, gipsy-seeming hair was oddly bunched upon one ear.

"How are you now?"

"Alive!" gasped the Captain. "Thanks . . . to you."

"The damned villains were too quick for me!"

"Faith," murmured the Captain, stifling a groan, "and me too!" Then, uttering a feeble, croaking chuckle, he raised languid hand to point with wavering finger: "Your wig! . . . your gipsy wig! Take care or . . . you'll lose it . . . my dear Gyfford!"

At this, though still somewhat spent with his recent exertions, Sir Richard contrived to chuckle also as he settled the disguising black curls back into place again.

"Thanks!" said he. "Thanks, my dear Archer."

The Captain drew a deep breath and tried to sit up, but finding this beyond his strength, lay still and closed pain-dimmed eyes.

"So you . . . you know, then?"

"Ay . . . I know."

"Since . . . when?"

"Last night," answered Sir Richard, stooping to wipe blood from the pallid face. "Ha, 'tis ugly blow you took here!"

"Bludgeon work, I think, but . . . my hat and wig saved me—somewhat. . . . And have you—Gyfford, have you told . . . Her?"

"No! . . . But rouse, man, rouse—you're shivering wi' cold—all a-quake!"

"I suppose. . . . 'Tis but to be expected . . . you will tell her, Gyfford?"

"Lord, sir, here's no place for talk! You're perishing with cold and so am I . . . you must to the inn —can you walk?"

"I can . . . try. Yet first, Gyfford, pray suffer me . . . a word. . . . I am, nay, I was 'Captain Archer.' 'Twas but for one year a . . . black year I confess. I was a young fool . . . ensign in Ogleby's . . . debts and the devil, Gyfford, so . . . took to the road. . . . One year! I—I have striven to . . . forget and . . . win back to honour and . . .

CHAPTER XXXVIII

RELATETH A CAPTURE

STOLID John Bly, the sturdy landlord, going by shadowy ways, halted suddenly, set down the unlighted lantern he bore, grasped his heavy, oaken stick more firmly and prepared for instant battle—for there were feet upon the road, slow, heavy-treading feet that stumbled frequently, yet plodded on resolutely nearer and nearer until one appeared who staggered beneath limp and sprawling burden; John stared and, uttering a half-strangled exclamation, stepped from his shady lurking-place.

"God love us . . . Sir Richard!" he gasped.

"So there . . . y'are at last, John?" panted a hoarse voice. "Bear a hand, will ye?"

"Lord . . . the Cap'n! Is 'e dead, sir? Is it murder?"

"Pretty near it . . . Gently now! Have ye . . . got him?"

"Ay, sure–ly, sir . . . Ecod but 'e—feels dead!"

"And heavier than . . . he looks, John. Quick now, get him indoors and to bed. Hot blankets and a compress to the cut in's head, then send for Samson. . . . Did the man Wentzelow come in?"

"Ay, sir, the word was Fallowdene Wood at twelve o'clock."

"Then I shall be late, it seems. . . . Can you manage him alone, John?"

"Lord, yes, your honour. I'll ha' the poor gen'leman snug abed in no time. But, sir, look to yourself. Murder's abroad, sure–ly—ah, and so's Oldcraft and his lads, dannel 'em!"

"Oldcraft? Ha . . . now I wonder!"

"There be my oak baston by the gate yonder, sir,

it should serve ye pretty tidy at a pinch . . . but,
Lord love ye, Sir Richard, go cautious, sir."

"Trust me for that!" answered Sir Richard, catching
up John's heavy staff and twirling it.

"Where'il ye lie to-night, sir?"

"At Weare, most like, for I want word with
Gregory."

"Then good luck to ee, sir! Don't venter across
the green wi' the moon so plaguy bright."

"Ay, 'twere wiser not. And mind, John, you'll send
for Samson at once!"

"I will, your honour."

Then, halting in the shadow of high hedge, Sir
Richard watched sturdy John tramp on, carrying
his burden with a surprising ease—that inert body,
rolling head and dangling legs so horribly suggestive
of death.

And it was with death in his thoughts that he now
turned back amid sombre trees and dense brushwood,
hasting on his trackless way.

He had gone some distance, guiding himself with the
unerring instinct of one long familiar with his sur-
roundings when from adjacent thicket an owl hooted.
Sir Richard stood still to listen and thus, after a moment,
heard the sound again; thereupon he whistled softly
and moved on until he reached a small glade, then a
voice hailed him softly, a hand came out in greeting,
a hairy visage smiled:

"Lord, brother, such din! I hears ye 'alf a mile off,
I does!"

"'Slife, Wentzelow, I'm careless fool. Is Truffeni
hereabout?"

"Under the oak yonder. But you looks dampish,
brother, dampish."

"Faith, 'tis why I'm behind time . . . come and
you shall hear."

In patch of moonlight, perched upon a gnarled root
of the ancient tree sat the old gipsy-woman.

"Ah, Truffeni," sighed he, sinking down wearily
upon the grass at her feet. "Kind friend, good mother,
there's comfort in the mere sight o' thee! . . . Events

move apace . . . devil's work." Here he sneezed, laughed, yet bowed head in hands like one sick to faintness. . . . Then an arm was about him, a cup at his lips, a voice in his ear:

"Drink, my chavo!" So he drank: deep and gratefully; and presently, his sickness passing, he looked up into the wise old eyes above him.

"Truffeni," cried he, starting to his knees, "there's a devil abroad . . . a thing desperate and without mercy—listen, friends!" And, crouched thus between Truffeni, the wise, and Wentzelow, the hairy, he spoke them briefly and to the point, nor did either utter word until this narration was ended; then quoth Wentzelow:

"And be the gen'leman dead, brother?"

"God knoweth—he fell swooning on the road.'

"Here," sighed Truffeni, "here is the bloody dukkipen I foretold him! Ay, and here shall be more blood unless —bend nearer—close, closer!" Then Truffeni began to whisper, quick-speaking and very softly; suddenly Wentzelow slapped hand on thigh and chuckled, while Sir Richard nodded and smiled grimly.

"And yet," said he, frowning thoughtful at the full-orbed moon, "there is ever a possibility I may be taken —how then, good mother?"

"Thou must not be taken, my chavo—no, no, 'twere to ruin all. Thou shalt come wi' us this night and sleep secure."

"Nay, Truffeni, rather must I watch—for though I lay secure, sleep I could not—knowing what I know. And the threat to my lady groweth hourly and I must be at hand. And now God bless thee, Truffeni, noble friend!"

So saying he arose and stood looking round about him on these darkling woods, their gloom pierced, here and there, by shafts of vivid moonlight.

"Fallowdene Wood!" he murmured. "'Twas here I played as boy. . . . 'Twas here Julian died."

"And for sufficient reason, my chavo! For evil begetteth evil, the harvest is reaped—soon or late! But now for thyself, be guided and go along wi' us— lie safe this night——"

"Nay," he answered, "good faith, 'tis but one more night—one day longer, Fortune should hold my friend till then!"

So saying, he waved his hand, turned and strode away, but glancing back, saw old Truffeni gazing after him with troubled eyes.

And now, having much to think upon, he went at leisured pace, sometimes pausing to gaze upon the luminous heaven or down upon the shadowy earth, lost in uneasy speculation of what the pregnant future should bring forth. . . . Another twenty-four hours and, if all went as planned, his innocence would be established, his honour vindicated. . . . And what then? She had doubted him, deep in her heart she doubted still. Well, in few short hours he would come back in triumph, her unworthy suspicions, her cruel doubts should be trampled underfoot. . . . And what then? Believing him blood-guilty wretch she had yet dared to protest herself his friend! Well, to the devil with such friendship! Better downright enmity a thousand times than endure such pitiful, doubting friendship. . . . So then, once he had proved his innocence beyond all chance of cavil, he would turn his back upon the world —shut himself up and devote his days to the regeneration of Weare, his tenantry and himself. Here he sighed, for somehow the prospect seemed strangely forlorn and desolate. . . .

He halted of a sudden, shivering violently for a chilly breath seemed all about him, deadly cold yet intensely vital. . . . What was it, in the name of God? He stared wide-eyed towards heaven and saw but the radiant sky, he looked to earth and found he stood upon a broad familiar path, dim yet dreadful to memory; for it was by this path Julian had walked to his death; this tree that loomed above him—it was here Julian had fallen writhing in mortal agony, to gasp his life away with urgent message but half spoken. A place of horror at such hour as this, and cold—cold with this dreadful, clammy chill that yet was so terribly vital, that somehow suggested Julian's very self—a presence growing ever more vividly alive until every

tree and bush, every leaf and twig became things hatefully intimate, giving forth an emanation that, moment
by moment, seemed to sap his manhood, his strength,
his very life. For this tree had pillowed Julian's dying
head, had drunk his life-blood . . . these leaves had
felt his last, gasping sigh. . . . Could Julian be here
then . . . the death-in-life—and trying to tell him
something, striving desperately to make him understand? Was it a challenge? Was it a mockery? Was
it a warning? Sir Richard stood appalled, striving to
hold fast his slipping reason; with sweating hands fast
clenched, with breath whistling through distended
nostrils, rigid stood he while Reason tottered. . . .
Could it indeed be that dead Julian's undying spirit
was here, close beside him, struggling thus fiercely
to send him some message beyond mere, mortal
comprehension? Slowly Sir Richard looked about him,
viewing all objects with quivering apprehension. . . .
Yonder dense-growing bush . . . it was beyond that
very bush the murderer must have crouched.

Suddenly as he gazed this bush was stirred gently
. . . leaves rustled behind him and, whirling about,
Sir Richard saw a vague face, caught at shadowy arm,
missed, staggered, was smitten to his knees, sank under
a hail of blows—to be trampled, buffeted inert and so,
dragged most unheroically away.

CHAPTER XXXIX

WHICH RELATETH YET ANOTHER CAPTURE

THE day being young, birds were carolling blithely as Helen stepped forth into the fragrant morning. For my lady's sleep, though profound, had been anything but dreamless; all night long she had been haunted of a face, somewhat vague, whose cheek bore a smear of blood, yet whose shapely mouth smiled, a little grimly to be sure, though the eyes (ah, these eyes!) deep-set, well-opened, held a look of such adoration as is, perhaps, seen only in dreams, and then, alas, but seldom! . . . There had been a chin to this dream face also, square and strong, whose self-confident jut reminded her of another chin, also square and strong—indeed it was this chin that had been the leading cause of so much after-effect, for, rousing from her dream, my lady had sat up in bed, broad awake on the instant, exclaiming to the nearest bed-curtain:

" Oh, good lack—how blind a fool am I!"

Having pondered which amazing fact awhile, she had leapt from bed, dressed in haste and now, despite the so early hour, here she was—out in the dewy morning . . . since gardeners, jobbing and otherwise, are all of them early risers, or should be.

And now, haunted thus by memory of this extremely odd odd-man, his features, in especial his eyes (ah, those truthful, tell-tale eyes!), and having debt of gratitude to speak forth, she made her way towards the kitchen-garden, his usual haunt, but found it empty desolation —this particular gardener rose late, it seemed. Well, so much the worse for him! Pensive, my lady rambled amid fruit and herb and vegetable, essayed an unripe gooseberry and, wry-faced, promptly ejected it, bit into an apple, shuddered and dropped it, and, finding herself thus beforehand with Nature, betook herself into the paddock, and so to the stables, whence issued a loud and intermittent hissing where George, of the heroic whiskers, novel adornments in clean-shaven age, was performing the Witch's morning toilette; but, becoming aware of my lady, he hissed no more, blushed instead, pulled his fore-lock and made a leg.

"Good morning, George!" said she, smiling gaily. "Have you seen the gardener this morning—the odd man?"

"Du 'ee mean Daffy Dick, my lady?"

"No!" she answered, in such voice that poor George jumped and dropped the curry-comb, whereat my lady actually giggled: "Nay, George," smiled she, "I mean the man Fullalove," then repeated to herself slowly and very softly: "Full . . . o' . . . love."

"Which that be 'im, my lady," quoth George, "me an' ol' Ben allus calls un Daffy Dick."

"Oh, do you—and why?"

"Becos 'e be a numps, ma'm, a poor half-witted chap, a nat'ral born fool."

"Oh?" said she again, fair cheek dimpling. "How long have you known him, George?"

"Only since he come to the 'ouse, ma'm."

"How came he here?"

"Which ol' Ben fetched 'e along one afternoon."

"Where is Ben?"

"A boltin' of 'is breakfus', ma'm."

"I beant, Jarge, no I beant," cried Ben, popping suddenly into view. "'Ere I be, my leddy, merry as any grig, ma'm, and wot's your leddyship's will o' me?"

"'Tis about the odd-man Fullalove, is he here, Ben?"

"Ay, ma'm, 'long of 'is cabbages, or should be."

"Well, he is not."

"The lazy wastrel! Do 'ee want 'im my leddy?"

"I wish to—thank him, Ben."

"Oh, ma'm? For wot?"

"Saving me from two wicked villains last night."

Here while old Ben stared aghast, and George agape, absent-mindedly performed upon his whiskers with

the curry-comb, my lady described last night's terri-
fying adventure.

"Lordy!" gasped old Ben. "Lord save's all! An'
'twere Daffy Dick, says you, as driv 'em off! And
'im no better nor a looby, a poor doddlish ninny-
cumpup!"

"But—is he, Ben?"

"Well—ain't 'e, ma'm? The way as 'e goggles!"

"How did you find him, and where?"

"Well, 'twere the mare—ay, 'twere the Witch as
brought us 'quainted-like, for, daffy soft or no, Dick's
got a way wi' 'osses—ah, pretty nigh as good as me!
And then, ecod, ma'm, 'e ups and clouts that theer
Oldcraft, arter which I took a likin' for the lad, and
'im lackin' a job and us needin' a odd man I brought
'e along."

"And, my aunt engaged him?"

"She did, my leddy, on the spot, and afore I could
say a word for 'e tu."

"Well, when he comes, pray tell him I desire a word
with him, Ben."

"Why so I will, ma'm, sure-ly."

Slowly and thoughtfully Helen retraced her steps,
but finding no sign of the familiar figure she sought,
wandered slowly and thoughtfully into the house, picked
up the latest volume of the *Tatler*, opened it, shut it,
and tossing it aside, wandered upstairs.

And now since dreams, it would seem, held so much
more than barren wakefulness, she determined to
dream again. So to bed she returned, and, falling
asleep, dreamed herself fleeing, very inadequately
attired, from hordes of gaping and relentless pursuers
. . . and awoke in a tangle of bed-clothes; and, being
heartily glad to find herself thus awake, smiled at poor,
woeful Betty, who chanced to be leaning above her
tumbled pillow.

"Oh, ma'm," she twittered. "I . . . oh, I had to
wake your ladyship, you did so moan, ma'm, so sigh
and tremble, ma'm, and toss, my lady."

"And small wonder, child—such horrors! For I that
do seldom dream dreamed wondrously last night, but,

striving to dream again, dreamed fantastical and indecorous folly. Pray, what's the hour?"

"Past three o'clock, ma'm."

"Heavens—'tis no wonder I starve! Come, dress me. Gemini, I famish!"

"There's a chicken, cold, a-waiting you below, ma'm."

"Then hurry for I'm ravenous as a plough-boy! Oh, alack, I'm distressingly human. And whiles I eat, I'll speak with the gardener of the new privet hedge, so bid him to me."

"Do ee mean Dick, my lady, the poor——"

"I mean the odd man, girl."

"But, ma'm, he's away—I mean he never come a-nigh the place this day."

"Oh!" said my lady musingly.

"But my lord's been—twice, my lady. Asking for you he was, but I dusn't wake your ladyship."

"You mean the Marquis?"

"No, my lady, he's out riding along o' Mistress Angela, and oh, ma'm, both so doting and lovesome! No, I mean the Viscount, ma'm.'

"Oh—him!" quoth Helen, frowning.

"He said he'd wait on you again, ma'm."

"Did he forsooth? Then go and tell aunt I'd speak with her."

"She's out likewise, ma'm—went a-driving in the chariot, she did, so soon as she'd read the letter."

"What letter?"

"One as was brought by Mr. Bly, ma'm—John, the landlord, my lady."

So presently Helen descended to her solitary meal, and had scarcely made an end than she espied a gleam of blue and silver beyond the open window and saw Viscount Brocklehurst was bowing his salutations.

"Ah—at last!" said he in quick, sighful reproach. "May I step in?"

"Nay," she answered rising. "I will step out."

But now as they paced the lawn together, though he uttered no word, she yet sensed in him such fevered agitation, such quivering repression that instinctively she drew away somewhat, viewing him with her clear

serene gaze; his restless hands, his pale face agleam
between the dark curls of his long peruke, features so
pale, so strangely worn and haggard that she spoke
on impulse:

"You are sick—ill, Viscount?"

"No!" he answered, turning upon her with quick
start. "No—and yet, in my mind yes—yes I am!
For the hour is big with good or ill for me, my—my
fate hangs i' the balance! Shall it lift me to heaven
or sink me to hell and black despair? Oh, Helen, 'tis
now—'tis now! My happiness, my future, my very
life is in thy hands."

"Oh, lud, sir——" she began, then caught her breath
for in that moment he was on his knees before her, a
wild, pitiful creature looking up at her with fearful
eyes, grasping at her with supplicating hands, crying
on her in breathless entreaty:

"Helen! Helen! You can give me life . . . or cast
me for death! Helen, be merciful!"

"Nay but—how, how?" she questioned. "What
seek you of me——?"

"Thyself . . . come with me . . . trust me—
marry me!"

Instinctively she recoiled, and then he was on his
feet and stood a moment, face hidden in his hands;
then he was smiling at her, but with pallid lips a-quiver
and the same fearful eyes, yet now his voice was gentle:

"Am I sudden? Seem I so, indeed? Yet dost know
I dote on thee. Think, madam, think on this and be
kind—a cruel Fate compels me suddenly hence—hence
for good and all, I must away. But thou, Helen,
thou'rt part o' me, thou'rt the very best o' me, thou'rt
in my blood—then how may I leave thee? I'd peril
my very soul for thee—thou'rt my love, adored beyond
life, beyond all fame and honour—then how may I go
and leave thee behind? Wed me, Helen, wed me and
I'll be thy slave! Come with me and I'll be a god
defying all——"

"Sir," cried she with imperious gesture. "Oh, my
lord, say no more, I beg, 'tis but pain to you and my
distress—for my answer you know already in your

heart . . . now as you have ever known. And thus
I pray you, with no more said, suffer that I bid you
farewell with kindest wishes for your future, wheresoever
it be, and prayers for your happiness."

"Future?" he murmured. "Happiness? Oh mockery
—for these you deny me! You . . . you would banish me . . . banish me to the outer dark. . . ."

"No, no, my lord, not I—pray heaven not I!"

"Yet you give me 'no'?"

"Because I cannot give you other."

"So then," cried he, in the same husky murmur,
"all . . . all's in vain! My schemes, my hopes . . .
all I have done, all I have endured . . . you would
make these all . . . all in vain! You . . . you
would plunge me to the very deeps of hell."

"Nay, sir," cried she, in swift indignation, "be you
more generous——"

"Generous? Why, Helen, I would give thee all I
am and hope to be, pledge thee my soul and body——"

"Ay," she retorted, "so much, my lord, to come at
your own selfish, so passionate desire!"

"Because I am but man and love you, and the love
of man for woman is, and ever must be, selfish."

"Yet, sir, I do dream of other nobler love and more
worthy!"

"Then 'tis dream you ne'er shall realise!"

"Then will I wed no man. And so, my lord, let us
speak o' this no more."

Viscount Brocklehurst drew a deep breath and
stood with haggard gaze bent earthward, while his
restless fingers fidgeted and fidgeted with his cane.

"In . . . in but a few hours," said he, at last, "a
few short hours, Helen, I . . I shall be far hence.
Madam . . . may I hope—venture to beg that your
kind thoughts may journey with me awhile?"

"Indeed you know they shall," she answered, giving
him her hand, "such thoughts, Viscount, as, if they
might, should banish all thy care, guard thee from
ill and teach thee happiness at last."

Mutely he bowed and very tenderly raised the warm,
soft fingers he held and touched them to cold lips.

"And so . . . farewell to Hope!" sighed he. "Wilt give me one o' thy so cherished roses, Helen, to bear with me for thy sake?"

So she brought him where the roses bloomed filling the warm air with their languorous sweetness, and bade him choose which he would have.

"Nay," he answered, glancing about him sombre-eyed, "choose thou, I . . . I shall cherish it the more."

Smiling, she plucked and gave him a scarlet, opening bud, and he stood awhile twisting it in nervous fingers.

"'Tis fair garden, this!" sighed he, turning to be gone. "I shall dream on't full oft. . . . You'll lack for one to tend it now t'other poor rogue is gone, and yet——"

"Gone, sir?" she repeated, opening lovely eyes. "Who? Pray what do you mean, Viscount?"

"Why, that he's taken—for some matter of poaching or smuggling or some such. But sure you've heard?"

"I've heard nothing. Pray who is taken?"

"Why, the gardener worked here . . . called himself, I think—Fullolove, though 'tis full of aches and pains he is at this moment, I judge him, poor wretch!"

And when they had walked some yards Helen spoke again, her voice serene as her look:

"Tell me all you know of . . . this poor wretch?"

"Well, he struggled with his captors, it seems, and took some scathe in consequence."

"Ah, you mean he lies hurt . . . wounded?"

"Somewhat. But, Gad, madam, such distress!" exclaimed the Viscount arching his eye-brows. "The poor rogue's humble welfare would seem to interest you—strangely!"

"Being one o' my servants, sir, no one—not even the law touches him unchallenged. I must see into this. Where is he?"

"I saw him lying by the heels at a little inn, a mere hedge-tavern hard beside the Long Man of Wilmington."

"You saw him?"

"The fellow Oldcraft showed me the pitiful wretch."

"Then will I see him also!" said she and set off towards the house.

"Aha!" sighed the Viscount. "'Tis a rarely fortunate rogue he to find such potent champion as thyself, Helen. You may soften even the rigours of the law, your rank and proud beauty do more for him than advocate most eloquent. Good fortune attend thee, Helen, and so farewell, my chaise waits and—alas, I must be gone."

"Stay, sir," cried she. "You know where he lies, you shall carry me thither if you will, Viscount."

"Ah, Helen, 'twould be purest joy to serve you, but——"

"Nay—wait, sir!" she commanded. "I do but stay to cloak me and leave word for my aunt, wait I beg!" And away sped Helen, forthwith, while the Viscount stood, sombre gaze bent earthwards again, twisting and twirling the rose in his ever-restless fingers; suddenly he uttered a stifled exclamation and, dropping the flower, stared at the slow-welling blood where a thorn had pricked him, and very deliberately set his heel upon the offending rose, crushing it deep into the sod—then looked up smiling as Helen reappeared, flushed, bright-eyed and so alluring in her glowing beauty that he drew a breath of stealthy rapture. . . .

Then side by side they hurried across the lawn and so, presently were gone; and nothing to mark their passing save the broken petals of a crushed and fading rose.

CHAPTER XL

CONCERNETH ITSELF WITH TWO CAPTIVES

THE ceaseless grind of rapidly-spinning wheels, the throbbing rhythm of swift-galloping hoofs—trees and hedges that flitted by to vanish in swirling dust-cloud; but Helen, swaying easily to the motion of the fast-travelling chaise, and lost in anxious thought, sat heedless of it all until—Viscount Brocklehurst laughed softly.

Roused by this sudden and most unexpected sound, she started from her reverie, and for the first time troubled to glance where he sat huddled in opposite corner, staring out of the window.

"Heavens, Viscount!" she exclaimed. "How you startle one!"

"Pray forgive me!" he murmured and, though his voice was so gentle, something in his air as he lolled thus, head persistently turned away, woke in her a vague disquiet; therefore she questioned him further.

"But—why must you laugh?"

"Because," he replied, still without glancing round, "being merest human I manifest my joy in human fashion."

"And where's your cause for joy, pray?"

"Are we not—together?"

"Have we much farther to go, sir?"

"Nay, we shall be there—all too soon."

"What is the name of this inn?"

"The ' Traveller's Joy.' "

"We have come a long way, surely?"

"I grieve it should seem so."

"Indeed, but 'tis farther than I thought."

"Oh, content thee," he sighed, "shalt see thy—thy Fullolove very soon." And still he lounged there,

"why force me thus to play the tyrant with thee—I—
that would be thy poor slave . . . live but to do thy
will—I that worship thee and ever shall. Oh, Helen!"

The chaise lurched violently and swung away from
the road towards a small, dismal building with a weather-
beaten sign above the door with the faded legend:

THE TRAVELLER'S JOY

by

JOB TUCKER

Before this gloomy "Joy" the chaise now jerked to
sudden stop, whereupon down from rumble clambered
two unlovely fellows whose growling speech and rough
garments smacked of ships and the sea.

"Wot's the word, your honour?" enquired one of
them, as they posted themselves on either side of the
chaise door.

"Summon Oldcraft!" cried the Viscount, but almost
as he was named, Master Oldcraft stepped forth of
the dingy tavern, smiling, bowing and rubbing his
hands.

"All's right, my lord!" quoth he. "I shall not
waste your lordship's or your lady's precious time—
not a moment! my lads are a-bringing him now," and
turning about, he whistled shrilly; at which summon
rose a clatter of horse-hoofs and from behind the tavern
his two fellows appeared, leading a horse whereon a
man was fast tied, a gipsy-seeming fellow who drooped
and swayed oddly with every motion of the horse.

"Bring him along, Bob, hurry, my lad, here's quality
to see the villain. So—that'll do! Now, turn up his
rogue's face, Tom!"

A square face and comely despite its pallor and the
blood which smeared cheek and brow.

"Oh . . . Gracious God!" gasped my lady, leaning out from the chaise-window. "Oh . . . 'tis
Richard!"

"Gyfford, lady?" enquired Master Oldcraft, gently.

"Yes . . ! yes. . . ! Oh, let me out!" And she
strove desperately to open the chaise door.

"And there's your identification!" said the Viscount. "Take him away."

"No!" cried my lady wildly. "Richard! Oh, Richard! what have they done to thee?"

The bloody head was slowly lifted, into the dulled eyes came a gleam of recognition, the powerful body writhed in its bonds.

"Oh . . . dear . . . dear Richard!"

The pallid lips smiled faintly, the battered head shook itself feebly and a hoarse voice whispered:

"Dick . . . always and ever . . . Dick full-o'-love for thee!"

"Away—take him away!" cried the Viscount, impatiently. "And up with you, Skag—up I say. Tell 'em to whip—and spur, I'd be at Barling Gap by sunset, the sooner we're at sea, the better."

"Plenty o' time, my lord," said Oldcraft, watching his battered prisoner led away, "so wait a bit, my lord."

"No, no, not a moment. You've got your man."

"Ay, I've got him safe enough!"

"Then we're quits so far."

"So far, my lord."

"Then, what, man, what is it?"

"Only this, my lord!" answered Oldcraft, showing a crumpled piece of paper. "Here's strange mention o' your lordship's name!"

"Eh, mine—mine, d'ye say?" cried the Viscount, reaching out imperious hand.

"Well, my lord, your lordship's name is wrote down here, though what a plague it all means——"

"The devil! Give it, man—give it to me!"

So the Viscount snatched this paper, scanned the message it bore, uttered a gasping exclamation of triumph, and was out of the chaise calling for saddle-horses, all in a moment.

"Who . . . how . . . where did ye get it?" cried he, flourishing the paper in Oldcraft's startled face.

"An old woman, my lord, a gipsy hag—creeping around here she was, sir, trying to come at my prisoner.

L

Ay, she was so! But I took her, my lord, and found this said paper on her, though what it means——"

"Aha!" cried the Viscount, with strange, shrill laugh, "have ye heard . . . have ye ever heard tell o' the Sword of Damocles?" Here, crumpling the paper in nervous hand, he laughed again, and so very strangely that Master Oldcraft backed away, staring.

"Horses!" cried the Viscount, turning away. "Horses d'ye hear—you, Skag—you will ride with me."

And now came Job Tucker, the landlord, a leering, bow-legged man, leading two saddle horses upon the nearest of which the Viscount was mounting when Master Oldcraft ventured to touch his arm:

"Where away, my lord?"

"The devil, man—that's my business!"

"Ay, but what o' your lady, my lord?"

The Viscount started and glanced towards the chaise.

"Look to her!" cried he, setting foot in stirrup, "keep her fast till I return."

"Not me, my lord, I must to Lewes wi' my prisoner."

The Viscount cursed pettishly and beckoned to the landlord.

"Have ye a place where my lady may lie secure, Tucker—secure, d'ye hear?"

The man leered towards the chaise and nodded:

"There be sich things as keys an' bolts, my lord, and me an' my man Sam. She'll be safe enough, I warrant me!"

Loosing his horse, the Viscount wrenched open the chaise-door.

"Come, my lady!" said he, and held out his hand, but Helen never moved. "Madam, pray trouble yourself to descend—this instant!" Helen never so much as glanced towards him. "Out—out with ye," he cried in sudden, wild fury. "Out, I say, or these men shall drag thee forth—ha, must they handle thee, madam?"

Avoiding the hand outstretched to her, my lady stepped from the chaise, and immediately, at gesture from the Viscount, was whirled up in powerful arms and borne into the dingy tavern, and thus, dumbly submissive with shame and terror, was carried upstairs and locked securely into a small and dingy chamber.

"Look to her, now!" cried the Viscount, pocketing the key. "Look well to her, Tucker, man, let me find her safe when I return or, by my soul, I'll be the death o' some of you."

So saying, he hurried downstairs, to find Jonas Skag already on horseback.

"Are you armed?" cried he.

"Sure-ly, my lord."

Then Viscount Brocklehurst swung to saddle and, calling on Skag to follow, galloped furiously away.

CHAPTER XLI

"MAKE a mock o' Titus, is it—ye dog? Clap me
i' the stocks would ye—ye murderous villain?"

They had stopped for refreshment at a little ale-
house, that is—Master Oldcraft and his comrades, Bob
and Tom, gulped their ale while their wretched prisoner
drooped quiescent in his bonds; indeed so still and
silent was he that Master Oldcraft sought to rouse
him with dexterous flick of his horse-whip.

"So—you'd try to play off your devil's tricks on
Titus—hey?" And again the whip cracked but still
the captive stirred not nor spoke.

"'E don't 'ear ye, Titus," quoth Bob.

"The villain's a-swounding, Titus," said Tom.

"Then heave yon bucket o' water over him!" said
Master Oldcraft, raising tankard to lip, while Bob
caught up the bucket forthwith and deluged the hapless
wretch. . . .

A gasp . . . a groan . . . and opening swooning
eyes, Sir Richard stared into the merciless, smiling
visage of Titus Oldcraft, glanced round about him on
the desolate country-side, and shivered.

"Sir," quoth Master Oldcraft, saluting him with
hat a-flourish in mockery. "You robbed me once—
me, Titus! Ay, you did so—d'ye mind it, sir? You
set Titus in the stocks! Ay, you did so—ye can't
ha' forgot, sir? Well, sir, Titus is a-going to set your
fine-gentlemanly neck in a noose, pretty soon, sir.
Ah, Titus is a-going to watch ye kick your fine-gentlemanly life out. Tit, Sir Richard, for tat, sir—tit for
tat is the motter for Titus. And now, sir, if you're
quite ready, we'll get a-moving."

Watched by awed landlord and one or two gaping rustics Master Oldcraft and his fellows got to horse and trotted off, their silent prisoner jolting helpless in their midst.

Evening was near—the wooded uplands stood dark against the sunset's ruddy flame, a vivid, far-flung splendour touching all things with a strange glory; it filled the narrow, winding road, the very dust glowed pink—it burned on the tree-bole, branch and twig, and threw up the sombre figure of the small neat gentleman in black and silver who stood beside the way, his arms folded and head bent like some philosopher lost in profound abstraction of thought.

"We shall be in afore the light fails us," said Mr. Old-craft, turning to feed gloating eyes upon his prisoner.

"And with your man, too!" chuckled Bob.

"Ay—with my man, Bob. When I go arter a man I get a man. Titus don't fail."

"Lookee yonder!" quoth Tom, pointing suddenly, "Wot's to do? Oo's 'im? See there!"

Now even as he spoke and pointed, the small, sober-clad gentleman paced slowly to the middle of the road and, halting there, stood with arms still folded, watching their approach beneath the shadow of his neat, three-cornered hat.

"Rum!" quoth Bob. "Wot's the lay, I wonder?"

"Out o' the road there!" cried Oldcraft, imperiously.

The stranger neither moved nor spoke, but stood there, arms crossed, booted legs firm planted, head bent, peering at them as they came.

"Ride the fool down!" cried Oldcraft, and spurred his animal to faster pace and then, as suddenly, reined in again, for the small, slim gentleman, uncrossing his arms, showed two purposeful hands, each of which grasped a levelled pistol.

"Eh! . . . damme, what's this?" demanded Old-craft, blenching. "We're officers o' the law . . . what d'ye want?"

"Your barkers—your pops, all of 'em!" answered the stranger, head still lowered. "Throw me your pistols—here, to my feet—quick, ye dogs!"

A moment's gaping dismay . . . the stranger took a slow pace forward, eyes glaring behind those unwavering muzzles . . . and then four pistols clattered into the dust.

"Now, dismount—all of ye, ye dogs!"

"Why . . . what more?" quavered Oldcraft, staring at this ominous figure with growing apprehension. "We . . . we are officers o' the——"

"Dismount! Down—ye dogs!"

Speechless and scrambling they alighted, all three.

"D'ye know me, Titus?"

"No . . .! But I guess you're the . . . Galloping Parson. . . ."

"That same. And shoot to kill. Now, tell your fellow-rogues to be gone."

"Eh—go, sir?" cried Bob eagerly. "Can us go, sir?"

"This moment or I'll drop ye."

Staying for no more, Bob and Tom turned about and incontinent, made off down the road.

"Oldcraft—look on me! I am Robin Leroy, the son o' that bright saint you and Jonathan Wild murdered—hanged him innocent, ye did, for the price of his blood——"

"No!" cried Oldcraft, in hoarse, pleading accents. "No—not me, sir—'twas never my work, not me on my oath! Jonathan maybe, but—not me——"

"Eight o' ye were concerned and six o' these are dead, and 'tis now your turn, and presently—Wild. . . ."

"Lord. . . . Lord God . . ." gasped Oldcraft, "y'never mean——"

"Titus, can ye pray?"

"No—no . . .! But, sir, you—you'd never murder me—you wouldn't——"

"If ye can't pray, I'll pray for ye. On your knees, Titus!"

Shivering, sweating, abject in his terror, Oldcraft fell to desperate pleading, but his frantic supplications were drowned in shrill laughter as, leaping with upwhirled pistol, Robin Leroy smote him to his knees.

"Titus, I'll count ten. Pray or—go without."

Then Oldcraft crouched, bowed his head, yet, with motion incredibly quick, snatched weapon from his breast and fired, but—like an echo to this shot came a second, and, without word or cry, Titus Oldcraft sank face downward in the dust and lay out-sprawling at the feet of his slayer.

Dropping his pistols, Robin Leroy slowly lifted hands and eyes to the radiant sunset.

"Lord," he murmured. "Oh, God of Justice, I beseech Thee . . . show mercy on . . . this evil rogue so lately dead, and give . . . I pray . . . kind welcome to the soul of him . . . now winging up to Thee." Thus stood he a long moment, hands reached yearningly aloft, his pale, lined face serene and glorified —then, as if racked by sudden spasm, his features grew convulsed, his fingers clenched and he crouched swiftly above the inanimate thing asprawl in the dust.

"Aha, Cain—so, there y'are?" he cried. "Ye'll shame and hang no more o' the guilty or innocent, ye dog! But Cain was marked i' the brow—so ho, come let's set Cain's mark on ye!" With fumbling hand he drew forth a pen-knife, opened it and, stooping lower, turned up that dead face. . . .

"Oh—for God's sake——"

Robin Leroy arose, dusted his knees, coughed suddenly and pressed a handkerchief to his mouth; then, walking with odd, mincing steps came to Sir Richard and cut him free of those cruel, galling bonds that bound him to the saddle.

Sir Richard slipped to earth, staggered and, sitting down, began to rub and chafe at his numbed limbs, staring the while into the eyes that stared back at him. . . .

"My horse . . . yonder——" the words ended in another fit of coughing. So Sir Richard, having found the horse tethered amid the thickets hard by, led it into the road and lifted the wounded man into the saddle, who, smiling down on him, fumbled in his breast and drew thence a small, silver-mounted pistol.

"Little Joseph!" he whispered. "Take it, friend, I don't need it. I shall never . . . die . . . in a noose!"

Smiling still, the stricken man nodded, coughed, and gathering the reins in failing grasp, ambled away towards the splendour of the sunset, and Sir Richard gazing after him, knew that, come what might, the Galloping Parson would indeed never die by rope and gallows.

CHAPTER XLII

"Fifteen golden guineas, Sam!"

"Lord, Mus' Tucker, a mort o' money it be!"

"Purty fair, purty fair!" nodded Job Tucker, giving a swirl to the ale in the mug.

"And a roight, proper gen'leman 'e be—eh?"

"For sure, Sam. Ain't 'e a lord and a vi-count?"

"Well, mates," growled their companion, cocking a weather-eye round about. "I be wishing as 'e were back again, 'tis glad I'll be to 'ave 'em safe aboard."

"But wheer's your 'urry, friend—tide don't serve till ten to-night."

"Ay, I know, but——"

"Lemme draw ye some ale."

"Avast, I fancy I 'ear summat! Belay now and listen!"

"What, d'ye mean the lady? Knockin' again, is she?"

"No, on the road—listen!"

A faint, rhythmic sound, now lost, now heard again . . . growing louder . . . fading away . . . swelling louder than ever.

"'Tis 'im at last!" cried the landlord. "Aha, and riding like a wild man, too! Better get them 'osses to the chaise, Sam!"

"'E sure du sound in mighty 'urry!"

"Ay, crowdin' every stitch o' sail, mates."

"And no wonder wi' such a 'andsome creeter waiting. Ecod, I never see a finer young woman."

"Though turble fiery, Mus' Tucker!"

"Well, being a man o' sperrit, I likes 'em fiery. She's a prime piece, Sam—ecod, wot eyes! Wot a shape —wot a——"

"Stand by, mates, the Vi-count's a-coming yonder."

"Ay, there 'e be!" cried Sam, pointing. "Lord, 'ow 'e du ride!"

"Ay, but," quoth the landlord, rising—"'e's coming from the wrong d'rection."

"Well, 'tis no wonder," cried Sam, "yon beant the Vi-count, Mus' Tucker!"

"Why then oo is 'e, Sam? I seems to know summat about—why dannel me, wheer's 'e a-coming to——"

For now, as they watched this rapidly approaching horseman he swerved from the road and, without checking his wild career, came galloping straight at them.

"In—in wi' ye," cried the landlord. "Jump, lads, jump!" and turning, all three, they tumbled into the taproom, pell-mell, but when they would have shut the door—there up-rearing was a foam-flecked horse with mighty hoofs lashing above the very threshold. Then his rider was out of the saddle and next moment the little dingy taproom, the inn itself rang and echoed with the sounds of furious combat, a wild uproar that waxed, waned and, suddenly subsiding, gave place to a portentous silence broken only by a voice that groaned and a voice that gasped.

"If only them white-livered dogs, 'adn't run and left me!" wailed the groaning voice.

"Where . . . is . . . she?" demanded the gasping voice.

"Aloft, mate. And if only them lubberly dogs 'ad stood by me——"

"Look . . . at this!" panted Sir Richard, showing a small, silver-mounted pistol. "Lie where . . . you are, or——"

"Lord love ye, mate—I don't want to move. I'm a lamb! But if them lily-livered dogs——"

But Sir Richard was off, stumbling up the dark and narrow stair.

"Helen!" he called, and was answered by a cry so wildly glad and eager that he thought very piteous to hear from any woman's lips and most especially—these.

"Richard. . . . Oh, Richard, pray—Oh pray come to me . . . they've locked me in. . . . Oh, Richard——"

"Then pray, ma'm, stand from the door and I'll endeavour to come at you." So saying, he backed away and hurled himself against the door, foot foremost, yet thrice thus he battered the stout oak ere it swung wide. . . . And then—almost before he knew it, she was in his arms, laughing and sobbing, shivering and clinging to him in a very passion of thankfulness.

"Hold me, Richard!" wailed she, in small, pleading voice. "Hold me fast, fast—hurt me, for Oh, Richard, alas I am but the merest craven, after all!"

"Faith, ma'm, I'll never believe it!" And though his tone was quite ordinary the expression of his battered face belied it. (And his eyes!)

"'Tis true, 'tis true!" she moaned, and clasped him the tighter, and before he could prevent himself he was stroking this lovely head that pillowed itself upon his ragged coat with such unwonted and most delightful humility.

"Oh, Dick," she sighed. "Oh, Dick Full-o'-love, thou'rt very damp!"

"A bucket of water!" he explained.

"And thou'rt a very dusty Dick!"

"S'bud, yes, ma'm, I shall spoil thy finery."

"Then prithee, spoil it! And not 'ma'm,' Richard! And thy heart beateth very fast, Dick!"

"I . . . I've been . . . busy!"

"Indeed I heard you—'twas like thunders and earthquakes."

"Come . . . shall we go?"

"Ay—but whither?"

"To the Moat House."

"No, no, 'twere madness!" And here, her hands stole up to creep and clasp themselves about his neck. "You would be seen and—if they took thee again!"

"'Twill nothing matter. For to-night, Helen, if all go well I——"

A hoarse voice bellowed loudly from the road.

"Oh, God pity me!" gasped Helen. "They are back . . . they are here again . . . the Viscount."

"Eh—Brocklehurst? God forbid! Come, let us go look!"

Hand clasping hand they crept from the room, and so to the front of the tavern whence they might peep down at the road.

A horse cropped the grass before the inn, while immediately below the lattice, wherefrom they peeped, stood the tall, unlovely figure of Jonas Skag.

Sir Richard peered down, measured the distance with his eye and, squeezing through the casement, had vanished before Helen might stay him. She heard a hoarse cry, and, looking down, beheld two forms that writhed and twisted. . . . Shrinking from the lattice she covered her face, and in that same moment heard a cheery voice calling her name; so she fled from the room and down the stair out into the soft twilight.

"Richard . . . ah, how could you?" she wailed.

"We needed the fellow's horse," he explained, "the poor beast I rode is well-nigh foundered." So saying, he swung to saddle and reached her his hand.

"Up with you, child—your foot on my toe—now!"

Mutely she obeyed and next moment was seated before him in the crook of his bridle-arm; and then spake a dolorous voice:

"Lord, mate, and wot o' pore Jonas—'ave ye killed 'im?"

"Nay, the hangman shall do that for him one day, belike. The rogue will be cursing lustily anon."

"Well, mate, you've the luck on't—but if only them lily-souled, lousy——"

But Sir Richard was off and away, riding at gentle pace and with sombre eyes watching the gathering dusk, and yet supremely conscious of the lovely face so very near his own, of the silky tress that tickled his neck, his ear, his cheek with such determined persistence, and of all the warm, soft, yielding, extremely feminine tenderness of her; and (moreover) if ever he seemed to become in the least regardless of all this

—there was that slyly-wanton curl to tickle and teaze him into proper heedfulness again; and as he was silent, so was she, and thus rode they through the fragrant dusk and never a word for a while; at last:

"Alas, thy poor face!" she murmured, and so tenderly that his arm instinctively tightened itself about her, and he made to speak, but—remembering with what very base persistence she had cherished the idea that he—a Gyfford of Weare—could stoop to murder, and how, in her secret heart she doubted his innocence at this very moment, he restrained arm and tongue together.

"Such swellings!" sighed she. "And scratches—though indeed I feared your hurts were greater."

"A little water will amend 'em," he answered, somewhat gruffly, wherefore she nestled to him a little closer, whereat he urged the horse to faster gait. And after they had ridden thus some distance, he spoke again:

"Ma'm," said he.

"Sir?" she answered. "And do not frown, 'tis no enemy you are clutching. Also I pray you remember this poor horse bears a double burden!"

"I do not forget it."

"Then why must you so hurry the poor, willing creature?"

"The evening falls apace. 'Tis some miles to the Moat House."

"Do you burn with such extreme impatience to be there?"

"Why, you must know . . . well . . . I . . . there is much to do."

"Then—why not do it, Richard, and be done?" Here he was obliged to wink by reason of that intrusive, silky curl.

"Because what is to do, if all goes well, is to be done at the Moat House."

"Why there, Richard?"

"Because my two best, my two most faithful friends await me there."

"And what is to do there, Richard?"

"A matter that something toucheth my future welfare."

"Pray, Richard, what matter?"

"That which shall, I hope, prove their faith in me no vain thing."

"Oh!" said my lady, frowning all unseen. "How sweet the honeysuckle smells this evening!"

"Ay!" he nodded, and became lost in gloomy abstraction.

"And your coat—so damp, so dusty—is discomforting pillow for any poor maid's cheek."

"I fear so!"

"And—dear heaven, you hold me like a sack o' wheat!"

At this, he clasped her more snugly but, heedful of the growing dusk, set the horse to even faster pace, whereupon my lady instantly sighed and moaned in protest:

"De-ee-ar goo-ood-ness!" she gasped. "'Tis savagely cruel to so bump and jolt a poor soul! Why! Oh, why such merciless speed?"

"To-night," he explained, "my two most kind, most faithful friends——"

"Who?" she demanded. "Who are these so kind and odiously faithful friends?"

"Madam the Duchess, your aunt, and Mistress Camlo, the gipsy——"

"They sound friends strangely assorted. And are these so marvellous faithful?"

"Beyond expectation!" he answered.

"Oh? And why must you so stress, so emphasize and harp upon the word. What mean you by 'faithful'?"

"Merely that such as kept their faith in my innocence all undimmed, were very few."

"Ha!" cried my lady, sitting very upright. "So, sir—having saved me from a villain, having me here at your mercy, holding me upon your heart, you will thus reproach me!"

"Heaven forbid!"

"Yet you dare to think I doubt you?"

"I dare to know you did."

"So—indeed, sir?"

"Thus—indeed, ma'm! 'Tis a matter betwixt us I never shall forget."

"Never, sir—never?"

"Why—how may I, Helen?"

"Oh, Richard Gyfford, now could I scratch and bite you, you become a creature detestable! So trot, sir, gallop—gallop, I beg, and deliver me from yourself so soon as you may."

"Why then," he answered, tightening his clasp about her, "hold fast, ma'm!"

"Never!" cried she disdainfully, and immediately clung to him as their willing horse bounded forward.

And thus with no more said, but clasping and clasped, they galloped homewards through the lengthening shadows.

CHAPTER XLIII

GIVETH FURTHER PARTICULARS OF AN APPARITION

Descending the stair, a radiant figure in her dainty laces and voluminous rustling silks, Helen beheld the up-lifted, soulful eyes of Mr. Trumpington, that sighful gentleman.

"Ah, madam," he murmured, hurrying forward to kiss her dainty, perfumed fingers, "you dawn upon th' enraptured sight like Beauty's revelation, th'embodied dream of poetical delight, Joy's apotheosis—your charms transcendent strike me dumb!"

"Oh, sir," she laughed, "never, sure, was dumb man so eloquent!" A stately bow, a profound curtsey, and, with her hand upon Mr. Trumpington's embroidered cuff, she sailed into the great withdrawing-room, where many candles shone bravely upon velvet coats, glossy wigs, gleaming shoe-buckles and jewelled snuff-boxes; for here the primest gentlemen of the neighbourhood were convened, and just now engaged in low-toned yet eager confabulation.

"Greetings, sirs!" said my lady, saluting the back-bending company with another gracious curtsey that set her silken mysteries billowing about her loveliness. "Indeed you are vastly welcome, but if there be any among you can ease a poor soul's curiosity, and say why we are here assembled at the Moat House so sudden, so secret and at such hour, I pray you speak."

"Why madam, a'Gad, y'must know, i'faith," lisped Mr. Threep, posturing. "There is a whisper, so to speak, a rumour——"

"There's a dozen!" boomed little Mr. Magnus.

"That we are to enjoy a charade——"

"A play-acting, madam!" murmured Mr. Trumpington.

"Or game o' hoodman-blind," quoth Mr. Threep.

"Tush, sirs!" cried Sir John Parret, rapping his snuff-box, "'tis no such—hem! I say her Grace would never convoke us for such—ha! I say, such fiddle-faddle!"

"Very true," boomed Mr. Magnus.

"Nay but, my dear Sir John," sighed Mr. Trumpington, his soulful gaze languishing meanwhile upon Helen's stately beauty, "here in our midst to bless our eyes is Beauty manifest, and our Duchess, God love her, hath ever some little, pretty, joyous device to charm and challenge our interest, some sweet, diverting, toy-dom, or——"

"Hey—toydom, sir, toydom?" quoth Sir John, strutting. "I never heard the word! I don't accept the word! I say—hum! I say d'ye think I'm one for such trifles? I, sir—to trip, sir, to—ha, to tumble about in such hoydenish business as—hum, as blind-man's-buff, sir? No, sir, I protest and dare assert 'tis for matter more serious Madam summoned me hither—some matter o' moment to us all, some matter doubtless touching our—hum——"

"That same," cried the Duchess, rustling suddenly in upon them, "that very same, me dear Sir John, whatever ye may mean. . . . And here's news for ye, gentlemen all—last night Richard Gyfford was struck down and captured."

"Eh—captured, madam?" cried Sir John, forgetting to be dignified. "Captured—ha? Taken is he—at last! But why—why was not I informed o' this—? Wherefore, madam, why—why should I be left i' the dark thus—a matter o' such moment—why was not I informed?"

"Perchance because ye were asleep, me dear."

"But to-day, madam? Here's all to-day passed and neither I nor my brother justices know a word!"

"Nay, not a syllable!" lisped Mr. Threep.

"Never a word!" boomed Mr. Magnus.

"Ah well, sirs, 'tis no matter—for the poor gentleman being captured last night, escaped this afternoon and——"

"Es-caped?" gasped Sir John.

"Gad defend us!" lisped Mr. Threep.

"Od rabbit me!" boomed Mr. Magnus.

"But . . . but, madam," stammered Sir John, "I . . . I don't understand——"

"Faith, Sir John, me dear, don't I know it?"

"But, d'ye say, ma'm, d'ye positively affirm, will ye actually tell me——"

"This, sir! Last night he was captured, this afternoon he escaped, and this evening he will, I hope and pray, be exonerated, his fair name vindicated for good and all, before your very eyes. 'Tis for this purpose I summoned ye here—nay, Sir John, pray silence and suffer me speech! I hope, ere the clock strikes, to show you all in a dramatical interlude that I'll call 'The Biter Bit.' The actors shall play their several parts as natural as life—especially one! . . . At least, b' the Powers, I hope so! So soon as the stage be set you will follow me into the morning-room where we shall sit very silent and very still,—the windows will stand open and you will listen and—watch the summer-arbour. But, sirs, there must be no talking, no, not even a whisper or our play is ruined, and 'tis a case o' life—and death!"

Here the Duchess consulted a somewhat ponderous gold watch, and—nobody spoke, even Sir John was silent.

"Come!" said she, rising suddenly. "You, Sir John, shall sit with me—your arm, pray! Helen and gentlemen, follow us!"

Soft-treading and with a strange hush upon them, one and all, they followed the Duchess and Sir John into an unlighted chamber whose long windows looked out upon the gardens, opposite which windows stood a row of chairs sufficient for the company.

"Sirs," whispered the Duchess, when all were seated, a very soft whisper and tremulous with anxiety and a very unwonted gravity. "Oh, sirs, if the dead are truly alive . . . if in Nature visions may rise to affright the guilty, avenge wrongs, and vindicate the innocent, I pray we may thus see, hear, and know the truth at last. And so—be hushed, breathe soft, look ye and listen!"

And now fell a silence that, as moment after moment dragged by, seemed but to grow the more irksome, more painfully acute, yet a silence none seemed able or willing to break.

The glimmering dusk, beyond the open casements, deepened to night, a windless dark wherein stars began to wink . . . a hush, a stillness, an all-pervading silence wherein the straining senses began to distinguish a thousand vaguely indefinable sounds blent and resolving into a heavy, ceaseless throb that was the very pulse of life itself. . . . Slowly this deadly stillness seemed to become more and yet more ominous . . . the deepening gloom seemed full of a terrified questioning—Who? What?

At last—stealthily—upon this awful troublous quietude crept a sound, regular, drawing nearer, growing louder. . . .

"Horse . . . horse-hoofs!" said someone in broken whisper.

"Or . . . the beating . . . beating of a fearful heart!" whispered the Duchess. "Hush! Listen!"

Hoofs clattering on the distant road, wonderfully clear . . . suddenly stilled.

"Now!" whispered the Duchess. "Ah—watch, watch!"

Stillness again . . . silence. And then in the garden's darkness a darkness that moved, a shadow that flitted through the shadows—swift, silent, purposeful.

"The arbour! See!"

A puff of greenish vapour . . . a glow, and, within the arbour's blackness, uprising from this gloom a be-wigged head, a face greenly luminous that seemed to hang suspended in air, blotched . . . frightful.

And then—the night-silence was split, riven asunder by a scream that dying gave place to loud babblement of frantic speech:

"Julian! . . . Julian—ah, no! . . . I never meant to kill . . . 'twas you forced me—forced me to it! . . . You——"

The feverish speech ended in a hoarse cry strangled to a dreadful choking. . . . Then, as if afloat in air, the head moved forward, the curling periwig vanished and there, down-bent, low to earth and still dreadfully aglow was the keen, hawk-like face of Old Truffeni.

CHAPTER XLIV

TELLS HOW OLD BENJAMIN MADE A BET

"A corpus, eh, John?" questioned old Ben, staring at his frothy tankard with eyes of awe. "Struck down stone-dead suddent-like arl at once-drackly-minute, same's a flash o' loightenin'—eh?"

"She told me fross-fross, Ben."

"Eh—oo?"

"Mrs. Camlo."

"But wot's 'er got to do wi' it?"

"Ah," nodded the stolid John, "wot, indeed! Lord, there's been all manner o' tales these last two days—black magic, speckitors, spells and phanitums an' I dunno wot all!"

"Stone-dead!" nodded old Ben. "Dead as mutton, and 'im a lord and a Vi-count!" Here he took a sip of ale with great apparent relish. "And t'think 'twas 'im as done the deed! To think 'twas 'im, in a mask an' S'Richard's cloak, stops 'er leddyship, my mistress, thieves 'er purse an' wissels 'twixt 'is teeth to put 'isself off on 'er for S'Richard! Oho, a raglar deep un and sharp as a gimblet!

"Though mind ye, John, lad, I wunt say as I didn't begin t'suspicion 'im noo and then, ye can't fule I! . . . But t'think 'twere 'im—and now dead!"

"Ah," sighed John, "and Cap'n Despard's a-goin' the same road."

"Eh, du 'ee mean as Cap'n 'll be a dead un tu, John?"

"So Doctor Samson do say."

"Another deader—well, b' the pyx these be loively toimes, John! Lookee, here be Mus' Julian dead, Vi-count dead, Oldcraft dead, th' Galloping Parson dead—as me an' Joel Bym found along by the four-wents—stiff an' cold, John, cold an' stiff—and now the

333

Cap'n a-goin' dead! Dannel me, but th'owd village be
a-lookin'up, lad—notororious be the word, John." Here
old Ben took a gulp of ale, nodded and smacked his lips.

"Ah, but murder and that-like beant good for my
trade, Ben. Here's two corpuses as I've 'ad on my
hands in less nor two months—which I says 'tis comin'
it a bit too much on any man!"

"Ay, two on' em, John, the killed and the killer—
Lordy Lord wot times . . . and S'Richard walkin'
bold as brass like any nat'ral, born fule—an' nobody
knowing 'e 'cept me."

"Wot, did ye know 'im, Ben?"

"Well—didn't I? Weren't it me as took an' be-
friended of 'e? Hast seen aught of 'im o' late, John?"

"No, Ben—shut hisself up at Weare, Gregory tells
me, won't see nobody neither—and no wonder!"

"But why shut 'isself away from me—an' arl 'is
other friends, John, lad?"

"Happen 'tis because his friends, most on 'em, shut
theirselves from 'e when most needed. . . . And
yonder is your lady, Ben, a-horseback. And a rare
booty she be!"

"Ah!" sighed the old man, ecstatic. "Just look at
th' action o' them legs, wil 'ee?"

"Eh—legs, Ben?"

"Ah! watch 'ow she picks 'em up! There beant no
mare like 'er in arl Sussex, nor nowheres else!"

And now, swaying easily to every graceful motion
of her beautiful mare, my lady came cantering across
the green and reined up within a yard of them:

"Pray, John," she enquired, glancing up at a certain
lattice window, "how is the invalid this morning?"

"Sinkin', my lady, sinkin' rapid. Don't know nobody
pore gen'leman, raving all night, my lady, and all
about death and Cap'n Archer, the highwayman, and
Sir Richard and hisself, and all on 'em drownding
together in th'owd millpool. Doctor be with 'e now
—no, 'ere 'e be!" quoth John as at that moment Doctor
Samson came hurrying forth to greet my lady.

"Sir," she questioned, bending from the saddle
anxious-eyed, "what is this I hear of Captain Despard?"

"If that he is dead, madam, the news is but a little previous," answered the doctor shaking grave head. "Alas, I fear the poor gentleman will be gone ere sunset."

"Dying?" murmured Helen, with another upward glance at the lattice overhead. "Oh, sir, can nothing be done?"

"Nought that I can do, madam, or any man."

"Has he no chance of life?"

"None, I fear. He needs a care unremitting, an attention unflagging, such as no man and no paid nurse can bestow. Given such——"

With an effortless ease Helen swung lightly to earth and, tossing aside her riding-rod, stripped off her gauntlets.

"Take the Witch home, Ben," said she, "and tell aunt I am remaining to nurse Captain Despard. And now, Doctor Samson, pray bring me to him."

So saying she hurried indoors with the little doctor eagerly attendant.

"Lordy—lord!" exclaimed old Ben, fumbling the mare's bridle and staring at John. "So . . . 'twas his honour the Cap'n as be her choice, arter all!"

"Ecod!" quoth John, rubbing square chin and staring at Ben. "And all along, I were thinkin' 'twas—some 'un else, Ben!"

"Eh, lad, but I could ha' told 'ee 'twas the Cap'n weeks an' weeks ago, I could."

"But . . . burn me, Ben, I could ha' took my oath 'twas—eh, but women be queer creatures! I could ha' took my Bible oath——"

"Lookee, John, I be a cautious man but—I'll lay a quart o' your best 'tis the Cap'n—alive or dead! A quart as my lady marries 'e—s'posing 'e don't die— so soon as 'e be fit—a quart!"

"A quart it be, Ben!" sighed John, shaking gloomy head, "though I'd sort o' hoped—ah, well!"

Here honest John sighed, shook his head again and trudged off about his business.

CHAPTER XLV

WHICH, BEING THE LAST, NATURALLY ENDS THIS BOOK

PULLING off coat and waistcoat, Sir Richard tossed aside cumbrous peruke, rolled up his shirt-sleeves, grasped the spade and fell to his customary toil; this labour to which he had devoted himself so entirely of late—namely, to make bloom again the garden which had once been his unknown mother's joy.

For two weeks had he wrought thus with a fiery zeal, and to-day the hedges showed trimmed and even; the paths, once choked with riotous tangle of weeds and briars, were now smooth and neat, while here and there fugitive blossoms peeped. Another twenty-four hours or less, and his self-imposed task would be accomplished and this revered piece of earth be as it had appeared when the light-tripping feet of that long-dead mother had blessed it.

Nevertheless, and though the day was hot, he dug with a certain grim fury, and when he paused, ever and anon, to wipe perspiring brow, his eyes were sombre, and viewed his goodly handwork with no degree of pleasure.

Now presently as he paused to take breath, bare forearm on spade, he heard the loud crackle of a fire, beheld its red glare and betook him into the little paddock adjacent where Gregory was burning a very mountain of weeds and tangled briars; and, as Sir Richard was glumly silent, even so was Gregory.

And when they had stared thus gloomily at the fire some while, they began to speak, thus:

GREGORY: If her sweet ladyship your mother might only see her cherished garden now I think she would smile and be glad.

SIR RICHARD: It . . . comforts me to so imagine, Greg.

GREGORY: (*Eyeing him somewhat askance*) Then . . . you've heard, sir, you . . . know?

SIR RICHARD: What should I hear, man? Since being proved no murderer my days ha' been all passed here at my task.

GREGORY: (*Groaning*) Ay—more's the pity! For whiles you played hermit thus and sulked, sir—ay, sulked, others have begun to live! Whiles you plied spade, others have plied their tongues, and to some purpose it seems.

SIR RICHARD: (*Sullenly*) Well, I'm no chatterbox.

GREGORY: (*Mournfully*) Ah, Richard—you that I've served since your first birthday, don't I know it! Hadst been readier o' speech here, long ere this had been some gracious lady to mistress thy desolate house o' Weare, to fill it with joy again and make of it a true home for thee. . . . But now——

SIR RICHARD: (*Pettishly*) Tush, man—tend thy fire!

Here a silence between them gloomier than ever while the fire crackles in derisive merriment.

SIR RICHARD: (*In kinder tone*) Faith, Greg man, I know thou dost love the old house.

GREGORY: Ay, verily, sir, its every stone and timber— so truly, so deeply that o' late I have begun to hope thee wed, to dream——

SIR RICHARD: (*Bitterly*) Nay, 'twas a nightmare!

Here another silence wherein Sir Richard watches the wreathing smoke ascend into the sunny air while Gregory watches him very wistfully.

SIR RICHARD: (*Pensively*) I understand Captain Despard is at last out o' danger.

GREGORY: And was out o' doors yesterday!

SIR RICHARD: I rejoice to know it.

GREGORY: Leaning—upon my lady Helen's arm!

Sir Richard takes up a stick and begins therewith to poke the fire gently.

SIR RICHARD: Well? . . She . . . also nursed him, I hear.

GREGORY: Samson vows she saved his life, and but for her most gentle care——

SIR RICHARD: (*Poking fire viciously*) So? She can be gentle then?

GREGORY: (*Reproachfully*) Sir, this we both know, and so now doth the Captain, passing well—for Samson says that from the moment the sick man realised her presence he fought desperately to live and so, came out of the very gates o' death. . . . And now——

SIR RICHARD: And now, Greg, now beginneth for him a new life—the which doth mind me! Go bring hither the third volume of Montaigne's Essays.

GREGORY: Eh—here, sir? . . . Montaigne's——

SIR RICHARD: Essays. The third volume. Upon the second shelf of the book-case beside the fire-place, left-hand side, in the library.

Left alone Sir Richard, leaning upon the stick, watches the fire with such profound abstraction that he never moves until, roused by a touch, he glances round to find Gregory beside him with a large volume open in his hands, thus discovering a thick wad of manuscript the uppermost of which bears the following superscription:

"*Hereinunder, proofs showing Captain George Despard to be the notorious malefactor and highwayman known as—Captain Archer.*"

"So you have read this?"

"I have," answered Gregory, his eyes very keen and bright, his gaunt features grimly resolute. "The book fell open as I drew it from the shelf and, having seen, I brought it so."

"Then you will forget it. Give me the papers."

"Wherefore?" demanded Gregory, closing the book.

"To burn 'em."

"You mean . . . sir . . . Ah, Richard, would you destroy this evidence then?"

"Utterly! Every damnable line!"

"Then, sir—listen! Nay, hear me! 'Tis said my lady Helen is good as betrothed to this man—is minded to wed this man—ay, he, that is no better than vile felon! This man that is——"

"Was, Gregory, was! Moreover, two such felons succoured me o' late! Come, give me those accursed papers—every one!"

"Richard. . . . Oh, sir, I tell thee she will wed this man—wed him!"

"Why 'tis no great matter for wonder. Save a man and wed that man, 'tis mighty like a woman."

"Sir, consider, reflect—but for this man she would be thine."

"She? Nay 'tis her fortune you mean—ha?"

"No, no, but for this one-time rogue, her heart would turn towards thee, Richard—I know it, boy! And now—now, with such evidence as this, we might——"

"Denounce him? Is this the way on't? 'Sdeath, man, are ye mad? Give me those papers——"

Sir Richard leapt and, seizing Gregory in compelling grasp, took from him the closed volume . . . next moment those fatal papers were blazing in the very heart of the fire.

"Zounds man!" quoth Sir Richard holding them down with the stick. "How dared you think it o' me? How could you? What's past and done shall be done with—ay, damme, the past shall never blemish a possible future. . . . If she'll wed him, none shall stay her. . . . She's no fool . . . and him I do believe to-day is man of honour. 'Tis not what a man was, but what he is, that matters. . . . But—you, Gregory! . . . 'Sblood, man, that you of all the world, should tempt me! . . . You that were my earliest playmate . . . my first teacher! You that I loved and honoured . . . you that saved me in the '15 . . . that I never knew stoop to aught unworthy! . . . Faith, man, I'm all amazed! . . . That you should counsel me to such——"

Gregory's head was bowed, his lean face hidden in clenching hands—something small and bright fell glittering. And then Sir Richard's long arm was fast about those bowed and heaving shoulders:

"Greg—Gregory! Oh Lord love thee, man! Why, Greg, old lad, forgive me . . . never weep or I too— ha, damnation! . . . I meant thee no unkindness, Greg—I spake thee i' the hot impulse o' the moment ——"

"And . . . wert right, Sir Richard!" he answered brokenly. "But, sir . . . oh, lad—thou'rt so lonely and know it not! The old house is so desolate and I had dreamed a goodly future for both . . . of gladness for thee, Richard . . . children to bear thy name ——"

"Why 'twas a fair dream, Greg! And i'faith, old friend, I will confess that on a time I dreamed some such. . . . But, what is to be must be and 'twere merest folly to repine, and yet——"

A flash of small brown legs, a sheen of glossy, black curls and there, slim finger beneath pointed chin, stood little Shuri curtseying to them demurely, looking from one to the other with great, wistful eyes.

"Kushto divous, prala!" said she, and held up to Sir Richard a somewhat grimy screw of paper; but, instead of taking this, he took her, swinging her aloft to ruffle her curls, pinch her cheek and kiss her proffered, rosy lips.

"Little elf," he smiled, "where have you lain hid so long?"

"In the wesh, prala, along o' the Hearns, the hairy ones. . . . But I comes back to-day and my grand takes me to your lady, and your lady gives me this —won't ye go for to take it, brother?"

So, with little Shuri perched jubilant upon his shoulder, he opened the paper and read as follows:

"This to apprise you, Odious Man, of a tea-drinking here, this day at four of the clock for purpose touching, very nearly, each and both of us. But what this is, come you and learn from the lips of "Your so unfaithful yet determined friend, "HELEN D'ARCY.

"Post Scriptum. Wear thy brown Ramillies wig, if it be in curl, it best consorts with thy so grimly visage."

He was yet staring at this missive when a dolorous voice hailed:

"Dick! . . . Dicky! . . . Oh, Richard!"

Setting little Shuri gently down, he beckoned to Gregory:

"Take her to Abigail," said he . . . "cakes, Greg . . . suckets, jellies and what not." Then, kissing the child's ruffled curls, he went back into the rose-garden and there beheld Mr. Trumpington, resplendent but forlorn, drooping dejectedly against the sundial, very dismally soulful indeed.

"What now, Trump?" he enquired.

Mr. Trumpington moaned, shook despondent head and spoke:

"Alas, Dick—all's over! Hope's flickering beam expires, my aspirations are frustrate all, my dream lies shattered for my soul's worship worships another . . . Dick, they've made a match on't—let me perish!"

"Who?"

"Our peerless D'Arcy and Despard."

"Are you—sure?"

"Beyond all hope of doubting, alas!"

Sir Richard turning away and reaching for his spade gripped it hard, and so leaning, began to whistle softly between his teeth while Mr. Trumpington moaned, shot a ruffle and sighed on:

"For perceive me, Dick, to your strong-souled woman, 'tis weakness doth ever appeal. To win such as Helen a man must needs become a very babe o' helplessness! And, alas, here's you, Dick, six foot o' rude manhood, vigour and strength, here's myself a very Achilles for virile courage—what chance then ha' we, in our pride o' health, 'gainst Despard in his sickness? Devil a bit! Thus to-day, Dick, within this very hour, at four o'clock I am bid to the Moat House to witness their betrothal—or some such calamity—and thither go I deject, with bleeding heart—to smile

and wish 'em joy—to watch another's hand possessive
clasp that hand adored—to see another's lips mayhap
press—— Oh, smite me dumb!"

"Amen!" growled Sir Richard.

"Ah, my poor Dick, 'tis plain, tis evident that, being
man, thou dost love her too. I know, I know—'tis
writ i' thy painful brow, thy smitten eyes, that desperate
clutch upon thy spade, thy mattock. So, Dick, being
comrades in amorous woe, let us together lament."

"Nay, Trump, I'm for digging!" he answered and
forthwith began, while Mr. Trumpington sighed and
drooped and watched.

"Oh, friend," moaned he, "is there forsooth comfort
in a spade? Shall a mattock amend love's shattered
dream? If so, bring me a spade!"

Sir Richard went on digging.

"And yet—Oh, Dick, Oh, Dick—to think on her . . .
our Helen—those matchless beauties destined for
another's arms!"

Sir Richard, plying his spade in sweating fury,
cursed soft yet deep.

"Another's joy, Dick, is our despair. Yet must we
hide our wounds and, concealing our agonies, face a
desolate world how best we may, thou in thy way, I
in mine—thou cursing above fierce-delving mattock,
speechless suffering, dumbly enduring."

"Ha!" exclaimed Sir Richard, pausing suddenly in
his labour. "Speechless, d'ye say? Zounds, man, your
dumbness deafens me! And if ye will consume, Trump,
why then consume, man, but i' the fiend's name—go do it
otherwhere."

"My poor Dick, thy grief doth make thee bitter,
sorrow tips thy tongue with gall—but mute in my woe
I leave thee, thou poor stricken soul, I go to feed my
yearning sight on charms that are—another's. So—
fare thee well!"

Long after Mr. Trumpington had sighed himself out
of hearing, Sir Richard leaned motionless upon his
spade, staring down at the new-turned earth; little
Shuri came to peep at him, but reading his face with
wise child-eyes, crept softly away. Came pretty Mrs

Abigail, her eyes even brighter than their wont, her dimpled fingers fast on Gregory's bony fist—but, beholding that forlorn and rigid figure, she shook her head, laid finger on rosy lip and, seeing Gregory's anxious look, kissed and led him softly away, whispering:

"He is best alone, my dear!"

Rousing at last, Sir Richard betook him to his labour again; he dug thus until afternoon languished to evening and evening to tender twilight. Then, casting by his spade, he sank upon that weather-worn marble seat whereon his young mother had sighed forth her gentle soul so many years ago; and there, sitting back, chin on breast, he stared upon the gathering dusk. A sound disturbed him, and he spoke, a little peevishly:

"Nay, Greg man, I've no mind for eating. I'll bide here a while. The garden is finished but——"

He glanced up, and started to his feet. . . . Helen was coming towards him down the path, cloaked to the dimpled chin of her.

"So you never came to me!" said she, in voice wonderfully tender.

"No, I . . . I couldn't!" he answered harshly.

"Art so—unforgiving?"

"'Twas no matter o' forgiveness, ma'm."

"You had my letter by little Shuri?"

"Yes."

"Well, Richard?"

"I was kept by . . . other business," he mumbled, not looking at her.

"Yes, you burned certain papers. Oh I know this of Gregory. I know, also, how you strove with death in that awful pool—and won! I know how, discovering shameful secret of one you deemed a rival, you kept it secret still. . . . Captain Archer, being man of honour hath told me all. . . . And so, Richard, here come I into thy mother's loved garden to beseech thy forgiveness. . . . Oh, dear Richard . . . my Dick Full-o'-love, wilt not pardon thy so poor, so humble, so unfaithful friend?"

She was down—down before him on her knees, and he saw her eyes bright with tears.

Awkwardly and speechless still, he raised her and she, letting fall her cloak, stood before him a resplendent vision bedecked with jewels that sparkled in her glossy tresses, gleamed upon her white bosom, glittered on dainty shoe—and yet none brighter than the tears that gemmed her lashes.

"Sir Richard, am I not bravely fine?"

"Yes."

"'Twas for thee—all for thee. Hadst but come this afternoon 'twas my desire to plight thee my troth before all those had so doubted thee—even as I doubted—though always was I thy friend, Richard, because this friendship o' mine, as I do know at last, was very love. . . . So, Dick Full-o'-love, if thou'lt have me . . . oh take me now—take me, in mercy's name—for heaven's sake——"

He swept her up to his heart, he bore her to the ancient marble seat—she was in his arms, on his knees, clasped fast against his heart.

"Helen . . . Oh, Helen!" he muttered. "I never knew . . . never guessed how much I loved thee, what life would mean . . . without thee until I thought thee lost!"

"Beloved man!" she murmured, touching his moist eyes with tender fingers. "Ah, my dear, my Dick full of love, from the night I struck this dear face with my hateful whip—Oh most odious me!—I knew myself thy very own—thine for ever, guilty or no. . . . But to-night—nay, prithee, kiss me not yet—to-night 'tis joy far beyond my poor telling to know myself so truly loved by one so brave, so honourable, so proud a gentleman as my . . . Gyfford o' Weare! And now . . . now, my Dick Full-o'-love . . . !"